Craving

Resurrection

Nicole Jacquelyn

Craving Resurrection
Copyright © 2015 by Nicole Jacquelyn
All Rights Reserved.
Formatting by Midnight Engel Press, LLC
ISBN-10: 1506165230
ISBN-13: 978-1506165233

No part of this book may be reproduced or transmitted in any form or by any means, electronic or mechanical, including photocopying, recording, or by any information storage and retrieval system without the written permission of the author, except for the use of brief quotations in a book review.

This is a work of fiction. Names, characters, businesses, places, events, and incidents are either the products of the author's imagination or used in a fictitious manner. Any resemblance to actual persons, living or dead, or actual events is purely coincidental. The author acknowledges the trademarked status and trademark owners of various products referenced in this work of fiction, which have been used without permission. The publication/use of these trademarks is not authorized, associated with, or sponsored by the trademark owners.

DEDICATION

To my Gram,

who shared her paperback copies of the Aces with all of her friends at the Senior Center. Thanks for being so proud of me—the feeling was mutual, gorgeous.

And to the friend who spells her name wrong.

I know it was hard to read.

I know you hated it sometimes.

I also know it wouldn't have become what it is without your help.

This one is for you.

ACKNOWLEDGMENTS

Mom and Dad: As always, thanks for the coffee and babysitting! Let's do this again soon ☺

My girlies: Thanks for being patient with me. I know it's annoying when you have to go to bed early on the weekends so mom can work! You two are by far my best accomplishments.

Sisters: Love you.

Toni: Thanks for listening to me ramble and complain and bounce around ideas. Now get to work, so I can do the same thing for you.

Ashley: You rock dude. Thanks for never sleeping so I can write you in the middle of the night and you respond in seconds. I would have lost my mind without you.

Donna: You're going to get an acknowledgement in every single book I write- because without you, this book wouldn't even be written… or it would still be an unfinished novella. You keep me on track, and I'm sure dealing with me is a lot like herding cats, but you're still patient and you still kick me in the tush to get me moving. You've been in my corner from the very beginning—I won't ever forget that.

My Betas: Kimberly, Gina, Tracy, and Aunt Deana- thanks for your input, your eagle eyes…and your crying voice messages. I needed those. Ha!

Nikki: Thanks for going over CRes with a fine-tooth comb. You practically spit shined this book, and it's a thousand times better because of your help.

My cover models who shall not be named: You guys went out of your comfort zone and totally kicked ass. Thank you so much.

Kara and Sommer: Once again, you've made my cover a thing of beauty. Thank you.

Dani: Thanks for always stepping up and making my chapter headings and paragraphs look awesome. You're usually working under a tight deadline, and you always come through.

Bloggers: Thanks for signing up, every time, to read and review my books. I know that blogging takes a lot of time and effort, and I hope you know that I appreciate every single word you write.

And you, person who's reading this: Thank you for reading *Craving Resurrection*. I hope you loved it. I hope it made your stomach churn and your heart race. I hope you loved Patrick and Amy as much as I do. Stick with me kid—I've got more up my sleeve.

Prologue

Amy

I wasn't nervous as I rolled through the open gate, though I did hope that I'd followed the right directions and an axe murderer wasn't waiting for me at the end of the lane. My new Prius was so ridiculously quiet that I could hear every crunch of gravel under the tires. I could even hear the crickets chirping out in the trees to my left—though that was likely made possible by my four rolled down windows. I hated driving with the windows rolled up this time of year. Everything in Oregon smelled so fresh in the spring with new flowers blooming and the hint of rain almost always in the air. It was so different from where I'd lived for the past twenty-odd years that I couldn't get enough of it.

The road forked like he'd said it did, and at the end on the left sat the big building I was searching for. I took a deep breath of relief when I saw the line of bikes backed up against it. Clearly, I was in the right place. Patrick had given me pretty vague directions when we'd spoken a couple months before, but I don't think he'd imagined me ever actually coming to his clubhouse—especially without speaking to him first.

His number had burned a hole in my metaphorical pocket for months, but I'd refused to call him. I wanted to get my life situated before I dealt with his shit, and I didn't think that was in any way unreasonable. Unfortunately, he'd disagreed.

I hadn't called him, but the man had been relentless, calling and texting me for months. After numerous texts that I had no hope of deciphering, I'd finally realized that his thumbs must have been too big for the tiny keyboard. Add to that the assistance of autocorrect and what I received were messages that appeared to be composed by a five-year-old, which was ridiculous considering how well read he was. It took less than a week for the messages to change from wondering how I was doing to bitching that I hadn't contacted him. The only reason I'd even known that much was because he hadn't been satisfied with texts; all phone calls had also been followed up with livid voicemails.

Like he had a right to expect anything from me.

I shook my head as I climbed out of my car and flipped my heavy silver hair over my shoulder. I'd pulled half of it back in a thick, loose ponytail near the base of my neck, and for a second, I wished I'd brought a larger rubber band so I could pull it all up and make it less conspicuous. A bandana wouldn't have gone amiss, either.

God, what was I thinking?

I'd worked hard to be where I was, and I'd been comfortable in my own skin for a long fucking time. I wasn't about to become self-conscious about something as stupid as my looks. I was strong, capable, and smart—those were the things that mattered. Besides, I looked damn good for a woman who was over forty years old. Yoga had kept me slim and good genes and clean living had kept my skin tight and my boobs perky. I wasn't going to cower, goddammit. I didn't cower for anyone.

There was an open door to the right of some large garage bays that were closed for the night, and I made my way there with my shoulders pulled back and my chin held high. I knew I should have been afraid of walking into a room of bikers I didn't know, but I wasn't.

I wasn't really afraid of anything. I think that might be what happens when you live through something you never imagined you'd survive. Everything else seems trivial in comparison.

The place was loud, with men in leather vests peppered around the room and half-naked young women of various shapes, sizes and ethnicities sitting on laps and preening for anyone who was looking. Good Lord, it was like a frat house with old men. I'm pretty sure I saw a movie like that once...

Focus.

"Amy, you look beautiful, as always," a gravelly voice murmured behind me, making me spin around.

"Charlie." I smiled huge as I took in his face, so much older than I remembered. "You don't look surprised to see me."

"Not surprised to see you, sure as shit surprised at what you're wearin.' " He answered with a grin, leaning in to kiss my cheek. "Knew he saw ya a few months back, but he didn't say a word about the get-up. When'd you become a fuckin' tree hugger?"

"Probably about the time you became president."

"Fuck, that long? Please tell me you still shave your shit." He leaned in to lift my arm to check for armpit hair and I couldn't help the loud, barking laugh that burst out of my mouth.

"Don't be a dick."

"Ah, still taking care of it I see." He winked, squeezing my arm gently. "I remember Poet going on and on about how you shaved your pussy way back when."

"Shut the fuck up!" God, I couldn't believe that he could still embarrass me with a few carefully chosen words.

"Who the hell..." A new voice came from the side and I took a deep breath as I turned to take the speaker in. She was wearing a Harley tank top and blinged-out jeans and I would have known her anywhere. "Holy shit. *Amy?*"

"Hey, Vera." I felt my throat get tight as her face broke into a huge grin.

"What the fuck are you doing here? Damn, you look good!" She smelled like vanilla perfume and cigarettes as she wrapped her skinny arms around me, and I couldn't help but hug her tight. I'd missed these two. Maybe if things had been different... no, I wouldn't think about that.

"Look at your hair!" she said, leaning back to run her fingers over my head. "Goddamn, it's gorgeous. You here to see Poet?"

"Poet? That's the name he uses?" I asked, rolling my eyes.

"Road name. Someone else picked it."

"Right." I nodded. "Yeah, where is he?"

"I'll get him." Charlie said quickly with a small smile.

"Slider," Vera warned.

"Slider?" I snorted. "I don't even wanna know where that came from. No worries, just show me where he is. I don't give a rat's ass what he's doing. I just need to talk to him real quick."

Char—Slider ran his hand over his slicked-back hair, and gave me a cautious nod before placing his hand between my shoulder blades to lead me through the room.

"You come see me before you leave!" Vera called out as we left her behind.

"Yup!"

He led me through a doorway and down a hallway that ran the length of the building, stopping a few rooms down, where I could hear someone giggling through the door.

"Poet, open up, brother!" Slider called out as I slid between him and the doorframe and pushed my way into the room before he could stop me.

Patrick must not have heard us, because he was on the bed, leaning back against the headboard with a small grin on his face as a woman in only a G-string told some kind of story complete with animated hand gestures. She was young, I could see that much, and she had a generic tribal tramp stamp on her lower back that he was tracing with the fingers of one hand.

Aw, how cute.

"'I missed ye' he said," I commented loudly in a thick accent, walking into the room as his head snapped up. "How'd I live so long without ye? Come home with me. Yer beautiful."

I sat down at the edge of the bed and sighed dramatically. "All lies."

"Who the fuck are you?" she asked, eyes wide, while Slider laughed, making no move to leave the doorway.

"Jesus Christ!" Poet hissed, pushing the girl off his lap.

"I've never loved anyone the way I love ye, lass." My voice dropped into his accent again, my tone growing more serious.

I shook my head slowly as I stood, finally raising my eyes to his and swallowing hard, letting him see exactly how I felt about the situation we were in. His jaw went tight and his eyes grew sad as he watched me, a thousand words unsaid between us.

When Slider realized the show was no longer a funny one and left the doorway, I allowed my gaze to travel over the woman eyeing me in annoyance, her long, red-tipped fingers barely covering her fake breasts. I wanted to stare right back and scoff at her gravity defying breasts and tiny hips, but I didn't let my eyes stray from hers.

I'd shoved my way into the room, interrupting a private moment, and she had no reason to be embarrassed. I refused to make her even more uncomfortable. She seemed nice enough while she was making Patrick smile, and even though a part of me hated it, she hadn't done anything to deserve disrespect from me.

Because of those things, I answered her as gently as I could.

"I'm his wife."

Chapter 1

Amy

All my life I'd been ordinary. Ordinary body: medium sized hips, five-foot-six barefoot, size seven shoes, average breasts—a C-cup on my good days or after a few extra Big Macs. I was neither fat nor skinny, but somewhere in between. Ordinary features: boring brown eyes and a nose a little large for my face, fullish lips, but nothing to write home about, and one of my front teeth was a bit crooked which caused a slight overlap that I hated and, therefore, my smile in every photo from the time I was seven and got my adult teeth was closemouthed.

The only things that stood out about me—not that they were really all that interesting—were the two fingers missing from my left hand and my long black hair. I couldn't remember ever actually having the fingers, so I never really missed them, and I'd inherited my hair from my dad. I loved it, and kept it really long. I'd never cut it much, just trims every six months to keep it healthy and so I didn't look like some sort of cult member with hair hanging to my ass. It was shiny and thick and reached just below my bra strap, so I could do anything I wanted with it. French braids, coronets, fancy up-dos, a long, silky ponytail, I'd learned to do it all.

It was one of the only things that I had control over, and it gave me something to hide behind in every new school and new city that we moved to. I'd lived in fifteen different cities by the time I was seventeen, and the most recent was Ballyshannon, Ireland.

We'd moved to the town only a few months before at the beginning of summer, and it was safe to say it was the hardest town to acclimate myself to. I'd lived in America my entire life, but I had dual citizenship in Ireland and the US because my mother was an Irish citizen. She'd gone to school in the United States, met my dad there, and the rest was history.

I'd always known I had dual citizenship, but actually having to use it was beyond belief. I was an American, dammit. It was what I understood, where I was marginally comfortable, where I believed I'd live my entire life.

I'd started at a private, all-girls Catholic school a few weeks before and I still had no idea how I'd ever manage to pass my classes. My teachers' accents were so thick that I could barely understand them, my peers looked at me like I was a freak any time I spoke, and the way they calculated my credits was completely different than the schools I'd attended back home. It felt like I was going to be stuck in Catholic school hell for the rest of my fucking life.

The only thing I didn't hate were the uniforms, though the plaid skirt and white blouse uniform felt a little like I was dressing for a porn shoot. It gave everyone a sort of equality—*we were all dressing for pornos*—that I hadn't had in my previous schools. It was insane the way fads changed between large schools in the inner cities and small schools in the backwoods. I don't know how many times I'd gone to school on the first day and looking like a complete weirdo compared to everyone else. Of course, at my new school all I had to do was open my mouth and the freak flag started waving yet again.

I was walking home, counting down the 128 days until my eighteenth birthday and wondering how I could save enough cash to get my ass back onto US soil, when a voice called out to me from the steps just a few houses down from the one we were renting.

"Would ye like to come in for tea?"

I didn't realize at first that the woman was talking to me. I'd never seen her before in my life, but when she repeated the question, my head popped up from behind my hair and she was staring straight at me.

"Me?"

"Well, I don't see anyone else, do ye?"

I searched the quiet street in confusion, but she was right. We were the only ones in the general vicinity. I can't lie, the first thing that popped into my head was 'Stranger Danger!' which was ridiculous, seeing as how the woman was inches shorter than me and skinny as a rail. I could totally take her. But why the hell was she inviting me to her house?

I stepped closer to her as she sat patiently, and I couldn't help but smile back at her when she grinned. She was cute, probably a bit older than my parents, with wrinkles at the edges of her eyes and deep grooves in her cheeks. Although she was smiling almost ear-to-ear, she looked... lonely. There was an exhaustion to her that didn't come from a hard day at work, but from a lifetime of hard days at work.

"Do you normally ask strangers to eat at your house?" I questioned as I got closer.

"Ach, no! But I've seen ye around. Always with yer head in a book, always hidin' behind that hair a yers."

I snorted at her very apt description.

"Always had a snack for my boy when he got home from school. Young ones need that after a hard day. Thought I'd offer ye the same, if ye'd like."

"I'm old enough to forage for my own food," I said with a smile, thinking *geez, she's nice*. "And I don't even know your name!"

"Peg," she answered with raised brows, waiting for me to reply in kind.

"I'm Amy. Nice to meet you, Peg."

We both grew silent after that, at a standstill as I considered her odd request and she watched me like a hawk.

"Well," she huffed, finally breaking the awkward silence. "How about ye make an old woman's day and give me someone to eat with?"

I knew what she was doing, trying to make me think that feeding me wasn't about *me* at all, but that didn't stop me from nodding slowly. "You're not that old," I argued. "But...okay, if you're sure."

I wondered if she knew more about my life than she was letting on as I followed her into the tiny house, but it occurred to me pretty quickly that it didn't really matter. My parents wouldn't be home from work for hours still, so it's not as if I had anyone to miss me. Plus, she seemed really nice. I'd learned over the past seventeen and a half years how to spot people with ulterior motives—it's all in the eyes—and she really didn't have any other reason for inviting me in. She was clearly hoping for a little companionship, and who was I to refuse that? I didn't have anywhere else to be.

I learned a lot about Peg as we ate, mostly because the woman was a chatterbox. I actually kind of loved how she filled the quiet, because God knows I didn't have much to say. She was Scottish, which explained the accent that wasn't entirely like the ones I'd been hearing, but she'd been living in Ireland for more than twenty years, so it was an odd mixture of both Irish and Scottish. She'd followed her husband to his hometown after their wedding, and though I never got a clear answer, it seemed she was still married, but they hadn't lived together for quite some time. Their son, Patrick, who Peg seemed to think walked on water, was away at University studying literature, and she'd worked at a local grocer for almost as long as she'd lived in Ireland.

She talked and talked and talked, and before I knew it, almost two hours had passed. I knew my mother would be home any minute, and though I didn't think she would even notice my absence, I didn't want to chance it. Who knows how badly she'd fly off the handle if she knew I hadn't gone straight home from school. My parents had never had clear rules for me, but every once in a while, I'd unintentionally do something that would set them off and the punishments were severe.

"I better get home," I said reluctantly, cutting Peg off as she went on and on about her handsome son. "My mom should be home soon, and she'd worry if I wasn't there yet."

Peg's brows furrowed for a moment as if she knew exactly what I wasn't saying, but almost as quickly as the frown appeared, it was gone and she was smiling brightly.

"Well, this has been lovely," she said as we stood from the table. "Would ye like to come again tomorrow?"

I grabbed my school bag off the floor, thinking about my answer before turning back toward her. "I'd like that."

"Perhaps tomorrow ye can tell me a little more about yerself. Seems I didn't let ye get a word in edgewise today!"

"I didn't mind." I replied shyly, my cheeks heating as I realized she'd noticed that I'd barely said a word the entire afternoon.

"I'll see ye tomorrow, lass!" she called as I raced down her cement front steps.

I made my way home with fifteen minutes to spare before my mom walked in the front door, and was quietly doing my homework on my bed when she came to check on me.

My mother was beautiful. She made sure of that, with weekly trips to salons and daily workouts to stay trim. But it was a brittle type of beauty, one that looked as if one wrong movement would shatter the entire façade. I think the shit her and my father snorted up their noses had something to do with that.

"Oh, good, you're home."

"Where else would I be?" I asked, rolling over to look at her.

"Good point." She brushed her hands over the light blue dress she was wearing, making sure nothing was out of place after her short walk home from the local realtors office where she was a receptionist. "Your father and I are having a guest over later, so be sure to stay in your room after you grab some dinner."

"Okay," I replied woodenly, refusing to show any emotion.

"Finish your homework."

She walked out of the room and I listened for her bedroom door to close before I dropped my head to the bed and struggled not to cry. It had been months since they'd had any 'visitors,' and I'd been hoping that it was all over since we'd moved to a new town. They'd put me into a private Catholic school, for God's sake, and we'd started going to Mass again every Sunday for the first time in years. I'd let myself believe that things would be different.

Stupid. Stupid. Stupid.

At least I had tea at Peg's to look forward to the next day, that was something. I leaned back up and returned to the math homework I'd been working on, but I wasn't able to focus.

As excited as I was to visit with Peg, I couldn't help the worry that pooled in the pit of my stomach. Our house was tiny, and I was going to have to figure out how to make myself as scarce as possible when their visitor arrived. I didn't even know if I could stand to be in my bedroom, which shared a wall with both the living room and their bedroom.

I glanced at my window and came to the conclusion that I would climb out after dinner. The nights were still pretty warm, and if I took my flashlight, I'd be able to read while I was out there. I wasn't sure how long I'd have to hide, but I was hoping I could still get a little sleep since I had school the next day. With that decision made, there was only one thing left to worry about.

How the hell was I going to discuss my life with Peg without hinting at all about my parents' lives? I wasn't clear on Irish customs, but I was pretty sure that hiring prostitutes—the younger the better—wasn't considered normal behavior for married couples with children.

If Ballyshannon were anything like the previous towns I'd lived in, nothing good would come from people knowing about their extra-curricular activities.

No one could know.

Chapter 2

Amy

I waited until I heard my dad come home that night and voices began filtering in through the wall connected to my parents' bedroom before I grabbed my comforter, a flashlight and my tattered copy of *Fahrenheit 451* and climbed out my window. There was a thick patch of grass beneath it between our house and the one next to it that provided me a safe little cocoon as I leaned against the wall.

I wrapped my comforter around me, pulling it up and over my head so I could turn the flashlight on without drawing attention to myself while I read. It wasn't ideal; I'd much rather be inside, but it worked. I was just glad our house had only one story, or I would have been shimmying down a frigging drainpipe to get away.

I read most of the book before my eyes grew tired, but I still hadn't seen or heard anyone come out our front door. I wasn't sure how late it was, but I knew from experience that sometimes 'visitors' stayed well into the night. I'd just have to wait them out.

I jerked awake with a gasp some time later when I felt someone shaking my shoulder. My feet were freezing, and I was soaking wet.

"What in God's name are ye doin' out here, Amy?" Peg scolded as she rubbed my shivering shoulders.

"I didn't want my parents to know I was awake reading, so I snuck out here last night... I must have fallen asleep." The lie passed my lips easily, but Peg's expression told me she didn't believe my bullshit.

"Now, ye remember when I said I'd seen ye around, dontcha?" she asked quietly.

"Y-yes." I was stuttering as she stared me down.

"I see most things that happen around here. Probably comes from havin' too much time on my hands..." She let that sink in as my eyes grew wide. "Seen that gash goin' in yer house last night with yer da."

I gulped, but stayed silent.

"Also saw her leave not an hour past," she told me with a nod. "Get on back in yer bedroom before ye catch yer death."

I scrambled to my feet, too relieved that she hadn't asked me any questions to ask any of my own. I gave her an impulsive hug before I picked up my flashlight that had rolled a little from my hiding place and crawled back inside. Then I closed my window as she walked away as if nothing had happened.

When I glanced at my clock, it was four in the morning. Thank God, I'd get a couple of hours of sleep in an actual bed before I had to get up again for school. I was so exhausted, I couldn't even think about how awful it was that Peg knew my secret.

***

I was distracted all day during school, my anxiety about what Peg had seen making me jittery and unfocused. I wasn't sure what would happen. Would she tell everyone? Ballyshannon wasn't a tiny town, but it seemed pretty close-knit. God, my life would be over if anyone knew, especially if my schoolmates' devout Irish Catholic families found out.

By the time I walked home that afternoon, I could feel hives beginning to form on my wrists and the tops of my hands. I think it was a family trait; both my mother and I dealt with the physical manifestation of stress. I was alternately scratching and rubbing my arms through my cardigan by the time I passed Peg's front steps.

"Thought ye were comin' in for tea!"

I stopped abruptly, and whipped my head in her direction. "Oh, um..."

"The offer stands."

"Okay," I whispered back, turning toward her house.

I didn't understand why she was still being so nice to me. She had to have some idea of what was going on. There was no way she'd misinterpreted the situation the night before; she'd practically spelled it out when she found me.

Peg held the door open as I walked inside slowly.

"Sit down! Sit down! I baked a caramel shortbread!"

"Why are you being so nice to me?" I asked quietly as I followed her into the kitchen. "I know what you saw."

"What does that have to do with anythin'?"

"Well... I just figured you wouldn't want me over again, since... you know." I mumbled back. I was so uncomfortable, my arms began itching almost all the way up to my elbows.

"Lass," she sighed as she stopped moving around the kitchen and placed a plate of shortbread in front of me before dropping down in the seat across the table. "What yer parents choose to do hasn't got anythin' to do with how I feel about ye."

"How you feel about me?" The pastry sat neglected on the table as I stared at it, afraid to meet her eyes.

"Well, from what I've gathered, yer smart." My eyes snapped up to meet hers. "Yer kind, thoughtful, pretty, and yer just plain sweet the way ye've catered to an old woman's whims like ye have."

"You're not that old," I replied automatically.

"And ye've got nothin' wrong with ye, no matter what yer parents choose to do in their own home." She smiled at me gently, and reached out to squeeze my hand. "Now, enough talk about those perverted parents o'yers."

I choked on her matter-of-fact assessment of my parents, and giggled as she winked.

"Well, just one more thing." She reached into her pocket and pulled out a shiny new key, setting it on the table in front of me. "Ye can't be spendin' the night outside, especially once the weather starts turnin' colder."

I looked back and forth between her and the key in confusion before her offer became clear.

"You can't give me a key to your freaking house! Are you crazy? I could steal all of your stuff! I could…I could murder you in your sleep! You don't know me!"

She laughed at my indignation, and swiped the back of her hand away from her body as if she was literally brushing away my comments.

"Got nothin' to steal!" she cackled. "Ye plan on murderin' me in me bed, well, ye could do that by climbin' in me open window, now couldn't ye?"

"I can't take a key to your house," I argued stubbornly. "No. No way."

"Ye'll take it," she snapped back. "Ye'll use it if ye have the need, and if ye don't, well, I'll have someone to water me plants when I go on holiday."

"You're going on vacation?"

"Well, I haven't yet, but that doesn't mean I won't in the future."

"Jesus Christ," I mumbled, causing Peg to reach across the table and flick my forehead. "What the hell?"

"Don't take the Lord's name in vain in this house. That's non-negotiable."

"God-shit-sorry!" I hissed and dodged as she tried to flick me again. "I won't!"

"Well, good then. Now can we eat? Ye said ye'd tell me about yerself today."

I watched in awe as she stood back up to grab her own decadent looking pastry then sat back across from me as if we hadn't been arguing for the past five minutes. The woman was quite obviously out of her mind, but I couldn't help but find it endearing. She may have been more trusting than anyone I'd ever known, but I could also tell that she was no one's fool. She'd known exactly what she was doing when she'd had that key made for me.

It was also more comforting than I would have ever admitted that she'd set a rule, even if it was as small as taking the Lord's name in vain. Her punishment had been swift and effective, and I knew in the future exactly what would happen if I slipped and said it again. It wasn't as if the flick had even hurt that badly, but it had gotten Peg's point across. The thought of disappointing her or making her angry was enough of a deterrent to keep my language clean when I was near her—the flick was more of a reminder.

My chest felt light as she nodded to prod me along.

"Well, I was born in Cheyenne, Wyoming of all places…"

***

After that first week, Peg and I settled into an easy routine. I stopped by nearly every day after school, and she was always waiting for me on her front stoop as I made my way home. She became the first truly comforting person I'd ever had in my life, and before long, I couldn't imagine my world without her in it.

We didn't talk about what was happening at my house; I refused to bring it up and she was too understanding to mention it, but I noticed the way she watched me more closely after one of my parents' visitors came.

But I didn't use her key.

It felt too much like taking advantage of her at first, and after that I was too afraid that she'd worry if she knew how bad it was getting. She must have noticed the women—and now men—traipsing in and out of our house at all hours of the night, but she never said a word and I didn't either.

It wasn't until two months later that I finally broke down, running barefoot to her house at two in the morning.

"Are ye okay, lovey?" she asked urgently, pulling me inside the house before I'd even grabbed the key from the string around my neck. She must have been watching for me.

That night, my parents had two visitors. From the different pitches of their voices, I'd guessed it was both a man and a woman, which wasn't out of the ordinary. However, as I'd sat against the side of my bed, my fingers in my ears and a book resting on my knees, I'd noticed movement out of the corner of my eye. Then I'd watched in horror as my doorknob turned slowly and silently.

If it hadn't been for the small slide-lock I'd picked up at the little hardware store down the street and installed myself, whoever was trying to sneak into my room would have succeeded. I'd stared frozen until the knob stopped turning, then hopped to my feet and practically dove out my window to safety and Peg.

"I'm okay. I'm okay." I repeated a few times, trying to convince us both. "I just got freaked out. I should go back. I overreacted."

"Absolutely not!" Peg shrieked. "Ye'll not go anywhere tonight."

I was still so shell-shocked, I just watched silently as she locked the front door and grabbed my hand.

"Ye can sleep in the second bedroom."

"But my parents…"

"They'll not know a thing unless ye want them to," she assured me, pulling a cord above her head to turn on the light in the small room. "I'll wake ye when I go to work and ye can slip back in yer room."

"I don't—"

"Don't ye argue with me!" Peg scolded, flitting around the room to find sheets and a quilt for the bed. "Ye'll just stay right here tonight, where I know yer safe."

"I probably overreacted," I repeated as she held the blanket and sheet up so I could slip inside. "It wasn't a huge deal."

"I don't care if ye were imaginin' green monsters. Somethin' spooked ye, and I'll finally get some sleep tonight if I know yer safe under my own roof." She leaned down to kiss my forehead, something I never remembered my mother doing, and stood back up to turn off the light.

"Sleep, my girl."

I fell asleep easily that night, the smell of Peg's house and the softness of the bedding and mattress comforting me like nothing had ever done before. She woke me like she'd said she would the next morning as she left for work, which gave me plenty of time to sneak back in my window before it was time to get ready for school. After that night, a pattern was established.

The next time we had visitors, I didn't wait before racing to Peg's house to climb inside the soft bed I'd come to love and listen to the most important parental influence I'd ever have snore softly in the next room. It didn't happen every night, or even every week, but every time my parents paid for a prostitute to visit our house, I went to Peg's. And every time, she met me at the door.

I never even had to use the key she'd given me in the months that followed; she always waited up to let me in.

Chapter 3

Amy

"Whoa! Who de fuck are ye?"

The voice coming from the edge of the bed startled me awake, and as soon as my eyes opened, I froze in terror. The man's face was shadowed as he leaned over me, and I couldn't even take a deep breath to scream before the light in the spare bedroom flicked on.

"Patrick! Stop scarin' the poor girl and get away from the bed!" Peg scolded, immediately calming me. Oh, good. Patrick. I knew that name. Peg talked about her son all the time.

I turned to give Peg a small grateful smile, but jerked my eyes back to the man when he kicked the side of the mattress.

"Who de hell is dis? Ye takin' in strays now, Mum?" he asked angrily, looking me over with a scowl. Damn, his accent was so thick it took me a second to realize what he was saying… and then I was pissed.

"Fuck off!" I snapped.

"Patrick!" Peg scolded at the same time.

"Ah, she speaks?" he replied sarcastically, scowling at me.

I glared back silently, unwilling to get into an argument with the prodigal son. I knew I was the interloper, and I was instantly terrified that his presence would ruin the safety I'd found with Peg. Even if he was being a jackass, he was her son and I was just the pitiful neighbor girl whose parents were too occupied with prostitutes and drugs to realize I was gone.

"Patrick Gallagher, this is *my* house and if ye don't stop glarin' at that girl, I'm goin' to beat ye bloody!" Peg hissed, surprising us both.

"What de hell, Mum?"

"Out!"

He didn't glance at me again, but threw his arms in the air, causing me to flinch back as he stormed out the door. What a dick.

"Ye alright? He didn't scare ye, did he?" Peg asked after he was gone from the room.

"Uh, a little." I laughed nervously. Was this when she'd tell me to leave? Shit.

"Ignore him. My boy's all bluster. Ye've got school in four hours. Try and get some more sleep, eh?"

My jaw dropped as she turned off the light and pulled the door mostly closed. Had she really just told me to go back to sleep? How the hell was I supposed to do that? And why hadn't she asked me to leave?

I sunk back down against the bumpy mattress and pulled the blankets to my chin as my mind circled around and around, going over what happened. I could hear their quiet voices in the kitchen while Peg banged pots and pans, but I didn't even try to listen to what they were saying.

I was too busy trying to ignore the flutter in my belly as I remembered Patrick's sharp jaw and full lips as he'd sneered at me. His cheeks had been flushed with anger, but I almost hadn't noticed because I'd been to busy tracing the freckles across his face. Dear God. Freckles. He was an asshole, clearly, but he was the most handsome one I'd ever seen.

***

I must have fallen back asleep at some point, because when I finally woke up the next morning, I could tell by the way the sun was shining through the window that I was really late for school. Peg always woke me up as she left for work so I could head back home to shower, but I wasn't really surprised she'd forgotten. She hadn't seen her son in months, and I was sure after the initial scene she'd been over the moon that he was home for a visit. She talked about Patrick all the time, and I knew she missed him like crazy while he was gone.

I slipped my feet into my sandals as I pulled my hair back into a ponytail. God, I hated mornings. I was dragging ass as I made the bed, fluffing the softest feather pillow I'd ever felt and smoothing down the patched-up quilt. I tried not to leave any messes while I was at Peg's. She worked really hard, usually exhausted by the time she got home in the afternoon, and I never wanted to make things harder for her. She claimed my presence in her life was God's blessing, and I didn't want her to change her stance on that by forcing her to clean up after me. A few minutes later, I was shuffling blearily into the living room.

"Mornin'."

I stumbled to a stop outside the bedroom, my eyes growing wide as I caught sight of Patrick's muscular bare chest and sleep-tousled hair.

Freckles on his chest.

Dear God, he had freckles on his chest.

"Me mum's at de shop."

My gaze dropped to the cup of coffee he was holding, his long fingers wrapped completely around the mug, and I swallowed nervously. I needed to get out of there before I had some sort of episode that ended with me passing out or peeing myself. "Okay," I mumbled, moving around him toward the door.

"Hey, Amy, right?"

My head snapped up in surprise. Why was he still talking to me?

"Sorry about dis mornin'. I haven't been home as much as I should, and de guilt of dat mixed wit' surprise at findin' a woman in me bed, well, I t'ought maybe ye were takin' advantage of me ma's good nature. Stupid, yeah? De woman's no fool." He said the last words on a smile, shaking his head. "Forgive me?"

"Yeah, okay," I answered quickly before he could take back the apology.

He'd been a complete asshole, but I couldn't really fault him for it. If I had a mom as sweet as Peg, I'd be hell-bent on keeping leeches away from her, too. Plus, I wasn't sure how long he would be there, and I was terrified if we didn't work out some sort of ceasefire I'd be stuck at the house with my parents for his entire visit.

"I better get home," I said with a nod, moving toward the front door again.

"Mum said ye were supposed to be in school today. Yer parents won't be angry yer not dere?"

After taking a moment to decipher his quickly spoken words, I realized he'd asked the same question that had been rattling around in my head since I'd woken up to sunlight through the window. "I can handle it."

"Ye don't go home until later, dey won't know right?"

Why the hell was the absence of the 'th' sound in his words so freaking hot? I'd been hearing it that way for months already. It's not like it was anything new.

"Uh..."

"Ye can stay here if ye want."

My jaw dropped, and he blushed when he saw my reaction to his words.

"Fuck, girl. I'm not tryin' to get in yer knickers. Just t'ought I'd help ye out. I'm too old for ye."

Did that mean if I were older, he *would* be trying to get in my pants? Wait, how did the conversation morph into getting in my pants? My palms began to sweat as he pushed himself off the sofa.

"Who—" my words stuttered as he stepped forward and we were suddenly very close to each other. "Who said I'd even want you?"

"Beautiful, might wanna look at me face if yer tryin' to convince me o'dat. Been starin' at me chest since ye walked out of me bedroom and yer voice has gone a bit...ragged." His cheeks dimpled, and he winked before stepping around me.

"Your bedroom?" My voice sounded strangled as I twisted to watch him walk away.

"Since I was a wean," he answered with a chuckle. "I'm havin' a shower. Yer here when I get out, we'll find somet'in' to do today."

The bathroom door closed behind him as I stood frozen. I'd been sleeping in his bed? Oh, my God. No wonder he'd walked right in.

I fell to the couch with a huff and dropped my face into my hands. I'd been sleeping in his bed more often than not for the last two months. Oh, shit! Had I been drooling on his pillow? And most importantly, if he was staying, did that mean I had to stay at my house?

It wasn't as if I could ask him to sleep on the couch so I could take his room. He wouldn't even fit on the damn couch. Not only was he too long, but I swear his muscles had muscles, and he was too broad for Peg's miniature sofa.

I whipped my hands away from my face in frustration and, to my horror, they were immediately tickled by little hairs. *Oh, no.* I reached up, fanning them next to my face and could have cried when I felt more hair brushing my palms. Shit! I'd pulled my hair into a ponytail, but I hadn't even thought to tame the flyaways near my face. Normally I didn't run into anyone before I'd had a shower. How could I have known he was lying in wait?

I knew what I would see if I looked in a mirror: a freaking horror show of dark fuzz curling slightly toward the ceiling like devil horns.

No wonder he didn't want to get in my "knickers." I looked like an idiot.

The bathroom door squeaked. "Don't leave, yeah?" he called quietly from the cracked door, making me shoot a startled look in his direction.

"Patrick..." I hedged, forcing my hands into my lap so I wouldn't try to brush at the flyaways and draw even more attention to them.

"Mates call me Trick," he replied with another wink.

When he closed the bathroom door again, I bolted off the couch and sprinted toward the front door. If I didn't leave before he finished showering, I had a feeling I'd be just another girl who lost all common sense at the sight of Patrick Gallagher's smile.

It was one thing to find him incredibly hot, but it was quite another to actually spend time with him… especially when I looked like crap.

Chapter 4

Amy

I was kidding myself if I thought I could avoid Patrick while he was staying at his mom's.

I hadn't been caught that morning. My mom had left a note saying that she'd gone to my room, but my door had been locked so she assumed I was sleeping and had left me be. Apparently, her and my dad would be gone for dinner so I had to 'fend for myself.' Like I hadn't been doing that every night since I was ten.

I spent most of the day working on homework that I'd neglected the night before, and trying to forge some sort of excuse for my absence from school. It was a Friday, so thankfully I wouldn't have to deal with the Sisters for a few days. Hopefully, I'd be able to legibly forge my mother's signature by Monday.

At three that afternoon while I was reading on my bed, I almost pissed my pants when someone began knocking loudly on my window. When I turned toward it, I found Patrick Gallagher's smiling face so close it was almost pressing up against the glass. Holy shit.

"What are you doing here?" I hissed, sliding the warped window open.

"Mum wanted me to come get ye. She t'inks yer angry about dis mornin' since ye didn't come for tea."

"Shit, I didn't realize it was so late." I stepped away from the window to grab a pair of shoes and my favorite sweatshirt. " I'll be right out!"

He disappeared from the window and I wrapped my hair in a knot at my neck before pushing one of my legs though the opening, then ducking and twisting to get the rest of my body through.

"What de fuck are ye doin'?"

My head flew up and knocked the windowsill hard in surprise.

"I told you I'd be right out!" I sniped, hopping down into the grass before rubbing the small knot on the crown of my head.

"Forgive me for assumin' ye'd go out de front door like a normal person."

"You're forgiven."

I refused to look directly at him as I walked past, too embarrassed to meet his eyes and totally annoyed that he'd surprised me twice. I wished he would just leave already so I could go back to my relatively safe and normal life. Before I'd reached the end of the house, my arm was grabbed firmly and I was swung around to face him.

"Is dere a reason ye don't care for me, or do ye generally hate all men?" His face was close enough to mine that I could taste the mint on his breath, and for a moment I was afraid I'd hyperventilate and swoon like a blushing maiden from one of my romance novels.

"I-I don't dislike you," I stuttered back, my heart thumping hard. "I don't even know you."

His grip suddenly softened and though I could've pulled away, I wasn't able to actually make myself do it. He was staring at me, cataloguing each of my features with his eyes, and I was frozen.

"Ye disappeared dis mornin'."

"I had stuff to do at home."

"Ye always take a shower and den read all day instead of spendin' time wit' a new friend?"

"Were you spying on me?"

He laughed, squeezing my bicep before turning me and wrapping his arm companionably around my shoulders as he began to usher me toward Peg's.

"Didn't have to spy—just guessed. I know de type. By yer reaction, I'll bet I was correct." He let go of my shoulders and dropped his hand to my lower back to guide me up Peg's front stairs.

"What type?" I asked, trying to focus on the conversation as his hand slid a little lower.

"Me type," he whispered as we walked in the front door.

Peg chose that moment to come rushing out of the kitchen, a small towel hanging over her shoulder. "Amy! Ach, I'm so sorry I forgot to wake ye this mornin'!"

"That's okay," I reassured her as Patrick moved around me to drop onto the sofa. "I was really tired, anyway."

"Well, come in and get yer snack, even though ye didn't spend yer day at school. I made yer favorite!"

"How was work?" I asked as I followed Peg out of the small living room. "You look tired."

"Eh, I'm always tired!" she stepped toward the counter then turned around with a flourish. "Strawberry shortcake!"

"Holy—" I ducked as her hand came flying toward my head. "You remembered! Thank you!"

I bounced on my toes until she'd set three bowls down, then wrapped my arms around her waist and lifted her off the ground. "You're really great, you know that?"

"Sweet girl," she murmured into my hair. "Now, put me down so we can eat."

We sat around the table, talking and laughing like we always did, but there was a significant difference with Patrick there. It was hard not to stare at his mouth as he told us stories about school and the mechanic shop where he worked, and it was equally hard not to groan in mortification every time Peg glanced between us with a small grin on her face. I'm not sure what she saw when she watched us bantering back and forth, but whatever it was had her acting like she knew something I didn't.

"It's five, Amy." Peg warned me suddenly, as I smiled at Patrick. Wait, *what*?

I jumped up hastily, tangling my feet in the legs of my chair and barely catching it before it tipped backwards.

"What de hell?" Patrick asked in confusion.

"Her parents get home soon, son." Peg replied quietly.

"So?"

"I'm supposed to be home before they get there," I explained hurriedly.

"Why?"

"I don't know, I just am." I slipped the chair gently into its spot against the table, and carried my dish to the sink where I began to rinse it out.

"Yer not allowed to have friends?" He persisted, following me to the small sink.

"Yes, I am…"

"Name one."

"Peg."

"Dat doesn't count, does it? Yer racin' home so yer parents don't know ye've been spendin' yer time here."

"That's not it at all!" I huffed, quickly drying the bowl in my hands. "I just have to be home when they get there."

"So dey know ye come here after school, den?"

I clenched my jaw as my irritation grew. Why was he pushing this?

"No."

"Well—"

"Patrick, leave it alone," Peg warned from the table as I moved to go around him.

"Why don't yer parents know ye come here? Why de big secret, eh?" he asked again, ignoring his mom completely. "Ye ashamed?"

Frustrated tears began to form at the back of my eyes as he moved with me, refusing to let me past him. "Don't want yer American parents to know ye've been spendin' time wit' de poor mick t'ree houses down?"

I reached out and shoved him hard in the chest, taking his second of surprise as an opportunity to slide past him.

As I reached the doorway and freedom, I spun back toward him.

"My mother's Irish, you prick." I said, lifting my chin. "And I didn't know you before, but *now* I don't like you."

I tore my gaze away from his and met Peg's over his shoulder. "I'm sorry, Peg. Thank you for the shortcake. It was amazing. I'll see you later."

It was a good thing he didn't try to follow me home, because I was livid by the time I crawled back through my bedroom window. The telephone was ringing in the living room, and I ran as fast as I could to answer it, picking up just as the answering machine message began to play.

"Hello?"

"That's not how you answer the phone, Amy."

"Hi, Mom. What's up?"

"Why are you out of breath?"

"I was working out."

"Oh, well that's good. You don't want to get fat."

There was an awkward silence as she waited for me to agree with her. It wasn't going to happen.

"Well, I was calling because your father and I have decided to spend the night out tonight. He met some friends through work and they've invited us over."

"Okay, well, what time will you be home?"

"Honestly, Amy? I just said we wouldn't be home tonight. We'll be back tomorrow mid-morning. You're almost eighteen. You can spend one night alone, for Christ's sake."

She'd used the Lord's name in vain as if it was nothing, and it reminded me of the house I'd just ran from. Suddenly, I didn't care if they never came back.

"Oh, okay. I'll see you tomorrow then." I mumbled.

"Speak up!"

"*Okay, I'll see you tomorrow,*" I enunciated obnoxiously. I was feeling brave, knowing that I wouldn't see her for almost twenty-four hours.

"You're such a fucking brat."

The line clicked and she was gone.

"Bye, Mom! Have a nice time!" I called sarcastically to the dead connection.

I set the phone in its cradle and looked around the house, suddenly unsure. It was really quiet, and I'd be there all night by myself…

I smiled huge and pumped my arms wildly above my head in jubilation. Then I carried my boom box to the living room and turned on some music, changed into a ratty pair of sweats, and went to the kitchen to make myself some dinner. I rarely had use of the kitchen for any length of time, so even though we usually had all the vegetables and fruits I could want, I never got to make anything elaborate or fun. My night was going to be awesome.

By the time I was done making beef stew from scratch, I was practically giddy. I couldn't wait to have my own place one day, to not have to worry about making too much noise or filling the house with 'food' smells—which was one of my mom's pet peeves. I was thinking about running over to Peg's to see if she'd like some stew when I heard someone knocking on the front door.

I wondered who it could be, maybe Patrick or Peg? I didn't really know anyone else. When I opened the door though, it definitely wasn't anyone I'd ever met.

I recognized his voice, though.

Chapter 5

Amy

"Hey, Allie, right?" the man said with a smile, crowding me back into the house before I could get a word in edgewise.

He wasn't huge, and he was good looking, but his voice made my skin crawl. I didn't mean to let him into the house. I really didn't want him anywhere near me, but he stepped so close that my immediate reaction was to take a step back, followed by another, and soon he'd crossed the threshold.

"What are you doing?" I asked, trying to hide the panic in my voice. I was practically an adult, and this was my house. I needed to just tell him to get lost and he'd leave.

"Yer mum gave me a ring, said ye'd be home tonight. Wanted me to check in, make sure ye were safe, eh?" he answered, raising his hands in front of him, palms up.

"Well, I'm fine. You can go."

"No hurry." He shrugged, then turned his face toward the kitchen, "Somet'in' smells good."

"I was actually just getting ready to leave, so…" My natural politeness kept me from yelling at him to get the fuck out, but my hands had begun to tremble in uncertainty as he looked me over.

His smile was charming, and I knew he was trying to seem as unthreatening as possible, but the fact that I remembered his voice had me choking back my revulsion. He needed to leave. He needed to get out of my house.

"Hey, hey, no need to be nervous, darlin'," he cooed gently, stepping toward me. "Yer mum told me it was yer first time. We can go slow."

He reached out to lay a hand on my shoulder, and I made a strangled sound in my throat at the implication, jerking away.

No. My parents were neglectful, sure, but she wouldn't send a prostitute to our house when they weren't home. They'd always made sure I was safe. I shook my head in denial. He was wrong. He was lying.

"I want you to leave. Right now." I ordered quietly, my voice trembling.

"Let's talk a bit first, eh?"

"I don't want to talk. Leave." As he stepped closer, I braced myself, refusing to step any farther back for fear he'd follow me and move even deeper into the house.

"I've been paid for de whole night, love," he assured me, "So we'll just do dis at yer pace."

Oh, God, he'd been *paid*?

My eyes began to water as he came closer, his persistence making me feel like a cornered animal. I didn't want him near me. Why wasn't he leaving like I'd asked him?

I don't know why I didn't fight harder, why I didn't scream at the top of my lungs and run for the front door. Maybe it was because I'd never before been in a position where I had to fight. I'd never imagined myself in that scenario, so I hadn't had time to prepare. And in all honesty, I didn't believe that he'd actually force me to do something I didn't want. I was in complete denial, even though my gut was screaming for me to do *something*.

He'd just wrapped his fingers around my hip when I heard a noise from the front door.

"Amy, me love, is dinner ready?"

I'd never been so happy to see someone in my entire life.

Patrick swung the front door open as if he owned the place and stepped inside, his body seeming even larger than the last time I'd seen him just hours before. He'd changed too, wearing old slip-on sneakers, baggy jean shorts and a white tank top that highlighted the defined muscles of his chest, shoulders and arms. Holy hell.

"I'll t'ank ye to take yer hands off me girl," Patrick growled ominously as he took in the scene.

The man's hand pulled away so quickly it was as if I could feel the air shift with his movement.

"It's just business, mate," the guy replied, taking a step back.

"Well, I know she doesn't need any of yer *business*, so get de fuck out." Patrick's voice had become even darker, and I could see his hands clenching and unclenching as they hung at his side.

"Yeah, okay. No problem."

The man scrambled for the door, practically tripping over his own feet, but before he left Patrick called out to him again.

"Ye take yer money and ye don't say a fuckin' word."

"Alright." He nodded.

He was gone within seconds, and I felt my whole body begin to shake as the door slammed behind him.

"De fuck was dat?" Patrick roared at me, his voice echoing against the walls.

"I don't know!"

"Ye don't *know*?"

"He just showed up!" I was trying to keep it together. I wanted to yell at him for being such an asshole...but I couldn't. I was just so grateful he'd shown up when he did. And I didn't care if it meant I was a wimp, or weak, or a complete idiot, I wanted him to fucking hold me so I could physically feel that everything was okay.

"Why de fuck did ye let him into yer goddamn house?"

"I didn't! I just—he—and then—" I was trying to explain it. I could hear the words in my head very clearly, but I just couldn't get them out. And then, finally, the damn broke and my teeth began to chatter as my eyes overflowed.

"Aw, sweetheart." Patrick sighed and came toward me, wrapping his arms around me tightly with one hand at my back and the other at the nape of my neck. "Shhh, it's okay now, love. Yer okay. Shhh."

"He scared the crap out of me!" I screeched into his chest. "Fuck!"

I felt him huff a small laugh into my hair at my outburst.

"I bet." He mumbled, "Fuckin' manky bastard."

I took a deep breath and leaned back. "I'm done. Holy shit. I'm fine, I'm okay." I laughed self-deprecatingly. "It's not like anything happened. Right? I'm such a fucking whiner."

"Ye know him, baby?" he asked gently, smoothing my hair away from my face with one hand as he kept me secured against him.

"No, I mean I recognized his voice, I think…"

"Den ye've no reason to be embarrassed for bein' a bit frightened. Mum told me about yer folks. He's in wit' dem, ye've got good reason to be worried." He warned, "I could fuckin' kill ye for lettin' him in de door."

"He just sort of pushed his way in…"

His head turned toward the door and he stared at it silently for a moment, before completely changing the subject.

"Ye cooked?" he asked with a quirked brow, his dimple peeking out as his lips tipped up.

"It's just beef stew. It's one of the recipes I know by heart." I pulled out of his arms and walked toward the kitchen. "But you don't get any."

"Why de hell not?"

"You were a total dick earlier!"

"Ah, was gonna come over and apologize… again. Was plannin' on doin' it in a bit, but den yer man showed up."

"He's not my anything."

"Sounded like he wanted to be yer *first*," he argued with a snicker.

"Oh, my God! Now you really can't have any, you asshole."

"I'm kiddin' wit' ye, girl. No need to get yer knickers in a twist."

"Has Peg eaten? I was going to see if she wanted some of this. I'm not sure how to cut the recipe down far enough to feed less than four people," I replied, completely ignoring the knickers comment. I turned the burner off and grabbed a couple dishtowels to lift the heavy pot off the stove. "I can just carry it over there."

He moved in behind me as I was talking and before I could grasp the handles, he was pulling me away. "Ye'll not carry a heavy pot of hot stew all de way to me mum's, ye eejit." Then he lifted the stew as if it weighed nothing and motioned with his head to get me moving.

When we got outside, I locked the front door while he waited patiently. He was watching me like a hawk, but his face was completely relaxed. It was odd.

"Do I have something on my face?" I asked, wiping at my mouth and cheeks as I joined him on the sidewalk and we began to walk. "Why were you just staring at me?"

"Just glad I was dere, is all," he answered in a low voice. "I'll keep an eye out, alright? Ye won't be bot'ered again."

"Thank you." I swallowed loudly. "I mean, I don't think he'd come back. Do you?"

"No tellin'. Ye'll stay at our place tonight, no reason for ye to sleep in dat house alone while yer folks are gone—"

"I'd like to argue, but I don't really want to stay there by myself," I confessed sheepishly.

"Wit' good reason. Dose locks are shite." He shook his head as I climbed the steps ahead of him and opened Peg's front door.

"I can't stay here forever, though."

"I'll make sure yer safe, even if I'm not here," he said, passing me carefully so he wouldn't burn me with the pot. Then he paused and turned his head to meet my eyes. "I'll not let anyt'in' happen to ye," he promised.

I nodded slowly, my eyes never leaving his. It was an asinine promise; he was away at school most of the time and my own parents were the ones who put me in that situation in the first place. But even though it had been only hours since we'd met and most of that time I'd spent completely pissed off because he was an asshole... I still believed every word he said.

"Are ye alright, dear?" Peg asked, hopping off the couch as we made our way inside.

"I'm fine, I made dinner—"

"What happened, why was that man—"

"Leave it, Mum," Patrick cut her off sternly.

"But Patrick—"

"I said to leave it." He stared at Peg in some sort of silent communication that I didn't understand. Then, to my surprise, she relented. Just like that.

"Well, I'm glad yer here," she said with a smile, "And ye brought dinner!"

She ushered me into the kitchen, chattering about nothing in particular, and I felt myself beginning to relax. There was just something about her that automatically put me at ease—as if nothing bad would happen as long as I was with her. As we sat down to eat, things grew more and more comfortable. They didn't bring up anything that had happened that evening, choosing instead to tell funny stories and local gossip. It was the best dinner I'd ever had.

"Well, do ye want to go or not?" Patrick asked as I stared at my empty bowl.

"What?" I'd been so lost in my thoughts I hadn't even heard the first question.

"I'm goin' to meet up wit' some lads to play basketball. Ye want to come?"

"Basketball?"

"Dat's what I just said. Ye a parrot?"

"You're such a dick!"

"Jesus Christ—fuck, Ma!"

"Don't ye use that language in my house, Patrick Gallagher!" Peg scolded as she tried to flick Patrick in the head again.

"Fine!" He stood from the table. "Let's go."

"To play basketball?" I still didn't understand. He was the least likely person I could see playing the game. I mean, he had a silver chain clipped to a belt loop on his pants that hung in an arc to the wallet in his back pocket… a *chain,* for God's sake.

"Kevie goin' to be there?" Peg asked as she took our bowls to the sink.

"Yeah, should be." He was still freaking looking at me.

"Go, then," she said to me with a smile. "Get out of here for a bit, yeah?"

Chapter 6

Amy

The neighborhood had an outside basketball court that I'd never noticed before. It was only four blocks away, but it wasn't on my route to school so it wasn't surprising that I hadn't seen it. I barely left the house unless I was going to the grocery store or school. God, that was pathetic.

When we got there, I was surprised to see just one guy waiting for us, dribbling a basketball between his hands. He was shorter than Patrick, but not by much, and he had blonde hair that was cut conservatively short. He was dressed for the game in track pants and a grey t-shirt, and when he saw us coming, his face lit up in a bright smile.

"Trick!" he yelled happily, walking quickly toward Patrick and wrapping his arms around him in a tight hug. I heard their murmuring, but couldn't make out what they were saying as I followed slowly behind Patrick, and by the time I'd caught up to them, they'd turn to face me, one of Patrick's slung around the other guy's shoulders.

"Dis is Amy," Patrick introduced, "Amy—Kevie. Stay away from him, he's a total arsehole."

"Ye cretin," Kevie replied, shoving Patrick away. "Hello, Amy. It's nice to meet ye."

He held out his hand to shake, but before I could lift my own, Patrick was knocking Kevie's down. "None o' dat."

We looked at him like he'd lost his mind, but Patrick's face was implacable.

"I cannot shake her hand?" Kevie asked dubiously, his eyebrows meeting in the middle of his forehead.

"Ye'll not touch her."

I knew my mouth was hanging open. I knew it, and I couldn't seem to close it as Patrick reached for my arm and pulled me to his side.

"Patrick—" Kevie was trying not to laugh, but he couldn't hide the smile causing his cheeks to twitch.

"Save it." Patrick ordered before turning to me. "Sit over here, yeah?" he asked, his voice gentling. I followed him for a moment, before turning my head back to Kevie.

"It's nice to meet you, too!" I called out, then stumbled as Patrick jerked me forward and spun me to face him.

"Don't," he said quietly, his face dipping down to mine until they were almost touching.

"What's wrong with you?"

"I shouldn't have brought ye here," he mumbled, his eyes sweeping over my face.

"Then I'll go back! God, why do I keep giving you chances to *not* be a dick?" I tried to pull away, but his hand came up and tangled in my hair.

"I don't want him lookin' at ye, I don't want him touchin' ye. I shouldn't have brought ye. I should have left ye wit' me mum."

"Is he bad? He seems nice." I rose to my toes to try and see clean-cut Kevie over Patrick's shoulder.

"Keep yer eyes on me."

"You're being an idiot. What the hell?" I reached up to try and untangle his fingers from my hair. I wanted to leave. The whole situation was just weird. He was acting like I was stripping or something, like that Kevie guy was going to lay me on the cracked asphalt and have his wicked— oh, shit. He was *jealous*.

"You're jealous?" I asked incredulously. "Are you out of your freaking mind?"

"I'm not fuckin' jealous!"

"Oh, yeah. Yeah, you are." I snorted.

"Yer such a pain in me arse! And don't snort, it makes ye sound like a pig."

"I bet Kevie would like if I snorted," I answered snottily, "Hey Kev—"

His hand slid out of my hair and covered my mouth before I could finish my sentence. I could hear Kevie laughing like we were the funniest thing he'd ever seen.

"Shut yer trap!" Patrick yelled back to him.

"God, why de fuck do I give a shite what yer doin'?" he asked under his breath. He looked so confused that I felt a little sorry for him. "Just sit dere, alright? I'll come get ye when I'm done."

His hand slipped away from my face and down my neck as I swallowed hard.

"I'm supposed to just sit here?"

"Ye can watch."

"Oh, joy."

"Can ye just shut de fuck up for two seconds?"

"Probably not."

"Yer—argh!"

He stomped away, pushing Kevie hard when he reached him and stealing the basketball out of his hands.

I was surprised at how fluidly they moved when they started the game. They weren't playing for points, and as long as Kevie didn't glance in my direction, they didn't play aggressively, either. It was more choreographed than that. They moved around each other like they'd done it a million times before, blocking and dribbling and shooting the ball through a hoop with an old chain net.

By the time they were finished, the sky was growing dark and my ass had long since gone numb. Patrick had also taken off his shirt. Damn.

"Ye ready?" he asked as he pulled the tank top from his waistband and wiped his face with it.

"I was born ready." I groaned and rubbed my butt as I stood up.

"Ye need some help wit' dat?" he replied with a smirk.

"No, I do not. Oh, hey, Kev—" My voice was sickly sweet as my eyes met Kevie's and before I could finish my sentence, Patrick had stepped forward and threw his shoulder into my belly, slinging me up until I was hanging over his back like a sack of potatoes.

"Let me down, asshole!" I yelled. "It was sooo nice to meet you, Kevie! We should do some—" I stopped on a startled breath when Patrick slapped my ass hard. Well, at least it wasn't numb anymore.

"Nice to meet ye, too, darlin'," Kevie told me with a smile, stepping back as Patrick spun around. "Yer losin' it, Trick."

"Christ." Patrick's hand tensed on my thigh. "I fuckin' know. I'll see ye soon, yeah?"

"Sunday?"

"Fuck off."

Patrick began walking away as Kevie's laugh echoed around the court. By the time we'd hit the second block, I was beginning to feel nauseous and the urge to lick Patrick's sweaty back as it flexed beneath me was becoming hard to ignore.

"Can you let me down already?" I asked calmly. "It's getting a little uncomfortable up here."

"Shite," he grumbled, sliding me down the front of his body. "Sorry, I probably smell like crap."

"You smell fine, but you're acting like a lunatic." I brushed my hands down my shirt and began to walk. "What the hell was that?"

"I don't fuckin' know." His cheeks were flushed scarlet as he glanced at me. "I didn't want him to touch ye."

"Yeah, I got that," I replied dryly. "It still didn't make any sense. You're the one who brought me."

"I know. I just—de t'ought of it turns me stomach."

We were silent the rest of the way back to Peg's. There wasn't much to say after that. I wasn't quite clear on the specifics, but it seemed like he liked me. A lot. And even though I knew I shouldn't enjoy the whole possessive thing he had going, I did. No one had ever been possessive or protective of me before, and in less than twenty-four hours Patrick had shown both traits.

"Yer home!" Peg exclaimed. "How was Kevie?"

"He's good, Ma." Patrick said, his eyes glancing from his mom to me.

"He's a good boy." Peg turned to me with a sad smile. "I see him every Sunday, but it's not the same as when he'd be playin' in the yard with Patrick every day."

"You see him every Sunday?" I asked. "Well, that's cool that he visits you when Patrick's not here."

"He doesn't visit me, dear." Peg corrected me as Patrick's face went pale. "I see him when I go to hear him give Mass."

It took me a moment to understand what she'd just said, my mind still reeling from Patrick's odd behavior. Then it clicked and my jaw dropped as the truth sunk in. I turned completely toward Patrick, who looked as if he wanted the floor to open and swallow him whole. "Kevie's a *priest*?"

Chapter 7

Patrick

I turned to my side, trying to find a comfortable position on my mum's couch. She'd had the stupid thing for longer than I could remember and I hadn't fit comfortably on it since I was twelve. Fuck it, I'd sleep on the floor.

I untangled the blanket I was using from around my legs and climbed to my feet. I would have just rolled onto the floor and slept where I landed, but I still had to move some tables and a footstool to make enough room for me to stretch out. It seemed that the older I got, the smaller my mum's house became.

The day had been so fucking odd I just wanted to go to sleep and fucking forget about it.

Amy…Christ. I hadn't seen that situation coming. Mum had seemed more upbeat recently when I'd called her, but I hadn't thought anything of it. When I'd found Amy in my bed the night before, I'd been so startled I'd almost screamed like a girl. I'd never had a girl in that bed—I respected my mum too much for that—so the sight of her had not only raised my hackles, but had also given me an almost instant hard on. What was it about the thought of fucking a woman in a taboo location that was so appealing?

Even in the dark, I'd known she was beautiful. Not in the traditional sense, maybe, but beautiful just the same. Poets wrote sonnets about her type of beauty. The kind you couldn't exactly pinpoint, but couldn't seem to look away from. And that hair... shit. The first thing I'd thought as she sat up and it tumbled down her back was how it would feel against my thighs. Now the thought made me feel like a complete dick.

When I'd found her with that nasty fuck earlier, the only thing keeping me from killing him was my ignorance of the situation.

I didn't walk into things blindly. Ever.

Except, it seemed as if that was exactly what I was doing with Amy. I didn't understand anything about her—yet I'd acted like a possessed man earlier that night around one of my best friends. I'd fought with, helped, flirted with, protected and teased her all day and she'd taken what I gave her and threw it right back.

None of it made any sense.

I was staring at the wall and trying to figure out what the hell was going on when the door to my bedroom clicked quietly shut, and the light flicked on. What was she doing? I watched quietly for the light to turn back off, but it didn't. Why wasn't she sleeping?

Before I could talk myself out of it, I was knocking quietly on the door and opening it slowly. If she didn't want me to come into the room, she had plenty of time to stop me...

Holy God.

She was sitting cross-legged in the middle of my small, childhood bed wearing a thin nightshirt that pooled around her thighs. Her arms were raised, and my eyes were drawn to her breasts, clearly free of a bra and moving gently as she messed with her hair.

God was punishing me. That was the only explanation.

When my eyes finally reached her face, I inhaled sharply. She'd pulled her hair into an elaborate braid that wrapped around her head, and for the first time I could see every angle and plane of her face and neck clearly. Gorgeous. Everything about her, from the way she was sitting, to the halo of dark hair, to her wide eyes staring at me in surprise.

That was it for me. That was all it took.

"I couldn't sleep," she murmured sheepishly. "I was trying out a new style I found in a magazine. Does it look okay?"

As she turned her head so I could see the back of her hair, she tucked a few wispy strands into the braid, and I lost all control of my mouth.

"Is it hard for ye to do all dat wit' yer fingers de way dey are?"

I had the overwhelming urge to cut out my own tongue as she turned quickly to face me.

"I—uh, no." She laughed uncomfortably and slid her hand under her thigh to hide it. "I don't remember ever having them, so..."

"I'm sorry. I shouldn't have said dat."

"It was an understandable question," she said reasonably. "I'm sure people are curious... they just don't usually ask about it."

She raised her other hand to start unwinding the braid, and I swallowed hard as her hair flowed back down around her shoulders. I took a step forward, watching it closely as she ran her palm down the length. Then I realized she was still self-consciously hiding her damaged hand under her thigh.

"Don't do dat," I ordered hoarsely. "Don't hide it."

"I just thought—"

"Whatever yer t'inkin' is wrong."

She was uncomfortable and trying not to show it and I was more ashamed than I'd ever been in my life. I'd done that. I made her feel that way—which had never been my intention. I shouldn't have been in there with her, not while I was trying to get my head on straight, but suddenly I couldn't leave her without somehow fixing the mess I'd made.

I reached down and pulled her hand from beneath her leg, keeping my eyes on hers as I lifted it up between us. She maintained eye contact and kept her hand relaxed in mine, but her pulse was racing at the side of her neck. Rubbing my thumb along her palm, I finally dropped my eyes to her hand.

Two of her fingers, her left pinkie and ring finger were both missing. They weren't completely gone, but ended at the middle joint, giving the impression that she'd only curled them out of sight. The skin was smooth, there was very little scarring and if she made a fist, it probably wasn't even noticeable that those two fingers were gone.

As I stared, she finally tried to pull her hand away with a huff of frustration. She didn't want me looking—her embarrassment was clear—but I wasn't about to let go.

And once again, I lost all sense of myself and did something stupid.

"What?" she gasped as I put her ring finger into my mouth and ran my tongue lightly up the side, ending the movement with a soft kiss. I repeated the motion with her tiny pinkie, then moved her hand up my face so I could kiss the palm of her hand.

"I was an idiot and I'm apologizin' for de hundredth time since we've met," I said, keeping her hand close to my face so she felt every breath on her palm. "It was insensitive to ask about yer fingers in such a way. In all honesty, I have no idea why I asked ye dat. It's none of me business, and yer hair looked beautiful so de question was irrelevant."

"I think you may be the oddest person I've ever met."

"I'm not usually like dis, believe me."

"You're still holding my hand."

"Do ye accept me apology?"

"There's nothing to accept. You were curious."

"I made ye uncomfortable."

"Only because I thought it grossed you out."

"Grossed me out?"

"Disgusted you."

"Dere's nuttin' about ye dat's disgustin'."

"Why are you still holding my hand?"

"I've no idea." I still didn't let go.

She went silent for a moment at my words, looking down at where

I held her hand in mine. I didn't know why I hadn't dropped it yet. I told myself that it was because I still felt the need to prove that her missing fingers didn't bother me—but that wasn't true. It was a part of the reason, but not the entire reason. If I were only trying to reassure her, I wouldn't have slid my fingers between hers until they were completely entwined.

"Want to hang out in here for a while?" she asked suddenly, her voice hoarse.

"It's late love, why aren't ye sleepin?" As soon as I'd said the words, I prayed that she wouldn't change her mind and ask me to leave.

"Can't sleep." She shrugged as if it was no big issue, but her eyes were drooping from exhaustion. "Come on, you're falling off the bed."

She scooted back on the mattress, gripping my hand tightly until she'd settled herself against the wall behind her. I didn't resist when she pulled me up next to her, even though I knew it was a bad fucking idea. I was twenty-two years old and she wasn't quite eighteen according to my mum—no good could come from sitting on a bed with her in the middle of the night, especially when she was wearing so little.

"I was in a car accident when I was two," she told me as I got settled. "My mom says my hand went through the window—that's how I lost my fingers."

"Dat must have hurt like a bitch."

"I don't remember it. They've just... always been missing, you know?" She straightened her fingers in mine and looked down at her hand. "I think most people notice, but no one ever says anything."

"Except eejits who blurt out any fuckin' t'ing dat pops into dere heads."

"Nah, just you."

"Ye just proved me—" I turned my head to look at her, and she was smiling impishly. "Ye pokin' fun at me?"

"Maybe a little."

"When's yer birt'day?" There went my mouth again, asking shit that didn't need an answer and I shouldn't be asking in the first place.

"What? Oh, next month."

"Eighteen, yeah?"

"Yep. Not that eighteen will be much different than seventeen."

Eighteen was very different than seventeen in my eyes.

"At least ye'll be a legal adult by den, yeah? Ye can move away from dose manky parents o'yers."

"Where would I go? It's not like I have a job or any money," she scoffed, shaking her head.

"T'ings have a way of workin' demselves out. Ye won't be dere forever."

"Did you move out when you were eighteen?"

"Nah, I had to stay wit' Mum for a couple extra years. I left for Uni when Mum got a promotion at work and could afford dis shithole herself."

"You work, though, right? As a mechanic?"

"Sure. Pays de rent on me flat and livin' expenses. Doesn't leave much after dat, dough."

"Oh." Her head was leaned back against the wall, but her eyes were closed and every twenty seconds or so, it was dipping a little to the side until she jerked it back up. She looked so sweet that way, with her mouth relaxed and her dark eyelashes fanning her cheeks. I imagined lying down and wrapping myself around her so I could run my fingers through her hair until she drifted off completely. I knew better, though. That road would take me straight to hell.

"Why don't ye go to sleep, love?" I asked, causing her head to jerk up again.

"No, stay for a while. I'm not tired."

"I'm watchin' ye fall asleep where ye sit. Yer tired."

"I can't stop thinking about that guy who came to my house earlier." She whispered groggily. "Every time I close my eyes, I think he's going to come back."

"Yer not at home, ye know he wouldn't get to ye here," I told her gently, my gut clenching at the thought of her lying in my bed afraid.

There was something inherently wrong with that picture. She should never have reason to feel afraid, especially while she was wrapped in my sheets.

"There's a window." Her voice was so quiet I had trouble hearing her, but when I finally figured out what she'd said, I had to stop myself from cursing out loud. There was a window at the foot of my bed that I'd had to stop crawling through when I'd reached puberty because it was so fucking small. The fact that she was afraid anyone over the age of ten could slip through it was a testament to how frightened she was. She'd hid it well, no doubt about that, but the truth often comes out in the dark of the night when one's so tired that their walls become nonexistent.

"Here, love," I said calmly, though my blood was boiling. I wanted to find that piece of shite and kill him, but I had other more important things to focus on at the moment. I reached up with my free hand and threaded my fingers into the hair at the side of her head, pulling her sideways a bit until she was resting against my side. "Sleep, I'll not let anyone bodder ye tonight. Ye have me word."

She sagged into me and I had to look away from her as she curled her legs to the side. She was wearing shorts that I hadn't seen when I'd first come in, but they didn't hide more than an inch of her long, smooth legs. I pulled the blanket up and over her to hide them. Christ.

She was going to be sore in the morning after sleeping sitting up the way she was, but I told myself over and over again that it didn't matter. I couldn't pull her into my lap and cuddle her more securely and I couldn't suggest she lie down flat. The sight of her spread out on my bed would completely dissolve any shred of decency I had left.

I didn't sleep that night as I sat with her. And if there had been any confusion before, it was gone then. I knew without a doubt that I was completely fucked.

Chapter 8

Amy

I woke up with a hard chest under my head and fingers threaded through my hair.

Patrick.

Opening my eyes cautiously, I took inventory of our bodies. I was on my side with one hand on his chest and the other still wrapped in his between us. Sometime during the night, we must have slid down the wall, because he was flat on his back on the bed with his feet resting on the floor. He couldn't have been comfortable, but his even breaths indicated he hadn't woken up yet.

As quietly and gently as I could, I untangled his fingers from my hair and slid away from him to climb off the bed. I couldn't believe he'd stayed the entire night with me, and I was more than a little apprehensive to walk into the living room.

Peg was out there and there was no way she'd missed that Patrick wasn't where she'd left him the night before.

Choosing between being in bed with Patrick when he woke up or facing Peg was easy though. I left the room silently, pulling the door closed behind me as I followed the noise into the kitchen.

"Want some breakfast?" Peg asked from where she was leaning inside the fridge.

"I should probably get home." I needed to get far away before I proved the medical field wrong and actually died from embarrassment.

"Stay! Havin' a special breakfast today!"

Before I could ask her why breakfast was so special, I felt a hand slide along my waist.

"Mornin', Mum," Patrick rasped as he walked past me. He leaned in to kiss his mom on the top of her head, and she smiled as if he'd just found the cure to cancer.

"Did ye sleep good?"

"Got a fuckin' kink in me neck."

"I bet," Peg said knowingly, glancing at me with a smirk. "Well, sit down! The food is ready."

We all sat down at the table as I tried hard to avoid both sets of eyes that were staring at me. *Nothing to see here, folks.*

"Ye'll say prayer, Patrick," Peg ordered, reaching out to grab both of our hands.

Great, now I was going to have to hold his hand again, when all I wanted to do was go home and brush my teeth and try to get over my complete mortification. I lifted my hand and limply placed it in his waiting one. I tried not to show any sort of reaction, but I stopped breathing when he ran his thumb over my fingers. The damaged ones.

My eyes met his as he began to pray.

"Bless us, O Lord, and dese dy gifts which we—"

The prayer was cut off as the door to the living room opened behind me and a man's voice called out in greeting.

"Margaret! Ye here?"

Patrick's hand dropped mine like it was on fire as he jumped to his feet. The veins in his neck were suddenly bulging, his face like stone.

"De fuck are ye doing here, Da?" he asked angrily, startling me.

"Watch yer mouth, boyo," the man admonished with a glare.

"Yer not welcome here."

My gaze flew between the two until I felt Peg's hand tighten in mine. When I turned to look at her, her normally rosy cheeks were pale and she was frozen in place and staring over my shoulder.

"Can a man not have a visit on his son's birthday?" the man asked jovially.

My thoughts of his complete obliviousness were cut off as I saw his hand clench and unclench at his side, a motion that was familiar because I'd seen his son do it repeatedly. He was nervous, maybe even scared. He turned his eyes to Peg, and I could feel the tension in the air as Patrick gripped the table's edge as if it was the only thing holding him back.

"Margaret, love—"

"Eyes on me, ye old bastard," Patrick roared, making me jump in my seat.

Peg began to dig her nails into the back of my hand, her body still stiff and still with an emotion I couldn't pinpoint. Terror? I didn't think that was right. There was something there, but I had no idea what it was.

When Peg's husband took a step closer to the table, I moved instinctively. My chair screeched across the floor as I stood, and for the first time since he'd arrived, the man's eyes went to me as I stepped in front of Peg, blocking his view of her. My arm was twisted oddly behind my back since Peg didn't seem ready to let it go, but I refused to acknowledge it. Instead, I met the man's eyes and lifted my chin.

"Sorry, dear. I didn't notice ye dere. Ye Patrick's girl?"

"Don't speak to her," Patrick hissed as he rounded the table.

"She's lovely," he replied, looking between Patrick and I.

"I swear to Christ, old man, one more word—"

Patrick's voice had taken on a wild edge, something that must have knocked Peg out of her stupor, because, with a small squeeze of my hand, she came to her feet behind me.

"Robbie, that's enough." Her voice was like a whip, slicing through the small kitchen. "Patrick, take Amy home."

"Mum—"

"Do as I say," she shot back, sliding around me.

Their eyes met for a second, another conversation passing between them with no more words spoken. With an audible swallow, Patrick nodded, then grabbed my hand roughly and pulled me with him around his father and out of the house.

"Was that your dad?" I asked breathlessly, practically jogging beside him down the sidewalk. "It's your birthday?"

"I don't have time for dis," he replied tersely, "Do ye have yer key?"

I nodded silently, duly chastised. He was sweating, and I knew it wasn't from our hurried walk to my house. I was missing something; there was a reason Patrick was so frantic to get me home.

I turned and unlocked my front door, and then he was suddenly in front of me and racing through the house while I stood stupidly in the doorway.

"Yer good. Lock de door and don't leave de house until I come back for ye," he told me with a quick kiss to my forehead. He started down the steps before turning to face me. "And close yer fuckin' window!" Then he was gone.

I'd been so eager to get home when I'd woken up, but suddenly I wasn't sure what to do with myself. I locked the door behind him and stood in the middle of the living room, looking around as if I'd never seen any of the contents before. I felt like I should take a shower or something, but I couldn't make myself move away from the front door.

What if he came back? What if he needed me? What if Peg needed me and I couldn't hear the door? The questions were asinine. I knew Patrick was fully capable of taking care of things on his own, but that didn't seem to slow my racing heart.

I wasn't sure what I'd witnessed at Peg's, but I knew it was bad. Peg hadn't seen her husband in years, and she'd told me that she preferred it that way. I'd gathered from small comments she'd made that the life he lived wasn't one she wanted to share.

So why was he there?

My mind wandered back to the look on Patrick's face when Robbie walked through the door, and all of a sudden I was reminded of the way he'd looked at the man he'd found me with the day before. I shuffled to the side and dropped inelegantly to the couch, raising my hand to my mouth as I thought of the many emotions I'd seen on Patrick's face in such a short amount of time.

Holy God, how had this become my life? My memory flashed from waking up to Patrick yelling at me, his bare chest, the way he'd teased me on our way to Peg's, the man who'd shown up the day before on some sordid errand for my parents, Patrick stepping into my house like some sort of avenging angel and making the guy leave… and finally the way he'd lifted my fingers to his mouth and slid them inside.

My stomach clenched at the memory.

Chapter 9

Amy

I'd long ago showered and was sitting on the couch reading when I finally heard a knock on the front door. It had to be close to three in the afternoon already, my parents had called to say they wouldn't be home for dinner, and I'd been pacing the house like a caged animal for hours. Part of me was infuriated that Patrick and Peg had kicked me out and ordered me to stay home, but another part—a small voice in the back of my head—was telling me that I needed to stay far away from the Gallaghers. Something was going on with them that was way bigger than the odd sort of friendship we'd formed, and I had enough of my own problems to deal with.

I hurried to the door and slid the lock back, but before I do anything else, it was being pushed open from the other side and there was Patrick. His t-shirt was stretched to hell at the neck, and his arms were crossed at his chest, causing the muscles to bulge. He looked... messy, unkempt.

When my eyes finally met his, I swallowed harshly. He was angry. Really angry, and I had no idea why. But before I could say a word, his hands were wrapped around my waist and he was pushing me roughly into the house. He kicked the door closed behind him right before my back slammed against the wall.

"What de fuck are ye doin' answerin' de door before ye know who's out dere?" he scolded before reaching up to grasp my jaw. "I coulda been anyone! Bad shite happens when ye aren't fuckin' careful Amy! Yer not livin' in America anymore. Yer in Ireland, yeah? Dere ain't no safe place in Ireland."

His voice quieted to a whisper on the last words, and his eyes squeezed shut as if he was in pain. I knew things in Ireland were bad and getting worse. I saw things on the news and in the papers all the time... but it hadn't really touched my life. I was an American teenage girl who rarely left the house, so it didn't really have anything to do with me. What the hell was going on? My throat grew tight as I watched him try to pull himself together, and without conscious thought, I reached up to cup my palm over his cheek.

His eyes opened and his mouth hit mine just seconds later, my breath hitching as his tongue licked into my surprised mouth. He tasted like peppermint candy and his breath was hot against the lower half of my face as he pulled back slightly and bit my lower lip.

"Touch me." He groaned frantically, leaning his forehead against mine as he let go of my body so he could pull my hand off his face and under the neck of his t-shirt.

I wasn't sure what I should be doing, but the aggression in his kiss had flipped some sort of switch in my brain, because without any conscious thought, I'd fisted one of my hands in his hair while the other wrapped around his back and dug in. His hands swept up and down my sides, eventually running down my ass and squeezing it gently as we kissed. I wasn't sure whether I should be embarrassed at where his hands were or climb him like a monkey, so I picked somewhere in between and slipped my hand under his shirt and scratched my nails up his back.

As Patrick moaned against my mouth and pressed his hips against mine, we heard the front door open once again and the sound of someone clearing their throat. I ripped my face away to glance toward the intruder and my face grew hot.

"Trick," Kevie called as Patrick dropped his forehead to my shoulder and relaxed his hands against me, sliding them to the top of my jeans.

"Get de fuck outta here," he mumbled toward my chest, causing my nipples to bead. Great, now my nipples were poking through my shirt, and right in front of a priest, no less.

I shoved Patrick away a step, and he finally raised his head. He'd cooled down in the few seconds since we'd heard Kevie's voice, and there was no trace of the desperation or anger he'd shown when he'd arrived.

"What are ye doin' here?"

"Got a call dat Robbie'd been into Maloney's for a pint, so I stopped by yer mum's. She sent me here."

"Well, everyt'in's fine, *Fadder Kevin*. Go on and baptize some babies or bless a fuckin' house."

"I'm not here as a priest," Kevie replied quietly, unable to hold back the traces of hurt and exasperation in his voice. "I'm here as yer friend."

"A friend wouldn't have stopped what I was doin'."

Kevie looked between Patrick and I, his jaw tight. "A good friend would've."

Patrick jerked, and his gaze flew toward where I was still standing unsteadily against the wall. I didn't understand half of what they were talking about, but I knew the instant Patrick regretted what he'd done. He looked ashamed.

"I'm sorry, lass."

"You're sorry?" I replied uncomfortably.

"Amy—"

I shook my head as he tried to talk to me, but I couldn't force myself to say another word. I was so embarrassed I just wanted to leave. Not only had the neighborhood priest caught us making out like the horny teenager I was, but with a few chosen words, he'd somehow made

Patrick regret it and me feel like a complete idiot.

"Me Da—"

"Really? That's what you want to talk about?" I practically yelled the words.

"Um, no. I don't really..."

"It's time for you to go." I moved to the door and opened it, staring at the men impatiently. "Well?" I swept my arm toward the street.

Patrick's nostrils flared at my attitude, but Kevie seemed to be silently laughing as he passed me with a nod. God, that priest was unlike any I'd ever met.

"We're goin' to talk about dis," Patrick ordered as he paused in the doorway. "I shouldn't have—"

"No, probably not," I replied before he could finish his sentence. "But it's no big deal."

He sighed in frustration as his fist clenched, "Yer only seventeen."

"Almost eighteen—but who's counting?" I waved my hand again to usher him out, but before I could evade him, he was gripping my chin and forcing me to meet his eyes.

"We *will* be discussin' dis. It's not at all what ye t'ink, but I need to go back and check on me mum and yer parents will be home soon."

I would have gladly dropped into the middle of a black hole in that moment, while he stood there staring at me and I tried valiantly not to cry. Patrick had given me the first kiss I'd had in two years, and within moments had completely crushed any enjoyment I'd gotten out of it. He hadn't just said he was sorry, I could tell by looking at him that he really *was* sorry. No matter what his reason for regretting the kiss, he'd tainted it.

"Sure. See you soon," I said with a nod, pulling my face away.

He left without another word, and after he'd gone, I spent more time than I should have leaning against the closed front door while I stared at the wall he'd pressed me up against. The most incredibly sexy moment of my entire life had been something he was ashamed of.

I decided then that I'd avoid him as much as I could until he left for school again. We didn't need to talk; it would be better for everyone if we forgot anything had ever happened.

Unfortunately, Patrick Gallagher had other ideas… and as much as I hated to admit it, I was beginning to realize that he usually got what he wanted.

Chapter 10

Amy

"**I**'m going to bed," I called to my parents from the doorway of my room.

I wasn't sure why I still did things like that—apprised them of my movements as if they actually cared one way or the other. I think it had become a habit, a way of making them acknowledge me in some small way. Even if they didn't care what I was doing, they couldn't escape the knowledge if I gave it to them deliberately. It was a subtle *fuck you,* one that wasn't noticeable from my tone or manner, but was there just the same.

They murmured back in response as they cuddled on the couch, my dad's arm wrapped tightly around my mom's shoulders in an uncommon show of intimacy. It made me shudder in revulsion, knowing that she must have made him very happy during their time away for him to treat her so gently. I refused to let my mind contemplate what she could have done with their 'new friends' that would warrant such behavior.

They'd gotten home right after I'd finished the sandwich that was my dinner, my mom giggling softly like a young girl as my dad led her through the doorway. I was sure that any other child on the planet would have felt comforted by the tableau, but it only made my stomach turn in apprehension. He was pleased with her, and she was glowing in his approval, and I hated knowing that whatever had happened was probably worse than I could even imagine.

Neither of my parents said a word about the man they'd sent to the house the day before. Other than the appraising look my mom gave me as she passed me in the hallway later, not one word was spoken about what or who I had done that weekend. It was as if nothing had changed, like the small bit of trust I'd had for them hadn't completely vanished like a puff of smoke from a cigarette on a windy day.

Like they hadn't betrayed their own child by paying a stranger to divest her of her virginity.

For the most part, I was glad that they hadn't tried to discuss it with me, not that I thought my dad would say a word about it. But a small part of me resented the fact that my mom continued on as if nothing had happened. What if it had been horrible? What if the man they'd sent me had hurt me? They had no clue what had gone down with the prostitute they'd sent, and they didn't seem to care. While it wasn't surprising, I couldn't deny that it hurt like hell.

I fell asleep easily that night, my parents' tired expressions divesting me of my worry about visitors in the house. I shouldn't have been so confident of their plans since things had been changing so quickly, but the events of the day made my entire body sluggish, as if I'd spent hours crying. Even if I'd been afraid, I wouldn't have been able to stay awake. I was exhausted.

When my mattress dipped later that night, my first thought as I slid into wakefulness was absolute disgust that I'd grown complacent in locking my door. But before that disgust could turn to fear, my arms were pinned by hands braced at my shoulders, pulling my blankets taut against my chest. Warm breath fanned my face as I opened my mouth to scream.

"Ye'll wake yer folks if ye scream," a familiar voice whispered,

"It's just me, love."

I relaxed into the bed as relief rushed through me.

"What the hell are you doing here?" I hissed, pushing at the blankets that held me immobile. "How did you get in?"

"I told ye de locks were shite."

"Let me up!"

He was silent for a moment while he considered my order. "What are ye wearin' under dere?"

"Are you shitting me?" I paused, waiting for an answer that never came, then huffed loudly. "A tank top and shorts, you pervert. Happy?"

"No bra?"

My mouth gaped like a fish as I stared at him, my face heating. "You're such a creep. No, I don't have a bra on, what woman sleeps with her frigging bra on?"

"I'm holdin' on by a t'read here, yeah?" he warned, leaning closer until I could see his eyes in the sliver of moonlight coming in through my window. "I know yer not seein' much right now, but me eyes have adjusted already to de dark. I've seen what ye sleep in, lass, and I'll not be seein' it again tonight, yeah? Else, me good intentions will fly out yer window dere."

"Okay," I replied. He was serious, and I was a mixture of extremely pleased with his words and completely mystified by them. "You want me," I commented stupidly to verify.

"Christ." He leaned down and rubbed his stubbly cheek along mine, his lips brushing my jaw. "I'd give anyt'in' to climb into dose sheets wit' ye, but I won't."

"Why the hell not?" My voice was too loud in the quiet night, and he hushed me by putting his hand over my mouth, unwittingly freeing me from the blankets.

"I've no argument wit' kickin' de shite out of yer da, but ye might not want to deal wit' de fallout of dat." He pulled his hand from my mouth and ran his fingers gently through the hair at my temple.

"Sorry! God, you don't make any sense. Why the hell are you

doing this?" My body was heating from the way he was touching me, and it seemed really freaking cruel that he would continue to move his hand along the side of my face when he had no intention of following through. I jerked my head to the side and away from his fingers. "Quit it."

His breath caught at my movement, and his head tilted to the side as he eyed the blankets that had pulled down my chest a few inches. They weren't low, my breasts were still completely covered, but a wide expanse of my neck and collarbone were suddenly bare. He jerked as he processed what he was seeing, which was really just an innocent patch of skin. However, the expression on his face was like I'd stripped myself bare.

"Holy Mot'er," he mumbled, lifting his hand to run it across my throat. "Do ye have any idea how appealin' I find ye?"

His voice was thick with lust, and my heart began to pound in excitement. The tension between us seemed to grow stronger as he continued to run his fingers all over the skin of my chest, sometimes so incredibly soft that I could barely feel it and other times rough enough that I knew there would be faint fingernail marks from where he had dragged them across me. We were silent as our eyes met and held, but neither of us moved as he continued to caress me.

Finally, I couldn't stand it anymore. My legs were tense under the blankets, my knees tilting slightly outward, and I needed so badly to arch my hips to try and find some friction that the restraint was causing my body to break out into a sweat. Before he could stop me, I'd shoved the blankets to my waist, the cold night air a relief that made goose bumps break out over my shoulders and my nipples bead tightly against my thin tank top.

He groaned deep in his throat and the sound gave me pause, realizing how far I was pushing him and the control he was exhibiting as he tried to hold himself back. His hand at my neck began to tremble as he watched it slide down to the top of my shirt. His eyes roamed over what I'd uncovered as he stood and turned toward me, his hand never leaving me.

His eyes finally met mine as he climbed on top of me, never removing the blankets that separated us from the waist down. My legs instinctively spread as his hips met mine. Perhaps I should have been more nervous than I was, but I was nearly eighteen years old. I wasn't ignorant to male/female relationships and all that they entailed, and I'd never been more attracted to anyone. I wanted him there, between my legs—and though I may not have been ready to have sex with him, I knew deep in my gut that it wouldn't get that far. I trusted Patrick implicitly, and it didn't matter how hard I'd pushed him, he'd never go farther than I was comfortable with.

"Yer goin' to kill me," he said quietly, as he braced himself above me.

His lips met mine before the words were fully formed and the second he'd finished speaking, his tongue was in my mouth, rubbing against mine. He tasted like cigarettes, something I'd never imagined I'd enjoy, but I couldn't get enough of him. There was something about the way he touched me, the way he held back even though I made it clear that I was all in—it turned me on even more. It gave me the courage I may not have had otherwise. I let go of the blankets at my waist, the need to feel his skin was so strong that I moaned into his mouth as my hands slipped under the front of his t-shirt where it was gaping between us.

"Yer beautiful," he whispered as his lips left mine and played gently against my jaw.

I tilted my head back to give him better access as he moved to my jaw. The sensation made me both shiver and burn, and when I felt the gentle scrape of his teeth, I couldn't stop my hips from rolling against his. The blankets were still between us, creating a barrier that I hated, but when I tried to push them out of the way his hips jutted sharply downward, immediately giving me the friction I craved and trapping the blankets more firmly between us.

"Ye'll leave dose dere," he ordered, giving no further explanation.

Our hips moved in tandem as he held my hands at my shoulders, bracing himself with his elbows. I hated the few inches that separated us then. I was no longer conscious of anything except the need to be closer, to rub my body against his and feel more of his skin.

"Please, Patrick," I whispered into his ear as he bit down gently on mine. "Let's just move the blankets. That's all." I brought my knees up as far as I could and laid them wide in an attempt to feel more of him, and my breath caught as I succeeded.

"Aye, move de blankets, she says," he chided into my ear, his voice taking on a bit of Peg's odd accent, "Dat's all, she says."

"Please. It's fine. Please." I didn't care how I sounded. I needed him *now*. I wanted to break his control so badly he'd give me what I wanted. I arched my chest up—my coup de grace—and just like I knew they would, the thin straps of my tank top became trapped under my shoulders and the front stretched so far that my breasts popped from the top. Who would've known that having a ratty old tank top that left me half bare if I twisted just right would come in handy some day?

Patrick froze completely above me, before slowly lifting his face to meet my eyes. He was angry. So angry, that I immediately flushed in embarrassment.

He closed his eyes tightly, his nostrils flaring and his mouth pulled up into a grimace before he lost whatever battle he'd been fighting in his head. I watched him, my hands still trapped under his against the sheets as his head tipped down and his eyes opened, staring at my breasts. He didn't move, but surprisingly, he didn't even need to.

Knowing that he was looking at me obliterated any embarrassment I'd felt and immediately ratcheted up my desire even farther. I began to move my hips against his tentatively, waiting for his response and, after a moment, he shoved down against me again. As he did, his head moved and suddenly my left nipple was between his lips and he was sucking it against the roof of his mouth. My breath caught as I tried to be quiet, but it was almost impossible to keep the noises from pouring out of my mouth. It all felt so *good*.

Until suddenly, it didn't.

Patrick dropped his hips, trapping mine against the bed and bit down on my nipple hard enough that it wasn't quite painful, but wasn't pleasant, either. That's when I lost the battle against sound and let out a mournful and pained whimper.

"Ye'll not move again, do ye hear me?" he asked harshly as soon as he'd let my nipple go. "I've made meself clear, yet ye keep pushin' and pushin'."

His tone was scathing, and I immediately felt tears hit the back of my eyes as I tried to pull my hands from his. I suddenly felt naked, the thought of his gaze on my breasts becoming something that turned me cold and made me panic.

"Let go!" I choked. "Let go! Let go! Let go!"

My words gained in speed and volume as I said it over and over again, but it only took seconds before his gaze turned from surprise to horror. He let go of my hands like they were on fire, and his mouth hung open as I pulled up my tank top and pushed at his chest.

"Leave me alone," I sniffled as soon as I was covered again. "Just leave me alone." I brought my arms to my chest to protect myself, curling my hands into fists at my neck.

"No," he said quietly, bringing one hand to cup the side of my face and leaving it there even as I tried to pull away. "Ye've got it wrong, love."

His voice was so gentle that my breath hitched, but I lowered my eyes. I didn't want to face him. I just wanted him to leave, so I could curl up into a little ball and pretend that I hadn't just made a colossal fool of myself.

"Amy, look at me," he ordered. "I'll not move until ye do."

I hated him a little bit then.

When I finally forced my eyes to his, the gaze that met mine was solemn.

"Dere are two types of women in dis world," he told me, rubbing his thumb along my cheekbone. "De ones ye fuck, and de ones ye marry."

My body jolted, and I wanted nothing more than to slap him across the face. I knew I was glaring, and I felt the tears drying into little hard lines against my temples where they'd run off my face.

"As much as I want ye, yer not a quick fuck," he said adamantly, lowering his face close to mine. "I've known ye weren't since de moment I met ye, yet I keep playin' wit' fire just to be close to ye. I knew better dan to kiss ye tonight, I knew dat t'ings would get outta hand."

"That's stupid."

"It's de truth. I'd like nuttin' better den to sink into ye, darlin'. But dat's not right."

"You yelled at me." My voice was shaky and I sniffled again.

"I'm sorry." He tilted his head until our foreheads were touching, closing his eyes. "It's not ye I'm angry wit.' Forgive me." His lips met mine softly in repentance, and I sighed against his mouth, my body beginning to relax.

He was like a hypnotist, controlling my emotions with a small movement or word. I knew it, yet I couldn't seem to stop it. It was as if my body followed his, my emotions mirrored his own.

As soon as his mouth lifted from mine, he crawled from the bed. When he stood, I couldn't help but stare at his hips where he was still hard and pushing against the zipper of his jeans.

"I'm leavin' after church wit' Mum in de mornin', so I won't see ye again before I go." He said, running his fingers through his hair. "It's probably for de best."

"So, this, us, it's over then?" I asked, rolling to my side to watch him as he moved to the door.

"I didn't say dat."

I finally looked away from his body and met his eyes in confusion. "You just said—"

He shook his head once as my words drifted off. Turning to open the door, he looked at me one more time over his shoulder. "I'll just have to marry ye."

Chapter 11

Amy

I knew from previous Sundays searching for Peg in the pews of our church that she attended a different one, but that didn't stop me from looking for any sign of her or Patrick the next day. He'd left me reeling the night before, questioning everything between us in an endless loop that hadn't allowed me to sleep. He'd have to *marry* me? I was seventeen, for goodness sake. I didn't even have my driver's license in Ireland *or* America. I hadn't even graduated from high school!

I also couldn't wrap my mind around the idea of there being two categories for women—fuck or marry. It wasn't the nineteen-fifties anymore. The sexual revolution had changed things, and frankly, the idea of saving virginity for marriage seemed archaic. Who wanted to wait to sleep with someone until after they were married? What if they were horrible in bed? Then you were stuck with them for life, especially if you were Catholic. There'd be no escaping.

I zoned out for most of the service, my mind wandering and causing my heart to race in both anger and confusion. My inattention didn't really matter, though; we always stood at the same time, replied at the same time, knelt at the same time, received communion at the same time. Catholic services were comforting that way, always the same, never surprising or different.

The days after that passed slowly, especially after I realized that Patrick must already be gone from Peg's and on his way back to college. It was like the spark that had been burning in my chest while I knew he was close was suddenly gone, and the days spread out before me under a dreary Irish cloud. The only sunshine during those days was Peg.

We dropped back into our normal routine pretty quickly after Patrick was gone. I met Peg at the same time every day after school and ran to her house under the cover of darkness on the nights my parents entertained. The only thing different about those times at Peg's were the days that she received a letter from Patrick. They always had a word or two for me in them, nothing profound or embarrassing, just a little something that assured me I was in his thoughts still. She let me read them sometimes, and other times she read them aloud, never letting me even glance at the page. I knew those letters contained things she'd rather I didn't know about, and I hated when he wrote them. I wanted to see his words, the small cursive handwriting that sometimes had crossed out letters and words as if he was thinking too fast for his fingers to keep up with and he didn't even have time to erase or start again. I *needed* to see the one or two lines he'd written especially for me.

The day of my birthday, I felt especially low. My parents had told me the night before that we had plans for dinner, and I dreaded the hour-long affair that I knew would include trying to politely converse with them as if they knew and cared about anything happening in my life. They'd had company the night before, and I'd held out as long as I could before the noises in their room had become so loud that I'd once again climbed out my window. Subsequently, my reluctance to run to Peg had caused both of us to stay awake late into the night, me because I'd been too afraid to go to sleep and Peg because she'd been too afraid *for me* to sleep. I'd promised her as I left the house that morning that I wouldn't do it again, and the bags under her eyes made me feel like a complete asshole as she'd left for work.

Peg wasn't waiting for me as I walked home that day, and my gut clenched in worry as I reached her bare front stoop. Was she okay? Even if it was raining, she was usually at least standing in the doorway as I'd made my way to her house. The sight of her had never been absent in the two months since Patrick had left again for school.

"Peg?" I called, knocking on her door before turning the knob slowly to find it unlocked. "Peg? Are you home?"

"In here, darlin' girl!" she called from the kitchen. The breath I'd been holding immediately left me in a relieved whoosh.

As soon as I got to the kitchen, I was greeted with the sight of a small cake complete with birthday candles. "Happy Birthday!" she yelled so loud I was sure the neighbors across the street heard her.

My mouth lifted in a huge smile as I looked around the kitchen. She'd hung up a homemade banner and streamers, and I could have cried at the trouble I knew she'd gone to.

"I can't believe you did all this." My heart felt light as I met her eyes.

"Of course I did! My girl is eighteen years today. It's cause for celebration!" She carried the cake to the table and set it down, careful not to let the candles burn out. "I'm sorry I didn't meet ye at the door. I wanted to have the candles burnin' when ye stepped in! Well, blow them out then."

I dropped my bag to the floor as I stepped closer to her, but I was in no hurry to blow out the candles. I hadn't had birthday candles in years. I wanted to savor the moment, to take it all in for just a second so I could remember every detail later. When I finally leaned down to blow them out, she started clapping delightedly, a wide smile on her face.

"I love you," I told her, my voice full of wonder.

"Sweet girl," she murmured with a soft look, "I love ye, too."

We sat down and ate the yellow cake she'd made, and as soon as I'd finished, she popped up from her chair to grab a small wrapped package from the couch.

"You didn't have to—" I started uncomfortably.

"Ach, I wanted to. It's the day of yer birth, the day God saw fit to put ye on this earth so seventeen years later ye could make yer way to me. It's worth celebratin', and it's worth a gift." She handed me the squishy parcel and stood, expectantly waiting for me to open it.

I couldn't help the look of confusion or the emergence of a grin that hit my face.

"An apron. Did you make this? It's beautiful!"

"Aye, I did. It's time for ye to start learnin' a little more in the kitchen. We'll start lessons after school tomorrow. Yer an adult, ye need to be able to feed yer family more than spaghetti and stew... not that those are anythin' to be ashamed of."

"I love it."

"Really? Yer sure?" she asked nervously.

"I'm sure."

"Right. Well, then, one more gift for ye."

"Peg, you shouldn't have got me—"

"Oh, this one's not from me," she replied with a sneaky smile, handing me a thin envelope. "Ye go on into the livin' room while I clean this up. Have a bit of privacy, eh?"

For Amy on her Birthday was written on the front of the envelope in familiar messy cursive. I barely made it to the couch before I carefully opened it, loathe to ruin even the envelope.

>*Amy,*
>
>*How far away the stars seem, and how far is our first kiss...*
>
>*I'd like to credit those words to myself, but I'll be honest and tell you they come from W.B. Yates. Don't try to find the rest of the poem, it's a bit of a depressing thing. Only these few words seem to remind me of you.*
>
>*I hope you're doing well. Mum says you're spending a lot of time with her. That's good. Spend as much time with her as you can, it's good for her and it keeps you away from*

those parents of yours.

I hope you have a wonderful birthday, sweetheart.

I wish I could write you pages and pages, but if I begin to do that I know that I will not be able to stop. I'd never get any work done that way.

Know that I am thinking of you constantly, especially on your special day. I wish I could be with you to celebrate.

Stay safe, darling.

Patrick

I read his letter over and over again, letting it seep into my brain until I could recite it word for word. He called me sweetheart again, and darling. My heart raced as I imagined him sitting at a small desk somewhere, finding just the right poem to quote and words to write. He hadn't crossed out one letter, as if he'd painstakingly chosen every word before he wrote it down.

"Amy, it's almost five," Peg warned me as she laid her hand on the top of my head. "Best put that away for now and head home."

"I wish I didn't have to," I mumbled, folding the paper back up and slipping it into its envelope.

"I know ye do. Do ye have special plans tonight?"

"My parents are taking me to dinner," I answered as I grabbed my bag and stuffed the letter inside.

"Well, I'm sure it will be lovely." It sounded as if she was trying to convince both of us.

"Probably not. I doubt I'll be over tonight, though. Even *they* wouldn't have people over on my birthday." I leaned down to hug her slight frame and inhaled deeply. "Thank you so much for my cake and my present."

"Yer welcome." She patted my back twice and then shoved me away gently. "Go on with ye then. Ye'll tell me about dinner tomorrow."

I left the house with a knot in my stomach that even thinking of my letter couldn't chase away. I didn't belong with my parents anymore.

Peg knew it, and I knew it. Yet I kept having to go back to them, and each time it became harder for me to do.

By the time my parents picked me up for dinner, the letter stuffed under my mattress had become yet another thing that depressed me. I loved it, every sentiment and curved letter… but it made me miss Patrick even more. I wanted to hear his voice. I wanted to smell the scent of cigarette smoke and feel the callouses on his fingers brushing against my face. And I hated that I was spending my birthday dinner with two people who hadn't given a shit about me for as long as I could remember.

"Why so glum?" my mom asked as we sat down in the fanciest restaurant in Ballyshannon. I hated that they'd taken me there. It was more for show than anything else. They wanted to see and be seen; the doting parents who took their daughter out for an expensive dinner for her birthday. It was disgusting.

"No reason." I smiled at the waiter as he left, then fiddled with my silverware.

"Well, cheer up! You're eighteen! Doesn't every girl wait impatiently for the day she turns eighteen?"

I smiled thinly in an effort to make her stop talking. Her voice was loud and obnoxious in the quiet room, the American accent she'd so painstakingly developed causing people to glance at our table. Exactly the reason she'd done it.

"A legal adult now, huh?" my dad asked in a voice appropriate for the restaurant we were sitting in. "How does that feel?"

"Pretty much the same as yesterday."

It didn't take long for the waiter to come back for our order, and soon after we were eating our meals silently, the requisite question and answer session over. It wasn't as if they ignored me, they just didn't have anything else to say. When you have little interest in the person across the table from you, it makes small talk virtually impossible.

It wasn't until dessert had been served that my father once again began to talk, and the ground seemed as if it was falling out beneath me.

Chapter 12

Patrick

"*I made a mistake,*" Robbie told us, sitting heavily in Amy's vacated chair. "*I'm not sure it happened, but de lads...*"

"*What de hell did ye do, Da?*" My stomach was churning at the sight of my father's hunched shoulders. I'd never seen him less than completely confident, no matter the situation—even the day my mum had kicked him out after she'd found out he'd been spending time with the O'Halloran brothers. He'd argued then, sure in his path even as she'd packed his suitcase.

He could have stayed. I'd seen it on his face that he knew he could get Mum to change her mind, but he hadn't. His respect for her and a goodly dose of pride had forced him to leave the house that day, and I'd only seen him sporadically through my childhood. It wasn't until I'd began at Uni that I began to see him more often, our paths crossing in a way that I knew hadn't been by chance.

I was now regretting ever laying eyes on him again.

"*I had a job, it was simple, eh? Go in, do it and get out. But it didn't happen dat way. Got out, alright. But fuck if dose slimy bastards hadn't made me look like a fool."* He rested his elbows on the table, clenching and unclenching his fists as he glared at them. When his eyes rose to meet Mum's, I knew that it was even worse than I'd imagined. *"I'm no longer trusted,"* he whispered.

Mum made a mournful noise in her throat and raised shaky fingers to rest against her forehead. My body suddenly felt as if the muscles would burst, my skin too tight for my body.

"What does dat mean?" I asked, slamming my fist on the table. "What have ye brought down on us?"

"I've not brought anyt'in' to de two of ye," he replied calmly, raising his hand to my mum, who'd begun to cry. "I'm not certain what will happen now. I've got to find a way to make me way back in. If I don't... well, I wanted to see me wife."

Mum sniffled and rounded the table, letting my Da pull her onto his lap. As she continued to cry, she pulled his head to her breasts and his whole body seemed to wilt into hers. I couldn't watch it.

I stood from the table quietly and they didn't notice as I left the house.

I thought about my Da's words as I nursed a Guinness in a pub near my house. I'd been there a while, just having finished my exams with what I was sure were barely passing marks. How a lad was supposed to focus on coursework when so many other things were happening around him was a mystery to me, but I'd continued on until the term was finished. I'd not have to take the classes over, at least that was something.

I should have been celebrating, but fuck if I could celebrate anything at that point. I'd seen my Da a few times since the day in my mum's kitchen, but we'd barely said a word to each other. Mostly we just passed each other in the street near the university. He didn't belong anywhere near there, but I never mentioned it. I knew he was making himself visible to assure me that things had not changed. He was still alive. For how long? That was anyone's guess.

I didn't want to know what was happening. I was glad, of course, that he was still alive, but I didn't want to be pulled into his life and the shadow that loomed above him. I was a scholar, for Christ's sake. I believed in a unified Ireland, aye, but fighting amongst ourselves was getting us nowhere. I believed things would change when we began to use our words instead of our fists, an ideal my mum had ironically beat into me when I'd fought with Kevie as a child. Brute force could change a man's mind, of course it could, but when two opponents were so clearly matched and unwilling to give up? It made for a long, bloody and unnecessary battle. One I wanted no part of.

My body felt languid as I tipped the last of my drink against my lips and I was relaxed for the first time in months until three men entered the pub. My back straightened at their arrival and every muscle bunched in preparation. I knew of them. The smallest of the three was the leader, higher in the ranks than my Da, but not at the top. His two followers were larger, muscled and stupid looking, and as I peered closer I realized the blonde one was from Ballyshannon. Kevie's older brother.

I'd been in that pub more times than I could count, but I'd never seen them there before. I'd idiotically thought that I could avoid it all there, that the tiny pub only two streets away from the university was somehow shielded from the things I tried to ignore. Naïve, perhaps, but I'd been frequenting the place for over two years and it was the first time I'd seen anything that would keep me from coming back.

My body grew more tense as the small guy leaned down behind a slight blonde woman who was laughing merrily with her friends.

She froze with one hand in the air as she heard his voice. She knew him, but it was clear she didn't like him. Her eyes went wide as she faced my way, but I knew she wasn't seeing me. I was tucked back at the end of the bar, and her eyes were unfocused as she began to nod at whatever he was saying. When his fingers began to dig into her shoulder, it took every ounce of restraint I had not to stand from my stool.

Instead, I watched as he let her go and went to a separate table with his men. As he got comfortable, ordering a pint loudly enough for the entire place to hear him, she began making excuses to her friends with a small, uncomfortable smile on her face. She left just minutes later, and in a moment of absolute stupidity, I followed her.

"Miss, are ye alright?" I asked quietly when I'd caught up to her a few blocks away.

She screeched in reply, swinging around to meet me with her hands held up in a defensive pose. I'd scared her... and Christ, she was gorgeous.

"What de hell is de matter wit' ye?" she scolded, her arms dropping as she looked at my face. I'm quite sure I looked like an idiot as I stared at her. She was flawless. Honey colored curls were wild and untamed around her heart shaped face and partially covering wide brown eyes with long curled lashes and a little bow mouth with a fuller bottom lip. Her thick sweater hid most of her torso from me, but it couldn't disguise her high breasts and slim waist that tapered down to an arse that seemed too wide and round to match the rest of her. Perfection. She was absolutely perfect in a way that stopped men in their tracks and caused women to scowl defensively.

"I know ye," she said. Then all of a sudden, she was blushing. Her blushing face was even better.

"Huh?"

"We have a few classes toget'er. I'm Moira Murphy."

"Sorry, beautiful, it's not ringin' a bell." Her face fell and I could have kicked myself. Fuck. I should have lied.

"Oh, well..." She ran a hand over her curly hair and laughed uncomfortably. "Right, well, yes, I'm fine and t'ank ye for askin.' I'll just be headin' home now."

She spun away from me and began walking briskly down the dark street before I pulled my head out of my arse and stopped her again. I couldn't let her get away. "Me flat's just around de corner," I told her, tilting my head to the side and giving her my most charming smile. "If yer not ready to go home just yet."

Things were a bit fuzzy as I waited for her answer. I'd been so fucking tired of waiting for the other shoe to drop, I'd had more than I should have at the pub. I knew I was playing with fire, but the thought of fucking with that man in the pub—the embodiment of every reason I'd not had a father as I grew, was too delicious to resist. I wanted to lash out. I wanted to fuck her so well that I ruined her for that asshole who'd ruined her night out. And frankly, I wanted to forget for a while that the shit around me was getting thicker and I was so goddamn homesick that I could barely follow through with the plans I'd had since primary school.

She was built for sex and the way she'd told me she knew who I was made me confident. She'd seen me, and she'd liked what she saw.

Moira looked back the way we came for a moment, then sniffed defiantly. "Alright," she answered, her voice confident.

Soon the only thought running through my mind was the unlikely chance that my level of consumption would hamper my ability to perform. The longer we were outside, the more fuzzy my head became, the last few Guinness' I'd consumed finally catching up with me. I wasn't even sure how we made it back to my flat with the way I was feeling. I'm sure it had been sheer will on my part. The woman had curves in all the right places, and a way of moving her body that assured me that she knew exactly how she looked.

I was so hot for her by the time we got inside, we didn't even make it to the bed before I was inside her. I was frustrated and angry and looking for anything that would make me feel better. We were ravenous, the both of us, and I was just drunk enough to think that she found me as appealing as I did her. It never once occurred to me that she'd have a different reason for ripping the clothes from my body.

I'd find out later that we'd both been running from things that night—the heavy weight of responsibilities, fear, threats, worries, and in her case, oppression. We explored each other long into the night, the need arcing between us leaving no room in our brains for anything beyond the ache for satiation. Exactly what I'd hoped for.

It wasn't until the next morning as I awoke to the telephone ringing on my counter, that the crushing weight of my responsibilities and unspoken promises broke through the haze of lust and alcohol. She was already gone, but my sheets smelled of sex and the perfume she'd been wearing, a reminder of what I'd done.

As I climbed naked from the twisted bedding, I rubbed my hand down my face. The interaction in the bar had been a clear indication that she was somehow connected to the life I was trying so fucking hard to stay away from, and the new worry was like a weight in my gut. She was a nice girl, the few times we'd spoken when our mouths were not otherwise occupied led me to believe she was intelligent, and she had a dry sense of humor that was at odds with her sweet face. If life was different, there was a good chance I would have pursued her. Her personality, however, didn't change matters. My only recourse was to refuse to acknowledge that it had even happened should I run into her again.

The decision made, I stumbled to the phone. I'd come too far to let heavy breasts and a warm cunt fuck up my life.

"Yeah?"

"Patrick, it's yer mum."

"Mum, why are ye ringin' me at…" I turned to check the clock on the crate next to my bed. "Seven in de fuckin' mornin'?"

My breath paused as she remained silent, not even chastising me for my language.

"I think there's somethin' wrong with Amy."

Christ Jesus. In all my recriminations that morning, I'd not once thought about the girl waiting for me in Ballyshannon. This would destroy her. I'd not made any promises, but Christ, I'd implied plenty. It was one more reason on top of an overwhelming list that convinced me I had to forget the night before had ever happened.

Suddenly, the flat felt as if it was closing in around me.

"Exams are over, I'm on me way."

Chapter 13

Amy

Time was passing at an alarming rate no matter how I tried to slow it, and I was sure that hiding out in my bedroom wasn't helping. I'd spent more time than usual with Peg, too, but that seemed to make things even harder, so I'd stopped making an effort. She was worried, but she didn't push me for answers.

I wasn't ready to talk about it. If I didn't say it out loud, I could try to pretend it wasn't happening.

My parents were too busy for their usual social calendar, which meant I was sleeping at home every night. I hated it and loved it at the same time, wishing I was at Peg's while still clinging to my small bedroom like a piece of driftwood in the ocean. I couldn't see my way out of the situation, there *was* no way out, and yet I continued to pray every night for some sort of help.

And then suddenly, help arrived.

I woke up that morning after a restless night of sleep to my bed tilting as someone sat down next to me. This was becoming familiar. The scent of mint, cigarette smoke and something unfamiliar hit my nostrils before I'd even opened my eyes, and I felt a lump grow in my throat. I recognized that smell.

"Hey, sweetheart," he whispered, brushing my hair away from my face. "Time to wake up."

My breath caught at the tenderness in his voice, and my heart started thumping hard in my chest. Embarrassment that he'd found me unwashed and sleep tousled warred with overwhelming relief that he was finally there. I'd missed him so much.

It was odd, really, how one weekend had completely changed the way I viewed things. I no longer went along with the feeling of apathy I had developed over the past few years. When your life changes so often, it's easy to stop caring about the new people you meet and the new places you go. If you know that sooner rather than later you'll have to leave somewhere with no choice as to when or why, you learn to see everything in a fog, easily changeable and forgettable. It's a defense mechanism—if you don't fall in love with a place, you're not sad to leave it.

Patrick had somehow brought everything into vivid detail. When I saw something, I wanted to tell him about it. I wanted to discuss the grocer where Peg worked. I wanted to bitch about the priest at my school who had a perpetual scowl on his face. I wanted to pull him out into the rain and jump in puddles with him just to see him laugh. I wanted to discuss books, and politics, and the way my fingers ached when it was cold outside.

I'd just flat out missed him.

"Hey." My eyes opened and I cleared my scratchy throat as I took him in. He was wearing a sweatshirt and jeans, his hair hidden under a knitted cap that I knew Peg had made him two Christmases ago. He looked like some sort of thug, with the hat pulled down low and his face scruffy… and he'd never been so appealing.

"Ye look like shite." Okay, maybe not that appealing.

"Thanks, dick." I closed my eyes and tried in vain to pull the blankets farther up my shoulders. "You can go away now."

"Ach, don't be like dat."

"Well, you look like a criminal," I grumbled.

Nice comeback, Amy. Fantastic. Really.

He burst out laughing, and I couldn't help but follow, pushing my face into my pillow. His laugh was deeper than his regular voice, thick and guttural, like it had come from deep in his belly, and the noise was infectious.

"Up and out," he ordered as his laughter drifted away. "Ye smell, and yer hair is…"

My face burned as his words trailed off. I knew what I looked like. Shit—just like he'd said. But I hadn't been able to find it in me to care until I woke up with him next to me. Suddenly, my refusal to get out of bed seemed silly and immature.

I didn't say a word as I pushed the blankets down and climbed out of bed, ignoring his sharp intake of breath. I'd worn very little to bed—just a tank top and some underwear—and even though I was sure I looked and smelled really gross, I was still baring a lot of skin.

My shower took a while. I hadn't shaved my legs in over a week and… oh, shit, my armpits! I hadn't raised my arms, had I? Gross. I had a hell of a time getting the knots out of my long hair and I also brushed my teeth. Twice. God knows I needed it. The entire time I wondered what he was doing there, in my house. It had been a little over a week since my birthday, and from his letters I knew he had tests at school that he couldn't miss. Was he done with them already? My school only had a few months left until graduation, and my stomach cramped at the thought.

What the hell was I going to do?

When I got back to my room in a warm flannel and jeans, Patrick had stripped my bed. The laundry was wrapped into a ball, and he was sitting on the bare mattress, leaning over with his elbows on his knees and his head tipped toward the floor.

"All clean," I announced quietly, grabbing his attention. "What are you doing here, anyway?"

"Ye've dark circles under yer eyes, and I've just found ye sleepin' like de dead at eleven in de mornin'," he said, ignoring my question. "What's goin' on, Amy?"

"Nothing." My reply was too fast—too sharp and definitive to pass as anything but a lie.

He searched my eyes for a long moment, then his gaze traveled down my body slowly before meeting mine again. "Mum's worried about ye."

"I—"

"Called me dis mornin', full o'tears, tellin' me dere's somet'in' wrong wit' ye," his mouth firmed into a straight line as he looked away from me. "Den I get here and yer sleepin' like de dead in de middle of t'day." He stood and I took an involuntary step backward. I'd forgotten how much bigger he was than me, and while it didn't frighten me, it did make me incredibly aware of the small size of my room. "I can see dat dere's somet'in' goin' on, yeah? I can tell by lookin' at ye. So why don't we cut t'rough de bullshite, and ye just tell me already before I lose me fuckin' mind."

My jaw dropped as I realized how wound up he was. His hands were flexing at his sides, and his head was tilted in question as he stared me down. I could even see his chest rising and falling hard beneath his sweatshirt, almost as if he'd been running.

The words came tumbling out of my mouth without thought.

"I'm eighteen. My parents are moving. Back to the states, I think. I'm not sure and they haven't told me. But they said I can't go with them. Well, they didn't say that exactly, it was more along the lines of, 'You're an adult now and can pay your own way, so we're moving.' They didn't specifically kick me out. They said I could stay in this house if I wanted, but I can't pay the rent and I don't have a job and I still have a couple months of school left and I don't know what I'm going to do." Actually saying the words aloud brought such a relief that I said the last sentence in one long wail, my words rolling over each other, and by the time I was finished, I could feel a sob bubbling up my throat. "Why would they do this?"

He didn't say a word as he stepped in against me, and before I could take another breath, he slid one hand around my waist and the other under my ass, boosting me up until I was wrapped around him. I buried my face in his neck as he began to walk through the house, talking quietly and kissing my temple.

"Dis is what has ye sleepin' t'day away? Shhh, now. Shhh, we can fix dis."

I'm not sure if he even shut the front door as we left, his long legs eating up the distance between my house and Peg's quickly. It was abnormally quiet as we entered, and I remembered that Peg was at work for a few more hours, but I didn't say a word as he rounded the couch and sat down heavily. His hand was rubbing up and down my back in long, sweeping motions, and I didn't fight him as he grabbed first one leg and then the other from around his waist and bent them at his sides so I was straddling his thighs. I was more comfortable that way, the position feeling anything but sexual as I burrowed even deeper into the front of his sweatshirt.

I was comforted in a way that I had never been before. The relief in telling someone that I'd soon be homeless made the situation seem *less* in some way, as if just the telling had made things less scary.

My body grew lax as he silently rubbed my back and the exhaustion that seemed to be my constant companion over the last week seeped even deeper into my pores. I wasn't sure how he thought he could fix things. I'd looked at the problem from a hundred different angles and found no solution…but his confidence was a soothing balm on my nerves, all the same.

As I drifted off with my face still pressed against his neck, I was overwhelmed with gratefulness that he was there. I also realized foggily that he smelled a little like Exclamation! perfume.

Chapter 14

Amy

"**D**ey've kicked her out of de fuckin' house, Mum."

"Is that the problem then?"

"She started cryin' straight off when I asked her about it."

"Ach. She knows she can stay here."

"Obviously not, since de poor girl has not even been gettin' out of bed she's so worried."

Their voices were low, but I still heard every word after Peg came bustling into the house after work. I was still in Patrick's lap, and my legs were cramping from being in the same position for so long, but I didn't want to move. He hadn't realized that I was awake yet, and I was enjoying the feeling of one of his hands in my hair and the other resting low on my back.

"Well, it looks like she's gotten a bit of rest now."

"She was until ye came bangin' in de door."

I jolted at his words and laughed a little at being caught. His hand slid out of my hair so I could lean back, and when I opened my eyes the only thing I could see was Peg's face.

Her jaw was set in a stubborn line, and her hands were on her hips as she stared at me.

"We'll pack yer things and move ye tonight," she announced with a nod. "I'll not hear another word about it."

She stomped off toward her bedroom as Patrick began to laugh beneath me, and I froze as his body jolted with his chuckles. He was rubbing against me in all the ways I'd ignored when we'd dropped to the couch hours earlier.

"Well, that was…" I wasn't even sure what to say. My bewilderment must have shown on my face because he suddenly stopped laughing.

"Did I not tell ye I'd fix it?" he asked calmly, laying his palm against my cheek.

"But why would she—"

"If ye've not noticed, me mum's adopted ye. Nuttin' for it now. Yer stuck."

"But I can't pay rent, I can't even buy a toothbrush—"

"Ye won't pay rent."

I jerked my body away from him and stood, running my fingers down my ponytail. I couldn't just live there without paying anything. It made my stomach ache to even think of taking advantage like that. Peg got along okay, but she wasn't exactly rolling in it. Feeding another person would be a strain on what little money she had left over every week.

"I can see de wheels turnin' in yer head. Stop." He rose to his feet so he was looking down into my face. "We'll straighten it all out later."

Then he turned his head toward the bedroom and called out to his mom. "We need boxes!"

"We've got some at the store." She replied as she came back out, then glanced down at my feet. "Ye'll need some shoes."

Before I knew it, we were in Peg's small car and on our way to the grocer, where we picked up enough produce boxes to pack my entire room. With the boxes piled next to me in the back seat, we drove back to my house. Packing up my few childhood mementos and books with the help of two other people was surreal.

I'd done my own packing for years as we'd moved from one place to another. My parents had always provided what I needed, boxes and packing tape and newspaper to wrap things in, but it had been handed over with the understanding that I'd do the work myself. We always rented places that were already furnished, so there was no bed or dressers to deal with, and the packing went fairly quickly. Soon the room was once again as bare as the moment I'd first stepped inside it.

Peg left to cook dinner and throw my bedding in the wash, and I was sitting on my bed waiting for Patrick to come help me with the last couple of boxes when I heard my mother's shrill voice in the hallway.

"Who the hell are you?"

I didn't hear Patrick's reply, but his thudding steps never faltered as he made his way back into my room.

"Are ye ready, love?" he asked as he stepped through the doorway, my mother close on his heels.

"Amy?" My mom's voice was incredulous as she looked around the room. "What in the world?"

"We've only got these two boxes left," I told her quietly, my throat tight in apprehension. "I can come back and clean the floors and window tomorrow."

"No, ye won't," Patrick chimed in with a glower.

"What do you mean? What are you doing?" my mom asked.

I stared at her in confusion as she stepped into the room. "You said I only had two weeks, so I'm..." I flapped my hands in the air, unsure how to phrase my sentence in a way that wouldn't set her off.

"You're *moving out?*" she asked accusingly, her eyes darting between me and Patrick.

"Christ, woman! What did ye expect when ye kicked her out?" Patrick yelled.

"I did no such thing!"

My eyes watered as I stared at my mother and tried to comprehend what was happening. She *had*. She had kicked me out. She and my dad told me that I needed somewhere else to live. Why was she acting like I was the guilty party? Did Patrick believe her?

"Let's go, love." Patrick said quietly, lifting his chin toward the last box on my bed.

"Amy Jennifer Henderson, you're not going anywhere!" Mom hissed at me, taking another step into the room. "Put that box down!"

I began to shake, the tone of her voice making me question my interpretation of the events of the last two weeks. It wasn't as if my parents had mentioned once in passing that I needed to find somewhere else to live. They'd reminded me every day that the clock was ticking, so why was she behaving as if she had no idea what I was talking about?

"Go, Amy." Patrick ordered again, jolting me out of my anxiety-induced stupor. I took two steps forward, stopping abruptly when my mother's nails dug into my bicep.

She opened her mouth to speak, but she didn't get a word out before Patrick was there, dropping the box he'd been holding and gripping my mom's wrist so tight his knuckles went white.

"Don't touch her again."

She let go instantly, her eyes wide as she stumbled back into the hallway and I was frozen in place as I watched her cradle her injured wrist to her chest. The situation was deteriorating so quickly, I didn't know what to do. I wanted to comfort her, but she was staring at me as if she hated me even as her eyes began to fill with tears.

Suddenly, Patrick's hand was firm against the small of my back, and he was ushering me down the hall.

"Your father will come get you!" she yelled to our backs. "Just wait until I tell him what you've done, you little whore! Get back here, Amy!" Mom screamed, completely livid as we continued through the house. Thankfully, Patrick's presence at my side stopped her from following me, because I wasn't sure what she would have done otherwise.

I felt the tears roll down my cheeks as we hit the cold air outside, and I couldn't help the shudder that ran through my body. Threats of my father's wrath had been something I'd cowered from for most of my life, and it hadn't magically stopped just because I'd be sleeping somewhere else that night. She'd been so horrible, and I didn't understand it. I was doing what she wanted! I'd done everything she'd told me to, and she treated me as if I'd wronged her in some way.

"She told me I had to move," I said, glancing up at Patrick's furious face. "I swear—they told me I only had two more weeks."

"I knew she was lyin'," he replied, giving me a reassuring nod. "She's just mad dat she didn't have de satisfaction of bootin' ye into de street."

My breath stopped at his observation, her actions suddenly so transparent, it caused an ache in my chest. How could someone be that vindictive, I wondered, to be angry that they weren't able to kick their child out with nowhere to go? Had she been expecting me to beg them to let me stay? I'd foiled whatever scenario they'd been envisioning, that was why she'd been so mad. It only made her threats about my father coming for me more frightening.

Peg was bustling around in the kitchen when we walked in the door, and she didn't notice us as Patrick pulled the box out of my arms and set it on the couch.

"Ye don't ever have to go back dere," he promised, pulling me into his arms.

"They're my family," I reminded him quietly. For better or worse.

"Ye've got a new one." His voice was resolute and a little bit raw, and as soon as he'd finished speaking he dropped his lips to mine, and kissed me hard. "I'll bring yer boxes into de bedroom."

Then he walked away, leaving me reeling.

It was all happening so fast that I couldn't settle on one emotion before another popped up and clouded my head. I was grateful, so overwhelmingly grateful that Peg was going to let me stay with her... but I was confused and scared, too.

Even though I'd gotten little from my parents over the years in the way of stability, they were still my parents. They'd still raised me from childhood and kept a roof over my head and food in my belly. I'd imagined finding somewhere to live and still being able to have some sort of contact with them, some kind of safety net—but my mom's reaction to my departure was a clear indication that any relationship was gone. They didn't want me.

I'd known Peg for only a few months, and though she'd never given me reason to doubt her, I still knew in the back of my head that she could throw me out at any time and I'd be homeless in an unfamiliar country. If my parents—the two people that should have loved me more than anything else—didn't want me around, why would Peg be any different?

Chapter 15

Amy

"Amy, yer goin' to be late!" Patrick yelled through the bathroom door as I smoothed my uniform over my hips.

It was my first day back to school since I'd moved to Peg's, and for some reason I was nervous. Peg had contacted the school to let them know that I was living with her in case my parents tried to cause problems, and I knew she was doing what she thought best, but the thought of everyone knowing my parents had kicked me out made me feel like I was going to be sick. God only knew what sort of stories people would make up about my living arrangements.

"I'm ready," I mumbled, brushing past him to get my bag.

"Don't ye look sweet and innocent."

"Shut up."

"Such a good little girl, on her way to school right on time."

"Shut up, Patrick!"

"How many times have I asked ye to call me Trick? I hope ye listen better in class den ye do out of it." His voice was teasing, and I knew what he was doing, but I still let him get to me.

"Sorry, *Paddy*," I replied, opening the door and sailing through it before he could reply.

"Ugh, don't call me dat." He called, locking the door behind us before jogging to catch up to me. "Dat's not me name."

His voice was so disgusted, I had to laugh. "Why Trick?"

"Because it's not Paddy."

"You're nuts."

"I t'ought it was cool, okay?" Patrick replied sheepishly. "When I was about eleven, I t'ought it was de absolute best nickname in de world and I refused to answer to anyt'in' else for a year."

"An entire year?" The thought of a little carrot-topped Patrick turning up his nose and refusing to answer to anything but the name he'd chosen had me in a fit of giggles.

"We're almost dere, and if ye don't want me givin' de Sisters somet'in' to talk about, ye'll quit laughin'," he warned as a red flush began creeping up his neck.

The heat in his eyes left no doubt as to the show he was about to put on, so I pressed my lips tightly together in order to hold the laughter back. He was so... charming. Every time I thought I knew him, he gave me something else to think about.

He'd also taken my mind off the nervous butterflies in my stomach.

"Here we are," he announced with a flourish as we reached the school. For the first time since I'd started there, I hated that the walk was so short.

"Thank you, Patrick," I said softly, leaning up to kiss his cheek before turning away and walking quickly toward the front door of the school.

"I didn't know ye'd be de one givin' de Sisters somet'in' to talk about!" he called after me, smiling as I turned my head to glare.

I turned back around and reached up as if to smooth down the back of my hair with my left hand, curling my pointer finger down as I did so, flipping him off as secretly as I could. A smile spread across my face as I heard him roar with laughter behind me.

"Dat's not how we do it here!" I lifted the pointer back up, and as I walked into the building I heard him yell, "Dere it is!" as one of the Sisters shushed him.

***

School was pretty much as I'd suspected. People were talking about me. I heard the whispers in the restrooms when girls didn't know that I was there...but surprisingly, everyone left me alone. I got the impression that the girls were almost in awe of me, which made very little sense. They hadn't given two shits that I was some exotic American when I'd first started, and I couldn't find a reason why moving out after I'd turned eighteen would garner any more of a reaction.

It wasn't until the second week of Patrick walking me to school that I finally understood what the fuss was about.

"Hello, Trick," one of the popular girls called flirtatiously as she passed me and Patrick in front of the school. We'd started waiting at the front of the school until the very last minute before we parted ways. I think he was growing anxious about leaving Ballyshannon, his trip home already longer than he'd planned.

He nodded to her with a smile, and I clenched my teeth so hard I heard my jaw pop.

"What the fuck was that?"

"What?" He looked at me as if I'd grown two heads. "Caitlin?"

"You know her?"

"We've met. Yes." His voice became amused, and rather than kicking him in the nuts like I wanted to, I tried to spin away. It was an overreaction to a frigging head nod, but it rankled just the same. I couldn't seem to stop the wave of jealousy that rolled over me.

We'd been cocooned in our own little bubble for over a week, and it had given me an unrealistic view of our relationship. In our bubble, it was just me, Patrick, Peg and sometimes Kevie. Up until that point, I hadn't had to deal with other girls vying for his attention, and knowing that Caitlin had probably known him much longer than I had made me green.

It was completely illogical, but that didn't make it any less real. *I was the one sleeping in his bed*—though he slept on the couch. *I was the one who was learning to make his favorite foods. I was the one helping Peg string up his boxers and undershirts to dry in the small backyard. I knew him better than anyone*, and it pissed me off that Caitlin thought she could flirt with him right in front of me. Even worse, he let her.

He was *mine*.

"Amy? What is it?" He wrapped his arm around my waist, causing one of the nuns to glare at us. "Why are ye angry?"

"I'm not."

"Ye are." He turned me around and searched my face for a moment before grinning slyly. "Yer jealous."

"I am not!"

"Oh, yes. Ye are. And ye've no reason to be." He grabbed my hand and started tugging me down the sidewalk away from the school. No matter how hard I tried to pull away, his grip didn't let up, and soon we'd made it around the corner and into an alleyway.

"I'm going to be late!"

He didn't answer me, but as soon as the last word left my lips, his mouth was on mine, his hands digging into my hair. His tongue licked inside, rubbing against my own, and I groaned as my body relaxed into his.

"Ye've no reason to be jealous," he told me between kisses. "I want ye."

"Then why haven't you kissed me in over a week?" I asked breathlessly. Our hands were roaming over anything we could reach without disrupting our clothing, and I somehow found myself pushed against the cold brick behind me as his hips ground into mine.

"Can ye imagine it?" he groaned into my neck, running his hands just under where my skirt met my thighs. "If I touch ye in de house, while no one's around? Dere'll be no stoppin' us den."

"Good," I whispered, running my hand down his back.

"No." His hands found mine where they'd begun digging into his ass, and brought them up, pinning my wrists at each side of my head. "We've talked about dis."

"That doesn't mean I agree with it!"

"Ye'll not give yer virginity away like a whore wit'out me ring on yer finger," he replied darkly.

I gasped in shock, and if he hadn't been pinning my hands, I would have hit him.

"You're such an asshole!"

"Would ye like to know how I know Caitlin?" he asked angrily. "Everyone *knows* her."

"I hate you."

"Ye love me, and ye'll marry me. All I'm askin' is for ye to fuckin' wait."

"Wait? Will you be waiting? You've obviously had sex already!" An emotion I couldn't place flashed over his face before it turned to a glare. He refused to give an inch, and I felt myself grow angrier and angrier until I couldn't stop the words that spilled from my mouth. "That's bullshit and you know it," I said, the words low and mean. "Maybe we should just stop what we're doing right now and we'll meet again on an even playing field."

"What de fuck does dat mean?" The veins in his neck bulged as he leaned closer to my face.

"Exactly what I said."

"Ye let anot'er man touch ye and I'll fuckin' kill him," he whispered back, angrier than I'd ever seen him. "Go back to school, ye fuckin' infant."

He pushed off the wall and stalked away without another word as I leaned frozen against the wall. I hated the way he made all of our decisions, sure, but I knew he was doing what he thought was best. I didn't know why I'd said those things; I didn't want anyone else. I'd instantly regretted my words, but my pride refused to let me call out to stop him from walking away.

Instead, I just stood in that alleyway for long minutes, miserable and trying not to cry.

***

I was so late to school, I should have just gone home, but I was too afraid to see Patrick again. I knew that his feelings weren't uncommon; there were still a lot of men who preferred their wives to be virgins when they married. It just seemed so unfair. Why did he get to have sex with whomever he wanted and was revered for it, while any type of perceived promiscuity on my part would label me a whore? It was so frustrating! That morning when he said he'd *known* Caitlin, I hadn't thought about the way he'd said it—like he was one of *many* she'd had sex with. The only thing that had registered was that she knew him in a way that I didn't, and that killed me. I just wanted to be closer to him and I wanted to stop feeling frustrated all the time.

I wanted to tether myself to him in that final way so I'd know he wouldn't leave me.

I barely made it through the day, so unfocused and depressed that I was asked repeatedly if I was okay. I wasn't, not in any sense of the word. My hands and arms had broken out in hives within the first hour of classes, and the physical discomfort made me even more miserable.

I could barely believe it, but I was beginning to miss the predictability of my life before I'd moved to Ireland. My parents had been awful, but at least with them I'd had a sense of familiarity. I'd been able to navigate that world on autopilot, secure in my position and the knowledge that eventually I'd be on my own and things would get better.

How wrong I'd been about the adult part. Being a so-called 'adult' didn't make things easier, it only meant that your problems were that much harder to solve. By the time I walked home from school, I'd worked myself up to the point that I was ready to apologize to Patrick about everything I'd said and done that morning.

He'd become my best friend, my only friend, outside of his mother. If I was honest, the thought of being with someone else hadn't seriously crossed my mind. I wanted only him. If I had to make some concessions in order for that to happen, I would do it. The rest of Patrick—the sweet, charming, protective part of him that I knew would never hurt me—was more than worth tolerating the controlling caveman that had made me so angry.

I had to believe that. I had to believe that the good parts outnumbered the bad and, if I was lucky, someday I'd stop worrying myself sick about the thought of waking up to find him gone.

Chapter 16

Patrick

My head was a mess.

There were too many things happening at once for me to focus on just one, and it felt as if, at any moment, I'd completely lose what little grasp I had on my sanity.

I'd been talking with Kevie almost nightly about the shit going on with my Da, and things weren't looking good. Kevie's older brother was a pretty high ranking soldier in the fight for a unified Ireland, and the conversations they'd had during brief trips to their mother's home didn't cast my da in a favorable light. The thought of Kevie's older brother coming anywhere near my hometown where Mum or Amy could come across him at any time made my skin crawl, but I was thankful for whatever news I could get.

I still wasn't clear on exactly what Da had done, but something had happened to make the boys question him. It wasn't good. Loyalty was a precious commodity among those men, and if you didn't have that, you may as well have a target painted on your forehead.

We'd also been getting calls to the house at all hours, and the minute Mum or I would answer, the line would disconnect. It was a fucking nuisance at best, and something far more sinister at worst. I wasn't sure what the person was looking for when they called, but I had two guesses. If it was my da they were hoping to contact, that meant he was in the wind. Not good for anyone. And if it was Amy's parents, well, I hoped they'd bugger off so we could have some peace. As far as I was concerned, they no longer had a daughter.

On top of all that, classes were starting again soon, and I needed to get back to Uni. My boss at the mechanic shop had let me take the time away, but that wouldn't last much longer, either. They couldn't just hold my place indefinitely. It wasn't the best job in the world, but I liked the lads I worked with and it was easy. I couldn't afford to let it go.

The thought of leaving my mum and Amy unprotected made my flesh crawl, but I couldn't stay based on a bad feeling. I had a life, school, and work. I couldn't just drop those for no solid reason, even though every day it became harder for me to envision going back. But what would I do in Ballyshannon? Work as a mechanic? That wasn't the plan and hadn't been for longer than I could remember. I couldn't support a family on a mechanic's wage without living like I'd grown up and I'd sworn to do better for myself than my da had. My wife wouldn't have to work her fingers to the bone to put fucking food on the table, and my children wouldn't wear handouts from the church.

Amy deserved better than that. She deserved to be cosseted.

The past two weeks with her had shown me things that I hadn't even realized I'd been missing.

She liked to do her hair in intricate styles, but she rarely wore them out of the house, preferring it down if she had to interact with people.

She was stubborn, believing that she was always right, but willing to give in to make others happy.

She laughed at commercials on the television that weren't meant to be funny, and read romance novels and classics interchangeably. She seemed to enjoy both equally.

She loved the freckles on my face and chest, and if she didn't think I was paying attention, she'd trace the ones on my arms.

She was a contradiction, both vulnerable and incredibly self-assured. She knew exactly who she was and didn't hide from that knowledge, but she didn't like the scrutiny of others.

She treated my mum like the Queen of England.

She treated me like a king... when she wasn't giving me shit about almost everything I did and said.

We could talk for hours and never run out of things to say, but could rarely agree on anything.

She could completely ignore things that she didn't want to face, and had skirted around any mention of her parents.

She challenged me and made my blood burn until I didn't know which way was up.

God, that girl drove me insane.

It was as if everything that made her who she was pulled at the opposite trait in me, drawing us together like magnets. She made me forget some things and remember others, and her presence gave me a peace I hadn't felt since I was a child. She calmed me in a way no one else had ever been able to do. She was simply...everything. Both my compass and true north.

I suddenly came to the shocked realization that I loved her more than anyone else in the world—myself included.

I'd been up most of the night trying to sort out how I'd protect her and Mum, my mind going over and over different plans and rejecting them while the phone rang sporadically. I'd felt like the walking dead by the time I'd escorted her to school. My body ached from the hours I'd spent on Mum's living room floor and I'd been short-tempered, anxious over the prospect of leaving them alone, and it took all I had to hide that shit from her. She didn't need to worry about things she couldn't change, and I didn't want her to. It was my job as her man to shield her from that shit.

So I'd painted on a cheerful face when she'd awoke and we'd almost made it to school without my façade cracking down the center. I could've kicked myself for getting into the situation in the alley, but to be fair, jealous Amy had been a sight to see. She'd been scowling, her face flushed, and I'd wanted nothing more than to take her home and fuck the jealousy right out of her, prove once and for all that she had nothing to worry about.

I couldn't, though. She should wait. I knew that eventually, when our kids were old enough to ask, that she'd want to tell them with a clear conscience that we'd waited until we'd said our vows. She may be full of hormones and grand ideas now, but the minute it was over, she'd have regrets.

She was my ideal, the most beautiful woman I'd ever seen—and though I knew it was dangerous to put her on a pedestal, I couldn't help it. She wasn't a woman you fucked before you said your vows in front of a priest, no matter how angry that made her.

Amy didn't want to wait and she thought I was an idiot for making her. I loved her, but she just kept pushing and pushing, and I'd finally had enough that morning. I was having a hard enough time keeping my fucking hands off her, and she wasn't making it the least bit easy. I was tired, worried, and turned on with no relief in sight… and then she'd decided to push just a bit further.

Threatening me with other men? Was she out of her fucking mind? It may have been the worst idea she'd ever had. I'd seen red when she started going on about how she'd, what did she call it? *Level the playing field?*

She'd let someone touch her over my dead body and not a moment before.

My stomach was churning when I'd left Amy in that alley, but I didn't even stop to look back at her. I couldn't. If I had, I'd known that the look on her face would have me right back where I started—in her arms—and we'd be riding that fine line again, or I'd do something to scare her, like take her over my knee and thrash the hell out of her.

I hated hurting her, but if I was honest with myself, I'd admit that I was also livid about her threats and it felt good to leave her worried.

How far did she think she could push before I pushed back? The tension in the house, both sexual and the fear of something terrible happening had us all on edge. I understood that she was feeling it, but that didn't give her leave to spew venom all over me.

Honestly, I didn't even know if Amy felt the oppressive weight of my mum's fear. I hadn't said a word about things happening with my da, and I doubted Mum had filled her in—she was too busy skittering around the house like she couldn't find enough to do until she dropped into bed exhausted. It seemed as if Amy walked around with her head in the clouds, completely ignorant to what was happening around her. Did she not realize that I was fraying like a badly knit sweater? I tried to shield her, but I couldn't understand how she missed the signs that something was looming on the horizon. Mum was acting like a maniac, Kevie was showing up unannounced at all hours, and I had bags under my eyes from lack of sleep—yet Amy moved blissfully along as if all was right in her world.

By the time I got home, I was almost dizzy with lack of sleep and fell into bed in a stupor. I couldn't remember how long it had been since I'd gotten a decent night's rest, and it seemed to be all catching up to me at once. I didn't even have time to appreciate the smell of Amy on my sheets before I crashed.

By the time I woke up, I could hear both of my favorite women talking in the kitchen and my anger had cooled completely. After a bit of sleep, things always seemed a little clearer.

It only took me moments to realize I'd slept the entire day away and I hadn't even gone to pick Amy up from school. She must have wondered where I was and if I was still angry with her. Guilt lay heavy on my shoulders as I walked slowly out of my room.

"Now, just lay yer arms in there," Mum said soothingly as I stepped quietly into the kitchen. "That'll help yer poor arms a bit, I'm sure of it."

Amy murmured something back that I couldn't catch because they had their backs to me, and it took me a minute to comprehend Mum's words.

"What's wrong wit' yer arms?"

Amy jumped, but Mum just turned to me with a smile.

"Ah, yer awake then! Hungry?"

"No, I'm not hungry. What's wrong wit' her arms?" I strode toward them quickly, imagining all sorts of horrible injuries.

"It's nothing," Amy said hoarsely, still looking toward the sink. "Just some hives."

"Hives?" I came to a halt, standing stupidly in the middle of the kitchen. Something was off. What was it? Mum was smiling like always, but I felt the tension she was attempting to ignore.

Amy was making no move to look at me.

"Amy, me love." I took another step toward her and watched her shoulders bunch with tension. "Sweetheart?"

"I'm just goin' to run up to the grocer, forgot some cabbage for tonight's supper," Mum commented quietly as she moved away from us.

As soon as the door closed behind her, I stepped forward again until my chest was flush with Amy's back.

"I'm fine, Trick," she said, shrugging her shoulders. "Just some itchy hives."

"Ye caught somet'in'?" I wound my arms around her waist and peered over her shoulder as she hunched a little farther into the murky water, her forearms almost flat against the bottom of the sink.

"No, I just get these sometimes."

Her arms were red as a tomato and from what I could see, covered in big blotches of raised welts.

"What in God's name?" I lifted one of her arms out of the water even though she pulled against the movement. When her forearm cleared the sink, I couldn't stop the noise that came from my throat. It was far worse than I'd thought and it looked incredibly painful. "What did ye do to yerself?"

"Nothing! It just happens."

"It doesn't just fuckin' happen! Yer arms are swollen to twice dere size!"

"It's not that bad. Stop being so dramatic," she snapped back, trying to rip her arm from my hand. When she gasped in pain at my firm grip, I immediately let her go. Shit. My fingers had left small white imprints in her flesh that quickly turned crimson again before my eyes.

She hissed as she laid her hand back into the water, and I gripped her belly in response, trying to brace her. Her arms looked like they were on fire, and I still couldn't understand what had happened.

"Talk to me, sweetheart. Tell me what happened."

"I already told you," she replied dully. "It just happens sometimes. I get hives, and they itch, and since I was wearing my uniform sleeves all day, any time I scratched them, they got worse."

"Why do ye get hives?"

"It just happens."

"Bullshite. I've not seen dem on ye before."

"Yes, you have, they just weren't as bad as they are now. They usually go away after a while."

"*Why*, Amy?" Our voices got quieter the longer we spoke, as if that could stop us from yelling, so by this time we were practically hissing at each other.

"I get them from stress or if I'm upset."

"Stress?"

"Yes."

"What are ye stressed about?"

She went silent at that, and my mind raced through the past few days, wondering if something had happened. Had her parents tried to contact her? Were they the ones who'd been calling at all hours? They'd left the house they were renting in the middle of the night—probably because they owed money to someone—and no one had heard from them since. No, she would have told me if it were something like that.

She didn't say a word as I tried to think of a reason for her stress. When I remembered our fight that morning, my gut clenched in apprehension.

"I did dis." It wasn't a question.

"No! No, it was just stress," she countered, backpedaling.

"I hurt ye."

"I hurt you back."

My arms tightened around her and she sighed as I rested my face against her neck.

"I apologize, me love," I whispered against her throat. "I was cruel."

"No, I was a bitch. I kept pushing. You asked me to stop and I ignored you. I shouldn't have said I'd be with someone else." Her words drifted into a whisper.

"De day ye stop pushin' is de day ye no longer want me. Dat's not somet'in' I ever want to happen, darlin'." I kissed her gently beneath her ear. "I was fuckin' tired, and I could feel me good intentions sailin' away in de wind, and I had to stop us. I went about it all wrong."

"I don't understand why—"

"I know ye don't. But can it not just be enough, for now, to allow me to make dese decisions?" My words were exactly what I should have said that morning... but my wandering hands were completely contradicting anything I was trying to get across.

"I don't want anyone but you," she said quietly as I bit down gently on her neck.

"I know."

My arms were still wrapped solidly around her waist, but I couldn't resist the lure of the bottom curve of her breasts. They were heavy against my forearms as she bent over the sink, and without thinking, my thumbs had begun sliding back and forth against the sides. She was so full there, thick and round and perfect.

My hips were snug against her arse, and I knew the exact moment that she realized my cock had become hard as stone. She froze, barely breathing as I kissed her neck, running my tongue against the pulse there. She tasted so good, a bit salty with a hint of something sweet. I couldn't help but imagine my mouth on other parts of her body, places where I knew the taste would be magnified.

The longer she remained frozen, the more I wanted to thaw her out. My thoughts were consumed with the idea of making her warm and willing against me, and for a few moments I forgot the frustration I'd experienced that morning over Amy pushing me for more. I couldn't think of anything except the fact that she wasn't responding to me like she usually did, and I wanted—no I *needed* her to, especially after her words that morning. Why wasn't she arching her hips like she usually did, or tilting her neck to give me better access?

"Patrick? We need to stop," she whispered, pulling her hips away from me timidly.

The words were like a bucket of ice water thrown over my head,

What the hell was I doing? My hands were completely covering her breasts, my fingers clenching against the resilient flesh, and I let go so quickly I could see them bounce a little as I glanced over her shoulder. After all I'd said, all the decisions I'd made for the both of us concerning sex and the fight we'd had that morning that had upset her so much that she'd broken out in hives…

I was the one who was supposed to stop things from going too far. *I* was the one who was supposed to protect her.

"I'm sorry," I mumbled, tripping backwards as I ran my hands over my face.

"It's okay. I just…"

"Ye've got whiplash from me givin' ye mixed signals? Fuck me." I shook my head in disgust.

"I just wasn't sure what to do."

"I know, lass. De fault was mine."

I sat down heavily in a kitchen chair and braced my elbows on my knees. Christ. I wasn't sure how much longer I could live like this. I wanted her. Badly. And I knew I couldn't live with myself if I took her.

I was living with the woman I wanted above all others, yet I couldn't allow myself to touch her the way I wanted to. I could barely touch her at all without becoming so turned on that I had a hard time remembering why I held myself back. It was a hell of a position to be in.

"It's time I go back."

"What?" She spun toward me in surprise, water splashing across the floor around her. "No! We'll just be more careful. I can—"

"Love, it's not anyt'in' yer doin' or not doin'. I've got to get back to school and work. Can't be stayin' here forever and livin' off me mum."

She stood there in the kitchen, wringing her red hands and her eyes filling with tears, while little tendrils of hair curled around her face from the steam.

She was as beautiful as the Madonna statue they kept in the church. Her beauty went so much deeper than her face or body; it was a manifestation of her innocence, the sweetness she showed everyone, the steadfast loyalty that she gave to others even though it had never been given to her.

And for some reason, she loved me. She hadn't said the words, but I knew it. She showed it in every action, in every secret smile and small brush of her hand against me when she thought no one was looking.

She was everything—messy and emotional and pragmatic and snarky and possessive and beautiful—and I couldn't go another day without making her mine.

I knew with sudden clarity that I wasn't going anywhere before I quieted the doubts I knew were running through her head.

I stood from the table slowly, my eyes never leaving hers and she sniffled even as she raised her chin proudly. She wouldn't beg me to stay or try to change my mind—that wasn't her way. She'd made her argument, or attempted to before I cut her off.

She didn't beg for scraps. It was beneath her to do so.

She expected everything, as she should. Lucky for her, I'd give her anything.

I stepped closer and raised my hands, resting them at the sides of her throat, my thumbs tracing her delicate jawline.

"Marry me." It wasn't a question.

The wind-up clock in the kitchen ticked at least fifteen times as she stared at me with wide eyes. I'd surprised her.

"Marry you? Are you insane?" she said finally.

"No. Marry me."

"I'm eighteen. I haven't even finished secondary! I can't just—"

"Marry me."

"Stop saying that!"

She gripped my forearms tightly in her slender hands, her nails digging in, and I couldn't help but smile happily. Finally, *finally*, something in my life felt right. This felt *right*. I'd anchor to her to me so securely, she'd never again think of a life without me.

The front door opened and my mum walked briskly into the kitchen, pausing as she caught sight of us.

Checkmate.

"Marry me."

Mum gasped in delight, and Amy's eyes closed in defeat.

Then her lips tipped up just a fraction.

"Marry me," I whispered again, pulling her face toward mine.

"Are you sure?" she whispered back, opening her eyes. "Absolutely sure? This isn't a game Patrick Gallagher, you can't just change your mind."

"I'm more sure of dis den I've ever been of anyt'in'."

Her eyes shifted from side to side, searching for something in my gaze, and I knew when she'd found whatever she'd been looking for. "Okay."

"Okay?"

"Okay, I'll marry you."

I heard my mum clapping her hands together gleefully, but I couldn't focus on anything but Amy's flushed cheeks and excited eyes.

I kissed her hard, pushing my lips against hers as I pressed my tongue between her teeth. I ignored the fact that we had an audience and were standing in my mother's kitchen. Nothing mattered but her.

I inhaled deeply, taking in her scent and the slight smell of the oats she'd been soaking in as one of her hands left my arm and wrapped around the back of my head. Her nails dug into my scalp as I stood taller and pulled her with me until her feet barely touched the ground.

I wanted her to remember how she felt at that moment— loved wholeheartedly, yet perched precariously on her toes and leaning on me for balance as I controlled our movements.

Chapter 17

Amy

"**Y**ou're still leaving?" I knew I was gaping like a fish, but I had a hard time trying to school my features. I was blindsided. We'd only just decided to get married, and I'd thought we'd have longer—that I'd have longer—to just bask in the excitement.

"I've still got responsibilities, love. More so now den ever."

Patrick continued packing his small duffel, pulling t-shirts and socks from the bottom drawer of the dresser we'd been sharing.

"But I thought—" My words broke off as I realized how ridiculous I'd been. Of course he hadn't been leaving to get away from me. How self-important I'd been to assume that.

"I've only got a few more classes before I'm finished. It'll go by quickly, especially while yer finishin' up yer own studies and plannin' for our weddin.' " He glanced up at me with a grin, and I couldn't help but mirror it.

We'd been discussing our plans most of the night, cuddled up on the couch while Peg knit in a chair next to us. It didn't seem real yet, the idea of being married. Where would we live? What would it be like to fall asleep next to Patrick and wake up the same way? Would sex be as awesome as I'd been imagining, or was the all the hype just bogus posturing?

I had a thousand questions and very few answers, but I couldn't help but be excited. I was getting married. *Married.* I'd never again feel like a guest who'd overstayed her welcome. I'd belong to Patrick. He'd belong to *me*.

"I'll be home again in a few weeks. Mum says dat she's sure Fadder Mark will be anxious to get de deed finished and he'll probably let Kevie do the ceremony, especially since ye've been sleepin' in me bed for so long already," he commented with a sly look as he zipped up his bag. "Ye've less den a mont' to find a dress and some sexy undergarments."

"Less than a month," I said quietly to myself as I dropped to the edge of the bed. "It feels so far away and so soon at the same time."

"I'd marry ye tomorrow," he answered quietly, sitting next to me and taking my hand in his. "Dis'll give ye time to be certain."

"I am."

"We'll see."

I laid back against the cool quilt, dragging him with me until we were lying side by side with our feet hanging of the edge of the bed. I could feel the heat of him from my knee to my shoulder, and for once I didn't feel the urgency to connect our bodies more fully. I was happy to be just breathing the same air as him and clasping his fingers between mine.

"Where will we live?" I asked dreamily, rolling my head to the side so I could watch him. "How many children will we have?"

"Here for now, I suppose, dough I'll be back and forth from Uni for a while." He squeezed my fingers between his own. "I'm sorry I've not more to give ye yet."

"That's okay."

"It's not, but I promise ye, some day ye'll have everyt'in' ye want. Once I'm done wit' school, I'll find some job—maybe teachin'—and we'll move far from dis place. Get us a house wit' a garden where ye can lie in the sun and bloom like de roses."

"What about Peg?" I loved this game we were playing. I wanted to know all of his dreams, all of the things he imagined for us. I wanted, for once, to picture a happily ever after.

"We'll take her wit' us. Perhaps I'll be hired in Scotland and we can bring her dere for a while."

"She'd love that."

"She would."

"She could babysit our kids while we go on romantic dinners."

"Keep dem overnight so I can fuck ye in every room of our house." His thumb began to trail over my fingers, never hesitating over the missing ones, as if he didn't even notice them anymore.

"I'll wind up pregnant again from all that fucking."

"Christ, it's hot when ye curse."

"Focus. We were talking about our children. How many will we have?"

"As many as I can plant in yer belly."

"Two."

"Six."

"Three."

"Four."

"Okay, four."

We lie there, smiling at each other for a long time, the future full of possibility and promise. I knew that things wouldn't be easy, life rarely was, but I couldn't imagine it being less than perfect if I was with Patrick.

He could make me giddy then livid within the space of a few moments, and I couldn't have loved him more. We fit somehow, the two of us. His overwhelming need to look after the women in his life matched my need for security, as if we were two pieces of a puzzle.

"Are you sure you have to leave tomorrow?" I asked quietly, dreading the answer.

"If I don't go tomorrow, I won't go at all. De lure of ye will be too strong to resist," he answered, turning to his side so he could brush his fingers through my hair. "I know it's been hard to wait…"

"Now we don't have to."

"Aye, we do. We've still a mont' until de weddin', we'll not be anticipatin' de vows." He lifted an eyebrow at my snort. "Be patient, me love. Less den a mont', and I'll be wakin' up to all dis beautiful hair wrapped around me."

I giggled like an idiot at the picture he painted, and he smiled at me indulgently as he waited for me to finish. No one had ever looked at me the way Patrick did—like everything I said and did was the most important thing in the universe and he didn't want to miss a moment.

"What would you do if I came down the aisle with my hair cut to my chin?" I teased.

"I'd marry ye, kiss ye hard and den spank yer arse before we even made it to de reception."

"You would not!"

"Aye, I would."

"You're full of it. You'd never hit me."

"I'll ask ye a question den. Do ye t'ink me mum would ever hit ye?"

"No. No way."

"But she flicks ye every time ye take de Lord's name in vain, does she not?"

"That's completely different!"

"So is a spankin' from yer husband."

"Bullshit!" I sat up in irritation. "I'm not a kid you can just spank when I do something wrong!"

"Dat could be argued…" he grumbled as he sat up next to me.

"Don't be a dick."

"Ye'd radder ye felt guilty for days because ye knew ye'd made me angry?"

"Of course not. But what about you? Do I get to spank you when you do something wrong?" The words sounded ridiculous as they came out of my mouth, which irritated me even further because it hadn't sounded ridiculous when he'd threatened the same thing. Overbearing and controlling, yes, but not ridiculous.

"Darlin', I have no doubt dat ye'll belt me upside de head more den a few times in de course of our marriage," he said with a smile. "And I'll let ye, because guilt'll be eatin' me alive."

"Do you plan on fucking up a lot?"

"I'll try me best, but I'm a man, yeah? I'm sure I'll do somet'in'."

He was wearing the charming grin that I had such a hard time resisting, and after a moment I was grinning right back. He was so...ugh, I didn't even have words for the way he made me feel.

He filled me to bursting with every emotion, and it was a novelty that I couldn't get enough of. I'd been floating along for what felt like my entire life—never belonging anywhere or to anyone, and within just months, Peg and Patrick had completely changed everything.

"Ye look tired, love," he said gently, pulling me out of my musings. "I'll go to de couch so ye can get some rest."

He leaned down to press a soft kiss on my lips, but the moment his lips touched mine, the urgency that had been missing while we discussed our future came back in a flood of sensation.

"Don't go yet," I whispered against his lips, "You're leaving in the morning. Don't go yet."

"Amy," he said in warning, groaning as I stood from the bed and immediately climbed onto his lap. "Dis is not a good idea."

"We're getting married," I reminded him, kissing across his jaw. "And you're leaving me tomorrow. Tonight we should celebrate."

"Do ye have any idea how hard it is not to push dose shorts to de side and sink into ye? Yer playin' wit' fire, engagement or not."

"You only said we couldn't have sex..."

"Yes," he hissed out the word as I made my way to the lobe of his ear. "What exactly do ye t'ink yer gonna get tonight?"

The question stumped me. What was I looking for? I wasn't sure, but I knew I wanted more. Even if he couldn't give me everything, I wanted something.

And frankly, I was getting tired of always being the aggressor.

"I don't know," I answered honestly, leaning back so I could meet his eyes. "You're the experienced one."

"Oh, so it's me decision den?"

"Well..."

"Dat's what ye said."

"Goddamn it, Patrick," I sighed, "If I left it up to you—" My words were cut short as I was flicked right in the center of my forehead. It completely stunned me for a moment; we'd been having what I thought was a serious and heated conversation and he flicked me in the forehead?

I must have looked as shocked as I felt because Patrick began laughing hysterically at whatever he saw on my face.

"What the hell?" I screeched after a moment of complete silence, throwing my body weight against him until his back hit the bed. I scrambled to hold him down as he continued to laugh beneath me, ineffectively trying to fight me off as I flicked at his head.

"Ye shouldn't take de Lord's name in vain, Amy," he tried to scold through his laughter, "I'll not have any wife of mine bein' blasphemous."

"Ha, ha. You're so funny," I said back through heavy breaths as we wrestled across the bed. "Can't say goddamn it, but I can say—" I paused, before moaning breathlessly, "Fuck me now, Patrick."

He froze beneath me, exactly like I knew he would, and I crowed in delight as my finger met the middle of his forehead with a hard thump. Ha! A little distraction and victory was mine.

He didn't even flinch as I flicked him, but the moment I put my arms over my head in a modified victory dance, he was rolling me underneath him.

"Say it again," he ordered seriously, pinning my arms above my head.

"What?"

"Say, 'Fuck me Patrick'," he ordered, shifting my hands into in one fist. "Say it."

His free hand slid down my leg to catch underneath my knee, and before I knew it he was pulling it up to hug his side and arching his body into mine. Our breaths were still labored from the wrestling match, and my chest felt tight as I tried to acclimate myself to the change in mood and the feel of him against me.

"Say it," he whispered, rubbing his lips over mine then pulling away as I tried to deepen the kiss.

"Fuck me now, Patrick," I whispered back, the words sounding so much more obscene when I wasn't joking.

"Ye need it, darlin'?" he asked as his hand slid under my tank top and curled around my breast. "I haven't been takin' care of ye. I was bein' careful." He rolled his hips against mine and a thousand pinpricks of sensation seemed to flare through the lower half of my body. "I don't have to be so careful anymore," he said with another roll of his hips. "I can give ye a little, now dat I know dat pretty soon I'll be so deep, ye'll feel me for days. I'll take de edge off a bit, yeah?" Another roll. "What have ye been doin' wit'out me? Ye take care of yerself in me bed?" Another roll. "Slip dose little shorts off and roll around in me sheets?"

If he hadn't been hitting me in exactly the right spot to make my mind go fuzzy, I probably would have cared that his words were making my cheeks heat in embarrassment.

"I have not!" I argued, lifting my hips to meet his. My hands were still pinned above me even though I pulled at them, and his fingers began to pluck at my nipple over and over, the sensation adding to what he was doing below. "I don't do that."

"Ye don't use yer fingers to get yerself off?" he asked dubiously.

"Not here! Your mom's here!"

"Me mum's here now, and I don't hear ye tryin' to stop me." I whimpered as he leaned back to his heels and lifted his hands from my body, but I wasn't disappointed for long. He was only leaning back so he could grasp the tank top at my waist and rip it over my head in one smooth movement. "Ye goin' to stop me?"

I shook my head silently as he tossed the shirt off the side of the bed, but when he leaned down toward me again I found my voice. It was hoarse, as if I'd been yelling and sounded almost scratchy to my ears. "Yours, too," I ordered.

His dimple showed as he smiled at me in approval, then with little fanfare he grasped the t-shirt behind his head and tore it off, sending it flying to the floor. His skin was smooth, with just a smattering of hair in the middle of his chest, and I ran my fingers through it for a moment before he took hold of my hands, trapping them above my head again.

"Hands to yerself, yeah?" he said. "I'll stop, but—" He didn't finish whatever he was about to say, instead lunging toward my chest with a groan and pulling my nipple into his mouth.

He sucked hard then softly in a confusing rhythm that I couldn't follow, then bit down tightly before soothing my skin with his tongue. My hips instinctively moved upward seeking his, and he met me with a hard thrust.

"Keep dem dere," he ordered, pushing down on my hands so I'd understand what he was telling me. "Christ, ye feel good."

"Watch your mouth," I chastised breathlessly as he moved to my other breast, giving it the same attention as the first. His hand slid down to my thigh, rubbing down to my knee and then back up slowly.

"Make me," he challenged, moving up to press his mouth to mine. His chest rubbed against mine as we writhed on the bed, and my breasts, still wet from his suckling met little resistance as they slid up and down with the force of his thrusts. My breath began to hitch in my throat as the pressure on my clit intensified, but before I could hit the peak I was reaching for, he pulled away, leaving me frustrated beyond belief.

If he left me then, I might have killed him.

"Shhh," he murmured into my mouth. "I need to feel ye."

His hand slipped up the side of my shorts, making me freeze in both anticipation and nervousness. Things were venturing into the unknown, and even though I wanted him, I was still a little...

apprehensive.

When his fingers reached the gusset of my underwear at the juncture of my thighs, I held my breath.

"Not inside. Not dis time, alright? We'll save dat," he said tenderly, leaning down on his forearm to cup my face.

I jumped as his fingers finally slid over my skin slowly, but his eyes held mine as he explored, and soon I was relaxing into the bed. His calloused fingertips on my flesh felt a thousand times better than what I'd been getting through our clothes and I was at the edge again only a few minutes later.

"Ah, darlin'," Patrick said, his voice breaking a little before he cleared his throat. "Feels good, doesn't it? Yer so swollen and wet. Almost dere, yeah?"

I nodded once before sliding into oblivion, my arms wrapping around his neck without thought as I rode the waves. They seemed to go on and on, magnified as he moved his mouth back to my breast, and tugged each nipple. The feeling lasted much longer and was much stronger than when I'd attempted to do the same thing on my own, and as soon as I was finished, I was anxious to do it again.

"Whoa. Too much, Patrick," I warned starting to pull away from his touch when the pressure intensified.

"I know," he assured me, laying his hand completely over me in a firm grip. "After a while it hurts a bit, eh?"

"Yeah. Holy crap." I pulled his mouth to mine, licking into his mouth, until eventually he slid his hand completely out of my shorts. I could feel him moving it around above me, but I didn't understand what he was doing until he pulled his lips away and looked down.

I followed his gaze to see him sliding his fingers against each other, and rubbing his thumb up and down the digits that were completely lubricated from my body. It was slightly mortifying at first, but the longer he stared at his hand, the less I felt that way. He was literally rubbing me into his skin, and I had a feeling that if he hadn't been braced above me with one arm, he would have been rubbing his hands together as if he was applying lotion.

"That's kind of gross," I muttered, not bothering to move away.

"It's not gross. It's lovely."

"Lovely?"

"Look at dat," he said, raising his hand until it was closer to our faces and I could barely catch the scent of myself. "Smell it."

"Dat's what yer body made to prepare for me. Dat's de reason ye'll take me easily, wit' no pain. It'll smooth me way, tell me when yer turned on, tell me when yer ready to take me. It not only prepares ye, but de scent of it—de feel of it—will prepare me, as well. One look, one sniff, one small touch, and I'll be stiff as a pike." He glanced up at me as I stared at him wide eyed. "Lovely."

"Lovely," I whispered back.

I knew then why he'd forced me to wait, why he'd gone to such lengths to keep our hands above our clothing and our kisses chaste. Because as he spoke, I wanted nothing more than to take him into my body.

"I love you," I told him.

"I know."

Chapter 18

Patrick

I left my mum's after an hour of goodbyes with Amy. It seemed as if the moment I stood to walk out the door, I just needed one more kiss—or she did—and the cycle started all over again. After I'd had my hands all over her body the night before, it was almost impossible to keep them off her that morning.

I knew the scent of her, the way she felt on my hands, the way she went silent and still just before she came, shuddering helplessly. I'd shown incredible restraint in not taking what I'd wanted so badly, but with the end of our abstinence in sight, I refused to give in.

She'd been everything I could have imagined the night before, a touch hesitant here and there, but otherwise almost aggressive in the way she'd moved against me. There were many things I loved about her, but I knew that if we didn't spark sexually it would be a miserable marriage for us both. I'd never doubted our chemistry from the first, but chemistry and willingness to reach for what you wanted in bed were absolutely not the same thing. Thankfully, it seemed with Amy that I'd gotten both.

By the time I got back to my flat that afternoon, any gratitude that I wouldn't be torturing myself by living chastely with Amy was long gone. I missed her already. I missed the warmth of my mum's house, the sound of her instructing Amy on how to prepare different dishes, the way my woman would brush innocently against me as if she needed just a small touch to ground her. I missed it all, and the flat that had once been if not *comforting*, at least *comfortable*, felt anything but.

I dropped my duffel near the door, grabbing a beer out of the fridge. I started classes again the next day, followed by my shift at the garage, but that night I had absolutely nothing to do. I made my way to my messy bed and sat my beer on the bedside table that was covered in water rings from the many beers that had gone before. I would lie in bed and read, I decided, striding to my bookshelf for a tattered copy of Robert Frost's greatest works. It was the only thing that might be able to take my mind off Amy and allow me to relax.

But as I pulled back the sheets in one hand and fell into the bed, a vaguely familiar scent met my nostrils. I jumped back up, my stomach roiling as I knocked over my beer in an attempt to get away from the bed.

I'd forgotten.

How had I forgotten?

That blonde girl. Moira.

Mother of God, what had I done?

I swallowed hard, staring at the bed in horror before losing it completely and ripping the offending sheets onto the floor. I didn't want them anywhere near me. I forced myself not to panic as I checked the wastebasket, finding used rubbers and their wrappers littering the inside. The sight made me literally sick, until my mouth was watering so badly that I had to swallow over and over again until the nausea dissipated.

I had to get rid of it all. I had to wipe it away as if it had never happened, I thought, as I tried to stuff the sheets into the small bin. I'd only once thought of my poor decisions while in Ballyshannon, during the argument with Amy in the alleyway, but at that time I hadn't been aware of just how much I may have fucked up.

We were engaged now—set to be married quickly, and planning our lives. If Amy knew that I'd fucked a woman just hours before I'd gone to her, she'd be completely devastated. She'd never want to see me again. I could argue that we weren't yet together, but I knew that was shit. There were expectations there, long before I'd brought Moira back to my flat. The excuse that I hadn't made any promises was despicable; it would be using semantics to try to justify my behavior, taking no account of Amy's feelings, or my own.

I don't know how long I stood there, staring at nothing, but it eventually grew dark before I moved again. I slid my feet back into my boots and threw on my coat before grabbing the bin full of bad decisions and taking it out to the dumpster that sat outside my building. I tossed it in with a curse, knowing that it wouldn't be so easy to get rid of the guilt that seemed to be burning like flames inside my chest. How could I have done such a thing?

I wasn't paying attention as I walked up the stairs to my apartment, so I didn't notice the two men outside my door until I was almost on top of them. I shuffled to a stop in surprise when they blocked my way, and as I looked up, my surprise turned into dread.

"Malcolm," I greeted with a nod.

"Trick," he answered, his expression not giving anything away.

"Can I help ye wit' somet'in'?" I looked between Kevie's older brother and his companion.

"Lookin' for yer Da," Malcolm informed me. "As a courtesy, we came here first."

The underlying threat was not as subtle as he'd like to believe. If I couldn't help him, he'd be on his way to my mum's.

"I just came from home tonight," I answered, "I've not seen me da in weeks. He know yer lookin'?"

"He does."

"If I see him, I'll let him know."

"Do dat."

I nodded again, then waited silently as they watched me for any sign I was lying. After years of listening to the other children snickering about the way my mum had 'run my da out of town', I'd learned to hide my feelings quite well. They'd not get one twitch from me.

"Good to see ye, Trick." Malcolm said after he'd decided to believe me, clapping me on the shoulder as if we were old friends.

"Ye, too," I replied.

I watched them walk confidently down the hall and into the stairwell before unlocking my front door and pushing inside. Jesus. I was having a hell of a night.

I strode to my phone, and as I gripped the receiver, I noticed that my hands were shaking with restrained nerves. I opened them wide and clenched them again and again before picking up the receiver once more and calling my mum.

Amy answered the phone.

"Hello?"

Her voice was like a punch to the solar plexus.

"Hello, me love."

"Patrick! I didn't think you'd call so soon!"

"I miss ye." I had to clear my throat twice before I could get the words out.

"I miss you too, baby."

"Baby?"

"Was that weird? I thought I'd try it out."

She was such a goofball. So completely unassuming. For the first time in a long time, I felt a lump in the back of my throat as if I was about to cry.

"No." I cleared my throat again. "No, I like it."

"Okay. Yeah, me, too."

"What are ye doin'?"

"Getting ready to watch a little TV with your mom while she tries in vain to teach me how to knit. What are you doing?"

I glanced at the bare bed and swallowed hard. "Just havin' a beer and gettin' ready to read for a while before bed."

"You're going to bed already? Are you eighty years old with gout and a broken hip?"

"No, I'm twenty-t'ree and have class and work tomorrow. Gotta rest up while I can."

"I can't wait until you're not so busy." She paused for a moment. "And home with me all the time. I really can't wait for that."

"Me, eider, love. I better get off to bed, but I wanted to hear yer voice for a moment."

"I'm so glad you called," she replied softly.

"Me, too." I rubbed my hand down my face as my shoulders slumped. "Is Mum around?"

"Sure. She's right here. Want to talk to her?"

"Please."

"Okay. I love you, Patrick."

"I love ye, too."

"That's the first time you've actually said it."

"I won't be de last."

"Good. Here's your mom."

There was a pause and some shuffling before Mum got on the phone, and I listened intently as she scolded Amy for dropping a stitch before she said hello.

"Hey, Mum," I called dully.

"Hello, my lad! Get home safe then?"

"Safe and sound. But I had a couple of visitors to me flat not long ago."

"Oh?" On the surface, her voice sounded nonchalant, but I could hear the panic threading through it.

"Malcolm was here lookin' for Da."

She sniffed into the phone.

"I told dem I just came from Ballyshannon and I've not seen him in weeks... but Malcolm mentioned stoppin' by yer place," I warned, just the thought of it making me want to race back home.

"Ach. I can handle Malcolm. I changed that boy's nappies," she snapped back.

"Mum, he's not de boy—"

"I know that, son. But I know nothin', so there's nothin' for him here. I'll tell him the same if he comes."

"Please be careful, Mum. Dese men won't be trifled wit'."

"Aye, I will."

"Keep an eye on Amy, will ye?"

"Of course. We've a weddin' to prepare for."

"I'll talk to ye soon, Mum. Ring me if ye need to."

"I will."

She disconnected without another word, and I was left once again standing in the flat I suddenly hated with a bed I wanted nothing to do with.

The next month could not go quickly enough.

Chapter 19

Amy

My future wife,

The days cannot move fast enough for my taste. It feels as if every minute takes an hour and every day a month.

I've had a hard time concentrating on classes and I almost dropped an engine on my foot at work yesterday. How would you feel about a groom on crutches with his foot in a cast? It may be a distinct possibility by the time I can come home to you.

Yes, home to you. My flat has become this depressing place where I brood and bemoan my loneliness like an Emily Bronte hero. I've never missed my tiny cot at Mum's more than I do now, knowing that is where you fall asleep each night.

Some days I wonder why the hell I made us wait until we were married, and others I'm filled with anticipation and a feeling of rightness that our wedding night will be the first time we come together.

I sound like a woman, don't I?

Ignore my ramblings. I'm tired.

Remember that you only have a few weeks left of school. Don't go offending the priests now, or you may never get out of there... even if you did think that he was trying to get a glimpse up your skirt. (Even writing that has me grinding my teeth.) Though, I'm sure by the time you receive this letter, you'll have already come to the same conclusion.

You flashes of anger remind me of Roses and Rue by Oscar Wilde:

"And your mouth, it would never smile,
For a long, long while.
Then it rippled all over with laughter,
Five minutes after."

Not much longer, my love, and I'll be there with you.
I'll slay all your dragons.
Love, Patrick

The weeks flew by at a rapid pace. There was so much to do and so many small details to finalize that it felt as if I was deciding on wedding favors in my sleep. We'd decided to have a very small service, just those closest to Peg and Patrick, and even though I knew Peg had hoped for something bigger, I was relieved. All my attempts to contact my parents had been in vain, so I would have no one on my side of the church except for some of my teachers from school.

My pews would be filled with black and white habits... at least I knew none of them would try to outshine the bride.

I talked to Patrick at least twice a week, sometimes more, and we sent tons of letters back and forth, sometimes overlapping so a question in one of my letters was already answered before I knew he'd gotten the one I'd sent. He hadn't been able to visit during the month like he'd hoped, but the things we talked about while we were far away from each other seemed to have created a stronger bond, anyway. It was so much easier to write our feelings down on paper—our fears and hopes for the future—that we seemed to have discussed a lot more than we ever had face to face. A part of me also reveled in the fact that I was receiving dozens of love letters that I could keep forever. Occasionally, his notes only contained a few lines, a poem or something he couldn't wait to tell me about—but other times they were long and heartfelt and made me feel like the luckiest woman on earth.

He'd finally come home the night before for our rehearsal at the church, and it had been extremely hard to keep our hands off one another. When I'd caught sight of him, stepping off a motorcycle I'd never seen before, Peg had gripped my arm like a vice in order to keep me from flinging myself into his arms.

He'd laid himself bare for me in his letters, and I wanted nothing more than to pull him into me and wrap myself around him.

Dinner at Peg's had been a lesson in torture, as she'd made us sit across from each other. She was adamant that we behave ourselves, and for the first time, became some sort of morality police to keep us honest. I think we were all afraid that after waiting so long, Patrick and I wouldn't be able to help ourselves. The thought being that we were so close to being married, we could act as if it already happened.

I could honestly say that I'd contemplated finding a way to get him alone more than once. The tension at the table was almost unbearable, and to add insult to injury, Peg had invited Kevie home to eat with us. He was officiating the service the next day, and if bursting with pride was an actual possibility, we would have been scraping pieces of Peg out of the sanctuary.

By the time Patrick left that night, we'd barely touched and had only said a few words to one another that were uninterrupted. I understood what Kevie and Peg were trying to do, but that didn't mean I agreed with it. I hadn't seen my fiancé in a little more than a month, and we were given absolutely no room to reconnect or even exchange 'I love you's' before he was shuffled off to Kevie's for the night.

By the time I got into the shower the next morning, I was strung tightly with nerves and the fact that I hadn't had any time with Patrick made things infinitely worse. Was he having any doubts? Was he as nervous as I was? Afraid he was doing the wrong thing? And my most terrifying thought—did he wish that he'd never asked me in the first place, and now felt stuck trying to do the right thing?

We were getting married. Married. And I still wasn't even done with school. I hadn't seen the world. I hadn't climbed the corporate ladder or gotten drunk or had sex. I'd done nothing at all to give me any life experience... yet beneath all that, I was still giddy with excitement.

It was an odd feeling, wondering if I was doing the wrong thing, but still willing to jump in headfirst. It made my hands shake and my palms sweat and my belly feel like it was crowded with a hundred butterflies.

I shaved my legs and my armpits before glancing down my body, chewing on the inside of my cheek. A magazine I'd been reading had mentioned trimming the hair down there to look more appealing, but I didn't have anything to trim it with and I'd felt too embarrassed to ask Peg where the small scissors were. I looked back and forth between the razor and my pubic hair for a moment before lathering up with soap and taking a deep breath.

Maybe if I just ran the razor lightly over the top of the hair it would trim it down a bit. I could make it just a bit less bushy and shave the edges a little so it looked more uniform. I ran the razor lightly over the frothy soap, coming away with a disgusting amount of hair that I quickly washed down the drain.

Okay that wasn't so bad.

I did it again and again, until I was sure that things would look fantastic. I set the razor on the edge of the tub and turned toward the showerhead to rinse off. That wasn't so bad. I bent at the waist to take a closer look.

Then I screeched in horror.

Dear God.

Oh, my God.

Shit.

Shit.

Fuck!

It was patchy. Patchy! It looked like my vagina had mange!

My hands started shaking as my eyes filled up with tears. What had I done?

"Are ye okay?" Peg called from beyond the door.

"No!" I yelled back.

Before I could change my reply, Peg had barged into the room and pulled back the shower curtain. I couldn't even raise my head to look at her, my eyes frozen on my mangled thatch of hair.

"What in God's name did ye do?" she asked incredulously.

"I don't know!" I wailed, finally looking up. "I tried to trim it! I just wanted to trim it!"

"Why on earth would ye do that?"

"I read it in a magazine!"

"I told ye to stop readin' those bloody things!"

"I know! Oh, my God. We have to postpone the wedding. We have to." I babbled frantically, water dripping down my face. "Patrick can't see me like this!"

"Ach, he'll see ye much worse."

"Not on my fucking wedding night!"

A small laugh bubbled up in her throat as she glanced back down, and I knew then that I would not be getting naked anywhere near Patrick for the foreseeable future.

"Ye'll just have to take it all off," she informed me as if it was the most reasonable thing in the world.

"What?"

"Take it all. Ye cannot leave it as it is," she answered, gesturing in the general vicinity of my hips.

"What if I cut myself?"

"I suppose ye'll just have to be very, *very* careful."

She pulled the shower curtain closed between us while I stood gaping at where she'd just been.

"And hurry it along, we've an hour before we have to leave for the church!" she called before slamming the door behind her.

I had no choice.

I lathered up and reached for the razor again.

After a few close calls, some very interesting contortions, and the loss of hot water, I'd finally shaved everything to the best of my ability. It felt odd without the protection of my hair, and every time my thighs slid against my lips it was like a little jolt, reminding me of what I'd done.

My long shower had seriously cut down on my preparation time, and Peg scrambled to get me ready. She blow dried and brushed out my hair while I did my makeup, complaining the whole time of my decision to leave it long down my back "covering the beautiful lines of my dress." I couldn't be swayed, though. Patrick liked my hair down. He couldn't keep his fingers out of it. The loose hair stayed.

We were five minutes late and both flushed with exertion as we finally left the house, but the short drive to Peg's church was thankfully enough time to calm both of our heated cheeks. Peg reached across the seats and gripped my hand hard before climbing out of the car.

"No need to be nervous."

I was shaky as we entered the side door so no one would see me, but by the time I stood at the large wooden doors at the back of the church, a feeling of unnatural calm had settled over me.

I was ready.

Chapter 20

Patrick

I stood at the front of the church, uncomfortable and sweating as I waited for Amy to arrive. I'd spent the morning sitting in Kevie's small flat near the church drinking a Guinness to steady my hands and running over and over my decision to marry Amy in my head.

I was nervous. Worried that I wasn't doing the right thing, that she was too young, that I was too young, that we lived in a place where life would never be easy, that we'd still have to live apart for months yet, that I'd wake up the next morning regretting the marriage—that she would, that somehow she'd find out about Moira and she'd never forgive me, but she'd be stuck with me, anyway.

I never voiced my doubts to Kevie. We were the first couple he'd ever married, and by the way he'd paced the floor mumbling to himself the night before, I knew he was almost as nervous as I was. If I said anything, I'd put him over the edge. I was afraid he'd feel the need to postpone the wedding to counsel us or refuse to perform the wedding altogether.

And even though my stomach was in knots as I climbed the steps to enter the vestibule of St. Joseph's, I couldn't stand the thought of waiting another day to marry Amy. The thought of never making her mine—of living without her—made me panic in a way I hadn't done since my father had left us.

There were people filling the first five pews, but I didn't meet anyone's eyes as I made my way to the altar to wait. I couldn't. I was completely focused on doing my part and not messing up this first part of our lives together.

I was wearing my only suit, an itchy wool thing that was a bit too small through the shoulders, and the brand new white shirt and dark grey tie beneath it felt as if it was strangling me. The neck was too tight, but I hadn't said a word as Amy had brought it out to me the night before. She'd painstakingly ironed it all under my mum's watchful eye, and she'd been so proud of it, I hadn't had the heart to say a word.

Unfortunately for my soon to be wife, the shirt she'd been so proud of was growing increasingly wrinkled as I sweated and fidgeted while waiting. I tried to stop my movements, but nothing helped. I was too anxious—so anxious that I could feel sweat dripping down my back and under the waistband of my trousers. My underarms were even worse, and I was suddenly terrified that I'd have to raise my arms during the ceremony and everyone would see the giant wet spots I was trying to hide. I didn't have to raise my hands, did I? I'd been to hundreds of weddings in my life, in that very church, but for the life of me I couldn't remember.

I clenched my eyes shut then popped them back open before anyone saw me. My normal composure seemed to have completely deserted me.

"Do not lock yer knees," Kevie whispered out of the side of his mouth. "Good way to pass out, dat."

I nodded gratefully, unlocking them and bending them slightly. I'd begun to feel a bit off, and I told myself that must have been the problem. Leave it to my best friend to catch me losing it while I tried not to let anyone see.

I turned my head to whisper back—I really wanted to know if I'd have to raise my arms during the ceremony—but before I could say a word, the organ began to play and my head whipped around to look at the front of the church.

And then suddenly, there she was, in a long white gown and a veil that only gave me small glimpses of her face.

I no longer felt like I was going to black out. Instead, as she moved toward me, I felt as if I could fly.

Chapter 21

Amy

I don't remember anything about the ceremony, except for the fact that it went on for far too long when all I wanted to do was kiss the hell out of my husband and during the ring exchange, we'd slid Peg's band onto my finger and then right back off again. My left hand was the damaged one, and with no knuckle to hold it steady, wearing a wedding band was pretty much impossible. My wedding ring finger would remain bare.

During every hymn, every reading, and every prayer, I stared at Patrick. I couldn't see anything else. He looked so handsome in his suit. His poor neck looked rubbed raw from the starch I'd put into his shirt collar, his hands fidgeted during the entire ceremony, and I watched a small bead of sweat run down his hairline—but none of that mattered. He was promising me forever.

Finally, Kevie blessed us as a married couple—it was still odd to see him in his robes—and we were married. Patrick's kiss was short and sweet at the end of the service, just a closed mouth peck on mine, but the way his hand gripped my fingers tightly as we turned to face our guests more than made up for it. Our vows were sealed and blessed, but I don't think either one of us was willing to let go of each other for even a second. It had been so long since we'd been able to touch, that even holding hands soothed me.

I couldn't get out of the church fast enough after we'd made our way down the aisle. People had stepped over to congratulate us over and over, and though it was very sweet, by the time the nuns from my school had lined up to say hello, I could have punched someone. Did no one see our impatience to get away? Did they not remember how it felt to be newlyweds?

Our small reception was being held in Peg's small house, and by the time we made it to the car, most of the guests were already headed that way. Even Peg had gotten a ride with Kevie before we were able to leave the church. I'd hoped that we'd have a moment to ourselves before the house was full of people, but that wasn't going to happen. It seemed as if the universe was working against us.

"Ye look beautiful, wife." Patrick said after minutes of absolute silence in the car. "I've never seen anyt'in' lovelier."

"You're not too bad yourself."

He made a sound of disgust. "Dis fuckin' suit is makin' me sweat like ye would not believe."

"I noticed," I replied with a small laugh.

"Ye did?"

"Even your face was sweating!"

"Do ye t'ink anyone else saw it?"

"Only Kevie."

"Well, dat's alright den."

"Why does it matter?"

"Because I felt like a fuckin' idiot up dere, sweatin' like a pig."

"Well, you didn't look like an idiot."

"Good t'ing no one was lookin' at me once ye arrived," he teased.

I smiled at him happily as he watched the road, and I couldn't believe my incredible luck. We were almost to Peg's when Patrick turned onto a street that was vaguely familiar. When he stopped the car and put it in park, I looked at him in surprise.

"Were you hoping for a game of basketball? I'm sorry, I didn't bring one with me. Couldn't fit it under the dress."

"If ye were tryin' to hide a basketball under yer dress we'd have quite a bit of explainin' to do," he answered, laughing as he pulled at his tie. "Christ, I can't get dis fuckin' button undone. It's too tight."

"Here, I'll do it," I offered, leaning toward him to slip my fingers underneath the fabric below his Adam's apple. "Good Lord, how could you even breathe?"

"Don't t'ink I took a breath until I saw ye."

"Aw."

"Shut it."

I wrestled with the button for a minute before it broke free, then ran my fingers over his poor neck. There were indentations where the collar had pinched at his flesh.

"Why the hell did you button it if it was so tight?" I scolded.

"Married less den an hour and she's already naggin'."

"We're married," I whispered, my lips curving into a grin.

"We are."

He lifted his hands to grip my head and then his lips were on mine. I moaned as he slid his tongue into my mouth, then relaxed my neck until he was completely supporting the weight of my head in his hands.

"I wanted to do dis de first second I saw ye," he said as he ran his lips across my jaw. "Standin' next to ye and not bein' able to touch ye was torture."

"I know, the ceremony went on forever," I complained.

"But de end was wort' it."

"You're mine now."

"Not yet." He chuckled darkly. "But later I will be."

I shuddered as his lips sucked gently on my neck. My nipples pebbled beneath my gown and I felt myself grow wet, the sensation reminding me of the mishap in the shower earlier.

"We have to get back to your mom's," I reminded him breathlessly as he worked his way back toward my mouth. "Everyone's waiting." His mouth met mine again, the kiss slow and surprisingly gentle, before pulling away.

"Why do dey have a party after de weddin'? Seems like an awful way to start married life, surrounded by people ye have to entertain instead of fuckin' like rabbits."

"You're so romantic."

"I am romantic," he replied immediately, offended. "I write ye fuckin' love notes."

"Oh, is that what they were?" I teased as he turned the car back on and backed out of the empty lot.

"Yes, dat's what dey were. I wrote ye poems!"

"You copied other people's poems."

"I'm a scholar, not a writer. Ye'd not want any poems I'd attempted to write."

"Oh, so you've tried before? Did you send other girls your poor attempts at poetry?"

The guests had been kind enough to leave an empty space to park right in front of the house, and after Patrick had pulled in and parked, he turned to me, his expression serious.

"I've not written anyone letters but me mum. Ever. Except ye."

"Why not?" I called as he climbed out of the car without another word, moving to my door to help me climb out.

"Because dey weren't de woman I was goin' to marry," he answered, then kissed me quickly, sliding his tongue against mine only once before grabbing my hand. "Now let's go celebrate for a while, so we can leave and celebrate on our own later."

The reception was fun, even though I was anxious to get Patrick alone. Peg grabbed me as we'd walked through the door, and spent hours introducing me to everyone who'd come to see us, from the couple who owned the grocery store Peg managed, to neighbors who'd moved away years previously. It was odd seeing Peg and Patrick interact comfortably with so many people, and it reminded me of how isolated we'd been.

Patrick took off to the corner of the yard as soon as Peg pulled me away, and he met my eyes a few times as I mingled, but we didn't have the chance to connect more than that. There were so many people in Peg's house and back yard that it was hard to even move from one place to another without having to stop and chat.

When I finally made my way back to him, I hesitated a few feet away. It was like looking at a person I'd never seen before.

At some point he had changed out of his white dress shirt and into a greyish green one, his tie gone, the button at his throat undone and his sleeves rolled to his elbows. He looked far more comfortable than he had earlier, and as handsome as ever, but there was something just slightly off. His cheeks were rosier than usual and he was smiling huge as he gestured wildly with one hand, the other clutched around the neck of a beer bottle. I couldn't help but smile when he laughed loudly, but before I could step forward, I watched him brace his arm against the wall beside him.

For a moment, I couldn't pinpoint what was bothering me. Then I realized with sudden clarity that my brand new husband was well on his way to being completely drunk.

I was happy that he was having such a good time. I was. But I felt a lump grow in my throat as he continued to laugh with his friends, nodding in thanks when one of them handed him another beer. I knew it was completely selfish, but I wanted him to be dying to get me away. I didn't want him having fun with his friends like he was out at a pub—I wanted him to be as anxious as I was to finally get away from prying eyes and into a bed.

I stood there dumbly, watching them laugh and poke fun at each other, until finally one of the guys noticed me and nodded in my direction. Patrick turned to face me with that same wide smile, before he started strolling toward me.

"Me beautiful, lovely, gorgeous wife!" he greeted loudly, wrapping his arms around my waist.

"Hey. Having fun?" I tried to match his happiness, but I must not have succeeded because his lips lost their curve as he looked at me.

"I'm havin' a grand time," he answered cautiously. "Aren't ye?"

"Of course. Peg's been introducing me for the past two hours to people I'll probably never see again, my feet are killing me because of these stupid shoes, I'm hungry, but every time I make it to the kitchen I get stopped by someone and I don't get the chance to eat, I haven't even spoken to you since we got here, and now you're drunk, and if I'm feeling what I think I'm feeling, you just spilled beer down the back of my wedding dress." My voice never lost its cheerfulness as I spoke, but his brows drew together as if he was trying to decide if I was joking. "I'm having an *awesome* time."

I reached behind me to find his hand, and took the bottle from his fingers before he could do any more damage. "I'm going to find your mom to see if she can get me out of this dress."

"Wait," he ordered, pulling me back against him. "I wanted to take it off ye."

I sighed, looking around the yard as people watched us. "I don't think you'd even be able to at this point, Patrick," I told him quietly.

"Dat's a load of shite." His fingers wound into my hair, pulling it tight as his hand reached my scalp. "I've had a few, but I'm not tanked."

"It's okay. Really. I'm just going to go see if your mom can help me. I'm really uncomfortable in this dress."

"I told ye I want to take it off of ye."

He leaned down and kissed me hard, sliding his tongue into my mouth with little finesse. His technique didn't matter in the slightest to my body, though. The minute his lips closed over mine, I relaxed into him. He'd been smoking not long before and the yeasty taste of the beer he'd been drinking mixed with the subtle taste of tobacco, the combination setting me on fire. I didn't even notice the yelling and whistling until Patrick started to sway my way and I was suddenly holding him up instead of the other way around.

"Patrick," I called, pulling my mouth away as he tried to right himself.

"Ye make me head spin," he informed me with a lopsided smile.

"Would ye like to come meet de lads? I want to show off me gorgeous wife."

My heart sunk as I realized he hadn't heard a word I'd said, but I smiled anyway. "Sure. Give me a couple minutes, okay? I'm going to find your mom real quick."

"Alright, me love." He kissed me tenderly on the forehead then grabbed his beer from my hand and spun from me to saunter away.

How could I be mad when he was having so much fun? He was an adorable drunk, and the way he usually looked at me seemed to be magnified with alcohol, turning it from loving to almost worshipful. No, I wasn't mad, not really.

I was just overwhelmingly disappointed and hurt.

Rubbing my left hand over the top of my right one, I searched the crowd for Peg, but couldn't see her so I headed for the back door. When I got there, I realized that people had started clearing out, and there were only a few stragglers left inside the house. Too bad the people in the yard seemed like they'd be staying a while.

My hands began to burn as I knocked on Peg's door, and I looked down to see a few small welts appearing as she opened it up. I couldn't stop the tears that rolled down my cheeks.

"What's wrong, sweet girl?" she asked, pulling me inside and closing the door. " I was just changing into something a bit less fancy so I could start cleaning up."

"Could you help me change?" I asked quietly.

"Well, didn't ye want—"

"I want to change now," I interrupted. "This dress is starting to feel really heavy and my feet hurt… I just want to get it off."

"Well, okay then." She opened up the door and marched through the living room while I followed behind her, and soon we were in my room.

"Turn around so I can get to those buttons."

A few more tears rolled down my face while she painstakingly unbuttoned every small button down my back, and I tried not to remember how I'd imagined hearing a ripping sound as Patrick lost patience with the small pieces of plastic and fabric. I'd giggled when I'd tried the dress on, imagining Patrick's frustration.

"Well, if I'd known I'd be the one doin' this, I would have advised ye to get the gown with the zipper," Peg commented with a huff, causing me to snort.

"If you just do a few more, I can get it off my hips."

"Okay, give me one more minute… there, see if that will work."

I brushed the sleeves off my shoulders and watched silently as the dress gaped in front and then slowly started to sag. Then, I clenched my jaw and shoved the bodice down over my hips until it billowed on the floor around me. I stepped out and sat on the bed, silently unbuckling my shoes and rubbing my sore feet.

Peg moved to the door, turning when I finally spoke.

"Would it be really rude if I stayed in here for a while?" I asked. "I'm getting a headache."

She searched my eyes before nodding twice. "That's fine, dear. Ye lie down for a bit. The only people left are too drunk to care where the guest of honor is."

Once she was gone, I took off the fancy, light blue bra I'd bought for my wedding night and slipped on a pair of Patrick's sweats and a large flannel shirt that was tucked into the bag he'd dropped off the night before. They smelled like him, and I pulled my head into the neck of the shirt like a turtle so I could take a huge whiff. It was the best scent in the world.

I crawled under the sheets that I hadn't thought I'd be sleeping in, and it didn't take me long before I was falling asleep with tears dripping occasionally off my face.

What a horrendous wedding night—the sun hadn't even gone down and I was in bed alone.

Chapter 22

Amy

I woke up later to the familiar feeling of Patrick sitting down on the edge of the bed, but I didn't open my eyes. I didn't want to see him. The memory of the reception was vivid in my mind, and I absently realized that my hands felt better, which meant the welts had gone away.

"I know yer awake."

"I'm surprised you are," I replied, opening my eyes.

He was hunched over, facing slightly away from me, looking down at his hands that were running along the satin of my discarded bra. He was still wearing what he'd had on before, but his hair looked as if he'd been running his hands through it, and the goofy smile was gone.

"I'm sorry," he said, finally raising his face so he could meet my eyes. "De lads were handin' me drinks, and I hadn't seen dem in a long time between bein' away for school and spendin' all of me time wit' ye... I lost track of time and how much I'd had."

"Is this how it's always going to be?" I asked quietly. "Me standing on the edges while you just go off and do whatever with your friends?"

"Of course not."

"I didn't know any of those people, Patrick."

"I didn't t'ink."

"It's our wedding day. Or it was…"

"Still is. It's about ten o'clock."

"You ignored me on our wedding day." The words came out garbled as I tried to speak around the lump in my throat.

"Aw, love. Don't do dat. Don't cry."

He dropped my bra as he stood, and I watched as he unbuttoned his shirt and pulled it from his trousers before tearing it off. Next came his shoes and socks, and then finally he was unbuttoning his pants and pushing them down his thighs until they dropped to the floor with everything else.

I let him pull the blankets back and crawl in beside me, and it was a tight fit in the tiny bed as we lay facing each other.

"What de hell are ye wearin'?"

"I didn't think I'd have company."

"Christ, how are ye not sweatin' yer arse off?"

He reached under the blankets between us, and shoved down on my sweats, tearing them off my legs before tossing them behind him.

"What are you doing?"

"I know yer angry. I'm not tryin' to fuck ye," he answered in disgust.

"Then what are you trying to do?" I asked as he leaned over me and unbuttoned my shirt.

"I just need to feel ye." He spread the sides of the flannel wide, then smoothed his hands down my sides. "It's been so long since I felt yer smooth skin."

"How did you know I was in here?" I asked as he lay down on his back and pulled my body against his side.

"Did ye t'ink I wouldn't notice dat me brand new wife went missin'?"

"You seemed busy."

"I wasn't." His arm tightened around my back.

"I bet your mom told you."

"She did."

"Did she give you hell?"

"I t'ought she was goin' to stab me in front of all dose witnesses."

"Good."

"Ye can't go askin' me mum to fight yer battles." He reached out to tip my chin toward him. "She's got no place in dis marriage."

I stiffened against him, pulling my face from his hand—angry and hurt all over again.

"I didn't ask your mother to say anything to you," I snapped back, pushing against his chest so I could sit up to and wrap the flannel back around me. "Someone had to get me out of that fucking dress!"

"I *told* ye I wanted to take ye out of it. I've been fantasizin' about dat very t'ing since ye stepped into de fuckin' church!"

"Then maybe you should have listened when I said I was tired! Maybe you should have stopped for one second to think about me, your wife! Instead, you went back to drinking with your friends." I choked back an angry sob. "Maybe if I hadn't felt like a leper when my hands started to break out, I could have stayed outside and you could have helped me with my dress!"

We were screaming at each other, and it was absolutely heartbreaking because it was the last thing I wanted to be doing. What had I done? Why had I married this man I barely knew? Where was the Patrick I loved? Why was I in bed with this stranger?

I tried to climb over him, but he was up and tossing me back onto the bed before I could get anywhere. Our chests were heaving, and I wanted nothing more than to lock myself away from everyone and cry my eyes out.

"I hated not bein' near ye," he said, pinning my legs with his and bracing his elbows near my head. He reached down to grab my wrist and pulled it between us, inspecting my hand before letting go and doing the same thing with the other one. When he was finished, he kissed it before placing it against his heart. "It felt as if I was comin' out of me skin when Mum pulled ye off to introduce ye to people. But at de same time, de closer we were, de harder it was to stop meself from kickin' every one of dose people out of de fuckin' house. I'm dyin' for ye. I've been dyin' for ye for mont's, and once I knew I could have ye, it was torture not to do so." He leaned his forehead against mine, closing his eyes. "I was just tryin' to distract meself wit' de lads. Dat's all it was. Just until it was over and I could have ye to meself."

"You hurt my feelings."

"I'll try not to do it again," he said earnestly, ghosting a kiss over my lips.

There was my Patrick.

"You looked so handsome today," I whispered, lifting my hands to his face. "I'm sorry I threw such a fit."

"I was an arse."

"You were, but you're not now."

"Forgive me? I'll make it up to ye."

"Just don't go out for a smoke or something and leave me giving birth on my own."

"I'd never do dat." He ran his hand against the side of my face, then threaded his fingers through the hair at my temple. "I'll never leave ye again."

"I love you." There was forgiveness in my words.

He sighed into my mouth, his shoulders sagging in relief. "I love ye, too."

His head tilted as his hips pressed down, and I spread my knees to make room for him above me as his tongue slid into my mouth. He groaned as I dug my nails into the back of his neck.

We were ravenous. We bit and licked and sucked at each other's lips and tongues, fighting for the dominant position, but it wasn't long before he'd gained the upper hand with a jut of his hips. We'd never had so few layers between us before, and my breath caught as he ground against my clit through our underwear. The feeling of him with so little between us incredible, made even more so by the lack of hair shielding my femininity. I could feel every single movement, every twitch and slide.

"I thought we were going to a hotel?" I gasped as he tore his mouth from mine.

"I cannot wait dat long." He leaned back on his knees and pulled me with him, lifting my arms above my head so he could slide off my shirt. "We'll go later."

"But—"

"Me mum's stayin' at Kevie's mum's tonight." He assured me, setting his palm on my breastbone and shoving gently so I fell backward. "She didn't want to intrude on our arguin'."

His smile turned devious, and then he was twisting around to shove all but the bottom sheet off the bed, mumbling. "We're goin' to need a bigger bed."

My nipples pebbled hard as he turned back to take me in, and my stomach became even more concave as I tried desperately to catch my breath. He was all muscle. His chest was muscular, and it tapered down to a rock hard stomach with a light thatch of hair swirling below his belly button. The muscles in his shoulders bunched as he reached out, and I shuddered as he laid his palm flat on my throat then dragged it down the center of my body until he'd reached the band of my light blue underwear.

"Ye bought de fancy undert'ings I asked for."

"Yes."

"Dere gorgeous, but dere comin' off."

He pushed the tips of his fingers beneath my underwear at my sides and slowly slid them down as I raised my hips from the bed. It was a smooth motion, slow and steady, until suddenly, he paused for a moment before ripping them down my thighs. I was startled, my body frozen at the unexpected move, but I didn't resist as he lifted one leg and then the other to pull the blue scrap of satin completely off.

He was staring.

"What did ye do?" he asked hoarsely.

The reason for his change in demeanor became clear and mortification set in. I laid my arm over my face.

"I tried to trim it."

"Dat's not *trimmed*. It's *gone*."

"I had a bit of a mishap," I replied sheepishly, peeking at him from under my arm. My body was cooling from the lack of stimulation and the conversation.

"Yer alright?"

"Yeah, I'm fine."

He was still staring at my pussy, and it began to get a little annoying.

"Are we done? It's getting a little cold in here."

His head whipped up in surprise and I glared at him. Couldn't he tell that I was getting embarrassed?

"It'll grow back!" I huffed in annoyance.

"No."

"No?"

"It's…" His fingertips traced down and over me, making me jolt. "Don't let it grow."

My body began to heat again as he traced over me gently, and goose bumps popped out all over. He slid back on his knees until my legs were propped up over his thighs, and suddenly his fingers were moving farther down and sliding through the slickness.

"Lovely," he whispered.

"Lovely," I groaned back, my hips tilting upward to give me better access.

"Are ye nervous?" he asked, barely sliding his index finger inside me before pulling it out again and repeating the motion. He leaned down to kiss my sternum, and I slid my fingers through his hair.

"No, I'm ready."

"Not yet, but ye will be."

His lips slid down my belly as the rest of his body slipped to the floor, and then he was gripping my thighs and pulling me down until my ass hit the edge of the bed. I wasn't sure what he was doing, but I had an idea, and any reservations I may have had were gone as he looked at me hungrily.

"Why do you keep staring?" I asked quietly, propping myself up on my elbows.

"I've only seen dis in magazines."

"You've seen other women before."

"Not bare ones... and don't bring up ot'er women in our bed."

"It's not a big deal."

"It is to me." He leaned down and ran his lips over the skin between my legs, making me arch sharply as he pulled away.

"De possibilities are endless," he said, pressing my legs farther apart until the sides of my knees almost touched the sheets. "If ye'd not shaved it off, I could still do dis—" He swiped his tongue up the center of me, making the muscles in my pussy clench hard. "And I could still do dis—" Then he flattened his tongue and rubbed it strongly against my clit.

"Oh, my God."

"But it wouldn't feel de same if I did dis—" He sucked one of my lips into his mouth and rubbed his tongue across it at the same time, ending with a small bite against my flesh that made me jump.

"I can see everyt'in'. Feel all dis soft skin," he murmured against me. Then he opened his mouth as wide as it could go and pressed it over my entire pussy, sucking gently. I could feel it everywhere, and my arms started to shake, but I kept them planted in the bed so I could continue to watch him.

His eyes were shut tight as he closed his mouth, rubbing his lips against me, but they opened back up when my hips began to roll beneath him. Everything he was doing felt so good, but I needed more. I needed something inside me. I needed friction. I needed *something*. I was panting as he lifted his face, pursing his lips to place a gentle kiss on my clit.

"Are ye ready?"

Before I could answer him, his face dropped again, and this time I wasn't able to hold myself up and fell to the bed.

His tongue rubbed small circles over my clit, bringing my orgasm closer and closer as his thumbs rubbed up and down the sides of my opening, the skin so slick that there was virtually no friction. Each time they came closer and closer to the center of me, until suddenly, one slipped barely inside.

My hips rocked against him as he turned his hand, then suddenly his thumb was gone and he'd slid his index finger all the way inside. I ignored the small pinch I felt as I got closer and closer, and my neck arched as he groaned against me. Finally, his other hand came to my belly, pressing down as if to brace me, and I shattered, yelling as I came.

I lay there boneless as he moved to his feet, only my eyes following the movement. He stripped his boxers off quickly, then leaned over me to smile at my dazed expression. He grabbed me beneath the arms and pulled me up the bed as I did nothing to help, and I smiled back as he climbed up between my legs.

"Yer not even goin' to look?" he teased, taking a hold of each knee so he could spread me wide.

"I think it's better if I don't see it beforehand. That way we won't be dealing with my virginal shock and awe and questions of 'how on earth will you fit?'"

"Ye've been readin' too many romance novels."

"I needed some tips."

"Don't be nervous."

"I'm not."

"Dat's why yer hands are shakin'?"

He grabbed one of the shaking hands in question, and raised it to his lips, kissing it gently before bringing it down between us.

"Feel how wet ye are," he said, running both of our fingers over my sensitive flesh. "Lovely."

"Lovely."

"Remember what I told ye? Ye'll take me easily wit' dis."

"I'm not nervous."

"Okay," he answered with a tender smile, letting go of my hand. Then he moved his body on top of mine more fully, bracing his forearm at my shoulder as I wrapped my arms around his back. His hand stayed between us, directing his cock to the correct angle, and then suddenly he was *there*.

"Still not nervous?"

"No," I whispered hoarsely, my pulse thrumming.

"Keep yer eyes on mine, wife."

He rocked his hips, gently at first, which got us nowhere, and then harder. I could feel him stretching me slowly, and it didn't hurt really, but it didn't feel good, either.

"Are you in?" I asked after a couple minutes of watching his jaw clench and sweat bead on his upper lip.

"Halfway."

"Oh, my God."

"Nervous yet?"

"No," I replied stubbornly, taking a shaky breath.

"Good." He arched his hips harder and suddenly there was a stinging sensation, and I was the one clenching my jaw.

"All done, me love," he whispered gently, leaning down to kiss me. I could taste my arousal on his mouth, but when I tried to turn my face away he gripped my jaw on each side, holding me in place. "Don't turn away," he said against my mouth. "Taste it. It's good."

I groaned as his tongue thrust in my mouth with the rhythm of his hips. I wasn't getting anything out of it, not really. I was sore and my thighs were beginning to hurt a little where his hipbones pressed against me... but he was *inside* me. It wasn't anything like I'd imagined, full of starbursts and fireworks and an orgasm that made my eyes roll back in my head. But somehow it was better, because this person—this gorgeous man who loved me—was my husband. And he was focused solely on me, kissing me, and rubbing my cheeks gently with his thumbs, and sliding in and out of me in a steady rhythm.

It wasn't long before he pulled his mouth away and rested his forehead against mine as he shuddered, jerking his hips uncontrollably. "I love ye, wife."

"Love you too, husband."

Chapter 23

Amy

We didn't leave for the hotel room Patrick had reserved until the next morning. Our wedding day had been so long and emotional, both of us had fallen asleep not long after we'd cleaned up. We only went a few towns over—there was no money for a fancy vacation—but I didn't care. I had three whole days of nothing but Patrick. I was in heaven.

By the time we got back, I actually *felt* married. It was just long enough that the exciting newness of it all had turned into a sort of newlywed bliss—still exciting, but more comfortable. More solid.

The Patrick I'd grown to love was back—attentive and sarcastic in equal measure and more physical than he'd ever been before. He was constantly touching me, a hand on my knee, on the small of my back, or wrapped around my shoulders. He kissed me constantly, when he was excited or happy or thoughtful. It didn't matter what we were doing, he was marking me constantly with his possession, figuratively—and literally—in the form of matching anchors we'd had tattooed where wedding rings would have been placed if that was possible. It was wonderful, and seeing the permanent mark on my hand made me giddy with love.

By the time we got back to Peg's I was more sore than I'd ever been in my entire life. Even sitting in the car for an hour had hurt like hell.

"Ye look like an old woman," Patrick teased as I climbed slowly out of the car.

"If you hadn't fucked me eighteen million times in four days, maybe I'd be a bit more spry."

"But t'ink of all de fun we would have missed," he said, pushing me gently against the car so he could steal a long, wet kiss. "Now it's back to reality."

"No," I moaned. "Let's go back. We'll live like gypsies."

"Yer home!" Peg called from the front door. "Did ye have a good time?"

We turned to face her, and she beamed back, clearly excited to see us.

"No, your son sucks in bed," I whispered to Patrick, which earned me a hard pinch on my ass. He pulled out of reach as I yelped and then grabbed our bags out of the back seat.

I walked slowly toward Peg and as I reached her, she snickered.

"Apparently, a little too much fun."

"Hey! A little sympathy would be nice." I scowled at her, but it didn't last long. She looked so happy, I couldn't stop from smiling back at her.

"Let's get ye into the bath with some salts," she said as she ushered me inside. "I know just how yer feelin'. Had a wedding night of my own once."

She settled me into the bath as we listened to Patrick putting my things away. The warm water felt fantastic against my raw skin and sore muscles. Why hadn't I realized that I was so sore? Probably because while we were away, Patrick had kept me in a perpetual state of arousal and willing to do anything to sate it.

We'd been both making up for lost time and preparing for time apart. Our few days had passed too quickly, and now I had less than twenty-four hours before Patrick had to leave again to get back to school. It felt like the end of the world, and I sniffled as I leaned farther into the tub water.

I hated the thought of being away from him for even a second.

"Hey, what's all dat about?" the man of my thoughts asked as he slipped into the room.

"You can't be in here!"

"What de hell are ye talkin' about?"

"Your mom's in the next room!"

"And we're *married*," he answered, raising his eyebrow.

"But—"

"Are ye feelin' any better?" he asked as he knelt by the tub, running the tips of his fingers through the water. His eyes roamed over my naked body as if cataloguing the love bites and fingertip bruises that covered me. Suddenly, he burst out laughing while I stared at him in horror.

"I'm sorry," he gasped, trying and failing to curb the laughter. "But yer—yer so concerned wit' me comin' in while yer bathin'!" He stopped to laugh loudly again, bending at the waist as he did so. "But didn't Mum just help ye in here? She's *seen* what we've been up to!"

"You're such an ass!" I cupped my hand in the water and shoved it toward him, causing a huge wave to fly over the edge of the bathtub and completely soak his face and chest.

He gaped at me, his wide eyes and mouth causing me to burst out in laughter of my own. Then he was up, kicking off his shoes and pulling his pants down his legs.

"No. No, Patrick! You can't—"

He leaned back and opened the door a fraction.

"Mum, I'm goin' to get in wit' Amy," he called, making my face flame in mortification. "We'll be out in a while!"

"Okay, dear!" Peg called back.

"I cannot believe you just did that," I hissed through my teeth, climbing to my feet.

"Sit back down."

"No, I'm getting out."

"Sit. Down." His voice had gone deep and stern, and I looked up in surprise to see him pulling off his t-shirt. I debated ignoring him, but there was no amusement left on his face. He was completely serious... and angry?

I timidly sat back down in the water and pulled my knees to my chest as I watched him finish disrobing.

"Pull out de stopper for a moment," he directed, stepping into the tub. He was standing right in front of me, and I reached behind me blindly to pull the plug while his erection seemed to bob in my face.

My mouth began to water.

"Dat's enough," he said after a minute, pulling me out of my stupor.

I stopped the draining water again as he reached down to tug on his erection, and my sore muscles clenched.

"I t'ink I've found one part of ye dat isn't sore," he said quietly, reaching out to rub my cheek and slide his thumb into my mouth. "Up on yer knees, wife."

I scrambled up, the water rippling around me, and as soon as my hands were planted on his thighs, his were in my hair guiding me toward him. We'd done it before, a few times, but never in that position.

I opened wide and the pool of saliva in my mouth made his entry easy. As I wrapped my lips around him, being careful not to get him with my teeth, he shuddered.

"Dat feels wonderful," he rasped, and I jolted, looking up to urge him to silence with my eyes. Peg could *not* know what we were doing.

"Open wider," he urged gently, his brow furrowed. "Take me deeper in yer mout'."

My eyes bugged at his obvious words, and I felt heat flush up my neck. He was doing it on purpose. If I opened any wider I'd have to unhinge my frigging jaw.

He might have been embarrassing me, he was still infinitely gentle as he guided my movements, and his mumbled words of praise had me heating and growing even slicker in the water. He was so gentle and obviously thankful that I was giving him a blowjob that I couldn't even be mad at him.

"Enough." His words were garbled as he pulled away. Suddenly, I realized how cool the water had gotten and how much of my skin was out in the cold air. I shivered as he carefully sat down facing me, his knees jutting above the edges of the tub.

"Not much room in here," he said with a smile, pulling me to his chest so he could reach around me to turn on the taps. "It's hot, don't lean back."

I nodded as he pulled me into his lap, my knees under his armpits and our bodies completely aligned from hips to chest.

"I'll not hide or sneak around. I pay me mum plenty to cover de rent on dis place, it's just as much ours as it is hers. " He told me seriously, one hand at the back of my neck and the other smoothing its way down to tease at my peaked nipple. "Yer me wife. We make love. Dat's de end of it."

He was hard beneath me, and with a twist of his hips he was sliding slowly inside, watching my face closely for any sign of discontent. I was still sore, but the throbbing ache of arousal overwhelmed any discomfort I may have felt. He felt so good when we were wrapped around each other that way.

"Alright?" he whispered.

I loved him so much in that moment.

"Lovely," I whispered back with a sly smile.

He met my smile with one of his own and he reached behind me to turn off the water. The motion pressed him deeper and I stuffed my head into his neck to keep from moaning out loud.

I was braced against my knees and bent completely in half in that small bathtub, and there was virtually no room to move, but we made it work. We rocked gently, kissing faces and necks and shoulders and arms until it was over and I was completely exhausted.

***

We spent the rest of the day together with Peg, watching old movies and cuddling. It was exactly what I needed after the long week we'd had. It had gone by too fast, though, and a part of me wished we could do it all over again. I dreaded Patrick leaving in the morning.

Peg was considerate of us, and spent a lot of time puttering around the kitchen and her small garden to give us a little time to ourselves, but I knew that she was dreading Patrick's departure almost as much as I was. There was something happening behind the scenes, something they weren't telling me, and it was making her more anxious than normal.

We slept naked and curled around each other that night, but my poor body was at its limit, so we didn't do anything else. It was nice to just feel our skin touching in various places as we lay in the small bed. Patrick made comments about finding a bigger mattress, but I hoped he wouldn't. I loved that we had so little room—it meant that we were always touching, no matter how we moved around in our sleep.

When he left the next day, I put on a brave face and refused to cry. It's temporary, I told myself. He's making a better life for us. He's working hard toward our future.

None of my affirmations gave me any sort of peace.

I missed him the minute he left the house.

Chapter 24

Patrick

Life fell back into a familiar rhythm, but everything felt off kilter.

I wanted to be home.

I ached constantly for Amy, which made me feel like the biggest fool who'd ever lived. I knew she was back home waiting on me, but our marriage seemed to have caused a new and stronger sort of possessiveness to take hold. I was jealous of anyone who came in contact with her when I couldn't. I found myself calling home more often than I could afford just to hear about her day and to listen for any mention of other men. I knew it was completely asinine for me to do so, but I couldn't seem to help myself.

I was driving myself crazy. That must have been why I hadn't seen the writing on the wall. I'd been so caught up in my wife that I'd let my guard down. Nothing had changed just because I'd gotten married, even though it felt that way for me.

"Patrick Gallagher," a man called out behind me as I started to open the door to the building I lived in. His voice sounded friendly enough, but the hair on the back of my neck stood on end and I braced as I slowly let the door fall shut and turned to face him.

I recognized Malcolm first. He was standing just slightly behind the man who'd called my name, and as I took in the four men before me, my stomach clenched in fear. They must have found out about the girl.

"Found yer Da," Malcolm told me with a nod. My stomach sunk. Not the girl.

"An interestin' man, yer fadder," the short man mused, looking me over. "Loyal as a bloodhound and about as smart as one. Odd dat his son spends his days inside a classroom."

My fists clenched at my sides, but I knew there was no way I could hit him the way I wanted to. I was outnumbered and unarmed. It would be suicide.

"What can I help ye wit'?" I asked calmly.

"We have some t'ings we'd like to discuss wit' ye."

"I'm not interested." I glanced at Malcolm, but his stoic expression didn't move.

"Ye haven't heard what I'd like to discuss."

"I know exactly what ye'd like to discuss. I'm not interested."

"Yer fadder will be...disappointed." The inflection in his words made my back break out in a cool sweat.

"Where is he?" I asked, even though I knew that was exactly what he wanted.

"He'd like to see ye," the man replied jovially.

He hadn't answered my question.

They began to move away, as if it was a foregone conclusion that I'd follow them. They'd cast the bait, and I bit. When I reached the sidewalk, Malcolm fell into step beside me.

"I heard ye've married."

"Yes." I absolutely was not going to talk about Amy with these men.

"Kevie says she's beautiful."

I didn't reply.

"I'll have to introduce meself next time I'm home," he prodded.

"Stay away from me wife," I replied sharply.

"No time for an old friend, den?"

"We were never friends."

We climbed into a small truck, Malcolm staying by my side in the back, and I couldn't help but wonder what would happen if they killed me. Would Mum know to take Amy and leave? Malcolm's interest in my wife made me so livid I envisioned killing every one of them before we reached our destination.

The man driving would be easy to take out, just a quick snap of the neck and he'd be gone. Malcolm's pistol was in his jacket on the side closest to me, and I wondered if I'd have enough time to pull it and kill him and the short man before they retaliated. I clenched the hand resting on my thigh twice, trying to calm my breathing. It wouldn't work. If I killed the driver, we'd crash. And even if the plan worked, more would come. They were like rats in a sewer, kill a few and the rest followed in a huge wave until you were overwhelmed.

I sat silent until we reached an older building across town. From the outside it looked like a bakery, but I knew we weren't there for pastries.

Inside the store, the men didn't stop to speak to the man behind the counter. With a quick nod in passing, we strode straight by him into the back, where a stairwell led us into a finished basement with a steel door.

My Da was sitting at a table with a couple other men, and he stood in surprise the minute I cleared the door.

"Patrick?"

"I told ye I'd bring him," the short man said. His tone was cheerful, but it was an eerie sort of glee.

"What's dis about Da?"

He shook his head slightly at me.

"Well, now. I only believed dat two men are better den one. And who better to work wit' ye den yer son?"

"He's made his own choices, Michael."

"He's made no choice," the short man replied. "Yer eider wit' us or against us."

My heart began to pound at his words. It was exactly what I'd been running from, and I should have known that eventually they would catch up to me. My Da had made this choice for me before I'd been able to wipe my own ass, and there wasn't anything I could do about it. Christ, if Mum hadn't kicked him out, he probably would have filled my head with propaganda and I would have been eager to take my place in the ranks. No matter the course that got us to that point, it was always going to happen.

My life—the dreams that I'd followed and worked for—flashed before my eyes, and I knew. I'd never live in a small cottage with Amy, filling her belly with babies before I trudged off to teach excited new students about the importance of classic literature. I'd been a fool, and it was finally time to face reality.

My hand began to clench at my side and I consciously relaxed it, loosening my body until none of my tension was apparent. Any sign of weakness would be seen by these men, and I couldn't afford it.

The short man made it sound as if I had a choice, but there was really no choice at all. I was their puppet or I was a dead man. And they'd effectively cut me off at the knees, because with one word about Amy, Malcolm had known that I'd never take my chances against them. She was a weakness they were willing to exploit.

"What's de job?" I asked quietly.

My da looked surprised and short Michael was smug.

"I hear yer good wit' a knife."

I glanced at Malcolm to see a small, weasely smile on his face.

"I'm fair."

"Dat'll do." Michael tipped his head then stepped forward to the table and laid his hands flat on the surface. "De police commissioner has been makin' t'ings... hard for me lads," he said, spreading photos of a house and a man out on the table. "We need to do somet'in' about it..."

My need to protect my mum while my da was gone had led me down a shady path for a few years as a teenager. I'd come to the conclusion that those who weren't feared were those who became the preyed upon. Our neighborhood had never been one of the worst, but it wasn't the greatest either, and I'd realized that even my da's reputation would not protect my mother and I. So, I'd become one of those who were feared.

I'd never carried a gun, I couldn't make myself go so far, but believing that fists alone would make my point would have been foolish. Instead, I'd carried a switchblade. I'd practiced and I was good with it. Almost as if it was a natural extension of my hand, I'd made my stand over and over with the local thugs who thought they could intimidate me. My reputation with a blade had eventually made it so that even if I wasn't in town, my mother and now Amy were safe under my protection. I hadn't had to pull my knife in over four years.

But I still carried it.

The implication behind Michael's words was clear. He wanted the man dead, and he wanted me to do it. We spent the day going over the police commissioner's habits and memorizing his address and by the time I left late that night, my future was set in stone.

Perhaps it had always been set in stone and I'd been too blind to see it.

When the time came, my Da tried to talk me into letting him take the kill, but I knew that was suicide. Da was on the outskirts already. If he took the job I was given instead of being a look out like he'd been ordered, we were both dead men. I had to prove myself... incriminate myself.

The idea was brilliant, really. With one job, they'd successfully assured both my Da's loyalty and my own. I became a murderer, and Da would do anything to protect his only son.

The police commissioner was the first man I killed. He was a drunk who lived alone. It was easy.

I vomited afterward.

I also vomited the next time.

And the next time.

And the next time.

But eventually it got easier.

And then I became numb to it all.

I'd successfully brought my father back into the fold. It was unfortunate that I'd had to follow him back in.

Chapter 25

Amy

Going back to high school—or secondary, as it was called in Ireland—was so weird. The conversations I'd listened to so intently before about boys and how far so and so had gone the weekend before suddenly sounded petty and immature. The girls all seemed like such babies.

A part of me wanted to speak up when a girl across the lunch table talked excitedly about how her boyfriend had wanted her to touch his 'you know' when they'd been out that weekend. The girls had made disgusted faces and it took everything I had to not tell them that eventually they'd be putting 'you know' in their mouths. I forced myself not to giggle into the sandwich I'd brought with me for lunch. Oh, the things I could tell them.

Life was just different for me, I had to remember that. Not better or worse, just different.

While those girls were kissing frogs and touching random 'you knows' looking for their happily ever after, I'd already found mine. Well, it wasn't exactly a happily ever after, but it would be. For a while, I'd been talking to Patrick nearly every day, but we'd resorted to letters after a while.

I wasn't surprised by it; phone calls were expensive and I knew he was busy…but it made the time pass slower when I no longer had his voice to look forward to at the end of the day. The longer I went without seeing him, the more disjointed my life felt. I wasn't a wife, but I wasn't only a high school student, either. I was someplace in the middle. I missed him so much that sometimes I had a stomach ache all day long, but it helped a little to know what we were working toward something. All I had to do was picture a small house on a quiet street and Patrick in a suit and tie getting ready for work, and it made things just a little more bearable.

I told myself I just had to be patient. It would all work out in the end.

***

"Peg, I'm home!" I called out wearily, dropping my bag onto the sofa. God, I couldn't wait to be done with school. Patrick had been gone for a month and I was sick and tired of living like a child when I was actually a married woman. I was ready to move on from that stage of my life. I was so ready, in fact, that I'd stopped by the local pub on my way home asking for a job. I knew I had to finish school, quitting wasn't an option, but I only had another month left before I graduated. I needed something else to do and a way to contribute somehow.

Thankfully, the owner of Dillon's was more than happy to hire me on. I think Casey Dillon had been friends with Patrick's dad at some point because I'd met him at the wedding reception, and I was pretty sure that's the only reason he gave me the job. The pub was practically empty when I'd walked in—there was no way he needed the extra help. I didn't start for another week, but after that I'd be stocking and serving alcohol from five to midnight Friday and Saturday nights. It wasn't much, but it was something.

I was so excited to tell Peg about my new job that I pretty much danced into the kitchen then came to a comically abrupt stop. My husband was there in the middle of the room, with a small smile on his face and his hands pressed deeply into the pockets of his jeans. I was stunned at first, and then racing to him. Within seconds, I was wrapped in his strong arms. I felt tears hit my eyes as I inhaled deeply and gripped the back of his sweatshirt. He smelled exactly the same, and I couldn't get close enough. I wanted to burrow inside his clothes so I could touch him skin to skin.

"Dat's a good welcome home," he whispered huskily into my ear.

His hands were shaking against my back.

"I missed you so much," I said into his neck.

He shuffled me backward, never letting me go as we made our way out of the kitchen and finally through the door to our bedroom. I knew we were being rude. I hadn't even said hello to the people at the table—but I couldn't find it in myself to care.

My husband was home. I wouldn't have cared if the pope himself was sitting at our kitchen table. I didn't have eyes for anyone but Patrick.

We fell onto our little bed in a tangled heap before I wrapped my legs around Patrick's hips as tightly as I could.

"Hello, wife," he said quietly, pulling away just far enough to meet my eyes.

"Hello, husband."

"Christ, I've missed ye."

I'm not sure which of us moved first, but soon, his tongue was in my mouth, rubbing over my lips and teeth as if to familiarize himself with it once again. My entire body relaxed into the bed as his hands moved over me, never sliding beneath my clothes, but sweeping over me with reverence.

It reminded me of before we were married, when we were dying for each other, but unable to take the final steps. We murmured nonsense against each other's mouths for long minutes, my hands sliding through his hair and gripping the back of his neck, but eventually reality intruded.

"Tea!" Peg yelled through the house. I could tell that she hadn't come to the door, but had called from far enough away that she wouldn't be able to hear what we were doing. Smart woman.

Patrick pulled away slowly, coming back for soft kisses over and over again as he stood up and pulled me up to a sitting position on the bed.

I couldn't stop staring.

He was exactly the same, but different. I recognized his face as clearly as my own; however, it seemed as if there were new lines around his eyes and his cheekbones had become a bit sharper. His hair was longer than I'd ever seen it, and it flopped over his forehead messily. He looked wonderful and extremely tired.

"We'd better go out dere," he said, glancing toward the door for only a moment before meeting my eyes again.

"Why are you home? How long are you staying?" It seemed as if the shock had finally worn off and now my mind raced with questions. He hadn't told me he was coming home.

"I came to see me beautiful wife for a few days, is dat all right wit' ye?"

His words were mild, but there was an underlying defensiveness to his tone that raised my hackles. What the hell? I immediately thought back to my questions, but couldn't find anything in my tone or words that would warrant a defensive reaction. If anything, my exuberance should have been a bit funny.

"What?" I asked, puzzled.

"Dere a reason ye don't want me home?"

My brows furrowed in confusion as he watched me closely. What was he talking about?

"Of course I want you home!" I jumped from the bed, but stopped short when he took a step back. "What the fuck, Patrick?"

I watched him take a deep breath and run his fingers through his hair, pulling the long strands back away from his face. He looked like he was trying to calm himself down, but I couldn't understand why he would act like that in the first place. Where was my charming husband? Why was he so angry?

He took a step toward me, and that time it was me stepping back.

"I'm sorry, love," he said, stepping forward again to reach me. "I'm just tired. I don't want to fight."

I let him pull me into his arms, but my body remained rigid. I wanted to wrap my arms around him so badly, but I was terrified he'd pull away again. I didn't understand how I'd made him mad in the first place, and the anxiety made my heart race.

I didn't want to fight with him, either. I'd missed him so much that I was past the point of jumping up and down with excitement that he was there—no, I didn't want to jump, I wanted to cry with relief that I could finally feel him against me. The overwhelming emotion of it all went beyond anything I'd ever felt in my entire life. He was finally there, in my arms, and it felt like he didn't even want to be there.

Patrick pulled me to the kitchen by my hand, as I tried valiantly to straighten my hair with the other. I didn't need to broadcast the make-out session we'd just had. When I finally sat down at my place at the table, I realized who exactly I'd seen out of the corner of my eye when I'd been too focused on Patrick to pay attention.

Peg's husband Robbie sat in the normally empty chair as if he'd done it every day for the past ten years, instead of living in a completely different town.

"Ye've met me da," Patrick said shortly, sitting down at the table next to me.

"Um, not really." My face heated in embarrassment at his blatant disregard of common manners. "I'm Amy. It's nice to meet you."

"Robbie," he replied back with a nod, lifting his arm across the table to shake my hand. "It's lovely to finally meet ye, too."

"Brought some pastries home," Peg announced cheerfully, bringing them to the table. "Didn't realize our men would be here."

It felt like I was in a Twilight Zone episode as all the people around me ate quietly as if it was any other day of the week. As if the last time we'd all been in the same room, Robbie and Patrick hadn't been ready to come to blows and Peg hadn't been on the cusp of a nervous breakdown. What the hell was going on?

"I'm glad ye two are gettin' along," Peg announced, looking between Robbie and Patrick.

Tension at the table rose as the two men glanced at each other, and I jumped in my seat as Peg's fork went clattering to the tabletop. Her entire body stiffened as she looked back and forth between them. I didn't understand what was going on, and all of a sudden I was really sick and tired of having no idea what was happening in my family. From the very beginning, I'd tried not to overstep, afraid that if I did my place at that table would disappear. But marriage, or perhaps time, had erased those worries. I wanted to know what the hell was going on. Now.

"No...Tell me ye didn't, Robert," Peg hissed. "Tell me ye didn't bring our boy into yer bullshite."

"Margaret—"

"Mum—"

The guilt shone plainly on both men's faces.

"How could ye?" she screamed, making the hair on my arms stand straight up.

"We did not have a choice!" Robbie said back, pleadingly.

"There's always a choice!"

"Mum—"

"Not a word out of ye, Patrick Gallagher!" Peg ordered, never looking away from Robbie.

"I didn't know until it was too late." Robbie insisted.

My mind was spinning and my stomach clenched as all three stood from the table. I was frozen in my seat as I watched it play out in front of me, terrified to know what they were talking about, but unwilling to try and calm the storm before I knew exactly what was happening.

"Ye could have done somethin'! Ye could have got him out!"

"Dere is nuttin'—" Robbie's arm swung out, and I flinched in my seat at the movement, "Dere is nuttin' I could have done. Dey would have killed me and pulled him in anyway, ye know dat I wasn't on de best terms!"

"That's not true!" Peg argued, wrapping her arms around herself and placing one hand over her heart. "I would have *died*. I would have *killed myself* if it meant that our son wasn't pulled into this madness ye've been so intent on being a part of." Her anguish was palpable, her small body shaking with anger as she took two steps forward and struck him across the face. "I begged ye!" Another slap. "I begged ye to keep him out of it!" Another slap.

Robbie didn't do one thing in his defense, just stood there and let her beat on him as I watched in horror. When Patrick started to move around the table, yelling for his mom to stop, his dad just raised one arm, motioning for him to stay back. Peg was sobbing, and I'd never before seen her so out of control. Her husband was twice her size, but he did nothing to stop her, even as his face turned red with handprints and his lip split where her wedding ring caught it.

And still, I sat, frozen to my seat. I couldn't make my body move. I couldn't organize my thoughts into any semblance of order. They were just a jumbled mess of dawning horror and disbelief at what I was witnessing.

What in God's name had Robbie pulled Patrick into?

Chapter 26

Amy

"What's going on Patrick?" I asked as he pushed me into our room. The screaming had gone on and on, until finally, Robbie had pulled Peg into his chest, comforting her as she slumped against him. He'd lifted her and carried her into her room, closing the door behind them and we hadn't heard a peep since.

Patrick hadn't met my eyes after his parents had disappeared, and now he was moving around the room, grabbing a fresh button down shirt out of the closet and doing anything he could to refrain from looking at me.

"Get dressed. I'll take ye to dinner."

"I want to know what the hell is happening." I insisted, crossing my arms over my chest.

"Get out of dat uniform and get dressed," he replied flatly.

"What the fuck is going on, Patrick?" My voice was getting louder as he turned his back to me, his shoulders tight as he pulled off his sweatshirt and t-shirt. Suddenly, he spun to face me, giving me a glimpse of his bare chest that I didn't have time to appreciate before he started speaking in a low, angry tone.

"Oh, *now* ye want to know? After all dis time, livin' here and eatin' our food and contributin' absolutely nuttin' to dis fuckin' house except extra dirty laundry—*now* ye want to know what's happenin' around ye?"

My jaw dropped in surprise and my heart started to race as he glared at me. My stomach began to churn at the derision in his stare, and I honestly thought for a moment that I was going to vomit all over the bedroom... contributing even more dirty laundry to the house I gave nothing to.

What could I say to that? What words could I use to fight against something I'd been terrified would happen? I'd been so conscious of what I was doing every second I was at Peg's. I'd cleaned and helped with the laundry and made dinner as often as I could, because I'd felt like an ingrate for not paying my share of the expenses. From the very beginning, I'd felt like a charity case, but I'd let them talk me into staying there because I'd had no other options and they'd assured me that they didn't think of me that way.

My eyes filled with tears as I began to gather the few pieces of laundry off the floor, in some sort of small attempt to make amends.

I just had to do more, I thought, my movements jerky. I just had to help out more, and then when I started my job the next week, I could help with the bills, too. I didn't want to be a burden. Did Peg feel that way, too? Oh, God. I was so fucking embarrassed. It was humiliating.

I glommed onto his words about my lack of contribution, completely disregarding the rest of our conversation. That was my fear—that I was taking advantage of someone that was spectacularly good to me, and eventually, they'd realize that I wasn't worth the time or energy.

I didn't even realize that he'd manipulated me in order to turn the conversation in a different direction. I don't think he'd anticipated my reaction though, because soon he was talking to me, trying to get my attention, but I couldn't hear him over the words in my own head.

I stuffed the dirty laundry into the hamper near our bedroom door as I strode out into the kitchen and began to clean up the plates and silverware on the table. I could get that cleaned up before Peg came out of her room, then she wouldn't have to do it. I turned on the sink and began to fill it with water for washing, and opened up the small fridge to see what Peg had planned for dinner. Some sort of casserole sat along the bottom shelf, and I felt a pang of anxiety that it was already prepared, but pushed through it. I could put it in the oven for her. That would help.

As I stuffed the dirty dishes into the sink and began to wash them, I heard Patrick come into the room behind me and I stiffened. I didn't want to talk to him. I was embarrassed and angry and ashamed that he thought I was taking advantage of them. I just wanted to be alone, so I could finish those dishes and then maybe dust the front room. Peg had a ton of little figurines and things that she rarely had time to dust—I could do that.

"Amy," he called quietly, and I remembered a different time that he'd come to me while my hands were in the kitchen sink.

"I need to finish these dishes," I answered. "Peg's already made a casserole, so I'll just put that in for dinner. No use wasting money."

"It's not a waste of money to take me wife out for dinner."

I laughed nervously. "Peg already went to the trouble. Plus, I have some things I need to do around here tonight."

"Yer almost done wit' dose dishes. Come on, put on a pretty dress and I'll take ye out."

His hand came out to squeeze my shoulder, and I pulled away roughly, my hands never pausing on the dishes. "I have other things to do, Patrick."

"More important den spendin' time wit' de husband ye haven't seen in a mont'?" he asked incredulously.

I wanted to go with him. I wanted that so badly. But his words had pushed some sort of trigger, and the thought of taking a night for fun made me feel crazy with anxiety. I needed to clean the house. I needed to contribute, to be better.

"Maybe tomorrow."

"No, get dressed. We're goin' now."

"Tomorrow, Patrick."

"Now, Amy."

I shook my head, refusing to argue with him anymore, and then suddenly I was pulled away from the sink and flipped over his shoulder. He carried me into the bedroom while I pinched at his back, too conscious of Peg and Robbie in the next room to yell at him like I wanted to.

"I told you I don't want to go to dinner!" I said after he'd put me down in our room and closed the door behind him. "I told you I have things to do!"

"Dey can't wait until tomorrow?" he asked calmly, watching me closely.

"As you so eloquently put it, I'm not contributing. I'm dead weight, right? So, no, I don't want to go out to dinner and waste more money."

"Dat wasn't what I meant!"

"It's what you said."

"Mot'er of God! Yer de t'ickest woman I've ever met!"

"Then go back to your other life if I'm so stupid!"

My words fell like an anvil between us and the room went silent. We were staring at each other, and I was wondering how the hell everything had gone so lopsided when Patrick's hand began to clench at his side. Over and over again, it clenched and relaxed as I watched.

"You're clenching your fist," I said quietly.

"I'm not goin' to hit ye." He sounded disgusted at the thought.

"No, I know that." I shook my head. "You do it when you're upset."

His hand instantly went limp at his side.

"Yer not dead weight." My head was nodding before he'd finished his sentence and he became frustrated at the placating movement. "No! I didn't mean it dat way… but, fuck Amy!"

He moved to the bed and fell heavily onto it, sitting with his elbows on his knees. He looked so exhausted that way, so weary. I wanted to hold him, but I wasn't sure that he'd even let me, so instead I sat down next to him, and the few inches between us felt like a mile.

"Ye've been so bloody oblivious," he said quietly, turning his head to look at me out of the corner of his eye. "I shouldn't have brought ye into dis."

He was beginning to scare me. "Tell me what's going on, Patrick."

"I tried to stay away from it. I swear it," he said lifting his hands, palm up in supplication. "I wanted to make a better life for us. A different life."

"I like our life," I assured him almost pleadingly. Was he going to leave me? I didn't think I could bear it if he did.

He shook his head, looking down at the floor again before he started to speak.

"Me da wasn't always a part of t'ings," he began. "When he and Mum got toget'er, he was workin' odd jobs in Scotland. But a while after dey were married, me nan got sick and me da brought Mum down here to live wit' her until she'd passed. Mum says dat de plan was for dem to stay just until Gran didn't need dem anymore, but after a while, dey'd built a life here. Da was workin' at a factory and Mum was home wit' me, and dey'd made friends and dey were comfortable. Out of nowhere, Da began comin' home talkin' about how t'ings were goin' to change. Makin' radical statements dat she'd known had come from someone else."

I laid my hand on his back as he took a deep breath, and that was all it took before he was pulling me into his lap and scooting toward the wall so he could lean against it.

"Me da fell in wit' some men dat me mum didn't approve of. Dangerous men who were willin' to go to any length to get what dey wanted. De worst t'ing about dose men was de power dey held. Generations of men who believed de same t'ing, who used dere money and connections to fight a silent war against dere enemies."

He was silent for a while, lost in his own thoughts. "I still don't understand," I whispered, feeling like an idiot.

"He's IRA, Amy."

"What?" the word was a breath, with no sound behind it.

"Me fadder has supported and worked toward a united Ireland for as long as I can remember."

"But—"

"Look around ye. Every person ye've met, every person ye've passed on de street and have seen at de grocery store—dey all have clear ideas about de situation here. Ye may not know dem, and dey may not broadcast dem, but dat doesn't mean dat dey aren't givin' every last bit of pocket change to support de cause dey're behind."

"Okay, so it's not a big deal then, right? I mean if everyone is supporting one side or the other, than why is it such a huge deal that your dad supports the IRA?"

Patrick grabbed my chin in a harsh grip and pulled my face toward his until we were practically nose-to-nose. It didn't hurt, but the meaning behind the motion was clear. He wanted me to pay attention.

"Me fadder is not a 'supporter.' Me fadder *is* IRA. He makes t'ings happen. T'ings ye'll never know about unless ye see dem in de newspaper."

The realization came in small increments as he stared into my eyes, until all at once I realized why Peg had lost it in the kitchen.

"You're IRA," I whispered in horror. "*You're* doing those things."

"Until de day dey put me into de ground," he confirmed with a slight nod.

Chapter 27

Amy

I stared at Patrick for a long time, cataloguing the freckles and the scruff of his five o'clock shadow and the blue eyes that saw everything. All things that I'd fallen in love with, and all things that didn't mean a single thing when it came down to real life.

Real life was hard. It wasn't only the actions that you followed through with, but also the ones you didn't. Real life was finding a small glimmer of hope when the world seemed to be falling around you. Real life was bills and housing and food on the table. Real life was knowing that the person you love and crave beyond all others had gotten himself into a situation there was no way out of, and there was absolutely nothing you could do about it.

"Lie wit' me," Patrick said quietly, pushing me off his lap.

We were silent as we undressed each other slowly, leaving on nothing but our underwear before climbing into bed. His hands were gentle as they pulled me against him and dragged the blankets up to our shoulders.

"What are we going to do?" I asked quietly after a few minutes.

"Continue on as we have been," he answered, rubbing his thumb over my anchor tattoo.

"Are you going to finish school?"

He didn't reply right away, and I slid my cheek against his body until my chin rested on his sternum. His eyes were sad as they met mine.

"I've already quit."

"Why didn't you tell them no?" I asked in frustration. He'd been so proud to be almost finished with school. He'd worked so hard for it, and then suddenly, all that work had been for nothing.

"Dese aren't men ye say no to," he replied calmly.

"But they left you alone before—"

"Dey must have been waitin' for de right moment."

"Let's just leave. We'll go to the US."

"Wit' what money? Dis is our life, Amy. Dis is our home."

"But what if—" His head jerked hard to the side, cutting off my words. That subject was closed.

"Are you going to get in trouble?"

"Only if I get caught."

"What have you done?" Panic was rising in my belly as different scenarios ran through my head. My Patrick wasn't a criminal. He was smart and kind and funny. He had a passion for the written word that astounded me, but was adamant that he had no talent of his own. He had a temper, but I'd never seen him become violent. He took care of his mother. He had more confidence than any man I'd ever met, and was so sure of himself that it translated into an acceptance of others.

"Do not ask me dat," he replied, cupping my head to turn it toward his face. "Not ever."

"Patrick?" I whispered.

"Not ever, Amy," he insisted. "Don't look for answers, ye'll not like what ye find."

My eyes filled with tears, and I tried to blink them away. "I'm scared."

"Ye don't ever have to be scared again," he replied instantly. "I'll not let anyt'in' happen to ye."

"I'm scared for *you*."

He sighed, and looked away from me, his eyes landing on the ceiling above us. "I'll be alright," he stated quietly. His hands began to clench and unclench in my hair.

"You're clenching your fists again, Mr. Gallagher," I said, leaning heavily into his body.

"I've tried to stop doin' it." His hand softened on my hair. "I don't even realize I am, half de time."

"Maybe you should try to do something else. Something less noticeable." I crawled up his chest until we were nose to nose, my arms bent and resting on top of him. "Like this." I tapped my fingers softly against his breastbone.

"I don't realize I'm makin' a fist, how de hell am I goin' to stop it?"

"Any time you think you might be getting anxious, tap your fingers." I tapped mine again in a short pattern. "Eventually, you'll do it automatically, and the fist thing will be gone."

"Oh, yeah? How do ye know dat?"

"Because I used to suck my thumb," I told him with a small smile. "I did it for a long time, until finally my parents started punishing me for it. So I figured out that any time I was worried, if I tucked my thumb into my palm I wouldn't put it in my mouth by accident."

"I've seen ye do dat." He said with a grin.

"Not very often anymore. But, it worked back then."

"I'll try it out."

"It'll work."

"We'll see." He cupped my cheeks in his palms and tugged me gently until my face was close to his. "I'll figure dis out," he told me seriously. "It won't be dis way forever."

"Will you have to leave again soon?" I ran my fingers over his eyebrows and down the sides of his face, soothing both of us with the repetitive movement.

"Not if I can help it. I have to take small trips back, but I t'ink I can spend most of me time here."

"That's a relief, at least. What's happening with your dad?"

"I've no idea. If Mum forgives him, he might stay here. If she doesn't, I guess he'll go back to his flat."

"This was what she was so afraid of all these years, isn't it? She didn't want him pulling you in with him."

"Yes." He settled me more comfortably over him, my legs on the outside of each of his and our torsos pressed together from hips to chest. "Dough, I t'ink it wasn't for nuttin'. If she'd have let him stay, I wouldn't be de man I am. Ye see? I wouldn't have de clear sight dat comes from watchin' somet'in' from de outside. I'd be full of zeal, ready to take on anyt'in' dey gave me wit' a sort of blind obedience dat dey'll never get from me now. She protected me de best way she knew how, and I'd like to t'ink dat it gave me somet'in' of a chance to keep me head around dose men."

"Why is life so freaking hard all the time?"

"It just is, me love. But it makes times like dis—wit' yer sweet body on top of mine while we talk and de sun goin' down outside shadin' de room—it makes dose times all de sweeter for it."

"I thought you weren't a poet?" I asked, tilting my face until our mouths were barely touching.

"I'm not. I've probably stolen it from someone and I just cannot remember." He pulled me deeper into the kiss as his hand slid down to cover one of my ass cheeks.

"I'll try not to be afraid," I told him quietly, as the room became darker with the setting of the sun. "I love you."

"I'll protect ye always," he said back, rolling slightly, switching positions so I was beneath him. "Dis is just a bump, me love. We've plenty of smoot' road ahead, I promise ye."

He leaned down to give me a soft kiss while I reveled in the weight of his body above mine, and before long the heat between us grew. My husband was home. No matter what life had in store for us in the future, no matter what he had to do to survive or what I had to live with—that was what mattered. The weight of him above me, the feel of his arms surrounding me, the wetness of his kiss as his tongue slid against mine, and the feeling of absolute joy I felt whenever he was near... those were the things I would focus on.

We were quiet as we pulled off our remaining clothes and Patrick took one of my nipples into his mouth. He made love to me slowly, with soft touches and smooth movements that made my eyes grow heavy and my skin break out in goose bumps.

Peg never made dinner that night. I'm not even sure if she and Robbie ever left her room. I think we all just wanted that night to hold our lovers close in the calm of the storm.

I had no idea then the lengths the men Patrick worked with would go if they felt the need. I was naïve. My biggest fear was that Patrick would somehow be taken from me, that he'd be picked up by the police or killed fighting a war that I didn't understand.

I didn't realize that the big bad wolf was closer than I could imagine.

Not even when Patrick turned from me as I fell asleep, pulling me in against his back as he lay facing the doorway to our room, a pistol in easy reach next to him on the floor.

Chapter 28

Patrick

I'd always thought my da was an idiot, but I couldn't help but respect the man. He knew everything about everyone, and he never forgot a face. We were on a job that was taking days instead of minutes, and I swear the man had the patience of a saint. I guess that had worked well for him in the years before I'd taken over his job.

They called him The Executioner. At first, it had been hard to reconcile the fact that the man who loved my mother so fiercely and had taught me to tie my shoes was a cold-blooded killer—but it hadn't taken long before I understood it to some degree.

He'd learned how to separate the two different lives in a way that was still a struggle for me after two months. It was as if he shut off one part of his brain when he was at home, and the other part while he was working—though I knew he'd struggled with that when I'd been brought in. In his mind, the two lives were completely different. He was two different men.

I wasn't able to compartmentalize my life that way.

Sometimes, it took all I had to wrap my arms around Amy when she raced to meet me the moment I got home. She couldn't see the blood on my hands, but I could. I felt like a monster... and those were on the good days.

I woke her in the middle of the night just to lose myself in her body. I sat at the pub where she worked just to watch her move around the room. I couldn't stand to be at home without her. I shook like a man with palsy when she left for school in the mornings, and found myself sitting on a bench across the street more often than not, waiting for her to finish for the day.

It was finally the day of her commencement ceremony, and I knew without a doubt that I was going to miss it. The man we'd been watching was moving around his house as if he didn't have a care in the world, and there wasn't anything I could do to speed things up and give him a dose of reality. His wife and three kids showed occasionally in the first floor windows, and we couldn't move until they were gone. It was bloody frustrating in the extreme.

We'd been sitting in the car all morning, and I had to piss so bad I felt as if my eyes were floating. I should have known that coffee wasn't a good idea when Da had refused a cup, but I'd been so tired I hadn't been thinking straight. Sleep was getting harder to come by as the days went on, especially on nights that I was away from Amy. I'd found myself plagued with either insomnia or nightmares, the two intertwining until I was no longer aware of how long it had been since I'd slept.

The morning was moving into afternoon when Da finally sat up a little in his seat and nodded toward the house. The wife and husband were moving between the house and the car, carrying what looked to be luggage.

Fuck.

He had better not be leaving town before we could get to him. My orders had been clear. Eliminate him before he had a chance to do any more damage than he'd already done. I wasn't sure whose ear he'd been whispering in, but the information we'd been given said he was passing things on that he shouldn't have been and it needed to be stopped.

We watched silently as the man kissed his children as they piled in the car, then stepped over to his wife to kiss her long and hard. I didn't quite understand what I was seeing until I heard Da mumble, "Well, fuck me," as the wife got into the car and drove away.

It was our chance.

We waited about a minute after the wife's car turned the corner before we stepped quietly out of our car and moved toward the house. It was a stroke of luck that the family seemed to have been going on some sort of trip. They wouldn't find him for days.

As we reached the side of the house, headed for the back door we knew led out to a small garden, we heard the shot. Both of us ducked down and searched the street, but nothing was moving.

"Jesus Christ," Da hissed as he stood to his full height and looked into one of the windows. "De man shot his bloody head off."

I moved in behind him to get a look and then wished I hadn't.

The man was sitting on his sofa, a hand-stitched afghan wrapped around him like a cocoon, with one hand out—holding the gun that was resting on his chest. He'd pulled himself so far into the blanket that he hadn't even tilted his head back before putting the barrel into his mouth and pulling the trigger.

He'd wrapped himself like a baby before ending his own life.

"He must've known we were comin'," Da said quietly, pushing me from where I was frozen. "It's time to leave. Now."

We made our way to the car in what seemed like slow motion, and for the first time in over a month I felt the urge to vomit.

It took us over an hour to get home, and we didn't speak one word during the entire trip. I was sure that my father had seen much more gruesome sights in the past twenty years, but he didn't seem any more inclined to talk than I was.

I had no idea how I'd articulate my thoughts if he had tried to speak with me. I was completely and utterly without words at what we'd just witnessed and it seemed odd to me that the scene had affected me so much. I'd killed. I'd taken other men's lives, but the sight of one man comforting himself with a blanket before he blew the back of his own head off seemed to have pushed me over the edge.

"It looks like yer mum and Amy are still at de commencement ceremony," Da said as we parked in front of our small house. "Shall we drive over dere and see if we can catch dem?"

I couldn't make myself form the words to tell him no. I couldn't say anything. I couldn't even move my mouth. I just stared at him blankly.

"Right. Let's get ye inside den."

He opened his door and climbed out of the car before leaning back in. "Get out of de fuckin' car Patrick," he ordered, knocking me slightly out of my stupor.

I followed him inside and stood by the couch, replaying over and over in my head the way the man had kissed his wife before she left. He'd known. He'd known what he was going to do, but she hadn't. She'd probably assumed that her husband had to work, or some other excuse he'd given to make her take a trip with three kids on her own. He'd made sure that they were gone, out of the house before we got there, and then he hadn't waited before taking care of his death himself.

I'd seen many men beg and plead for mercy and promise their own mothers for a chance to live. I'd never before seen the courage I had that morning.

"Let's go, son," my da said gently, pushing me into the bedroom, and shoving me slightly onto the bed. "I'll tell Amy ye weren't feelin' well."

He pulled off my coat and boots, then flipped back the blankets on the bed and motioned me to crawl inside. Once I was there, he covered me slowly then leaned down to kiss my forehead like he had when I was a child.

"Put it out of yer head," he commanded quietly. "He made his own decisions, and he paid for dem."

I lay there silently for a long time after he'd gone, breathing in the comforting smell of Amy and trying to marshal my thoughts into some sort of understandable pattern. Then I slid my hand down the side of my leg and began to tap the rhythm that Amy had taught me the month before.

Chapter 29

Amy

Life was a mixture of incredible highs and frightening lows. Since Robbie had moved back in with Peg, Patrick and I were looking for an apartment or a small house of our own. Peg's house just wasn't built for four adults, and it felt like we were tripping over each other constantly.

My job at Dillon's pub was working out well. I was getting more and more hours every week and had been setting aside most of my pay in a coffee can inside our dresser. The only downside was that Peg and I worked pretty much opposite shifts, so I barely got to see her anymore. I couldn't complain too loudly, though, because Patrick had found mechanic work at a used car dealership and spent most nights after work sitting at the bar to keep me company.

We were living. That was the only way I could explain it. Finally, after months of surviving in that weird limbo, we were finally building a life. It wasn't what I'd imagined, and I wasn't sure how the hell we would manage if Patrick got me pregnant like he'd been trying to, but we were finally together and that fact made me practically giddy.

I didn't ask about Patrick's other job. He hated it and he'd come home looking like he hadn't slept for days, even if he'd only been gone for a few hours. It made my stomach burn, and I'd been drinking so much milk to try and soothe the feeling that I had gained at least five pounds. I wanted to help him somehow, to take away the shadows in his eyes and get him at least one full night of sleep—but I couldn't. There wasn't anything I could do for him.

Sometimes, he'd walk through the front door and come directly to me, pulling me away from whatever I was doing and taking me straight to bed. Other times, he'd pass right by me on his way through the house, completely silent as he went into our room and shut the door solidly behind him, knowing I would follow. His moods were unpredictable, he barely slept, he carried a gun that I'd never seen before, and he spent most of his time at home glued to my side, even if he wasn't speaking.

But it wasn't all bad.

He also brought me flowers home. He brushed out my hair. On rare occasions when we had the house to ourselves, he'd run a bath and tug me in with him. He took me out to dinner, taught me how to play basketball, sat beside me in church and held my hand throughout the service.

He showed me he loved me in a million different ways and I tried to do the same for him. I think we were happy, as happy as we could have been under the circumstances.

***

"Hey, gorgeous, can I get another beer?" The American accent coming out of the stranger's mouth had a wide smile breaking out across my face.

"Sure!" I chirped back, tossing down the rag I'd been using to wipe off the bar. "What were you drinking?"

"You're American." The man leaned over onto his elbows on the bar and smiled back. "What the hell are you doing all the way over here?"

"She goes where her husband is." Patrick must have seen our

interaction, because he'd come up behind the stranger and moved smoothly around him.

The man started to laugh. "That makes sense." He lifted his hand between them. "I'm Charlie."

"Patrick," my husband said with a nod, shaking Charlie's hand. "Me wife, Amy."

"Nice to meet you, Amy."

"She's workin.' Ye can talk to me."

I felt my face heat over the way Patrick was behaving. He might as well have pissed on my leg. The guy was just being nice, and he hadn't even tried to flirt.

"I think you've got the wrong idea," Charlie said, chuckling.

Patrick's fingers began to tap on the bar top, and before I knew what I was doing, the palm of my hand slapped down over them, pinning them to the polished wood. "Knock it off, Patrick," I warned through my teeth.

"Vera!" Charlie yelled across the pub. "Come over here, baby."

A thin woman around my age stood up from where she'd been sitting surrounded by a big group of rough looking men and strutted toward us, her eyes never straying from Charlie's. "Whattya need, baby?"

"Patrick and Amy, meet my wife, Vera," Charlie said proudly.

I snickered, looking over at Patrick, whose expression hadn't changed.

"Nice to meet you, Vera."

"Whoa, you're American."

"Born and raised."

"Well, shit," she pushed Charlie out of the way and slid onto a barstool. "It's nice to finally hear someone who sounds like home."

"Where are you guys from?" I asked, wiping my hand down the cool wood of the bar top.

"I'm from Washington, but Charlie's from Oregon, so we live there. How about you?"

"I've lived all over. Moved here less than a year ago, though, and it looks like I'm staying since I married an Irishman." I smiled at Patrick, who still hadn't said a word, and watched his eyes go soft.

"Well, hello there, handsome," Vera said, following my gaze to Patrick. "Vera."

"Married," Patrick replied, making me want to flick him in the forehead.

"Yeah, I got that from your wife."

"Get your man a beer, Amy," Charlie said, sitting on the stool between Vera and Patrick. "On me."

"I'll buy me own," Patrick argued.

"After the first one you will. I just made a new friend and I'm gonna buy his ass a drink."

"Yer delusional."

"I'll grow on ya."

"He will," Vera piped in, nodding her head. "I didn't even like him at first."

"Sounds familiar," Patrick mumbled.

"You just watch, man. You'll dig me."

My gaze shot between them as I watched them banter back and forth, and for the first time in weeks I saw my husband's shoulders lose a little of their tension.

"What are you guys doing in Ireland?" I asked Vera as Patrick and Charlie started talking about motorcycles.

"We're on our honeymoon. Well, sort of." She sighed. "His club had some business over here, so Charlie brought me along, promising a romantic getaway. Romantic ... shit. You see the big one over there, bigger than all the others? His room is next to ours in the house we're staying at, and when he busts ass at night, we can fuckin' smell him through the vent."

I snorted. "Sounds romantic, for sure. Club?"

"Motorcycle club."

"Oh," I whispered, not really sure what being in a motorcycle club entailed.

"It is what it is. That's life, ya know? I married him knowing that this was how it would be, no use bitching about it now."

"I can understand that," I replied quietly, glancing at Patrick.

"Yeah, your man's got that same look about him."

"What look?"

"That hard look. You know, always ready for something bad to happen—almost like they expect it." I nodded. "It's worth it, though, I think, living with that look. Because *we* get the other looks, too, the sweet ones and the sexy ones and the exhausted ones. They only share *those* looks with us."

"I like the sexy look best," I murmured as Patrick glanced up and met my eyes, his lips tipping up a fraction until his dimple came out.

"No doubt." Vera laughed.

"Is your husband a mechanic?" I asked, deciding to change the subject.

"Sure, he works on bikes and shit."

"Patrick's a mechanic, too, but I think he works mostly on cars."

"That right?" she glanced over at the men. "Well, maybe they'll hit it off and then me and you can hang out more while we're here. I've been bored outta my mind."

"Sounds good to me," I answered with a grin. I knew plenty of people, but I think Vera was my very first girlfriend in Ireland.

We chatted while I worked, our husbands moving off at some point to talk to the rest of Charlie's friends, and I learned that Vera had run away from home at sixteen. She was a year older than me and had been with Charlie off and on for the past two years, the last 'off' ending with a marriage proposal. They hadn't been married long, but it sounded like they'd been living together for a while. She didn't have that starry-eyed newlywed look about her that I knew I still had. It was a more full-bodied look, comfortable, solid.

The night went by more quickly than it usually did, and before I knew it, I was closing down and locking up. My boss let me work a couple nights a week on my own, usually when it was slow and he knew Patrick would be there. I loved those nights, when Patrick and I would work together to close up. It gave us a few minutes alone that we wouldn't have had otherwise in our packed house.

"Give me a call this week and we'll hang out," Vera said, moving in for a hug. "I'm so glad we met."

"Me, too."

Vera and the group of men walked boisterously down the quiet street as Patrick wrapped his arm around my shoulder and led me home.

"Ye like her?" he asked in a low voice, the quiet wrapping around us like a blanket.

"Yeah, she was nice. Too bad she lives in the US." I wrapped my arm around his waist. "Charlie seemed cool."

"Yeah, he's not bad. De lads he came wit', dough... I don't want ye seein' dem alone, alright?"

"Okay."

I wanted to ask questions, but I knew better. If Patrick didn't want me to see them by myself, there was a reason for it. It wasn't worth it to me to argue.

"I can't wait to get home, I'm so tired," I moaned, leaning into his side.

"Dat's too bad," he whispered back, leaning down so his breath brushed across my neck, "I was hopin' we wouldn't sleep for a while yet."

"Is that right?"

He reached for my hand and pulled it across his body to rub it against the front of his jeans, "I'm dyin' for ye."

"Poor baby," I said back huskily with a wicked smile. I could see our house in the distance and broke out into a run as his carefree laughter floated out behind me, making my heart skip a beat.

I had my key in the lock when he caught me and my breathless laugh was loud against the door when he pressed his body against my back.

"None o'dat." His hand covered my mouth to keep me quiet as he ushered me inside. "Ye have to be quiet or ye'll wake de house."

We walked with his body pressed tightly against mine all the way to our bedroom, one of Patrick's hands covering my mouth and the other cupping my breast under my coat, flicking and pinching at my nipple.

We made it to our room in only seconds, but I was already slick and ready as he closed the door behind us.

"Don't move," he ordered, pulling my coat down my arms. "Have I told ye today how beautiful ye are?"

"Not today."

"I apologize for lettin' ye go all day wit'out hearin' it."

"Can I move yet?"

"No."

Patrick pulled my snug t-shirt over my head, immediately unhooking my bra and pushing the straps all the way down my arms until it dropped to the floor. He was still behind me as he wrapped his arms around my waist to unbutton my jeans. "Kick off yer shoes."

My breath became choppy as I kicked off my shoes, and as soon as I had my balance, he was pulling off my jeans and underwear in one swift movement, leaving me in nothing but a pair of white socks I'd stolen out of his drawer that afternoon.

"Bend over de bed," he said huskily, pulling the scrunchie out of my hair so it spread in waves over my bare back.

"Oh, so I can move now?"

"Smart mout'."

He grabbed a handful of my hair and walked me forward until my knees hit the bed, but when I tried to lower myself he stopped me.

"Legs straight, wife." I loved it when he called me wife that way, all growly and fierce like he was reminding me who I was to him.

"Dat's right, now bend," he said softly, putting one hand on my belly to situate me how he wanted.

The muscles in the backs of my legs protested the position, but I didn't complain as I heard first his jacket and then his shirt fall to the floor behind me. I was braced on my elbows with my head hanging between my arms when I felt him move to his knees behind me, gripping my legs gently as he moved them farther apart.

"I've been waitin' all day for dis," he said, his breath hitting the back of my thighs. "Daydreamin' when I should have been workin'."

His hands moved up the backs of my thighs until they met between them, and I whimpered as I felt his thumbs pull me apart. The first touch of his tongue against my flesh made me jump, and he made a soothing noise in the back of his throat as he moved in again, licking me delicately at first and then harder as my hips began to undulate.

We'd done almost everything we could when it came to sex; Patrick wasn't shy and he wouldn't let me be, either, but every time felt new, the orgasms stronger as inhibitions fell to the wayside and we grew more comfortable with one another's bodies.

I bent my knees, relieving the tightening pressure of my thigh muscles, and arched my back so I could push against his mouth, completely lost in the feeling of his lips and tongue against me.

"Dat's right, me love," he murmured against me, "take what ye want."

His hands were gripping me tightly as I moved against him, and then suddenly, a sharp slap hit the meat of my ass, the sound echoing throughout the room.

"What the fuck, Patrick?" I hissed, my head whipping up in shock.

"I told ye I'd spank ye." Another slap on the opposite cheek had me trying to pull away. I couldn't believe him.

"I didn't do anything wrong!"

" 'Knock it off, Patrick'," he mimicked me, spanking me again. "Slapped me hand down on de tabletop like a child."

"You deserved it!"

He began to laugh, and I struggled away from him. I was angry that he'd slapped me and even more livid that he'd ruined my impending orgasm.

"You're such a dick!"

When I turned to face him and dropped to my ass on the bed, he was still kneeling there on the floor wearing a wide smile. It was one I hadn't seen in what felt like a very long time, and I felt my anger drifting away.

"I love dat yer back to arguin' wit' me," he said simply. "For a while it felt like ye were too afraid to cause any waves, so ye were just goin' along wit' whatever I wanted."

I opened my mouth to respond, but nothing came out. I *had* been like that when he'd first moved back, but I'd realized after a while that I couldn't behave that way. It just wasn't me. Did I want Patrick to love me? Of course. Was I willing to be a doormat to secure that love? No way in hell.

"I can't believe you hit me."

"Ach! It was a love tap."

"You slapped my ass hard! Three times!"

"And it felt good, didn't it?"

My eyebrows lifted in surprise as I paused.

"I bet yer arse is red as a cherry right now, all hot and tender," he coaxed, leaning forward to place a kiss between my breasts. "A little pain feels good, yeah? Like when I bite ye here?" he turned his head to the side and pressed his teeth against the side of my breast. His hands slid up the tops of my thighs, one veering to grip my hipbone and the other trailing down until the tips of his fingers were pressed just barely inside me. "Or when I take ye hard," he rasped, thrusting inside forcefully.

My head tipped back and my eyes closed as his fingers curled forward inside me. He moved his mouth between my breasts, biting and sucking hard at my nipples while his fingers continued their movements, and before long I was holding back the moans that threatened to burst out of my mouth.

Right as I felt that final swell that I knew would take me to the promised land, Patrick's fingers and mouth were gone, and he was flipping me to my belly before pulling me up to my hands and knees.

"Me handprints look good on ye," he said breathlessly as I heard his belt clinking. He placed his hands on my burning cheeks and pressed outward, opening me up. Then with one hard thrust he was planted inside me and I was yelling sharply into the blankets beneath me.

His hips moved jerkily until he got a rhythm going, and a warm feeling grew in my chest at his obvious lack of control. I loved knowing that he was as affected as me.

"Ye were made for me," he said into my ear, wrapping his hand in my hair as he came down over me with one arm braced above my shoulder. "I'll never love anot'er."

When I looked back on that night later, I sometimes wondered if I would have changed the way we came together. If I would have rather made love to him face-to-face so I could watch as his eyes grew cloudy, and his face flushed with his orgasm. If only I'd made him flip us back over so I could run my hands across his chest and map the freckles across his cheeks with my eyes. I decided eventually that I wouldn't have changed a thing, though.

The way he took me wasn't sweet or tender, it was fucking in its rawest form. I was pinned beneath him and unable to touch him, but I'd also been surrounded and protected and his words against the side of my face were the purest declaration of love I'd ever heard.

Chapter 30

Patrick

Christ, I was tired.

I'd been gone from home for almost a week, which meant I'd gotten very little rest. I was still having trouble sleeping without my wife, and my dependence on her presence made me angry. I was the man. I was the husband. My need for her shouldn't surpass her need for me—but that was exactly what it felt like. She went on about her days when I was away, as if she hadn't a care in the world, while I grew shaky and out of sorts the minute she was out of my sight.

It was frustrating as hell.

I got back to our house late that night, and everything was quiet as I made my way inside. I'd stopped by Amy's work, but apparently she'd taken the night off because she was feeling ill. I hadn't talked to her in a few days and I was anxious to make sure she was okay. I hated the thought of her not feeling well while I wasn't there, even though I knew my mum would take care of her.

When I crawled into bed beside her, she was sleeping heavily and I could feel the fever on her skin. I wrapped my cool body around hers, and breathed deeply, my anxiety lessened even with proof of her illness.

"Patrick?" she whispered.

"Go back to sleep, love." I rolled over to face the door and felt her curl up against my back with one hot hand on my stomach.

"I think I caught a cold from Vera."

"I know. Go to sleep now. We'll talk in de mornin.' "

I felt her nod against my back, and less than a minute later her body relaxed into mine.

I wished I could roll back over and let her rest against my chest, but I didn't dare. I was too tired and I was afraid to fall asleep that way, vulnerable on my back, with her body shielding mine. We hadn't slept that way since I'd started working for Short Michael, and I didn't ever see there being a time where I'd feel confident enough to do so again.

Too many things happened when you weren't prepared. I'd seen that first hand—I'd been the thing that happened.

I'd never be caught off guard, especially while my wife slept trustingly against me.

***

I woke a few hours later to quiet voices and movement around the house. Mum had work that morning, and my da had started waking up with her so they could have a few moments of privacy before she started her day.

I'd never understood their relationship, and I didn't think I ever would. They'd spent so many years apart, but it seemed that it took only days before they fell into a loving relationship that rivaled how they'd been when I was young. My mum smiled and laughed and looked at him with tenderness, and it had been difficult to adjust to at first. Eventually, though, I'd come to the realization that their relationship wasn't my business. I'd been taking care of my mum for so long that it had been hard to let go, but she'd wanted me to. She needed him in a way that a son could never fill. She needed her man, and as odd as it was for me, I had to accept that she was happier than I could ever remember.

I heard the front door open and close as Amy moved slightly behind me, and I relaxed into the bed again, pulling her arm more tightly around my waist as her hips met my ass.

I'd just closed my eyes again when I heard it.

The house shook as the thunderously loud noise hit my ears, and I was up and out of bed before I was fully aware of what was happening.

"Patrick?" Amy called frantically as I threw open the door to our bedroom and raced toward the front door.

"Mum!" I yelled as I ran outside and caught sight of the burning mass of metal that had been my mum's car. "Mum!"

I couldn't see anyone near it, but the minute I got close enough to search more thoroughly, the car next to it caught fire. I stumbled back when a wave of heat blasted against my bare chest. Both cars were burning then, lighting up the early morning and breaking through the quiet with the sound of creaking metal and odd popping noises.

"Jesus Christ," I gasped in horror. I glanced back at the house and felt my heart stutter in my chest.

"Get in de fuckin' house!" I yelled at Amy, running toward where she was silhouetted in the doorframe in nothing but one of my t-shirts. "Get inside!"

I wrapped my arm around her waist as I reached her and practically threw her inside. She'd been so close, fuck me, she'd been so close.

"What's happening?" Amy cried, pulling at the skin on my arms as I tried to turn away from her.

"Patrick?" The voice was quiet, a shell-shocked whisper that barely reached my ears, but had me automatically turning toward it.

I stumbled toward the back of the house and found her.

I'll never forget my mother's ravaged face as she met my eyes from where she was kneeling on the floor of her room. She knew. The minute it had happened, she knew.

"He was heatin' up the car," she whispered brokenly, her hands raised palm up in front of her.

"Oh, my God," Amy whispered behind me.

I was frozen as I stared into my mother's tear-filled eyes, but my wife wasn't. When I didn't move, Amy shoved past me and dropped to the floor next to her.

"You're okay," she said over and over again, as she pulled my mum into her arms. "Patrick will take care of things. You're okay." Amy began to cry as Mum's wails filled the house and my body came back to life.

I'd been so worried about making sure that Amy was safe that I hadn't even tried to save whomever was in the car.

My Da. Maybe I could still save him.

I could hear sirens in the distance, so I tossed my pistol into a drawer on my way outside and ran to my mum's car. It was still burning, the flames shooting into the sky, but I forced myself to get close enough that I could see inside the driver's window.

I didn't see him at first, but as I got close enough that I could feel little embers burning my skin, I finally found him.

He was inside still, lying across the seats, and I felt my entire body go numb as I took three stumbling steps backward.

I didn't bother trying to get him out. He was quite obviously already gone.

Chapter 31

Amy

The days after Robbie's death were unbelievably hard.

I hadn't known him well. His personality didn't invite deep conversation, but I'd lived with him for months and he'd loved the same two people that I did. He'd been a quiet guy, very polite, and he'd worshipped Peg.

Watching Peg in agony was one of the hardest things I'd ever gone through because I didn't know how to help her. She'd become a shell of the woman I knew, and seemed to walk around in a fog when she actually made the effort to get out of bed.

Patrick had gone so deep inside his head that he was barely there, even when he was sitting right next to me. He didn't sleep. He carried a pistol with him at all times and seemed to be waiting for something. I felt him drifting away, farther and farther, as he tried to come to terms with what had happened.

As if you could ever come to terms with something so violent.

I didn't understand it all. The whispers and the comments from neighbors went right over my head, but I knew with certainty that if Patrick didn't get his shit together quickly, things would only get worse.

Three days after we had Robbie's funeral in the same church we'd been married in, I'd had enough.

I knew Patrick was devastated. I *knew* how devastated he was. But Peg wasn't getting out of bed, and Patrick wasn't going in to work, and something had to happen. Life hadn't stopped, but the two Gallaghers had. They'd come to a complete standstill, and I was terrified out of my mind.

"Peg, are you hungry?" I called quietly into her darkened bedroom. I didn't want to wake her up if she was sleeping, but she hadn't been eating very much. Her slight frame couldn't afford to miss any more meals.

"I'm goin' to sleep for a while longer," she called back, her voice scratchy. "I'll have somethin' a little later."

I sighed in defeat, but left her alone. Who was I to force her? She'd just lost the love of her life, and I had no idea how I'd react in that situation. Even the thought of Patrick dying made my stomach turn.

I made my way into the kitchen and began making one of the only breakfasts I could prepare without completely ruining. I was the first one up that morning, but I'd heard Patrick moving around after I'd slid out of bed. It wasn't as if he'd been sleeping.

He came into the kitchen behind me, resting his hand on my hip as he kissed the back of my head.

"Smells good."

He sat down at the table with a cup of coffee, and we didn't say a word as I finished cooking. He didn't say much anymore, and I was afraid if I opened my mouth I'd either burst into tears or start screaming. I took long, deep breaths to calm myself down.

"You have to go to work today." I told Patrick as I brought his plate of fried eggs to the table.

"I will."

"I have to go in tonight, too." I tried to hold a conversation with him, keeping my voice level in an attempt to get back to some kind of normal, but his monotone answer was like hearing nails scratch across a blackboard. "You should come straight home, so someone is here with Peg."

"I'll come by de pub."

"No, Peg needs someone here."

"I said I'll come by de pub."

His voice still hadn't lost the flat quality I'd come to expect, and I wanted to scream in frustration.

"No, you won't!" I snapped, unable to keep the temper out of my voice. "You'll come home and take care of your goddamn mother!"

Patrick's jaw clenched and a red flush ran up his neck as he began to tap that stupid pattern on the tabletop with the tips of his fingers.

"Stop it!"

"Ye t'ink ye can dictate to me?" He asked incredulously, standing from the table. "I t'ink ye've forgotten where ye fit in dis house."

"Fuck you." I hated the words spilling out of his mouth, but got a small surge of satisfaction at the emotion I'd finally evoked. "I'm the only one doing anything around here. I get it, okay? I know you guys are hurting. But no one is telling me what's going on, we no longer have a car, none of us have worked in over a week…"

"Ye want to know what's goin' on?" he asked, leaning over the table until he was inches from my face. "It was a warnin.' Only no one has contacted me to tell me what de fuck dey were warnin' us about. I've no idea where de next hit will come from. What will be next? Mum? Ye?"

I began to shake as a red flush of anger spread up his neck. I'd instinctively known that what happened to Robbie hadn't been random, but hearing it spelled out turned my fear into a physical thing, a pressure on my chest that made it feel as if I couldn't breathe.

"I'll be at de pub tonight." Patrick said, his voice calming. "Tell Casey dat ye'll be a few minutes late because I'm walkin' ye over."

"You said we'd be okay," I whispered back. "When I told you I was scared, you said you'd handle it."

His eyes clouded over before they shut entirely, and his head dropped down in defeat. What the hell was going on in our lives? How was this normal?

I didn't understand how people could live like that. I didn't understand why a man would willingly choose a side in a war with no winner, putting himself and his family in danger. For what? What the fuck could be *that* important? I knew then with absolute clarity why Peg had kicked Robbie out all those years ago. She loved him, but sometimes you had to jump ship if you wanted to save yourself.

"I don't want to do this," I said quietly, standing from the table.

The words hit him like a blow and he reared back in surprise.

"Do what?"

"I don't want this life. I don't want to be worried every time I leave the house. I don't want to bring children into this shit!"

He let me move around him, but followed me into the bedroom.

"So what? Yer goin' to leave me?"

"I don't know."

"Ye don't *know*? Where de fuck would ye go? I'm yer goddamn husband."

We were yelling, facing off inside that tiny bedroom. My mind was a jumbled mess of contradictions. I loved him, but I couldn't see a way for him to ever get out of the mess he was in. I wanted to leave. I wanted to take Peg and Patrick and leave the country—go far away where no one would find us. But that wasn't reality.

The reality was that I was married to a man whose time was limited. It didn't matter if the IRA believed his loyalty and continued to use him. There would still come a time that the things he was doing would catch up to him, and he'd either go to jail or he'd go in the ground. It was heartbreakingly inevitable.

"I wish I hadn't married you."

His back hit the wall as he stared at me in horror. "Do not *ever* say dat again."

I began rubbing at my hands as we stared at each other in the silent room. He looked like hell. His face was gaunt, with dark circles under his eyes and he hadn't shaved his face in so long it had gone beyond a five o'clock shadow and had turned into a scruffy looking beard. His clothes were clean, but they seemed to hang off him oddly as if they no longer fit. He was unraveling before my eyes, and I didn't know what to do.

"I love ye," he said, breaking the silence. "I love ye more den anyt'in' or anyone on dis earth. I'll figure dis all out. I just needed a few days, dat's all. I just needed to get me head toget'er."

I nodded, unsure of what would come out of my mouth if I attempted to speak.

"Don't do dat, me love," he said in the same tone, stepping toward me to take my hands in his. "Ye'll make dem worse."

I glanced down to see barely raised welts on my hands, aggravated from where I'd been rubbing them.

He pulled me into his arms then, and the comfort of his scent and his strong muscles resting against my body were impossible to ignore. I wished we could stay like that forever, safe from the rest of the world in our tiny room.

"I'll better be off if I'm goin' in to work," Patrick said, pulling away slightly. He leaned down to brush my lips with his, and the heat of his mouth seemed to spread throughout my body in a large wave. He'd barely touched me in over a week, and even though the move hadn't been sexual, it still made me a little needy. I leaned onto my toes as our lips brushed again, and when he felt me reaching, his tongue slid out nervously to lick across my bottom lip.

We moved into a sensual kiss without thought, rubbing and sucking at each other's mouths. It wasn't a prelude to anything, there was no urgency in it, but I don't think anything could have been more perfect at that moment.

"Charlie and Vera will be over today," Patrick informed me as he finally pulled away with a squeeze of my hips. "He'll stay until I'm home tonight."

I thought about my new best friend while I watched Patrick begin to change for work, pulling on a ratty flannel that was covered in grease stains and an old pair of jeans. I'd spent time with Vera after the night we'd met, having lunch and following her around while she shopped for souvenirs, but it hadn't been until my life had become so out-of-control that I'd realized how deep our friendship went. She was loyal, unflaggingly so, and a car blowing up in front of my house hadn't seemed to change her opinion of me in the slightest.

Vera acted as if it was normal. She was conscious of our grief, and helped out as much as she could, but she didn't go overboard. She wasn't whispering and looking over her shoulder like the neighbors had been in the days after Robbie's death. She'd just pitched in when she could and sat with me for hours, even if I didn't have anything to say.

She'd arrived every morning for the past week, sometimes with Charlie and other times with the big, smelly guy she'd pointed out in the pub the night we'd met. She'd stay all day, helping with chores and gossiping about movie stars while Charlie sat on the couch watching television with a silent Patrick or the big guy sat on the front stairs outside. She was just there, with no hidden agenda or preconceived ideas about us.

She was the best friend I'd ever had.

"I'm sorry I said I wished I didn't marry you," I said as Patrick sat on the edge of the bed to pull on his boots. "I'm not sorry."

"I know yer not." He tugged me into his lap. "I know yer scared, darlin'. Just stick wit' me, eh? I'll fix dis."

"I wish you didn't have to work today." I laid my head on his shoulder and pressed my forehead into his neck.

"First she orders me to work and den she says she wants me to stay home," he announced to the room, sounding like my old Patrick.

"I know, I'm all over the place lately."

"Maybe yer pregnant?" he asked, laying his hand on my belly.

"Not this time, Mr. Gallagher. I'm just coming off my period." It still surprised me how comfortable I was with sharing intimate details of my body with him, but it had been that way almost from the start. He knew everything about me, every curve and mole had been mapped. My body held no secrets anymore.

"We'll have to work harder dis mont'," he teased gently, pulling me closer.

"I'm not sure we should," I mumbled into his neck, already sure of his reaction. "Maybe—"

"De church is very clear on birt' control, wife."

"It's a stupid rule. Do you really want to bring our child into our life right now?"

"It's not up to us to decide which rules are meant to be broken."

"It's my body."

"Is it not me decision too, den?"

"Of course it is." I sighed, annoyed that I'd even brought it up.

"I know dat I've not been de best man, especially in de church's eyes," he said into my hair, rubbing my back softly. "But I cannot agree wit' puttin' t'ings into yer body to stop ye from havin' a child. Me child. To me, it would be like refusin' a gift from God because it wasn't convenient for us. Who's to say dat we'd ever be offered de gift again?"

"Your reasoning is medically unsound, but I understand your point."

"Medically unsound? Ye've been readin' again, I see."

"It's been quiet around here."

"I know it has." He tightened his arms around me then tapped my back twice, signaling for me to stand up. "I've got to move or I'll be late."

He kissed me goodbye, just a quick peck on the lips, and was gone. I really did hate that he had to go to work, even though I'd been dying for him to go just an hour before. We may not have figured anything out, but I felt marginally better about things once we'd discussed them.

Knowing that Patrick was working on a solution instead of just staring at the walls made me feel almost optimistic. As long as we were together, we could figure it out, I told myself. We just had to be careful for now, until we knew what we were dealing with.

When I made my way out of our room, Peg was sitting at the kitchen table eating a piece of toast. I couldn't stop the wide smile that spread across my face as I realized she'd actually gotten dressed and had brushed her hair. It seemed as if both my favorite people had decided to re-join the living that day, and I couldn't have been happier for the small steps they'd taken.

I spent that morning with a small smile of relief on my face, just knowing that it was going to be a good day.

I've often wondered how my instincts could have been so poor.

Chapter 32

Patrick

"I'm sorry."

My boss's quiet words followed me out the door. I couldn't have replied without choking the life out of the weasely little fuck, so I ignored him.

I'd lost my bloody job. Fucking hell.

They'd let me finish work on the car I'd started before my da was killed, but as soon as I'd finished, they'd given me the boot. Fucking bastards were afraid of their own shadows, it was the only way they hadn't been pulled in to any side of the war that seemed to be tearing my entire life apart. They were sorry, sure, but their fear had been more important than any reservations they had about letting me go.

Mother of God. We were fucked. Mum hadn't been working, I had no idea when she'd be ready to go back, and now this. My stomach burned at the thought of asking Amy for the cash I knew she kept hidden in our sock drawer, but there was no other way to keep a bloody roof over our heads.

I may as well have just sliced off my balls and handed them to her.

I slammed into the house, letting the door bounce off the wall, and the first thing I saw was Amy standing in the tiny entryway, going through some mail.

"Patrick? Why aren't you at work?"

"De bastards fuckin' let me go!"

"What? Why?" Her shoulders slumped and I hated everyone in that moment. Why the fuck couldn't life ever be fucking easy? Why couldn't we catch just one break? Just one! I was failing her, and I'd become the man I'd sworn I'd never be, dependent upon my wife's labors for food on the table and a roof over our heads.

"Dey're afraid to keep me on. Afraid one of dere cars will blow sky high if dey're associated wit' a Gallagher."

"Shit," she whispered, her eyes wide and worried in her face. "Baby—"

"I'll figure it out," I promised her, my gut burning at her expression.

"I know you will."

I wrapped my arms around her, and calmed my breathing by huffing in deep breaths of Amy-scented air. My body was practically shaking with anger, but I had to keep it together. I had to figure all of the shit out, and there was no way I could do that intelligently if I was riding on emotion. I needed to be logical.

"You thought any more about my offer?" Charlie asked from where he was watching us on the couch. "It stands."

"We'll discuss it later," I said warningly. I didn't want to get Amy's hopes up, but Charlie had offered to bring my family to America. His father owned a big motorcycle shop, and he'd offered me a job there. I was pretty sure his club owned the shop along with the men who worked there, and I didn't know if I wanted to be beholden to anyone like that.

According to Charlie, it wasn't like that at all. They were a family whose loyalty was unquestionable. They took care of each other. Woman and children were off limits, always, and they protected each one as if it were their own.

I liked Charlie. During the time he'd been in Ireland, I'd gotten to know the man pretty well, and his word was good. But I'd never seen him under fire. His loyalty hadn't been tested. My family's lives couldn't depend on a man that I'd known for only a couple of weeks.

It did sound wonderful, though. I couldn't lie and say that it didn't. It was a new place to build, men who would watch my back, a new life for Mum and me and a place where Amy would feel a little more at home. Still, I was leery. I would be exchanging the devil I knew for one I didn't.

Someone began knocking on the door and before I could drop my head wearily to Amy's shoulder, my instincts had kicked in and she was shoved behind me. My gun was pulled out of the back of my jeans and Charlie was on his feet within seconds. He lifted his head toward the door, and I nodded once before stepping forward to open it up.

I'll never forget the sight that greeted me.

Chapter 33

Amy

She was bloody.

Her curly, golden hair was matted and knotted with it.

She was shorter than me.

She was pregnant.

And her hands were smaller than mine. The one I could see looked tiny clutching the back of my husband's work shirt.

But she was bloody. I had to focus on that.

Her face was swollen, her lips split in three different spots. There was blood beneath her ear, but I couldn't tell if it had come from there or had been smeared from one of her other scratches.

She was sobbing. Scared. Holding onto Patrick like he was the only thing that could save her.

"I'll call my dad and have him send Doc over. Thank Christ the old shit came with us," Charlie said as he looked out the door and then shut and locked it.

"Yer Da has a doctor?"

"Close enough."

I stood frozen as everyone broke into action around me, until Vera pinched my side hard. "Put it away. Swallow it all up until we know what we're dealing with."

I nodded vaguely, still watching as Patrick tried to soothe the hysterical woman.

"Now Amy," Vera ordered as she moved past me to get to Patrick.

"We need to lay her down somewhere until we know what's wrong," Vera told Patrick calmly over the sound of the woman's crying and Charlie talking to his dad on the phone in the kitchen.

Patrick nodded as Peg came rushing out of her bedroom. She must have heard the commotion, there's no way she wouldn't have. The woman was fucking loud.

"What's going on?" she asked me, her voice full of worry.

"I don't know." It all seemed like it was happening somewhere else, like I wasn't even present.

I watched as Patrick gently lifted the woman into his arms and moved around me and Peg. He paused at the couch for a moment, and his face looked pained as he glanced at me for a split second before carrying the woman into our bedroom.

It snapped me out of the stupor we were in, and I raced to the kitchen to wet a rag. Maybe if we cleaned up a little of the blood, it wouldn't seem so bad. Head wounds always bled a lot, and the split lips and the scratch on her cheek hadn't even scabbed over yet. I followed Vera and Peg, who had burst into action once she'd gotten a good look at the woman, but when I reached the doorway I couldn't go any farther. The room wasn't built to hold so many people, and it seemed even smaller than normal as I watched detachedly as Patrick sat next to the woman on the bed, brushing her hair carefully out of her face.

I took a small step, scooting around Vera so I could hand the woman the wet towel in my hand, but froze the minute she began to speak.

"I didn't know where else to go," she told Patrick hoarsely, her voice ruined from the wailing she'd been doing. "I didn't know what to do."

"Shhh. Yer alright now," he soothed her.

"Michael found out. I tried to hide it." More tears leaked out of the corners of her eyes. "But I got too big and he finally noticed."

I watched Patrick swallow hard, never looking away from the woman's face.

"I tried not to tell dem it was ye. I swear it." Her eyes implored him as I began to feel lightheaded. "But I just couldn't take anymore."

I gripped the doorframe hard, willing myself to stay upright. This was wrong. All of it was wrong. Patrick was going to speak up at any moment, and everything would become clearer.

"We need to strip her down and see what we're looking at. Out, Patrick," Peg said sharply, refusing to even look in his direction.

"Mum—" his voice cracked. That small break in his words destroyed everything I'd thought, believed and known about my relationship with my husband. It took less than a second.

"Out," Peg ordered again, ignoring the shame in his voice.

As Patrick hushed the woman again, speaking quietly while attempting to pull away from her, I wrenched myself away from the room. I couldn't watch it any longer. I needed to get away from him.

I sped through the house, only to be caught around the waist by Charlie. "You need to wait and hear him out, girl. Don't be stupid and leave when we don't know what we're dealing with."

I ripped his arm off me and changed direction, stepping through the doorway of the bathroom just as Patrick came out of our room. I didn't stop. I didn't even turn my head in his direction.

I couldn't even look at him.

"Amy—"

His words were cut off as I quietly shut the bathroom door and turned the flimsy lock. My legs gave beneath me, and I slid to the floor without even turning on the light. I didn't mind the darkness.

It was quiet in there—a step away from the insanity that had taken over my home. Why had I been so giddy that Patrick had brought everything into clear focus again? Why had I let them pull me in, why had I let myself be pulled? Why couldn't I have just continued on in the life I'd been living? There were no highs or lows in that life. I'd been comfortable there, before Peg and Patrick. I'd been numb.

I pretended for a split second that everything was back to normal again.

Robbie was watching television while Peg fixed dinner, and any moment Patrick would be home from work. Then the fantasy was shattered as the door vibrated against my back.

"Amy, let me in." Patrick began knocking and trying to turn the doorknob. "Please, me love. Please, let me in."

I didn't say a word. I didn't have anything to say. Nothing. There was not one word in the entire dictionary, not one word in any language that seemed appropriate at that moment.

He'd slept with that woman. He'd slept with her and gotten her pregnant. The pain in my chest was too excruciating to bear. I couldn't even cry. I just sat there staring into the darkness.

"Let me explain, me love. It's not what yer t'inkin', I swear it. Please, please, please let me in. Let me hold ye. I need ye, Amy. Please, open de door."

Patrick continued to knock on the door, at one point threatening to break it down, but he didn't get in. He just stood outside, begging and pleading and threatening and cajoling me to speak with him.

As if I had anything to say.

Eventually, he moved away from the door and I heard other voices in the house. Charlie's dad must have shown up with the doctor.

I didn't care.

I didn't even care what happened to her.

I knew that made me a monster. She was pregnant, and in pain, and someone had beaten the hell out of her. But I still didn't care. I wanted her to disappear and I wasn't picky about how that happened.

"Let me in, lovey." Peg's voice drifted through the door, but I still didn't move. "It's just me. Open the door."

I couldn't make myself get up off the floor.

"Charlie?" Peg's voice was muffled as she turned away, but the walls were so thin in that fucking house that I could still hear her. "She's not answerin' me. Can ye take the door off the hinges? I'm afraid if we try to break through it, she'll be hurt."

"Sure," Charlie replied.

I heard him start fiddling with the door, then more voices in the living room.

Suddenly, I couldn't bear the thought of all those people seeing how absolutely devastated I was. Oh, poor Amy, her husband fucks around on her. Poor Amy, who still isn't pregnant, but her husband's side piece is. Poor Amy can't even get up off the bathroom floor because she's so upset.

Fuck that.

I climbed to my feet as a familiar feeling of disconnect ran through me. I wasn't poor Amy. I'd dealt with far worse things in my life. I'd grown up with parents who either didn't give a shit or outright disliked me, who'd been neglectful at times and cruel at others. I'd moved from one place to the next, never able to make any real connections with anyone. I could deal with proof of Patrick's infidelity.

It was nothing. He was nothing.

What had he said before? *It was just a bump.*

I opened the door to Charlie's surprised face, and gave him a thin smile. I was fine. He didn't need to take the door off.

Patrick, Peg, Vera and a couple older men were standing in the kitchen discussing something quietly as I made my way to the couch. I kept my torn up copy of *Fahrenheit 451* on the bottom shelf of one of Peg's side tables because Robbie had started reading it when the house was quiet. I didn't let myself think about that. I was fine.

I opened it up to a random page in the middle, then changed my mind and flipped back to the first page. I had a feeling I was going to be there a while.

"It was a pleasure to burn..."

"Amy!" Vera plopped down on the couch next to me. "Shit, girl.

I've been calling your name."

"What do you need?"

"Huh?"

"Did you need something?"

"You're just gonna sit here and read while all of this," she waved her hand around in front of her, "is going on around you?"

"That was the plan."

"You okay?"

"Yep. Fine."

"I mean, I wouldn't be. I'd be freaking out big time."

"I'm good."

She looked at me like there was an alien climbing out of my head. "What are you doing?"

"I was trying to read."

"No, *what are you doing*?"

I pretended that I hadn't heard the emphasis she'd put into her words and scowled at her. "I was reading, and now I'm talking to you. Soon as you're done, I'm gonna get back to reading."

She shook her head in amazement. "You're nuts, you know that, right?"

"I prefer apathetic."

"What the hell does that mean?"

Before I could reply, Peg was calling my name from the kitchen. It was a smart move on her part, because she knew that I'd answer her.

I slowly turned down the corner of my page, even though I'd read the thing a million times and it didn't matter where I started up again, then placed it back on its little shelf. Vera stayed behind as I made my way toward Peg, but she followed my movements with her eyes as if she was still trying to figure me out.

"What's up?" I asked Peg, strolling into the kitchen.

"The lads are makin' some plans. Ye should be in here for this."

"Okay," I replied easily, sitting down at Robbie's spot and folding my hands on the smooth wooden table.

The men watched me warily as they crowded around me.

"Ham," the man who must have been Charlie's dad said, reaching out to shake my hand. "That's Doc."

"Nice to meet you, I'm Amy."

"Trick's wife," he replied with a smile. He seemed nice.

"For today."

Patrick took a step forward, but out of the corner of my eye, I saw Charlie's hand grip his shoulder hard as if to stop him.

"So what's the plan?" I asked calmly, looking directly at Ham. What a weird name.

"We leave on a steamer in two days," he said, pulling out a chair and flipping it around so he could straddle it. "Got two spaces open—we can only take two of you with us then."

"That seems easy enough," I replied.

"Gotta leave two behind."

"So take Patrick and the girl."

"I'm not leavin' ye and Mum, are ye out of yer mind?" Patrick exploded, stepping forward to slam his palm down on the table.

"The girl has to leave, right?" I asked Ham, completely ignoring Patrick's outburst. Why was I calling her a girl? The woman had a baby in her belly, for Christ's sake. "So she's one of the people, automatically."

"Gotta get that girl outta here before they realize where she's gone," he confirmed with a nod. "Doc set her arm, but she won't be up to fightin' anyone off for a while."

"Okay, well if Patrick doesn't want to go with her, then I guess Peg goes."

"I can't just leave ye here," Patrick interrupted again.

"I'll not leave ye to take care of that whore." Peg's comment was quiet but resolute.

"Mum—"

"Ye've made yer bed, son."

"Jesus Christ," he said softly, running his hands through his hair.

"We've got contacts on another steamer that leaves at the end of the week," Charlie chimed in. "Whoever stays back can leave on that one. It's only four days difference."

"It's settled then, Patrick and the woman—" Peg said.

"Her name is Moira," Patrick corrected quietly.

Peg paused and turned to look at Patrick.

"I don't care if her name is the fuckin' Virgin Mary!" she yelled at him, finally losing what little composure she had left. "How could ye? I taught ye better than that! Ye think it's okay to be fuckin' other woman while yer wife's home in yer bed?" She reached out and slapped him across the face. "How could ye do that to Amy? Amy, who's been nothin' but good to ye! Dealin' with yer travelin' from home and leavin' her here more often than not! She's waited on ye! She's done nothin' that other girls were doin' because she was waitin' on yer sorry arse to come home to her, and what do ye do? Tell me, Patrick Gallagher! Say it! What did ye do to her?"

"Enough." My words were quiet, but they rang out like a gunshot through the room. "You don't need to stick up for me, though I love you for it. This isn't getting anything done, and we need to plan."

Peg had angry tears rolling down her cheeks, and Patrick looked like his world had just ended. I realized that they were hurting with the cool detachment that I'd developed throughout my childhood. It was all too much on the tail of Robbie's death. They looked so overwhelmed.

I felt bad for them, but that was pretty much the extent of my emotional reaction.

"So Patrick and—" I cleared my throat and glanced at Patrick, who was looking at me with a stricken expression. "Moira will take the first steamer, Peg and I will come at the end of the week."

"I'll stay behind and go with them," Doc spoke up for the first time. "Girl in there doesn't need me for the trip, and you all need to get back home with that steamer. Don't feel right leavin' them here alone."

Ham watched him for a minute and then nodded. "You'll stay with the women."

"If there's an open spot, then Amy can go with ye on the first one," Peg argued.

"Not going to happen," I answered flatly. There was no way in hell that I was going anywhere with Patrick and that woman.

"I can—" Patrick began to speak again.

"No." I stared him down until he gave in with a defeated nod. We weren't going to get anywhere if we continued on about who went with who. The plan was set—Patrick and Moira on one and Peg and I on the other. The end.

"Okay, is there anything else we need to go over?" I asked Ham. I had work in an hour and I wasn't even sure how I'd get my clean clothes out of the bedroom Moira was sleeping in. I couldn't believe that I was still going to work as if my life as I'd known it was gone. Then I brushed that thought away. I was fine and I needed the money.

"Pack light, only things you can carry. Leave everything else in the house as-is. Trip to North Carolina will be rough, so make sure you bring some pain relievers and shit with you. Maybe some Dramamine."

"We're going to North Carolina?"

"Just stoppin' there. We'll ride the bikes to Oregon."

I nodded and stood from the table, done with the conversation.

I'd never been to Oregon.

Chapter 34

Amy

"Are ye ever goin' to speak to me?" Patrick asked quietly from the couch as I walked in from work that night.

Charlie and Vera had walked me to Dillon's and had stayed for my entire shift to keep watch. It had seemed a bit overboard, but I didn't really mind it. They'd gone out of their way to act as if everything was normal, and I'd been grateful for the reprieve. We'd all agreed that mentioning anything out of the ordinary wasn't a good idea since we weren't sure who was looking for Moira.

It had been fucking wonderful to pretend she didn't exist for a few hours.

Unfortunately, the minute I'd walked through my front door, reality intruded.

"What do you want me to say?" I asked tiredly, taking off my coat and hanging it on the hook by the door. I needed to remember to take it with me when we left.

"I don't know, Amy. Somet'in'. Fuckin' hit me. Yell at me. Anyt'in.'"

"I can yell if you want, but I'm not sure it would do any good.

Would that make *you* feel better?" I walked around the couch and sat in the chair next to it as Patrick ran his hands over his face.

"It was before we got married," he said softly.

"She's not that pregnant," I replied flatly.

"I'm not lyin.' It was before I'd even proposed to ye."

"Not long before."

"No," he answered painfully, and suddenly I had to know everything.

"How long before?"

He didn't answer, just stared at me as if memorizing my face.

"How long before, Patrick?"

"De night before Mum called and told me somet'in' was wrong."

The words felt like a punch to my chest, and suddenly I was afraid that I'd never be able to breathe again. I'd been so scared that night. I remembered lying in my bed, begging silently for Patrick, but too afraid to reach out. To think, just the next day I'd thought that my prayers had been answered when he'd come and taken me away.

"Yeah, not long before," I whispered to myself.

"We were not toget'er den. If we'd been toget'er, I—"

"I was waiting for you," I cut in, my voice barely recognizable it was so quiet. "You kissed me and said you wouldn't fuck me because you were going to marry me first. I was devastated the night before you came home. I remember so clearly, because I hadn't been out of my bed all day and my mom had come in to tell me that I wasn't finding a place to live by rotting away in my bed. And then the next morning, you were there... like magic."

The scenes played like a movie in my head, and by the time they were finished, I couldn't help the hysterical laugh that came out of my mouth.

"I was so stupid. So fucking naïve."

"Don't say dat. Yer not stupid. Ye were never stupid."

"I made comments about your experience," I spoke over him, "I pushed you because I was angry, and the entire time you were fucking other people. No wonder you didn't mind waiting until we were married."

"Dat's not how it was."

"So fucking stupid." I shook my head, scrubbing my hands over my face.

"It was one night. One night. Dat's all. I was pissed—"

"You're really going to use the drunk excuse right now? Really, Patrick?"

"I wasn't in me right mind—" I gripped the arms of the chair, but he was off the couch and kneeling in front of me before I could push myself to my feet. "Please, Amy. Please, *listen*."

I leaned back in the chair as far as I could and wrapped my arms around my chest. I didn't want to hear what he had to say. My stomach was churning and my heart was racing… but a part of me ached to know it all. I needed the details, so I could try to make sense of the whole thing.

He loved me. I knew he did. How could he do this?

"I began me night early at a pub near me flat. I was alone. I was missin' home and me da had just come to Mum's to tell us dat he was in trouble. Me classes were goin' poorly and I'd just finished me exams." His hands were gently gripping my thighs, his thumbs rubbing back and forth in an unconscious gesture. "I was havin' a shite week. Den dese men came in de pub, and I recognized one of dem. Local IRA, not high level, but not low level eit'er. Somewhere in de middle. Dey stopped at dis table full o'women, and I couldn't hear what was said, but one of de women stiffened and den left de bar."

He swallowed hard and his chest began rising and falling as if he couldn't catch his breath.

"I followed her," he whispered, "I stopped her to ask her if she was okay. She knew me, but I didn't recognize her. She liked me, I could tell by her body language dat she'd been watchin' me for a while. It was so easy. I wasn't t'inkin' clearly, I barely remember gettin' back to me flat. But I'd seen her wit' dose men in de bar, and in me muddled brain it had seemed like de perfect revenge. I wanted to punish dat man in de bar—fuck dem de way dey'd fucked me. It meant nuttin'! It was a *mistake*, but it was only *one night*."

I clenched my jaw, but a raw noise of pain still burst out of my throat.

"One night, but not only once, huh?" I asked hoarsely, looking away from him.

"Forgive me," he begged. "Please. Please. I love *ye*, only ye. Forgive me."

"No."

I didn't look at him, but I heard his sob as his head dropped to my knees.

Chapter 35

Patrick

I made my way into the large house silently, the key Moira had given me barely making a sound as I'd unlocked the front door. There was one thing that had to be done before I left Ireland for good.

I'd expected some kind of guards or maybe even a few large dogs, but all I encountered as I made my way through the house were darkened rooms and the low hum of the furnace. I knew he was there because his car was parked in the driveway, and it amazed me how little he cared for his own safety.

I'm sure he believed he was untouchable, and in most circles he was probably considered so… but I had nothing to lose. I was leaving to go halfway across the world in a matter of hours, and in just a few days the only people I cared about would be following behind me. His reputation was no longer relevant. His arms couldn't reach me.

I moved on silently to Moira's room and found the bag she'd told me would be under her bed. I quickly located the music box her mother had given her as a child and stuffed it into the bottom of the bag before pulling shirts and pants from her dresser. When I got to her underthings, my stomach cramped. I shouldn't be touching them. It was wrong. I shouldn't be touching any woman's underthings that weren't my wife's.

As soon as I was finished, I set Moira's bag outside the door to Michael's room and stepped inside.

He was asleep on his back when I found him, his arms tucked under the blankets like a child and his face slack with slumber. The look was almost innocent, and it was hard to imagine that the minute he awoke, he'd look like a completely different man.

I stepped up beside him and quickly hopped onto the bed, pinning his arms to his sides with the blanket he'd so kindly wrapped himself in. The moment my weight hit him, his eyes snapped open and it only took seconds before he realized that the blankets and my legs had completely trapped him.

"Ye'll die for dis, ye fuckin' bastard," he said menacingly, trying to work his arms slowly out of the blankets.

I could feel his every move, but I didn't stop his almost imperceptible struggle. I wanted him to feel it. I wanted him to know that he was trapped.

"Do ye know why I'm here?" I asked, flipping open my blade before resting it on my thigh.

"I'm guessing me whore of a sister somehow got out of her room," he growled, his legs beginning to kick at the blankets. It was really too bad that he insisted on having such a tightly made bed.

"Ye almost killed me child," I said quietly.

"Yer bastard, ye mean?"

I clenched my fist around the handle of my blade and reminded myself that I wasn't finished yet.

"Did ye set up de blast dat killed me da?"

He froze beneath me.

"It wasn't meant to kill him."

"I'd come to that conclusion meself."

"It was just a warnin.'"

"A warnin' dat would have killed me mum."

"We're in a war, Trick. Sometimes—"

"Spare me yer rhetoric!" I hissed through my clenched teeth. "Ye killed me da and ye nearly killed me child."

"Moira is me sister. It's me job to punish her for wrongdoin's."

He believed it. All of it. I could see it in his eyes. He thought that beating a woman almost to death was an acceptable punishment, that it was alright to kill a person's spouse as an effective way to keep him in line.

He believed that the end justified the means.

"Immanuel Kant was a philosopher," I began slowly as he watched me in confusion. "He believed dat people should be viewed as de ends, not de means."

I paused and watched as he tried to understand the conversation's change in direction. He was nervous and afraid and began to shake beneath me.

"For dat reason alone, I'll allow ye to pray."

"What?" he asked in horror.

"Beg forgiveness."

His eyes widened in fear as he lay frozen for a long moment.

"Our Fadder," he sobbed, "who art in heaven—"

I cut his words and his neck with a deep slash of my knife from ear to ear. Then I climbed off the bed and wiped my blade down on the corner of his sheets.

For the first time, I didn't feel an ounce of remorse, and I wondered briefly when I'd become such a monster. Then I made my way back outside, locking the front door and climbing onto my motorcycle so I could go home.

***

I sat alone in the silent house for a long time after I got back. I'd fucked up so badly that I knew any chance of righting my life was completely gone. I'd never again step foot in my own country, I had little money to start a new life, and both my mother and my wife hated me.

I couldn't blame Amy for her anger. One poor decision, one mistake, and I'd broken all trust between us. It didn't matter that we hadn't yet made any promises to each other. I'd known the morning after my night with Moira that I'd made a horrible mistake, but it had been too late then to right it.

I wondered if Amy would have forgiven me if I had told her after it had happened. Perhaps she would have fought me, but eventually forgiven me—I'd never know. But I did know that if I had the chance to go back and tell her, I still wouldn't have.

She wouldn't have married me. She would have allowed me to work back into her good graces, but it would have taken time, time we didn't have. Because Moira showing up at my door, pregnant with my child, was inevitable. And when that happened, I would have lost Amy forever.

I took comfort in the fact that Amy and I had already spoken our vows. I had a hold on her that was unbreakable. It made me a bit nervous that we were headed to the United States, where people seemed to divorce on a whim, but I didn't think she could get one without my consent, so I tried not to worry.

I had more pressing matters to worry about.

I was leaving the country of my birth to build a life in a place I'd never been, with a woman I barely knew but was carrying my child, and I had to leave my wife and my mother behind. I'd barely slept.

Amy and Mum were sleeping together in my mum's room and Moira was asleep in the bed I'd only ever shared with my wife. That knowledge made my guts clench in shame.

My wife hadn't deserved to be pulled into this mess. I'd kept so much from her trying to protect her that she'd unknowingly climbed aboard a sinking ship, and the most horrible part of it was that I wouldn't have gone back to change it.

I knew she deserved more, but I'd never give her up.

"Mum," I called, walking slowly into her room. "Wake up, it's time."

I made my way to Amy's side of the bed, and brushed her hair away from her face. Dried tears had made a few strands stick to her cheeks, and as I pulled them away, I leaned down to kiss those spots.

She wouldn't have let me that close if she was awake, and I didn't feel one ounce of shame for taking what I could.

"What time is it?" she asked sleepily, before stiffening where she lay.

"Goin' on t'ree. We need to leave," I answered, the words like invisible razorblades in my mouth.

It felt wrong to leave her. All of it felt wrong. I couldn't tell if it was just because I hated to be away from her or if my instincts were trying to tell me something. The anxiety was making me sweat.

"Is she awake?" my mum asked as she climbed out of bed, her tone a clear indication of which "she" she was referring to.

"Not yet."

"Better go wake her."

I nodded, but couldn't force myself away from Amy's curled up form. It felt wrong. My head was screaming at me to do something, but I didn't know what. Christ, I felt like I was being torn in two.

Amy scooted to the edge of the bed, and I had to take a step back so she could climb out from under the blankets. When she got to her feet, she mumbled something about getting dressed and grabbed a stack of clothes off my mum's dresser before moving around me and walking into the bathroom.

I brushed my hair away from my face and followed her out of the room. I needed to get moving. The ship we were riding on wouldn't wait because I hadn't given Moira enough time to get ready.

"Hey, wake up," I said gently, reaching out to gently shake Moira's shoulder. "It's time to go."

I'd explained our plan the day before on one of the rare occasions that Moira had been awake to discuss it. She seemed to sleep a hell of a lot, but Doc assured me that it was normal. Between the pregnancy and the beating she'd taken, she needed the extra rest. So far the baby had held fast, and after the first twenty-four hours I'd begun to feel a mixture of relief and… I couldn't say it was disappointment. That wasn't right.

I would never be glad for my child to die, no matter how it was conceived. However, when she'd continued on with no sign of a miscarriage, I'd finally realized that there was no turning back. This woman who had seemed so nice and smart and beautiful when I'd first met her was actually going to have my child… and I didn't love her. Not even the slightest bit.

And the woman that I loved more than life would not give me my first child the way we'd dreamed.

"Patrick?" Moira answered as I continued to pat and shake her shoulder. "Is it time to go?"

"Soon," I answered, looking over her bruised face as I turned on the light. "How are ye feelin'?"

"Like absolute garbage," she whispered, rolling onto her side before gingerly pushing herself up. "I'm so sorry for all of dis, Patrick. I didn't know ye were married or I wouldn't have come."

"Not yer fault," I reassured her, dropping down to sit on the edge of the bed. "I wasn't married when I met ye. Hadn't even proposed yet."

"Ye work fast."

"I would've married her de day I proposed."

"What are we goin' to do?"

"I've no idea." I rubbed my hands over my tired eyes. "Let's get to Oregon, we can sort it all out den."

I didn't realize how close we were sitting or how it would look, until I heard my wife clear her throat from the doorway.

"I just forgot a sweatshirt," Amy mumbled, averting her eyes as she walked into the room.

I jumped from my spot on the bed, but the damage was done. She didn't look at me once as she pulled her clothing out of our half-empty dresser drawer. Her hands were shaking, but she ignored us as we watched her shuffle through her things until she found what she was looking for.

I'd already packed my things into a duffel that rested at the end of the bed, and as she walked back out of the room, I picked it up and slung it over my shoulder to follow her.

"I brought ye de t'ings ye asked for," I told Moira, who was looking at me in apology. "We'll have to buy ye some new clothes once we get where we're goin.' Ye'll not fit in dose for much longer." I gestured to the bag by the door.

"T'ank ye," she whispered. I nodded once and tried to smile, but I was sure it looked more like a grimace.

When it was finally time for us to go, my entire body was tight with tension. A part of me wanted to tell Amy to pack a bag—that she'd be going with us. But I couldn't leave my mum alone, no matter how much I wanted Amy with me.

She was across the room with Vera and they were hugging each other goodbye with low promises to see one another soon. I was glad that she'd made such a good friend, and even more glad that her new friend would be in Oregon with us as we tried to settle in.

"I'll walk Moira out," Mum said, glancing at Charlie, who was standing at the open front door. Then she turned fully to me and used both hands to pull my face down to hers. "I'll see ye in a few days. I love ye, even when yer bein' an eejit." I felt a lump form in my throat as she kissed me quickly on the lips, and I pulled her into a tight hug. "It'll all turn out in the end," she whispered into my ear. "Ye'll see."

With a quick pat on my back, she let me go and led Moira, Vera and Charlie out the door, leaving me alone with Amy.

We stood awkwardly facing each other and I didn't know how to cross the gap between us.

"I'll see ye in a week, yeah?" I asked her, breaking the silence.

"Yeah, it'll be nice to be on home soil again," she replied uncomfortably.

Fuck this.

I stepped forward and gripped her arms, pulling her against me before she could protest. Wrapping one hand securely around her waist, I moved the other to the hair at the base of her neck so I could tip her face toward mine.

"One week," I said, my voice raspy. "I'll see ye in one week, and den we're goin' to figure dis out."

"I'm not sure there's anything—"

I refused to listen to her tell me that we couldn't be fixed and I stopped her words with my mouth. She stiffened as my teeth bit into the fleshy part of her bottom lip, but I didn't stop, and soon she was relaxing against me and sliding her hands under the back of my coat to grip the t-shirt underneath.

"I love ye," I said harshly before pressing my tongue into her mouth. "We will sort all of dis as soon as ye get to America."

Tears began to roll slowly down her cheeks, and I shuddered. How the hell was I supposed to leave her?

"We'll sort it out," she agreed, bringing her hands up to cover my cheeks. "I love you so much."

"I love ye, too. Me beautiful wife," I groaned back, thanking God that whatever I'd said had finally gotten through to her.

I'd find a way to earn back her trust. I had to. There was no other option.

I loved her more than anything else on earth—more than my mother, more than myself. I'd do whatever it took, jump through whatever hoop I could, beg on my knees if I had to.

I would not allow her to pull away from me.

"You have to go," she whispered achingly, running one of her fingers over my eyebrow. "I'll see you in a week."

"Be careful. I took care of Moira's brudder, but ye still need to be careful, yeah?" I kissed her hard. "I don't want to leave ye."

"It's only a week," she reassured me, and I wasn't sure how our roles had become so reversed that it was as if she was comforting me. "That's not so long."

"Trick, we need to go, man." Charlie called, popping his head inside the front door.

"I love ye," I said again hurriedly. "If I get dere before ye leave, I'll call ye."

"Okay," she said, nodding even as I kissed her. "Now go." She planted her hands against my stomach and pushed me away, but I immediately grabbed her hair in both hands and pulled her back, kissing her harshly.

"Trick! Let's go." Charlie called again.

I tore my mouth from Amy's and dropped my hands from her hair. I knew that if I held her for a second longer, I wouldn't leave. I'd fuck everything up worse, because I'd refuse to take one step from her side.

I grabbed my duffel from the floor and threw it over my shoulder before looking back at the woman who held my entire world in her hands. Her arms were wrapped around her waist, and her shoulders were bunched up nearly to her ears as she huddled against the wall, watching my every movement. I wanted to go back to her. Everything in my body was screaming for me to reach for her again, but I knew I couldn't.

Instead, I nodded at her and pursed my lips in a kiss before turning my back and striding toward the door.

I didn't look back again. I didn't have the willpower.

Years later, I wondered what I would have seen on her face if I'd glanced back just once.

Chapter 36

Amy

It was my last shift, though no one in the pub knew it. Three days had passed since Patrick had left, and though I missed him, I also felt a little numb about it all. I had to pull all that numbness in around me like a cloak. Thinking about Patrick alone with Moira made me want to scream and rip my own hair out. It was agony… so I didn't think about it. Late the next night, Peg, Doc and I would be headed for the steamer that would carry us to the US and my husband, who I was sure was waiting impatiently for our arrival.

I wasn't nervous, not really, but I'd had this weird energy running through my body that entire night and it made me feel like I was going to jump out of my skin. Intuition? Maybe. But I couldn't tell if it was because we were going to be on a freaking boat in the middle of the ocean for days, or if it was because I was so anxious to see Patrick again.

I was still so angry with him.

I'd had so many different emotions since he'd left. I was angry, sad, confused, nervous…jealous. God, it felt as if the jealousy would completely eat me up from the inside.

I hated Moira for taking away the one thing that I'd known I could give Patrick, the one thing reserved for me and me alone. She was having his child. *His child.* And here I was after months of marriage with nothing in my belly but a seething mass of emotions. It wasn't fair.

I knew that life wasn't fair, of course I did. But the whole situation with Moira was just too much for me to handle. I wanted to cry and scream and scratch at the hives that had become a constant reminder of my husband's infidelity every second of every day. Instead, I just kept living like nothing was wrong and I pulled that cloak of numbness tighter around me.

Underneath it all, I just missed him so badly. Having him away at college was nothing like knowing he was somewhere on the Atlantic Ocean. I had no way to even contact him.

My night was finally almost over, and I was thinking about the things I needed to pack as I carried some garbage out the back door of the pub. I tried to ignore the hair prickling on the back of my neck as I lifted the dumpster lid and threw out the bag of trash, but something had me reaching up to rub it.

Then everything went black.

***

I woke up tied to a chair in the middle of a living room I'd never seen before, facing a man sitting on a flowered sofa. He looked familiar, but I couldn't place him, and I had a hard time focusing my eyes because my head was pounding with every beat of my heart.

"Yer finally awake," he said calmly, sitting completely still except for the way his lips moved when he talked. I opened my mouth to answer, and that's when I realized there was something wrapped around my head and pulled tightly between my teeth.

"It's a belt in yer mout'," he commented as my eyes grew huge in my face. "So ye won't bite yer tongue."

Why the fuck would I bite my tongue? Where was I? Oh, God, it was like every horror movie I'd ever seen. Don't go out to the dumpster alone, you fool! Run the other way!

"Amy Gallagher. Wife of Patrick Gallagher, 'De Butcher of Dublin', de papers call him." He finally leaned forward to rest his elbows on his knees. "I've been waitin' to talk to ye."

I tried to mumble back that I didn't know who he was or what the hell he was talking about, but the words came out as a bunch of gibberish. I didn't know why he wanted to talk, but I'd talk to him about whatever he wanted if that meant he would let me go.

I wasn't thinking about escape—I knew I was trapped. But maybe if I gave him what he wanted he wouldn't hurt me. Maybe he'd let me go. I clung to that hope as he lifted one finger as if I should wait, and walked out of the room.

When he returned, he was carrying a ball peen hammer, some scissors, and a pair of pliers.

"I can see why Trick wanted ye," he said conversationally, setting a small table to the right of my chair and laying the tools on top of it. "Yer quite pretty. Nuttin' like me fiancé, but dere are few woman as beautiful as her."

My eyes followed his movements as I barely breathed, and at the mention of his fiancé, my eyes shot to the door.

"Oh, she won't be here," he commented, catching the movement of my eyes. "I'm not quite sure where she is at de moment."

He pulled a chair in from the kitchen and sat down so close that our knees were touching. "I was hopin' ye could help me wit' dat. Nod if ye'd like to help me," he ordered with a smile.

I nodded frantically, willing to do anything for him to let me go. He wanted me to help him find his fiancé? I'd search for her myself.

"Wonderful," he said, reaching behind my hair to gently loosen the belt and pull it down until it was resting against my collar bone. "Would ye like a drink of water?" I nodded again, as I tried to moisten my mouth with saliva. My mouth was so dry that my tongue was sticking to the top of my mouth.

"Dere now, dat's better," he said, after he'd lifted a glass of water to my mouth. "I'm so glad dat yer willin' to help me. Dat makes everyt'in' so much easier."

He set the water down on the table and then turned to face me again.

"Where is Moira?" he asked, reaching out to run his fingers through my hair.

His fingers caught in the tangles of my hair and I shivered in revulsion as panic hit me harder and more quickly than it ever had in my life. For a moment I was completely silent as I gaped at him. This was because of *Moira*?

"I don't know," I answered honestly. I wasn't sure if they were still on the ocean, where they were on the ocean, or even if they'd made it to North Carolina.

He made a chastising noise with his mouth, and I realized then that I should have asked who Moira was. By answering the way I had, he knew that I knew something.

"Please, please, I don't know," I pleaded quickly as he stood and grabbed the scissors off the table.

"Every time ye lie, ye'll be punished," he replied, gripping my hair and pulling until my neck was arched over the back rung of the chair. I fought to bring my head forward, but all that did was make the position of my neck hurt worse.

He began to use the scissors on my hair, and though I was relieved that he wasn't hurting me, I couldn't stop the hysterical sobs that ripped out of my throat. I couldn't see how much he cut off, but I could feel the cold edge of the scissors against my scalp over and over again, and by the time he was done, I could actually feel cool air against the crown of my head.

"Dat was not so bad," he scolded, sitting down calmly in front of me again as he discarded the scissors. "Butcher paid a visit to Michael, did ye know? Left his callin' card, so to speak, so I know he's got her somewhere and yer his wife, so I'm sure ye know where he's keepin' her. Maybe even feelin' a bit out of sorts with his bastard in her belly? So why don't ye tell me, hmmm? Where is Moira?"

"I don't know! I swear I don't," I told him, looking directly into his eyes. His pupils were like pinpricks, and I was suddenly afraid that he wasn't only crazy and angry, but that he was on something, too.

He sighed deeply, and I watched in terror as he pulled the table so that it slid under my left hand, between the arm of the chair and my fingers. He moved his tools around, setting them just so. When he picked up the hammer, I felt my entire body freeze in terror.

I didn't see it hit my index finger. As he raised the hammer, I'd instinctively shut my eyes against what I knew would happen.

It didn't change a fucking thing, though. I still felt the cold metal crush the bone as I bit my tongue and then screamed, blood pouring out of my mouth and down my chin as I lost all control of my bladder.

I'd never felt such pain before. It was radiating up my arm in waves that I couldn't control, and when I tried to curl my hand into a fist to protect the other digits, his large hand slammed down on top of mine, making me howl once again.

"Where is Moira?"

"I don't know," I whimpered, trying to pull away from him and making the chair wobble underneath me. I was frantic, pulling and twisting against my bonds, but they held fast.

I wasn't even trying to protect her. At that moment, I would have given the man her and Patrick's coordinates if I had known them—but that was the problem. I *didn't* know where they were, and I was in so much pain that I couldn't see past the literal interpretation of his words.

The hammer slammed down again on my middle finger, and I screamed in agony once more, but when he asked again where they were, I gave him the same answer.

The next finger was so short that when he took aim and hit it, I felt the bottom knuckle break.

His question never wavered, and neither did my answer. I felt him position my smallest and most delicate finger on the table, and I was so dazed from the pain that I didn't even fight him. My head was rolling across the top of the chair as I prayed that I would lose consciousness.

I didn't.

The hammer fell again.

When he loosened the rope around my wrist so he could position my thumb along the tabletop, he finally asked the right question.

"Where did he take her?" His voice was still calm, but I could hear the frustration behind it. I watched detachedly as he tightened the rope around my wrist back up.

"North Carolina," I mumbled, finally seeing black spots dance around the edges of my vision.

I was losing focus on his face, but I noticed when he began to turn red and the veins in his neck began to bulge. I didn't flinch when he flung the hammer across the room, or at the sound it made as it lodged in the wall.

I also didn't move when I realized he was untying me from the chair. I barely flinched as he laid me on the floor and tugged my wet jeans and underwear down my legs. And when he left me there, bare from the waist down and cradling my broken hand to my chest, I finally, blessedly, passed out.

I'm not sure how long I was on the floor, but I woke up to him murmuring. "Disgustin'," he said, and something about an eye for an eye as he used a wet towel to clean me. My hand was still curled limply against my chest and I couldn't focus on anything else except the pain. It was taking over my entire body, making my teeth chatter and my legs shake against the cold wood floor.

I barely noticed when he lifted me from the floor and laid me on the couch. I was drifting in some weird space where I'd come to briefly in order to see his livid face, and then fade away again as if I wasn't even in my own body.

I'd like to think that I would have fought him if I hadn't been so out of it, but I'm not sure that I would have. The memory of what he'd done to my hand was so sharp, the pain so intense, that even if I'd had my wits about me, I wasn't sure I would've tried to stop him.

I probably would have lay there, exactly as I did, and whimpered as he pushed inside me. It hurt, but it was nothing compared to the agony in my hand.

I'm almost grateful for that—the pain and the disconnection—because it didn't allow me to focus on the triumph in his face, the way he groaned as he pumped away, or the way he laid my unresisting leg over the back of the couch so he had more room to move as he changed my life forever.

I just hurt all over and I wanted Patrick.

I heard the front door open, but I was too out of it to pay any attention as the man finally pulled away and left me spread out on the couch.

He was buttoning his jeans leisurely as a familiar voice called through the house.

"Mum, are ye here?"

Footsteps grew closer, but I still didn't move. I didn't feel anything. I was completely numb, aside from the pain that had moved all the way up my arm and had settled like a weight pressing on my chest.

I met Kevie's eyes with my dull ones as his mouth dropped in absolute horror.

"Malcolm, what in God's name have ye done?"

Chapter 37

Amy

I don't remember how I got home and I don't remember Peg's reaction. I assume that Doc bandaged my hand, but I have no memory of him doing that, either.

The first thing I recall was waking up in my bed, while Kevie sat watching me from a chair that had been dragged in from our kitchen.

"Yer awake?" he asked quietly as I tried to remember how I'd gotten there.

It came back to me in flashes, the memories becoming heavier and heavier as I curled onto my side and wrapped my body protectively around my hand. I could hear Doc and Peg speaking in the kitchen, which calmed me somewhat, but my face burned in shame as Kevie leaned forward to meet my eyes.

"I'm so sorry dis happened," he said, his hands wrapped up in a rosary as if I'd interrupted his prayers when I'd woken up. "Me brudder—"

"That was your brother?" I asked in confusion, my throat sore from screaming.

"Yes."

My body tensed again as I watched him try to martial his features into something that didn't resemble complete devastation.

"I cannot apologize enough for what he's done," he whispered, his eyes brimming with tears. "I don't know what demon has taken hold of him, but I fear dat he's past de point of any help."

"Did you kill him?" I asked curiously, feeling surprisingly sorry for the man.

"Of course not," he replied, and all sense of sympathy left me.

"What did you do?"

"I dressed ye and brought ye home," he answered, his cheeks growing red at the word 'dressed'.

"Where is your brother?" I glanced at the window. Patrick had told me no one could fit through it, but at that moment I wasn't sure if I believed him.

"I believe he's still at our mum's. She's at her sister's for de weekend."

"That was your mother's house?"

"Yes."

"And you just left him there, to what? Watch some television? Make a little dinner? Have a beer?"

"I had to get ye home. Yer hand—"

My hand's throbbing seemed to intensify as he pointed it out.

"Did you tell Peg where you found me?" I asked in suspicion. "Peg!" I yelled. "Peg!"

"Do not say a word!" he hissed quietly as we heard he steps moving toward us.

"Yer awake!" Peg cried as she came to the bed, pulling me up slowly and wrapping her arms around me as she burst into tears. "My poor baby."

I met Kevie's eyes over Peg's shoulder, and barely held back the shudder at the glare on his face.

"What happened?" I asked Peg, never looking away from Kevie's face.

"Ye don't remember?" she asked in surprise, then hugged me even tighter. "Thank God. Thank God."

"The priest here says he found ya in the alley behind the bar," Doc said, coming into the doorway. "Says he thought you'd want him to bring you back here instead of the hospital." His voice was laced with suspicion, and I couldn't help the relief that ran through me. He didn't believe it. He knew something was off.

"I'm just glad I was takin' de short cut to Mum's from de church," Kevie said, his jaw clenching.

"I'm so glad yer home," Peg whispered into my ear, "What would I have done? My poor girl."

"I'm a little hungry," I lied, leaning away from Peg's arms. "And I'd really like a shower."

"Of course!" she shot up from the bed, jostling my arm. "I'll start some breakfast."

She left the room and I turned to Doc, who hadn't left his post. "Can I have a minute with Kevie?"

He stared at me for a long moment, and I honestly thought he was going to refuse, but then with a small nod of his head, he stepped out of the doorway.

"Why did you lie?" I asked, knowing from the shadow outside the door that Doc hadn't gone far.

"If ye try to—" Kevie shook his head and stuffed his rosary beads into his pocket. "Do not go against me brudder," he warned, "Ye'll not come out of it unharmed."

"I have nothing to lose."

"Ye cannot honestly believe dat," he argued.

"I could send him to prison."

"Yer delusional," he hissed leaning forward until I was forced to move back or our faces would be touching. "De police in Ballyshannon wouldn't even arrest him, ye bloody idiot. No one would believe yer word over Malcolm's. *No one.*"

"But they'd believe you. You're a priest. They'd believe you." I pointed out quietly, watching as his face moved from a pleading expression to completely void of emotion.

"I'll not help ye put me brudder in prison," he said resolutely, standing from his chair. "Keep yer accusations to yerself if ye know what's good for ye."

He left the room as I began to panic.

I had no recourse. There was absolutely nothing I could do. I couldn't go to the police, Patrick wasn't there, Charlie and Vera were gone… and I'd have to live knowing that at any time, Malcolm could come back to me.

Suddenly, I was overcome with a wave of disgust and I frantically pushed the blankets away from my body with my good hand. As I stood from the bed, the sore flesh between my thighs burned in protest, and I felt tears burn the backs of my eyes. I smelled like urine and sex.

"Need help?" Doc asked, looking at me kindly.

"I want to take a shower." I lifted my right hand up to run it through my hair, and that's when I finally remembered that it was gone. Tears dripped down my face as I looked at Doc. "I forgot," I explained, running my fingers lightly over the patchy hair on my head. "It looks bad, doesn't it?"

"You won't be winning any beauty pageants," he confirmed, "but it'll grow back. Hair ain't nothin' worth worrying about."

I opened my mouth to argue, but what was the point? It was gone.

"I'll shave the rest off, if you want. It's gotta be better than having patches all over like that."

I think I nodded, and I didn't resist as he ushered me toward the bathroom.

I'll never know what he said to Peg that day when he went to get me painkillers from the kitchen, but I do know that she never bothered us as he shaved my head with a cheap razor from beneath the bathroom sink. He was careful. His hands touched me as little as possible, and when they did, it was as if I'd break at any minute.

I'm not sure why I didn't balk at Doc helping me shower. Maybe it was because he treated me like a child. Maybe it was the air of calm that he exuded. More than likely, I was still in shock. For whatever reason, I didn't panic once as he turned on the shower and sat on the toilet seat to help me get undressed.

My hand was pretty much useless; any time I moved it, I had to force myself not to gasp in pain, so Doc had to do most of the work. After he removed my shirt and bra, he pulled my pants to my ankles and helped me step out of them.

"Christ!" he hissed as he tried to remove my underwear next.

I began to shake as he wrapped his big hands around my hips and dropped his head forward in sorrow.

"I thought maybe—but then you didn't say nothin' so I hoped—" His voice was strained as he shook his head slowly from side to side. "I should have stripped you down while you were out," he said to himself. "I fuckin' knew better."

I was thankful he hadn't stripped me while I was unconscious. Who knows how I would have reacted to that on top of everything else?

"Thank you," I said in a small voice, laying my good hand on the top of his head. "Thank you for leaving my clothes on."

"Don't *thank* me!" his words were harsh, but his hands were still gentle on my hips. "Motherfuckingsonofabitch!"

He took in a deep breath and let it out slowly as I stood awkwardly in front of him, and after a few moments, his calm façade was back.

"You've—your underwear—the blood—" he took another deep breath then began again. "The blood has dried. I'm not sure how badly you're hurt, but your panties are stuck to your skin with blood, and I don't want to rip them away in case things are even worse than I think they are."

My stomach turned and I was afraid for a second that I was going to be sick. I swallowed it down and nodded at him to keep going.

"I'm going to put you in the shower like this so the water can wash away some of the blood," he looked at me for acceptance. "Keep your hand out of the spray if you can. I wrapped those fingers good, but fuck if I know if I made them worse or not. You probably need fuckin' surgery, but we can't take you to a goddamn hospital in this hellhole. If you get those bandages wet, I'll have to change them and it'll hurt like hell, okay?"

"I won't get them wet," I assured him as he grabbed my elbow to steady me while I stepped into the tub.

"I'm so sorry this happened to you," he said after silently keeping an eye on me for a few minutes as I let the hot water roll over my body. "I should have been more prepared. I knew somethin' felt off, but I thought you'd be safe at work."

"It's not your fault," I said flatly.

"I should have—"

"It's not your fault. Can you help me get these off now?"

He nodded and reached for my underwear, pulling them slowly away. Thankfully the water had done its job, and all I could feel was a stinging sensation as he moved them down my thighs.

"I know you don't want to do this. Fuck!" He threw the underwear out of the spray before continuing, "I need to check you, alright? I need to make sure you're okay down there."

I didn't think that anything was significantly wrong down there, but I had no way to know. I hated the thought of Doc seeing me—of anyone seeing me. It made my skin crawl with revulsion. He was being so kind, far more gentle and apologetic than I knew he was comfortable with, but that didn't stop the churning of my stomach as I agreed.

I stood there, one foot on the side of the tub, holding onto his shoulder to keep from falling, and burned with mortification.

It had been only hours since the only man who'd ever seen me without clothes had been my husband. It was demoralizing and degrading to let Doc look at me, but I knew I had to just let him do it. I'd been bleeding. Bleeding. And his eyes showed nothing but respect and sadness as he quickly looked me over.

When he was finished, I climbed quickly out of the shower and wrapped myself in a towel.

At some point after wanting to die of shame, I'd become angry. So very, very angry.

"I'm sor—"

"Stop saying that!" I snapped before dropping my head. Doc was an innocent party, he didn't deserve my wrath.

"Go eat and then get some sleep," he said calmly, opening the door to the bathroom so I could walk out. "We have to be ready to go by ten."

I stopped abruptly at the edge of the living room as Peg caught my eyes from her place in the kitchen.

"I'm not going to North Carolina," I informed them both. "I have some money stashed. It's enough to buy us some plane tickets to the US if either of you wants to go with me."

I looked back to Doc. "Thank you so much for your help today. I don't know what I would have done if you hadn't been here, and none of this is your fault."

I turned back to where Peg was walking slowly toward me. "It's Patrick's fault," I said, and watched her face fall. "I don't ever want to see him again."

***

I walked gingerly to my room and proceeded to get dressed and packed quickly, anxious to be gone from there. We left for the airport an hour later, and I carried nothing with me but the backpack I'd used for school, filled with clothes and the wad of cash I'd fished out of my hiding spot.

Peg decided that she would go with me, but Doc said he needed to take the steamer so he could meet Ham and the rest of the guys in North Carolina. I didn't care.

I was content to go by myself, but a part of me was glad I'd have Peg there. She took care of all the arrangements, buying the tickets to New York City with the cash I'd had hidden for a rainy day in my sock drawer. It was a good thing that she and Doc were so willing to step in for me. A really good thing.

Because the moment I'd announced that Patrick was at fault for all that had happened to me, I came to the awful realization that it was true. It was absolutely true. And it was too much for me to handle on top of every other thing I'd endured over the past week.

I didn't speak at all for the rest of the day.

Not on the plane to New York, or when Peg tried to discuss where we'd go from there.

I still hadn't spoken when we climbed onto a bus in Port Authority on our way to Texas, or when Peg rented us a small house on the outskirts of Austin with the money Robbie had given her just days before he died.

I didn't speak for months.

Not one word.

My voice was frozen in my throat. I had nothing left in me to say.

Chapter 38

Patrick

I was practically vibrating with excitement when we pulled our bikes into the parking lot of the pub where we were meeting Doc and the women. The last week and a half had been hell, and I was anxious to get it over with.

Moira had been sick as shit the entire trip, and I'd been uncomfortable as hell trying to comfort her while maintaining an appropriate distance. It was an odd situation we found ourselves in, and I couldn't help but feel very, very sorry for this woman who was carrying my child. She didn't deserve to be alone with a group of people she barely knew, especially when the only woman who could have helped had refused to say one word in her direction.

I was glad Vera was so loyal to my wife. I was. But I could have fucking killed her for refusing to even acknowledge Moira when she was so sick. I'd been helpless to do anything but talk quietly to the poor woman and occasionally rub her back until she fell into an exhausted sleep. Even that had made my skin crawl like I was doing something wrong.

It didn't help matters that I'd barely slept. I couldn't—not without nightmares plaguing me. Every scenario—from the things I'd done to things that I prayed would never happen—had flashed through my dreams. It had been easier to stay awake, but after a week with only a few hours of sleep I was feeling a bit fuzzy about the edges.

We'd left Moira and Vera back at our hotel while we met up with my women, and I hoped that their forced interaction would help them find some common ground. Unfortunately for all of us, Moira was going to be around for a long time and I knew as soon as Amy showed up things would become even more uncomfortable. I hoped that maybe things could settle down between the two women before Vera saw my wife again and her loyalty was brought to the forefront.

My wife. God, I missed her.

I couldn't wait to get my hands on Amy again. It felt like I'd been waiting an eternity for her to arrive. I didn't even care that she'd had time to stew and probably become even more angry with me. As long as she was with me, I was willing to wait a lifetime for her forgiveness.

When we walked into the pub, the first thing I noticed was the grim look on Doc's face. My stomach clenched in apprehension when I realized he was alone.

"Where are dey?" I yelled frantically, searching the mostly empty bar.

"Patrick—" Doc said.

"Where is me wife?"

"Calm down, son," Ham warned, gripping my shoulder. "Let the man talk."

My teeth came together with a crack as I waited anxiously for Doc to begin speaking again, and it seemed like hours before he opened his mouth.

"They're not here."

"What de fuck are ye goin' on about?" I yelled again, grimacing as Ham's hand dug into my shoulder.

"Amy wouldn't come," Doc said flatly. "Your ma wasn't about to let her go off on her own, so she went with her."

"Ye left dem in Ireland alone?" I roared, and before I could take a single step forward, a huge pair of arms wrapped around me, holding me in place.

"No, *you* did. *I* put them on a flight to New York before I left."

My body relaxed in relief before tensing once again. "I have to go," I said frantically, trying to pull away from Ham's arms. "I have to go."

"They're not there," Doc informed me, causing me to freeze. "I'm not sure where they were headed from there, but your ma said New York was too expensive. She said to let you know that she'd write you at the club as soon as they got settled."

My vision filled with red as Doc calmly told me that my wife and mother were traveling by themselves across a country they didn't know. It didn't even occur to me that America was where Amy felt most at home. The only thing I could imagine were the two most important people in my life stranded and afraid—alone somewhere with no one to help them or protect them. I was so unbelievably scared that it immediately turned to overwhelming anger at the man in front of me.

The sound that came out of my throat was inhuman, and I lunged, taking Ham with me as I went for Doc's throat.

I was out cold before I even made contact.

***

"**Y**e didn't have to knock me out," I told Charlie, as I nursed a beer at the bar. "I wouldn't have killed him."

Charlie snorted beside me. "He would have killed you, you moron."

"Fuck off! Yer a right prick, ye know dat?"

"I don't understand half of what you say, you realize that, right?" he answered with a laugh. "I'm not kidding. The man knows human anatomy better than I know my wife's pussy. He could kill you with a fuckin' toothpick."

"What de hell do I do?" I asked in defeat, drinking the watered down beer in front of me. American beer was fucking disgusting.

"It's time to go home, man," Charlie informed me with a slap on the back as he got to his feet. "Nothin' you can do in this shit hole, and your mom's gonna write to the clubhouse, yeah? Could be she's already sent the letter. No way to know until we get there."

I nodded, following him out of the bar on unsteady legs that I tried to disguise.

No one could know how fucking terrified I was that I'd never get that letter.

***

"Where de fuck are ye, Mum?" I said into the phone, trying to turn my back on the crowded room behind me.

It had been three agonizing weeks since that day in the pub, and I'd finally received a letter that morning in the mail with a telephone number where I could reach Mum. She hadn't said anything about Amy, and I prayed that wherever they were, at least they were still together.

I was livid and frightened. Everything was different in Oregon, the fucking roads, the money, even the language. Christ, we all spoke English, but there was quite a difference between how I spoke it and how they did. The slang was fucked, the beer tasted like shite, and I'd been going out of my mind with worry.

"Don't use that tone with me," Mum warned, before sighing. "I'm sorry it's taken so long."

"Where are ye?"

"I'd love to tell ye, but we both know the minute I did, ye'd be on yer way here and I don't think now is the best time."

I sputtered, completely caught off guard by her words. Not the best time? What the fuck did that mean?

"Explain yerself," I said, glancing over my shoulder to make sure no one was paying any attention to the way I was losing it.

"Amy is not ready to see ye."

"She's me wife, goddammit!" My voice rose and I could feel my temples throbbing as I tried to calm myself.

"Yer wife willna speak to ye. She doesn't want to see ye," she replied apologetically.

"And yer just goin' to play her game den, is it? Whose Mum are ye?"

"Don't ye dare, Patrick Gallagher!" Mum's voice went from calm to furious in a moment. "Ye've made yer bed, and ye know it. I've got a heartbroken girl here who refuses to speak, I don't have time fer yer male posturin'!' "

"Refuses to speak?" I asked, confused as fuck. "What are ye goin' on about?"

"She's not said a word since we left Ireland," she replied, her voice going quiet again. "I'm not sure why, but—"

"Tell me where ye are, Mum. Tell me where ye are and I'll come take care of it." I was pleading now, the fear in Mum's voice causing my heart to race as I remembered Amy when I'd found her at her parents' house, unwashed and afraid. Even then, she'd matched me word for word. I couldn't imagine anything that could make her stop speaking for any length of time.

"I'm sorry, son. I'm afraid ye'd make it worse."

"Mum—"

"Call again in a few days—"

"Mum!"

"I love ye."

"Mum!"

She hung up and I pulled the phone away from my face in disbelief before throwing it against the wall.

"FUCK!"

I scrubbed my hands over my face, then glanced at the phone that was hanging by its curly cord over the top of the bar. I couldn't even call back if I'd wanted to; I'd smashed the thing to pieces in my rage.

What the fuck was happening? I'd make her worse? I was her bloody husband! I loved her more than anyone on the entire fucking earth. I'd do anything for her.

"Is everyt'in' okay, Trick?" Moira asked quietly, coming up behind me to set a hand on my back.

"Not now, Moira," I mumbled, shrugging her off.

I had to get away from this place. I glanced up to see half of the room watching me curiously, and began tapping my fingers in a familiar rhythm against my thigh. I realized all of them were watching as I lost my mind, and my face fell into an expressionless mask.

"Let's take a ride, brother. Yeah?" Charlie called as he passed me, thumping me on the back.

Yes. That was exactly what I needed.

I followed him outside and climbed on the bike Ham had loaned me until I could work off a trade.

My wife was hurting and silent somewhere and wanted nothing to do with me.

It was the lowest point in my life.

Chapter 39

Amy

I had nightmares.

To be completely honest, they didn't happen every night. They only happened on the nights that I actually slept.

I was a mess. Peg and I had rented a small house, not unlike the one we'd had in Ireland, and I'd barely left it since the day we moved in. I just... couldn't. Peg had found a job pretty quickly in the produce department of the local grocery store, which meant we had money to live, but me? I barely contributed at all.

I cooked and cleaned like a stay at home housewife, but I could barely walk outside to grab the mail at the end of the driveway. Anytime I stepped outside, it felt like I was being watched. Logically, I knew the chances of Malcolm finding me in the small Texas town were nearly impossible. We'd changed busses so many times that the FBI would have a hard time pinpointing our location.

However, fear wasn't logical—it wasn't easily overlooked or pushed past. Instead, every day I had to push myself a little farther. I'd go to the store with Peg for groceries, or to the library for books. I'd step out onto the porch while Peg was at work and count to sixty, then one hundred, then I'd set the timer on the stove for five minutes, rushing back inside with a racing heart and sweaty palms as soon as the designated count was over.

I didn't even *look* the same. The weight I'd lost in my misery had sharpened my cheekbones, my hand was still taped because I couldn't bear to look at it, and… my hair. It had begun to grow back in, which made me look a little less like a freak, but it was silver. Every single strand had grown back in gray. The premature graying must have been genetic, but I couldn't help but feel that it was a mutation caused by trauma. I could barely look at myself in the mirror. It was an outward physical sign that I'd never be the same again. I hated the way I looked, hated the way I couldn't seem to get past my fears and memories. I hated the way my fingers throbbed in some sort of phantom pain, pain that I didn't even recall having when I'd lost two of them as a child.

Peg had no idea how to help me. I think she may have felt just as lost as I was. She didn't coddle me, that wasn't her style, but she never pushed me, either. She was just there, ready for anything I needed and willing to do whatever she could to help. She continued to talk to me like I was normal, like I had any opinion on which bed to buy at the local thrift store—which we'd gone to before the agoraphobia had kicked in—or what I'd like for dinner, even though I never answered her.

She tried. God knows she tried.

It had been two and a half months since we'd left Ireland and I hadn't spoken a single word since that day.

My body was healing, but my mind seemed to be stuck in those first few days after the attack. Certain things would set me off, like the trip to the hardware store a couple of blocks away, or the floral print couch Peg found at a yard sale for free.

Then, out of the blue, Peg decided to try something different to get my attention. She'd heard some co-workers discussing a lady that did acupuncture to treat everything from eczema to high blood pressure. I'm not sure if she thought I'd balk enough at the thought of some stranger sticking dozens of little needles in my body to speak up, or if she'd thought it would actually work—but two days later, she told me that I had an appointment.

The fear of leaving the house was getting better. I wasn't ready to take a cross-country trip, but I was able to leave the house for short periods as long as I was with Peg. I called it progress, though I'm sure Peg would have just called it annoying.

The acupuncture place was calming. There was some low nature sounds coming from the boom box in the corner, some incense burning on two different shelves, and the acupuncturist seemed high. Okay, maybe she wasn't high, but the woman was seriously calm, far more calm than I'd ever seen anyone. It was like she'd taken both happy pills and some sort of downer... life was good, but she wasn't going to get all riled up about it.

Everything went okay, and I wasn't even nervous. She sat me down in a comfortable chair after Peg told her I was mute. Fucking mute? I just didn't talk. It wasn't like I couldn't.

Of course I didn't correct her. It wasn't until she went into her whole little spiel that I finally had the urge to speak. No, that's not quite right. I didn't have the urge to talk, I just wanted to scream bloody murder. It was six words. Just six words left me screaming inside my head.

"Any chance you might be pregnant?"

She glanced between Peg and I, knowing I wouldn't answer, but just as Peg opened her mouth to speak...

I nodded.

It was one sharp jerk, an almost involuntary movement, but it changed so much.

The acupuncturist rambled on about different parts of my body she wouldn't touch in case I was pregnant, and I met Peg's eyes, seeing in them the same fear I was feeling. We were both counting back, trying to pinpoint when and how long.

It was silly. I knew when. I knew exactly when.

The acupuncture had actually helped a little, and I think it might have helped a lot if I hadn't had such a devastating realization right there in the office. I nodded in agreement to coming back for another appointment, and attempted a noncommittal smile as the lady gave me a list of times she taught yoga at the local YMCA. There was no way I'd go to a public place like that, but it was nice for her to offer.

Peg didn't say anything about it after we left. It was as if we'd both agreed to ignore it, at least until we wrapped our brains around it.

Two days later, I heard Peg talking in the living room while I lay on my bed. She did that a lot—talked even if I wasn't in the room. I think sometimes she just got sick and tired of the quiet and had to do something to fill it. It was a feeling I could completely understand. I was sick of the quiet too, but I had no idea how to change it.

My lack of period was a solid indication that I was indeed pregnant, but I didn't have any other symptoms. I wasn't sick, or hungry, or peeing all the time. I just hadn't had a period. For a few hours, I'd tried to pretend that the stress had just messed up my cycle, but I couldn't let my mind linger on that scenario for long. I'd become a realist sometime between getting married and being abandoned in Ireland, and I knew deep in my gut that I was carrying a child.

Peg's voice got closer to my bedroom door, and I was startled to hear another voice as she opened it. A familiar voice.

"Yer hair," he gasped in confusion, looking between his mom and me for an explanation. "What did ye do?"

"I don't know what to do anymore, Patrick," Peg said quietly, looking at me in apology. "I know I told ye to wait, and I still think that was the right thing, but… it's good yer here now."

She patted him on the back before stepping out of the room and closing the bedroom door quietly behind her.

"I've missed ye so much, me love," he said sweetly, moving toward me only to come to an abrupt stop as my hand flew up between us. I only wanted to stop him so I could get a handle on the emotions battling for supremacy in my brain, but the movement was so sharp it almost looked like I was trying to hit him.

It was so good to see him. He looked great. He was letting his beard grow out and his hair had gotten longer, too. But he barely looked like the man I'd married, and that made me nervous, even though it shouldn't.

As I was cataloguing all of the changes in his appearance, he seemed to be doing the same thing because I watched as his eyebrows drew down into a frown and he gently reached out to touch my still taped-up fingers.

"What happened to yer hand?" he asked quietly. "What de hell is goin' on?"

I didn't answer. Of course I didn't. Any thought of doing so had been erased with the glaring reminder of my injuries... and the reason for them.

"Answer me," he said, jamming his hands into his pockets like he didn't know what to do with them. "Amy? What de fuck?"

I didn't look away from him as his worry turned to frustration and then anger.

"Mum!" he called, watching me closely. "Get in here, Mum!"

The door opened quickly, and there was Peg, with tears in her eyes.

"I thought for sure—"

"What de fuck is goin' on?" he asked incredulously.

"Ye need to tell him," she ordered, her eyes full of sympathy. "He deserves to know."

"What do I deserve to know?"

"I'm pregnant," I said, the words scratchy and a bit wobbly.

He looked back and forth between Peg and I as if he was trying to gauge our sincerity, and then I watched as the most beautiful little grin spilt his lips. He lifted a hand to run his fingers over his beard, and it was evident that he was trying to keep a handle on his excitement. As much as I loved watching the transformation come over his face, I couldn't let it continue.

"It's not yours," I said flatly.

Peg let out a pained gasp and fled the room, but it took Patrick a little longer to fully comprehend my words.

"What a horrible t'ing to say," he rasped in disbelief.

I laughed bitterly. "Horrible, yes, but also true."

"Why would ye—"

"We didn't have sex after Robbie died," I cut him off. "I had my period after that."

He gaped at me for what seemed like forever, and I knew he was trying to come to terms with the information I'd just given him. I saw the exact moment he realized the full extent of my announcement because his face morphed into an expression I'd never seen before.

"If ye were attemptin' to pay me back," he said, "Ye could not have done a better job of it."

I laughed. For the first time in months, I laughed, and I did it so hard that my whole body was shaking and my breath was wheezing in and out of my chest. I was hysterical, unable to curb the noise even as he stared at me in disbelief and disgust.

"Filthy slapper," he said, his hands coming out of his pockets. He stepped forward menacingly, and my laughter finally cut off in shock as he leaned forward.

Then he spit in my face.

I didn't wipe it off.

I *was* filthy. I was disgusting. But so was he.

He left that day, slamming out of the house before my tears had even washed away his saliva from my face.

He'd had no idea. None. He'd looked right past my shorn off hair and mangled hand. And that's what was so heartbreakingly funny.

My pregnancy was most definitely payback.

It just hadn't been mine.

Chapter 40

Patrick

She'd wrecked me.

I didn't understand how she could have fucked someone else after I left. She'd only had a few bloody days to do so, but there was no way I'd misinterpreted her words. She was pregnant, and it was not by me. Unless it was the Lord's child, she'd had another man between her thighs.

Repeating her words over and over in my head made the ride home seem hours shorter than the ride to Texas had been. When I'd been anxious to see Amy and Mum, the ride had seemed to be unending. However, as I pulled into the driveway of the small house I'd been able to afford on my pay from the garage, it was as if the trip had taken mere moments.

There's a saying, 'Hell hath no fury like a woman scorned'. The words have been bastardized a bit since William Congreve first wrote them—but the sentiment was the same.

She'd been angry at me—with good reason—and she'd paid me back in kind.

The thought of another man's hands on her made me shake with fury. I couldn't even fathom it, and more than once during the ride I'd had to pull off the side of the road to be sick. It made me want to hurt someone. It made me want to hurt her.

Fuck her and her disgusting American views of marriage and fidelity. Fuck her short hair and her missing fingers and her accent.

I'd never speak of her again. It was the only way I'd survive without her, because as much as I hated her—I loved her still, and that made me angrier than anything else.

The house was quiet as I unlocked the front door and stepped inside. It was late and Moira hadn't known I was coming home so soon, so she hadn't left any lights on in the house.

What had I been thinking, renting one place for all of us? Had I been planning on living with both my wife and Moira in the same house? The decision seemed incredibly stupid as I pulled off my boots.

I moved down the hallway as quietly as I could, but Moira's voice still called out from her open bedroom door.

"Trick?"

"I'm back," I replied quietly, stopping in her doorway for a reason I couldn't name.

"I didn't expect ye back for a while yet," she said sleepily, raising up to her elbow and resting her head on her palm. "Is everyt'in' alright?"

I didn't know how to answer her. Was everything alright? No. However, there was no way to explain the situation without being completely insensitive and cruel.

The next words were out of my mouth before I could stop them.

"Can I sleep wit' ye?"

Her eyebrows rose in response, but she didn't turn me away as she watched me silently. After a few moments, I dropped my hand from the door. It hadn't been kind of me to ask, especially not after I'd just rode thousands of miles away from her to visit another woman.

"Yes, ye can," she replied as I began to turn away.

I looked back at her face and nodded once as I pulled off my shirt. I knew that I probably smelled like crap, but I was suddenly so exhausted that I couldn't even make myself have a shower. I dropped my jeans and climbed in as she moved over to give me room.

I stared at the ceiling for a long time with Moira wrapped around me, sleeping deeply. She was a good woman—built for the life we'd made in the few months we'd been in Oregon. She got on well with everyone, always looked beautiful even as she grew larger, and was genuinely kind to me even when I didn't deserve it.

I closed my eyes and begged not to dream of my wife.

As far as I was concerned, Amy was dead.

Chapter 41

Amy

That first year was horrible. It took months and months of speaking with a free counselor at a rape crisis center, hours of yoga, and long talks with Peg before I felt anywhere near back to normal, and even then... well, normal was relative.

I'd realized that I had to get my shit together after Patrick had left that day and I'd found Peg crying quietly in the kitchen. She'd suspected that something more had happened to me in Ireland than she'd been told and my insistence that Patrick wasn't the one who'd gotten me pregnant was the confirmation she'd dreaded. I hated telling her about it, and I'd barely skimmed the details, but she knew enough by the time I was done that she'd been both relieved that I'd finally opened up and completely livid at what I'd gone through.

I understood both emotions. I was angry, too, but life as I knew it would never be the same—not ever. And I realized then that I was going to have to figure out where I went from there. In a little over six months, I was having a baby. I needed to get my shit together.

So I did. It was one of the hardest things I'd ever done. I worked at it. Therapy was *work*, and it *hurt*, but I relished it—because with each passing week, things became a little clearer. My fears became a little easier to live with. My nightmares tapered off from every night, to once a week and then once a month.

I learned to think of Malcolm as a man, a very bad man, but not a monster that was hiding around every corner. I learned how to defend myself. I learned how to stop looking over my shoulder every second.

I learned how to live in the new normal I'd created.

And then, out of the ashes of the person I used to be, my son was born.

I named him Phoenix.

***

"I can't believe how small he is," I said dreamily to Peg while I watched Phoenix nurse.

Breastfeeding calmed me in a way that therapy and yoga never had. It made me feel connected to something bigger, something more important than myself. It was odd really, because in the month leading up to Nix's birth I'd been riddled with anxiety about it.

I knew that breasts weren't purely sexual from a biological standpoint, but that didn't mean that breastfeeding wasn't a trigger for me. It was. I didn't understand why it bothered me so badly, especially since my shirt hadn't even come off during the rape. I didn't have to understand the trigger, however, for it to have meaning, and by the time Nix was born, I'd broken out in never-ending hives again at just the thought of trying to feed him anything other than formula.

I was miserable as I tried to think of any excuse I could not to breastfeed my child, and guilt ridden over giving him formula when I was perfectly capable of nursing him myself. My hang-ups filled me with self-loathing and the hormones coursing through my body made everything so much worse.

Eventually, someone noticed my odd behavior, and before I left the hospital one of the nurses walked into the room with a counselor trailing behind her. She was someone I'd seen around the crisis center, and she'd known me immediately by name. I'm not sure if Peg had called them, or if the nurses had, but I'll never be able to thank that woman enough for the way she helped us.

The first time I nursed Phoenix, I cried the entire time. Not because it felt wrong, but because breastfeeding him was another one of the things that had almost been taken from me as a result of that night. It was freeing. It felt like I was fighting back.

"He'll be grown before ye know it," Peg answered with a small smile, folding towels on the couch next to me.

"Have you heard from Patrick yet?" I asked, though I knew she hadn't.

When Patrick had left over a year ago, he'd been livid. I understood it, and as time went on, I'd forgiven him for it. Therapy had helped me let go of the anger I felt toward my husband—the resentment and the blame. The things that had happened to me were not his fault, and I knew in my heart that he would have done anything he could to stop it. It was just... life. I'd been targeted by a psychopath, and it wasn't anyone's fault but Malcolm's.

That didn't mean that I agreed with Patrick completely cutting Peg out of his life. Me, I understood. He didn't know the situation and he believed that I'd betrayed him in the worst possible way. For a long time, I hadn't wanted anything to do with him, either. But Peg loved him and she missed him, and I thought he was acting like an asshole for refusing to answer her letters and phone calls.

"He'll come around," she answered me sadly. "He just needs some more time."

"He's being an idiot," I commented stubbornly, moving Nix to the other breast. "A stubborn idiot."

"Well, he isn't the only one," she replied.

"He has a family, Peg."

"When the hell are ye goin' to start callin' me Mum?"

"He has a family, *Mum*."

"Yer his family," she argued. "He'd be back here in an instant and ye know it."

I looked down and smoothed back Nix's wild black hair, ignoring her words. Perhaps Patrick would come running if I told him the whole story. Maybe he'd even move to be near us... maybe he'd raise Nix as his own. But as I gazed at my son, I knew I'd never be the reason that Patrick left his child. I couldn't do that to him and I couldn't do that to his daughter that Doc had mentioned one of the times Peg had called their garage.

"We're just fine without him," I announced, ignoring the pang in my chest that the words invoked. "It just wasn't meant to be."

"Yer both a couple of stubborn eejits," she grumbled as she stood up and walked away.

God, I was so grateful for her.

Chapter 42

Patrick

"A toast!" I slurred, a goofy smile on my face. "To loyal women and babbies who look just like dere das!"

"Hear, hear!" Slider called back from across the room.

I'd been making that exact toast and several similar ones all night long. I knew I was probably past the point of being annoying at that point, but I didn't give a fuck.

Moira had given birth just two days before, and I had a beautiful daughter with a head of bright red hair.

Mine. No doubt about it.

Becoming a father was like nothing I'd ever known before. It was terrifying and exhilarating and exhausting all at once, and I couldn't contain my joy. I wanted to tell everyone I came across about this beautiful creature that I'd made, and more than one woman at the grocery store had nodded in amusement as I'd told them all about her.

My Brenna. The smartest and most gorgeous baby that had ever been born.

I was pissed, completely and utterly drunk.

My mum had called again that day, and I'd refused to answer even though I'd been dying to tell her about Brenna. Dear God, I missed my mum—but speaking to her, even briefly, would open back up a chapter in my life that I was trying very hard to forget. I couldn't have one without the other, and though I tried to tell myself that I'd moved past Amy's betrayal, the drunken stupor that had started at three in the afternoon was a clear indication I hadn't.

Instead, I was making toasts to women who were loyal and babes who looked like their fathers. I was a bloody idiot.

I stumbled against a table, and braced my hand on the top of it, looking up to meet Ham's serious face.

"Might want to slow down, Poet," he warned oddly.

Poet, a name that I'd seemed to have fallen into within my first few months at the club and had followed me as I patched in. The name was fine, a lot better than some of the others. But I hated the memories it evoked.

"De night is young," I said back cheerily. "A toast—"

I stopped speaking when a large body stood up next to me abruptly.

"If I hear one more word come out of your mouth, I'll lay ya out," Doc said quietly, his body tight with anger.

He was staring at me, really staring, and the menace rolling of his body was unbelievable.

"De fuck?" I asked stupidly before snapping my mouth shut.

I remembered the day in North Carolina when Charlie had warned me about Doc, and since then I'd seen his expertise in handling the human body on more than one occasion. He was a fucking walking textbook on anatomy, and I knew even in my clouded brain that if I didn't take his warning, there was a very likely chance he'd make good on his threat.

"You have no idea—"

"Doc," Ham growled warningly.

"No," Doc snapped back, not even bothering to glance in the President's direction. "You have no fuckin' idea what you're talking about, boy. None. Your head is so far up your ass it's a wonder you know night from day."

"What are ye goin' on about?" I asked, taking an unsteady step backward. His tone and the sureness of his words were making me nervous, and I felt my palms begin to sweat. What the fuck was he talking about?

"You left your wife in Ireland to take off with the woman you had on the side," he hissed. "You want to talk about loyalty?" The veins in his neck were throbbing.

"Come on, brother," Charlie said, coming up on my side and wrapping his arm over my shoulder. "You look ready to pass out and I'm not dragging your ass to bed later."

He turned me away from the table and started walking me toward the back hallway, and though I didn't protest, my head turned so I could watch Doc as we left the room. He stared me down until I could no longer see him.

The whole encounter had been odd as fuck and I tried to focus on remembering his words as Charlie tipped me into bed and left the room. The club didn't get in the middle of brothers and their women. Not ever. That wasn't what they were about. So to have a member speak up like that was completely fucking strange.

***

I woke up the next morning with my heart racing, and as soon as I'd showered and remembered the night before, I knew I needed to speak with Doc. I was angry and embarrassed that he'd threatened me in front of the entire club, and I wanted to know why the fuck he would do it. My life outside the club wasn't his business. There was a clear line that wasn't meant to be crossed, and he'd jumped the bloody thing.

"Doc!" I called out as I saw him walking out of the garage. "Got a minute?"

I didn't think he was going to acknowledge me as he walked into the sunshine, but as he hit the grass outside, he paused and turned to look at me.

"What de hell was dat about last night?" I asked, stopping a couple feet from him. "Ye have a problem wit' me?"

"Forget it," he answered, dismissing me as he pulled a cigar out of his shirt pocket.

"Ye had somet'in' to say, now say it," I argued, annoyed that my accent was thickening with my frustration. It was a tell that I hadn't been able to get a handle on yet.

"What you do is your business," he said calmly. "Just don't like hearin' you bad-mouthin' a good woman."

"A good woman?" I asked incredulously, my eyebrows rising. "Amy?"

"You got no fuckin' idea what you're doin'," he said shaking his head. "Playin' house with your side piece, then comin' to the club and fuckin' drinkin' yourself into a stupor so you don't have to remember where you should be and what you should be doin'."

"I'm not playin' shite."

"Do what you need to do, Patrick," he said, my Christian name sounding odd coming from him. "But keep your mouth shut in my presence. Won't give you another warnin'."

"Ye have a hard on for me wife? Dat what dis is about?"

His hand was around my throat and his fingers digging into my windpipe before the last word was completely formed.

I hadn't even seen it coming.

"You worthless piece of shit," he hissed, spit from his mouth hitting my face as I tried to pry his fingers from my throat. "You fuckin' left her there!"

I could hear men yelling as they caught sight of us, but all of my attention was focused on Doc's mouth and the words flying out so fast I had a hard time keeping up.

"You left her to be fuckin' tortured. You left her to be raped. Then you come back here and run your mouth about her? That poor girl that never done anything wrong but make the mistake of loving a worthless piece of trash like you?"

"Let him go, Doc," Ham said quietly, his words no less than an order.

Doc relaxed his hand and I finally took a wheezing breath as I dropped to my knees. The world seemed to be moving in slow motion, all around me men were yelling, but I couldn't hear anything above the roaring in my ears.

I closed my eyes and the memories came before I could stop them.

Amy kissing me goodbye like she couldn't bear to let me go.

The trip to North Carolina.

Doc alone at the meet-up.

Mum's letter.

"I've got a heartbroken girl here who refuses to speak."

Riding to Texas.

Amy's taped up fingers.

"She's not said a word since we left Ireland."

Amy's shaved head.

"It's not yours."

Spitting on her.

"I've got a heartbroken girl that refuses to speak."

"It's not yours."

"I'm afraid ye'd make it worse."

Dear God, what had I done?

The noise that came out of me was like nothing I'd ever heard before, and I didn't know how to stop it. I sounded pathetic, and I knew that the men were looking at me. I knew they thought I was a pussy.

I didn't care.

I couldn't stop the sound. It was the only thing that drowned out Mum's voice.

"I've got a heartbroken girl that refuses to speak."

I wished Doc had killed me.

Chapter 43

Amy

When Nix was four months old, I went back to school. I wasn't sure what I wanted to do yet, but I knew that a college education would be important when it was time for me to start a career. Peg had been more than willing to bring in all of our income, but I hated the fact that she worked so hard and I got to stay home. I hated taking advantage of her and I knew that if I went to school, I could eventually find a great job and support her for once. I couldn't wait for that day.

About a month after I'd started my classes, I was on my way home when Nix started to scream in the back seat. I sighed, and pushed my hair away from my face. I would never again plan my classes so I arrived at the school's daycare right before Nix's afternoon feeding. If I stayed at the daycare to nurse him, we'd get home almost an hour later than normal, but it never failed that if I tried to race home before I fed him he'd start screaming within a mile of our house.

"It's okay, son," I crooned loudly over his wailing. "Almost there, bud!"

I rolled onto our short, gravel driveway, and was out of the car as soon as I'd placed it in park.

"You're okay," I said, pulling him out of his seat, "Good grief, it's like I haven't fed you in days!" He looked at me for a second, all noise paused, then screamed again while I laughed at his frantic fingers gripping and pulling at my shirt.

"Okay, let's get inside."

I turned to the front door and stopped short.

Patrick.

I watched his face as his eyes landed on my son, screaming and squirming against me, and I could barely breathe.

He looked good. More muscular than he'd ever been before, his beard reaching the top of his collarbone, and tattoos peppering his defined forearms. God, I'd missed him. Missed him and hated him for so long.

"Your mum's at work," I finally choked out, bouncing Nix, who didn't give a shit that I was freaking out.

"I—" Patrick ran his fingers over the top of his hair that was pulled into a stubby ponytail at the back of his neck. "Can we talk? It looks like ye need to get her inside."

I startled, looking down at my son's cream one-piece outfit, and smiled fondly. I guess it was a little hard to tell…

"He's a boy," I replied, finally continuing toward the house.

"Shite, I'm sorry," Patrick replied, his face turning red.

I laughed a little at his discomfort. Leave it to a baby to break the ice.

"Well, he's not in blue and he's kind of pretty," I said with a small smile. "How would you know?"

I let us into the house and moved right toward the couch in the living room, grabbing a thin receiving blanket on my way. Nix wasn't going to wait any longer, and after five months, I'd lost most of my anxiety about breastfeeding him in mixed company. Patrick would just have to deal.

We sat at opposite sides of the couch, and I ignored Patrick as I threw the blanket over my shoulder and Nix's head, quickly pulling up my shirt and unclasping the front of my bra. The house was so quiet that we both heard as Nix latched on hungrily, and I felt my face heat as the slurping noises ensued. Christ on a cracker.

"He was hungry," Patrick said quietly, chuckling a little.

"He gets pissed when he has to wait for a feeding," I replied, looking up to finally meet Patrick's eyes for the first time in over a year.

My breath caught in my throat and I quickly looked down again. He was looking at us so tenderly that I had a hard time holding back my tears. Shit.

"Why didn't ye tell me?" Patrick asked hoarsely. "Why wouldn't ye say anyt'in'?"

My head snapped up, and I looked closely at his face.

"Who told you?"

"Doc—" he cleared his throat, rubbing at his eyes. "Doc said ye were raped?"

"I don't want to talk about it."

"But why? Why didn't ye *tell* me? I came for ye. I love ye." His hand reached out as if to touch me, then dropped to the upholstery between us. "Doc told me, and I wanted to come back for ye, but Brenna was just born, and *fuck* Amy, after how I'd behaved, I didn't think ye'd want to see me."

I swallowed hard, months of therapy forcing me to tell him the truth as I tried to ignore the tears in his eyes. "I blamed you. I hated you."

"What?" He seemed so confused that I'd blurted it out that way. Not that he'd necessarily disagreed... but he hadn't been expecting my answer. He obviously had no idea what I was talking about, and that's how I knew that Doc hadn't told him everything.

"I don't blame you anymore," I answered, shaking my head. "It wasn't fair. I know that now—but at the time, well, things were messed up for a while."

"Is it because I left ye?" he asked desperately. "I didn't want to leave ye! Ye know dat. I begged ye to leave first! God, I would have done anyt'in' for ye, ye have to know dat. Ye have to know dat I'd—"

"Shhh," I whispered to Nix as he startled at Patrick's loud voice.

Patrick ran the palms of his hands over his eyes, and I noticed the wedding band covering his anchor tattoo.

Nothing in that moment could have hurt worse.

"None of that matters anymore, does it?" I asked gently, gesturing with my chin toward his hand. "I guess things turned out the way they were supposed to."

Nix popped off my breast then, but I was frozen, watching as Patrick's eyes dropped to the ring on his finger. He ran his thumb over it and swallowed, then looked at me sadly.

"It's not legal. Moira just wanted—" his words cut off as Nix lost patience with me and tugged the blanket down over his face.

Half of my breast was bare, and I scrambled to pull my shirt down over it to hide the blue-veined skin.

Patrick made a low noise in his throat that I ignored as I turned Nix and situated him at my other breast with the blanket once again covering both him and my chest. My bra was still hanging on my shoulders, and I knew my nipple was hard under the t-shirt, but I didn't let myself think about it or bring more attention to it as I tried to hide it.

"Yer bigger," Patrick commented, his voice barely audible. "And ye've—"

"Stop," I demanded, raising my hand up between us.

"Yer right," he said with a nod. "I'd just imagined ye dis way so many times before. Our child at yer breast... dough ye did not bot'er coverin' up in me daydreams. Christ, how did we get here?"

"Life," I replied with a sad smile.

"I suppose so."

"Phoenix Gallagher, yer nan is home!" Peg called cheerily as she came in the front door, slamming it behind her. "Where are ye two—Patrick!"

"Hey, Mum." Patrick said, standing from the couch with a nervous smile on his face.

"My boy!" She stepped into him and wrapped her arms around his waist, and for a split second I was jealous that she got to do so, but I didn't. "Don't ye ever do that again!" She slapped him on the belly, then wrapped herself around him again, crying.

"I won't, I promise," he replied, meeting my eyes over her shoulder.

"Are ye hungry?" she asked, leaning back to look at him.

"I could eat," he replied with a chuckle, "And I brought ye photos of yer granddaughter."

The smile that lit up his face as he mentioned his daughter was so bright that I felt caught in it and unable to look away. It was joy and pride and contentment in physical form.

I'd never do anything to jeopardize that.

***

"So yer in school now?" Patrick asked as he sat on the other end of the sofa that night.

I'd just gotten Nix down for a few hours at least, and I'd pulled out my textbooks to try and get some schoolwork done. I couldn't put my life on hold, even though there was a man in the house that I could have watched and listened to for hours. Homework didn't get turned in if I didn't actually do it, and I couldn't afford to take any of my classes over again.

"Yeah, I started a couple of weeks ago."

"I remember when ye couldn't wait to be finished."

"Priorities have a way of changing when you're a single parent," I replied with a polite smile.

I wished so badly that things could go back to the easy way they were before, but I knew it would never happen again.

Too much had changed since I'd seen him last. Too much had changed since I'd left Ireland for good.

I'd changed.

I no longer knew how to banter back and forth with him.

"What are ye studyin'?"

"Business," I answered with an exaggerated expression of disgust. "Boring—but it will get me a job when I'm finished."

"Ye seem like yer doin' really well," he said, smiling back slightly. "I'm glad."

"We're doing alright," I said with a shrug, looking back down at my book.

A part of me wanted to look back up, to catalogue every single one of his features so I could replay it in my mind after he'd left. But there was another part, a stronger part, that refused to give him any of my attention. I loved him, I didn't think that would ever change, but I couldn't get past the fact that he'd ruined my life and then started a family with someone else.

As if I was so easily tossed away.

"I'm so sorry—" he started quietly.

"Don't. Don't, Patrick," I ordered cutting him off. "I don't want to talk about it."

"I love ye—"

"Go back to your family." I looked at him then, the handsome boy that had turned into a man almost overnight. "We both have new lives, let's just leave it at that, okay?"

He stared at me, waiting for me to say something else, but I was all tapped out. I knew that one day things wouldn't hurt so bad. I knew that one day I'd be able to look at him with fondness, remembering what we had and how full of dreams we'd been.

But I couldn't see any of that now. All I could see was every single thing I'd lost.

He left that night and I didn't cry. I was stronger than that. It didn't matter how much I still loved him. At the heart of me, I was still that girl who was used to people disappearing from my life. He was just one more face that I'd have to learn to live without.

And I did. I learned to live without him—until years later, when he came to me. I must have been a glutton for punishment, because the moment he needed me again, I opened my arms wide and let him back in.

It was as if I couldn't help myself—his emotions still had a way of gaining a reaction from me, even after years apart.

Chapter 44

Patrick

I raced toward Texas like the devil was chasing me.

For the last two months, I'd sat with my eight-year-old daughter while she cried for her mother… and I felt as if I was coming apart at the seams.

I hadn't started out loving Moira. How could I? I'd loved another so much, there hadn't been room for the woman carrying my child. There hadn't been room for anyone but Amy, and I'd so single-mindedly focused on getting her back that I'd had little to give Moira.

It had all changed, though, first when I'd thought Amy had fucked someone else and I'd gone straight home and into Moira's bed. And then, the moment I'd seen that redheaded beauty placed on Moira's chest, covered in nastiness, but still the most beautiful creature I'd ever seen.

No, I hadn't started out loving Moira, I'd never been in love with her, but I *had* loved her. Christ, I'd loved her as much as I was capable with the other half of me living in some small Texas town. My chest felt as if it would cave in at any moment as I got off the highway.

There was only one person I wanted. Even if I knew that it was the last place I should be, I found myself pulling into her driveway.

My bike wasn't even shut off before she was standing on the porch, her hand shielding her eyes from the sun.

"Patrick?"

I knew why she was surprised to see me. Hell, I hadn't seen her in six years. Mum had moved into a small apartment, and I'd had no connection to Amy except for the photos of her and her son that Mum had placed next to photos of Brenna and I all over her home. Amy and her son were always conspicuously absent during the times I'd brought Brenna to see Mum. She'd never even seen my daughter.

"I'm so sorry, Patrick," she said kindly as I moved toward her. "I'm so sorry about Moira."

Her words wrapped around me, sinking into my skin like razor-sharp talons.

She meant it. She was actually sorry that I'd lost the woman who'd taken me away from her.

I lost it.

I reached her on the porch and pulled her to me, my fingers digging into her back as I pressed my watery eyes against her throat. I shuddered when her hands slipped under my cut to grip my waist.

This was the only place I wanted to be. I couldn't bear to let go of her.

"It's okay, sweetheart," she whispered in my ear, her hands running lightly over my lower back. "Shhh."

I gasped, my breath heaving in my chest as I tried to pull myself together. What was it about this woman that made me lose control of myself? It had been that way since the moment I'd met her, and almost ten years later, that still hadn't changed.

"Why don't you come in?" she asked, pulling away slightly to grab my hand. "Nix is at a friend's house for a sleepover."

She turned away, and I tried to wipe my face off with my free hand as she pulled me into the cool house. My fingers tapped my thigh as I took the time to look her over, from the thick ropes of gray hair that hit the top of her back to the slim waist and round ass covered by worn out jeans.

"You hungry?" she asked, never letting go of my hand as she turned to me with a small smile.

My mouth was on hers before either of us knew what I was doing. It was harsh, our lips pressed roughly against our teeth, but it only took a second before her hands were gently brushing through my hair. It calmed me in an instant, and I pulled away slightly to meet her eyes.

They were clear and wide—gentle and understanding—and my breath hitched as I leaned forward again, giving her plenty of time to pull away.

She didn't.

She left her hands in my hair as I kissed her lips softly, learning the contours and texture again after so long.

"I'm sorry," I whispered into her mouth, not even sure what I was apologizing for. The years we'd spent apart? The way I'd kissed her so roughly? The fact that I'd just lost the woman who'd torn us apart and I was using her to console myself?

"It's okay," she said immediately. "You're okay."

I groaned and pushed her against the wall, crowding her with my body until one of my thighs was pressed between hers and she was the one who was groaning.

"I've missed ye," I said harshly, kissing her neck as guilt filled my chest. *"Christ."*

She pushed me away abruptly, and I was suddenly afraid as I met her eyes.

"We don't take the Lord's name in vain in this house," she said, reaching up to flick my forehead.

My surprised laugh turned into a sob, and I hid it by grabbing her around the waist and pulling her into me so I could press my trembling mouth against her throat. I licked and sucked at her skin. It tasted different than it had all those years ago, and I wondered briefly if it was age or having a baby that had changed it.

I lifted her up, and she wrapped her legs around my waist as I carried her down the hallway, past the room covered in Power Ranger posters and through the door I knew instinctively was hers.

Her bed was covered in a quilt that I knew my mother had made, and before I set her down, I ripped it off the bed. I didn't need any reminders that what I was doing was wrong.

I was using her, and for some reason I couldn't understand, she was letting me.

We fumbled and bumped into each other as I tried to strip her jeans off and she went for my cut. Christ, our hands had no idea where to go and we were moving as if we'd get caught at any moment—frantic and desperate.

By the time we were both naked, Amy was completely silent, even her breath had ceased.

"So many tattoos," she said softly, running her fingertips over my arm and down my hand until she'd reached my anchor and the silver ring that rested at the base of it "You didn't cover it."

She sounded surprised by that, and it baffled me.

"Of course not," I replied.

There were tears in her eyes when they met mine, but they didn't fall as I pushed her into the bed and crawled on top of her.

"Yer gorgeous," I said reverently as I knelt above her, covering her breasts with my hands. My heart was racing and my breath was ragged as I weighed them in my palms. She was bigger there, more slender in her waist and more wide through her hips and thighs, giving her an hourglass figure that she hadn't had when we were kids.

I immediately needed everything at once and I laid down on top of her so I could reach it all. I barely noticed when her chest stopped rising and falling beneath mine. When she still didn't move, I leaned back from where my mouth had been on her nipple. God, I loved that new taste.

Her history came back to me in a rush, and I pushed my hands against the bed to get off of her.

"I'm so sorry!" I practically yelled as I tried to move.

"You're okay!" she assured me. "I swear, you're fine. I'm not scared, I was just… taking it all in, you know?"

"Aye. I feel dat way meself."

I kissed the small smile off her face, and leaned down until I was on my side. I couldn't stop my wandering hands as they moved over her curves, and she moaned low as I finally reached the place between her thighs.

"So wet," I teased, as she gave an embarrassed smile.

"Lovely," she whispered back.

My balls throbbed at the word, and I felt my skin flush in one hot wave. I rolled over on top of her and pulled one leg over my arm until it was resting in the crook of my elbow and she was wide open to me.

"Lovely," I murmured into her mouth as I thrust hard inside her.

"Shit!" she gasped, her hips coming off the bed.

"Did I hurt ye?" I began to pull out, and her free leg was suddenly wrapped around my ass.

"Don't stop," she groaned. "Keep going."

I was beginning to sweat, and for a split second I hoped I'd remembered to put on deodorant that morning. Then I cursed myself silently for acting like an idiot. Who the fuck cared what I smelled like? I was inside the love of my life—there was no room for anything else in my head.

I felt like a kid with his first woman as I thrust in and out of her, watching her face so I could relearn what she liked and what she didn't. I wanted it to last forever. I never wanted to leave her body, but eventually whatever I was doing must have pushed her over the edge, because she went completely still beneath me and then shuddered over and over again.

I came only a few thrusts behind her, my arms shaking from holding myself above her, and my heart beating as if it was trying to escape my chest.

I fell beside her and pulled her against my chest, wrapping my arms and legs around her.

That's when everything came back to me.

"You okay?" she asked as I went stiff.

"Fuck knows," I answered honestly.

"You will be," she assured me, laying her head against my shoulder.

Her hands soothed me as I thought about what the hell I was doing.

I hadn't been able to focus on anything but getting to Amy, but I hadn't thought of what I'd do when I'd actually reached her. I hadn't planned on fucking her. It honestly hadn't even crossed my mind during the long ride from Oregon. I'd just needed to be near her, however that played out. I'd needed the comfort of her presence, the assurance that she was still out there in the world, happy and healthy and whole.

"I'm a right bastard, aren't I?" I sighed, kissing the side of her head.

"You're not so bad," she replied, running her fingers over my side. "Sometimes, the things we need don't make sense to anyone else. That doesn't mean that you're wrong to need them."

"Why did ye let me in?"

"Because you needed me."

"Because I needed to fuck ye?" I asked harshly, immediately regretting my words. I was angry at myself, not her.

"No," she answered seriously, leaning up to look at me. "Because you needed *me*. You could have fucked anyone. Don't try to make this about something it wasn't."

"I'm sorry."

"So am I. You've had a hard time of it," her American accent had slipped a little since we'd began talking, and I couldn't help the small sense of satisfaction it brought me. She was an American, she always had been, but occasionally I could hear Mum's odd mix of Scottish and Irish in her voice.

"I'm not sure what to do now," I confessed, reaching down to pull the sheet over us.

"You keep living and you take care of your girl."

"What about ye? How can I—"

"Patrick, no," she said, shaking her head. "We had our time, and I'd give anything to go back… but that's not possible."

"Of course it is."

"No, no it's not. I have a child. A *son*. And our life is here. Your life is with that club, and with your daughter."

My chest began to ache in a way that I'd become familiar with. I didn't want to hear what she was saying. I didn't want to think about anything else but the fact that she was right there with me, in my arms for the first time in so long.

I interrupted her words with my mouth, and proceeded to distract her.

I knew it wouldn't change anything, but I needed to stop thinking, if only for a little while.

I knew I'd be leaving the next morning without her.

I also knew I wouldn't be welcome again.

Chapter 45

Amy

My hands were shaking as I watched out the window, waiting for Patrick to arrive.

I hated it. I hated that I was so anxious to see him, even though I had more important things to worry about. I hated that he was driving to the small, two-story house I'd saved and scrimped for until I could afford the down payment, but still looked as beaten down and weathered as it had three years ago when I'd been full of dreams to repaint the walls and refinish the floors. I hated that I'd made Nix go to his best friend's house so he wouldn't have to endure the same agony I was in.

I hated most of all that Peg was dying in the small, downstairs bedroom in my house, and there was absolutely nothing I could do about it but wait.

It had been eight years since the day Patrick had come to my house, hurting and confused after Moira's death. I'd seen him occasionally in passing after I'd made him leave the next morning, and even more often after Peg had gotten sick, but I'd still never met his daughter.

According to Patrick, she'd been too upset after her mother's death to go very far from home, and by the time she seemed to be healing, Peg had refused to see her because she was so sick. She'd didn't want to be the cause of more pain, the crazy old broad. I couldn't understand how she could ever believe that knowing her and losing her would be worse than not knowing her at all.

Mum. She was Mum to me now, and my chest ached as I thought about how she'd taken care of me for half my life. I'd never heard from my parents again after they'd left me, and looking back, I'd barely missed them. How could I when I'd been pulled under a wing so kind and full of love as Peg's?

Tires crunched outside and I was brought back to the present. A truck was coming down the road, but I couldn't see who was inside it. I placed Mum's hand on the quilt she was wrapped in, and stepped quietly out of the room. There was no need to wake her if it was just someone who'd taken a wrong turn. None of the roads near my house were marked, so it happened more often than I liked.

The door was open, letting in a cool breeze, and I pushed the screen out of my way as I stepped onto the porch… and felt my legs buckle beneath me.

Memories flew through my head as my stomach lurched and I anxiously reminded myself of every technique I'd learned to calm my breathing.

What in the fucking hell was that man doing standing in my driveway?

"Amy?" Patrick asked, racing toward me from the driver's side door of the truck.

I waved him back as I caught my breath, gripping the post that held up my porch railing.

"Get the fuck off my property," I growled, looking at the second man.

"I'm just here to—"

"I don't give a flying fuck what you were doing. Leave."

The white clerical collar at his throat made me want to vomit—it was a response I'd had to train myself for years to get over. It wasn't socially acceptable to puke every time your mother brought you to Mass.

"What de fuck?" Patrick asked in confusion, stepping forward once before stopping himself. "He's just here for Mum's last rites. I thought she'd like to see a familiar face."

"I can guarantee your mother would do something to land her an extended stay in purgatory if she got one look at *him*," I retorted, feeling stronger with Patrick standing between me and the priest.

"Kevie?" Patrick asked, looking back toward the truck. His expression was a mask of absolute confusion, and in that moment I hated that I'd never told him the whole story about my attack. Watching Peg deteriorate was already breaking my heart, and I was afraid that seeing Kevie again was going to push me over the edge.

Kevie stepped forward, his face a mask of pious calm, and I wanted nothing more than to string him up in the nearest tree. I knew how to tie a fucking noose, I'd learned it for a history presentation in college. I still couldn't move past the fear, though. If Kevie knew where we were, then Malcolm might know, too.

It was too much.

"I'm sorry me presence offends ye, Amy," Kevie said calmly, "Very sorry. I did not realize dat after all dis time…"

"Are you fucking kidding me right now?" I hissed, hiding my shaking hands in my armpits as I crossed my arms. "After all these years? Look at my hand!"

I raised up the fingers that had bent and twisted from arthritis and poorly set bones. It was gnarly looking, and when I pressed both hands together, they looked like they belonged to two different people. While Phoenix was growing, I'd made it into a game—'the claw.' No matter how sore the joints felt, I'd tickle him with my left hand until he was practically peeing his pants.

I'd turned the disfigurement into something joyful, but standing just feet from Kevie had me looking at it in disgust once again.

"Your presence will offend me until it's buried six feet under," I announced flatly. "Even then, I hope you rot in hell."

Patrick's face was like stone and his fingers began tapping his leg as he turned to Kevie, "What's goin' on, Kevin?"

"Ye don't—" Kevie asked before turning to me. "Ye never told him?" He swallowed hard and turned scared eyes back to Patrick.

"No," I replied flatly, his frightened expression like a balm over the resentment I'd felt for years. "I didn't tell him that you're the one who found me after your brother tortured and raped me. I didn't tell him that you told me no one would believe me, and if they did, they wouldn't care."

Kevie's face fell, his remorseful eyes refusing to leave me even as Patrick spoke.

"Ye knew?" Patrick asked, meeting his oldest friend's eyes. "Ye fuckin' knew and ye never said anyt'in'? I've spoken to ye hundreds of times in de past fifteen years. Malcolm?"

I noticed then, while listening to them talk, that Patrick had lost a lot of his accent while we'd been in America. It wasn't something that I'd ever thought about, but hearing both of them at once made it clear how much thicker Kevie's accent was. Patrick still sounded like Ireland, but his inflections and pronunciation had become more and more Americanized. He also sounded more and more like Peg as we got older. I guess a mother's voice really is the most important sound a child hears as they grow.

The thought made my stomach clench as I glanced toward the window to Mum's room.

"How close are yer neighbors?" Patrick asked menacingly.

"We don't have time for this, Patrick," I replied softly. "Just make him leave, okay?"

He stared at me silently for a long time, taking in my long dreadlocks and the summer dress I was wearing, before nodding and turning back to Kevie.

"Yer already a dead man," Patrick said calmly, before swinging his arm out. Kevie's body bounced as he hit the hard-packed dirt.

"Are you just going to leave him there?"

"No, I'm gonna tie his arse up and let him lay in de fuckin' sun all day in de back of me pickup. De fuckin' prick." He spit on Kevie's unconscious form then raised his eyes to me. "Ye got a rope?"

"What did you just do?" I asked, stepping backward as he moved toward me.

His eyes met mine, and he wrapped his fingers around my hips as he stopped on the bottom step of the porch. "I just slayed a dragon," he said seriously.

I sobbed once, and my shoulders relaxed as he reached up to brush his thumb across my cheek. "My hero," I whispered back.

"Always," he replied, squeezing my hip before stepping around me.

He called someone from his cell phone as soon as he'd led me into the house, and I walked away as he spoke to whoever was on the other line. It made me nervous, having Kevie passed out and tied up in my front yard, but I wasn't stupid.

Patrick wasn't an accountant. He'd been a part of an outlaw motorcycle club for the past fifteen years. I knew he would take care of everything, and I was willing to let him do it.

As I sat back down next to Mum's sleeping form, I tried to decide how I felt about the scene I'd just witnessed outside. Patrick was going to kill him—I knew that with absolute certainty. The way he'd moved, the tone of his voice, the way his eyes had met mine afterward... I knew that Kevie would never make it back to Ireland. The fact that I had no overwhelming feelings of horror or fear made me pause in my chair, considering the scene in my mind once more.

No, I still didn't feel anything.

I'm not sure if it was because I had no room for anything outside of the fear I had about Peg's death, or if it was because I trusted Patrick to handle it... but I felt nothing about Kevie's impending demise, or even the matter in which he died.

The man had gone on to reside over his own parish, for God's sake. He'd ignored his psychopath brother torturing me and had gone on to live as if he was without sin, as if he was worthy of the trust his parishioners placed in him. It made me sick to think of all the women Malcolm may have hurt, while their priest advised them to say nothing. No, I didn't feel anything but relief that Kevie was going to die, and if that was wrong, I didn't care.

Because Kevie never returning to Ireland meant that there was no way he could tell Malcolm where I was.

And Patrick…well, obviously nothing would end my love for him. After all the things he'd done, killing the man outside seemed insignificant.

"Dere will be men here soon to pick him up," he whispered in my ear as he stopped behind my chair. "Ignore dere presence—dey'll not come into de house."

I nodded, "Are—are you sure he won't wake up?" My hands were shaking slightly from the altercation, and I breathed deeply in order to get control of my emotions. I wasn't in Ireland and Malcolm wasn't in Texas. I knew there was nothing to be afraid of, even as my stomach twisted.

"Yer safe, me love," Patrick whispered back, making me jolt. He leaned his face into mine until our cheeks were touching. "I'll never let anot'er t'ing happen to ye. But, know dis—we will be discussin' de t'ings ye left out all dose years ago."

That wasn't a conversation I was prepared to have, but I wasn't about to argue. I nodded again, and let him kiss my cheek before reaching out to brush Peg's wispy hair from her face.

"Mum, it's time to wake up," I called gently. "I've got a surprise for you."

Patrick was silent as Peg gradually woke from her drug-induced nap, but his hand reached out to grip the back of my shirt as she opened her eyes and turned toward my voice.

She was so much worse than the last time he'd seen her—and I wished I had told him before he got there that the tumor in her brain had completely taken her vision.

"Amy?" She asked, gripping my hand.

"Hey, Mum. I brought you a surprise."

"My handsome grandson?"

I smiled as tears filled my eyes, "Nope, your handsome son."

"Patrick?" her hand reached out in front of her, and I covered my mouth with my palm as Patrick stepped around me so she could reach him.

"Hello, beautiful," he said softly, raising her hand to his lips to kiss it.

"Oh, I'm so glad yer here." Her accent had gotten deeper after the first week without her sight, and I wondered if it was because without seeing where she was, she simply forgot.

"I missed ye," he said, his eyes shut tight in pain.

"Ach, I missed ye, too. Always too busy for yer mum."

"Never." He leaned forward to kiss her forehead, and I dropped my face into my hands, unable to watch any longer.

"Amy?"

"Yeah, Mum?" I wiped at my face frantically even though she couldn't see me, and cleared my throat.

"Where's Patrick's gift?"

"Me gift?"

"Yes," I groaned playfully, making Mum snicker. "She insisted on buying all of our Christmas presents before she couldn't see anymore. The only problem with that is she has absolutely no patience, so she won't wait until Christmas to give them out."

"No patience? Ha! No time, more like," Mum commented, making Patrick take in a sharp breath.

"Oh, none of that," Mum scolded, squeezing Patrick's hand in her frail one. "We both know that I'll be gone soon, no use pretendin' otherwise."

"You don't have to be so blunt about it," I scolded, standing from my chair angrily.

I hated when she acted like dying was no big deal, absolutely hated it. It was the cause of all of our fights for the past five years. How could she act as if we'd all just go on without her? How could she act as if *I* could just go on without her? She was my best friend, my confidant, occasionally my co-parent and always the mother I'd never had.

There would be no moving on from her death. Not for me.

I was stopped short on my way to the door, as Patrick wrapped one hand around my waist and pulled me into his chest. His light kiss on my forehead had my whole body relaxing once again, and I took a few moments to get my emotions under control.

With that one gesture, he'd cautioned me that this was not the time to be angry. He'd assured me that he knew exactly how I felt. He reminded me that I wasn't alone in my grief.

"I'll go get Patrick's present," I said calmly to Mum.

"Thank ye," she replied, all evidence of her cantankerous mood gone.

Patrick and Mum were talking quietly as I came back in with the wrapped gift, but both went silent as I got close enough to hear them.

"Here you go, prodigal son," I said drolly, tossing him the package I'd wrapped two weeks before.

"Did ye just *throw* his gift?" Peg asked indignantly.

"No, Mum," Patrick and I said at the same time, making all three of us burst into laughter.

"Eejits," she grumbled.

Patrick tore the paper slowly, and a small smile lifted his lips as he realized what he was holding.

"T'anks, Mum," he said softly, leaning over to kiss her on the lips. "Dis is a wonderful gift."

"For my wonderful boy," she said back, patting his cheeks. They both had tears in their eyes as she rubbed her fingers over his cheek and down his nose, moving them up again to smooth his eyebrows and run softly over his lashes and the wetness there. "Read to me?"

"Sure."

He sat back in his chair, and I stood to give them some time alone.

"Amy, lie with me for a bit, my girl," Peg called out before I could leave the room. "Let's listen to my boy remind me of home."

I crawled in bed with her and laid my head on her shoulder, wrapping my arm around her tiny waist as she ran her fingers over my forearm.

"*I ya gae up to yon hill-tap, ye'll there see a bonie Peggy—*" Patrick began, stopping as Mum spoke.

"I love Robert Burns," Peg said, relaxing into me as the movement on my arm stopped.

"You just like your name in there," I teased, making her smile.

I heard Patrick clear his throat, then he started again from the beginning,

"I ya gae up to yon hill-tap,
ye'll there see a bonie Peggy;
she kens her father is a laird,
and she forsooth's a leddy..."

He finished the poem and started on another as Peg drifted off to sleep, and I listened to his clear voice as his accent grew thicker with each word. It wasn't the one I remembered from our youth; it was Peg's, and my throat grew tight with tears the longer he went on.

"She's asleep, Patrick," I said quietly.

He just shook his head, and continued without pausing. He kept reading as the men he'd called showed up and took Kevie away, as I got up to get him a bottle of water when his throat grew hoarse, as I climbed back in bed with Mum, and as the sun began to set in the sky. He didn't stop, not for one moment.

***

"**P**atrick?" I called fearfully, meeting his tear-filled eyes after the sun had completely fallen. "I don't think she's breathing."

"Come here, me love," he ordered gently in a scratchy voice. I leaned up to follow his instructions, then froze as Mum's chest rose one more time.

"Come to me," he said again.

He raised his hand for me to take and I slid off the bed, walking numbly toward him, my eyes never leaving Peg's chest. When I'd reached him, he pulled me into his lap, settling me across his thighs as he wrapped one arm around me and I pressed my forehead to his throat.

We were close enough that I reached out and grasped Mum's hand in mine, running my fingers over the back of her fragile bones.

I could feel the vibration as Patrick began to read again, and I watched in agony, with tears dripping down my face, as Peg continued to struggle for breath, not once waking up.

We stayed that way long into the night, until finally, without fanfare and with her son reading her to sleep, Margaret Gallagher left us forever.

Chapter 46

Patrick

I crawled into Amy's bed as the sun finally began to rise, curling my body around her sleeping form. It had been the longest night of my life.

Amy had been practically comatose after Mum had passed, unable to do the smallest thing to help me. I'd found the phone number to hospice and the funeral home on the refrigerator and by the time they'd arrived, I'd had to pry her out of the room so they could take Mum's body away for burial.

Mum's *body*. No longer simply her, but suddenly a *thing*.

My mother was dead. A part of me couldn't fully grasp the meaning of those words, but the rest of me felt heavy in a way I'd never experienced before. I'd felt loss before, my da, men I'd lived with, and a woman I'd loved—but I didn't think that anything had ever come close to the feeling of knowing I'd never again hear my mum's scolding voice.

I missed her already, and I wished for a moment that Brenna was with me. I didn't think she even really remembered my mum, she'd stopped visiting so long ago. It was a shame that she'd missed so much time with her nan, but when Mum had insisted that she didn't want to see my girl, I hadn't argued. I understood why she'd felt the need to stay away, even if I hadn't agreed with it. Brenna had already lost too much in her short life—I hated the thought of her losing even more.

As my eyes grew heavy, I rolled to my side so I faced the door to the bedroom, tucking a still sleeping Amy against my back. I had so many questions filling up my mind that I wasn't sure if I'd be able to sleep, but I knew I wouldn't be getting my answers that morning. My wife was devastated—completely broken—and I knew deep in my gut that if I brought up the past while she was in that frame of mind, I might never get the answers I was looking for.

***

"Who the fuck are you?"

The angry words woke me from a deep sleep and I automatically went for the pistol that should have been on the floor next to the bed. Shit. I'd left it in my truck.

"What are you doin' in my house? Huh? Where's my nan?"

I looked up to see a large kid staring down on me from the doorway, a shotgun in his arms and no shoes on his feet. His skin was light, his body was in that unfortunate stage where it was getting taller but not yet wider, his hair was almost black and his nose was a bit big for his face. I knew immediately who he was, and I had to force myself not to cringe when I saw Malcolm's eyes staring back at me.

"Mum?" he asked in confusion as Amy sat up behind me.

Shit, I didn't know if I should force her back down or let her talk some sense into the kid—I didn't want to get my ass shot.

"Phoenix Robert Gallagher, if you don't put that damn gun away, I'm going to beat you bloody!" she snapped, her voice husky from sleep.

"Mum?" Damn, it was fucking odd hearing him call her mum in that Texas accent.

"Get out, Nix," she ordered. "I'll be there in a minute."

He nodded and glared at me as he stepped out the door, and as he began to walk away, she yelled at him again. "Nix, close the door and lock up the gun!"

The door slammed with a loud bang, and suddenly I was lying in a quiet room with the most beautiful woman in the world.

"How ye doin', love?" I asked, rolling to my back so I could look at her.

"I feel like shit, how about you?"

I snorted at the apt description, then gave her a nod. "About de same. Can't believe she's gone."

"Me, either. And now I've got to go out there and tell my son."

"I t'ink he already knows."

"Yeah, but I'm still his mother... he needs the confirmation from me."

"Want me to go wit' ye?"

"No, can you stay in here for a while?" She looked sorry for asking, but I sure as hell understood her reasoning. The boy had just held a fucking gun on me. He wouldn't want me witnessing the moment he learned his nan was dead.

"Sure t'ing, gorgeous."

"Stop being charming," she grumbled as she rolled away from me and off the side of the bed onto her feet. "I'm immune to it."

"Ye care if I get a couple more hours of sleep?" I asked, not even sure that I'd be able to sleep, but afraid if I was awake she'd kick me out before I was ready.

"Nope, stay as long as you want."

"Appreciate it."

I watched her move around the room, pulling on a pair of sweatpants with some odd looking mascot on the side of them, and a long blue robe with frogs printed all over it. She moved as if I wasn't even there, braiding those long ropes of hair and slipping on some socks that didn't match.

"Why'd ye do dat to yer hair?" I asked for the first time.

"It grew in that way," she answered in an odd tone.

"No, de dreadlocks. Why'd ye do it?"

She paused for a moment at the door, then turned to look at me.

"Do you remember the way you used to run your fingers through it?" She asked with a bemused smile, then waited until I nodded in confirmation before she continued. "It wasn't the same after it was cut off. It was rough and ... I couldn't stand the thought of anyone rubbing their fingers through it."

"So now they can't."

"Right."

She left then, and I lay on the bed wondering if the real reason she'd done it was because she didn't want *me* running my fingers through it.

Perhaps it no longer mattered.

Chapter 47

Amy

"How did you get into my safe?" I asked as I strode to the coffee machine on the counter. God, I felt like I hadn't slept in weeks. My entire body felt heavy.

"I know the combination," Phoenix grumbled, tapping his fingers on the tabletop. "Who's the homeless guy?"

"He's not homeless, don't be an ass."

The conversation was irrelevant, but I let him continue. We were talking around the elephant in the room, neither of us ready to face it just yet.

"His beard is down to his chest and his hair is longer than yours."

"He's Nan's son. You've met him before."

"I don't remember him," he argued, crossing his arms across his chest.

"He's known you since you were a baby," I replied watching him closely.

"What's his name?"

"Patrick."

"Patrick what?"

I knew where the conversation was going, and I swallowed hard against the tightness in my throat. Shit. I wished so badly that Peg was there at that moment. She'd know what to do. A wave of grief rolled over me and I closed my eyes until the sharp pain calmed a little.

"Gallagher," I answered.

Nix looked at the table, his shoulders stiff and his entire body practically thrumming with pent up emotion.

"Is he my dad?" he asked quietly, like he was embarrassed to even be asking. Sometimes it felt like he was already an adult and I was just a nuisance in his life, but other times, like right then? He felt like the little boy who'd been afraid of his teacher in kindergarten and had cried every time I dropped him off that first week.

"Oh, no. No, baby, I'm sorry, he's not."

"I don't understand," he replied, shaking his head.

His black hair was messy and hanging in his face, and as I watched it fall into his eyes, I had the overwhelming urge to take him in my arms like I had when he was little and brush all of that wild hair out of his face.

"It's a long story, you sure you want to hear it?" I asked as I poured creamer into my coffee and sat across from him at the table. I didn't want to talk about it, but if this was how he chose to spend the morning instead of talking about the huge, gaping hole that we now had in our lives... I wouldn't argue with that.

"I don't have any plans."

I laughed a little at his nonchalant reply, and nudged him with my foot.

"When I was a little older than you are now, my parents and I moved to Ireland—"

"No shit?" he blurted, suddenly sitting up straighter.

"No shit," I confirmed, "and watch your mouth. Anyway, we moved to Ireland and that's where I met your nan." I shook my head, and felt a small smile pull at my cheeks. "I thought she was a crazy woman at first. She stopped me on my way home from school one day and asked me in for tea."

"You hadn't even met her before that?"

"Nope. Are you going to let me finish, or are you going to keep interrupting?"

He scrunched up his mouth and motioned as if he was locking it up, before throwing the invisible key over his shoulder. Goofball.

"So, to get the whole effect, you have to understand that my parents pretty much sucked. They were too busy with drugs and prostitutes to pay any attention to me."

Nix's eyes grew so wide they looked like they were going to pop out of his head, and I knew it was taking every ounce of willpower he had not to comment. I laughed, feeling lighter than I had in the last three weeks.

"So, Peg invited me in, and pretty much took me under her wing. After a while, I was sleeping at her house more often than I was home. One night, her son came home from Uni—their college over there—and he was pissed that some girl was taking advantage of his mom. I was freaked, but it didn't take long before he realized that I wasn't out to get anything from Peg."

"It took less den twelve hours," Patrick commented from the entryway of the kitchen, a small smile on his face. "Sorry, I smelled coffee."

"If he can cut in, I can cut in," Nix announced, letting out a huge breath of air as if being forced not to talk had made him hold his breath, as well.

"He was there, you weren't, kiddo," I argued, pointing at him.

"Yer mum was de prettiest girl I'd ever seen," Patrick said over his shoulder as he grabbed a cup of coffee. "I was infatuated from de first."

"He's full of it."

"I am not!" Patrick sat down at the table while Nix's head flew back and forth between us. "Ye should have seen her in her school uniform."

"I went to an all-girls Catholic school and had to wear the uniform—plaid skirt and knee socks," I informed my son.

"Not a visual I want," Nix groaned and slunk down into his seat.

"Anyway, we eventually got married," I said, rubbing my thumb over the tattoo on my finger.

"You're married?" he yelled, his mouth dropping open in surprise.

"Yep."

"Then why isn't he my dad? Why aren't you my dad?" Nix asked, on the verge of completely losing his shit. I guess it wasn't the best morning to lay it all out for him. God, I was a shitty mother. I didn't know what the fuck I was doing half the time.

"It's not—"

"No, let me take this one," I said to Patrick, cutting off whatever he was about to say. I'd not allow my son to know the full events of that year. Not for any reason, ever.

"We got married, but soon after that Patrick's dad—Nan's husband Robbie, who you're named after—was killed in a car bombing outside our house."

"Holy shit!"

"Yeah, it wasn't pretty," I said softly, glancing at Patrick as we both remembered that morning.

"God, that must have sucked," Nix said, slumping back down in his seat.

I nodded in agreement. "Then soon after that, Patrick's wild oats came back to haunt him." At Nix's confused face, I explained a little more clearly. "He'd slept with someone before we were married, and gotten her pregnant."

"You dick," Nix said to Patrick, who was running a hand down his face.

"Aye, ye've got de right of it."

"We decided to get out of Ireland with some friends of Patrick's, but we had to leave in two different groups. Patrick took his baby mama—" I paused when Nix snorted at my terminology, "then Nan and I were supposed to go in the second group and meet up with him."

I looked over and met Patrick's eyes while I finished my story. "I was angry, livid really, so before we left Ireland, I slept with someone else to get back at Patrick—and then I refused to follow him to Oregon. Your nan and I took a plane to New York and rode the bus down here instead."

Patrick's eyes closed tight, as if in pain, and I so badly wanted to reach across the table to hold his hand—but I didn't. He didn't deserve my comfort—not for this.

"Dang, Mum. Bad move."

"Not really, I got you, didn't I?"

"Yeah, lucky you."

"I know, I just love smelly socks and the way you stink up the bathroom so I can't shower for an hour afterward."

"Shut up, Mum!" his eyes flew to Patrick in embarrassment.

"Oh, please. I lived with the man—he could give you a run for your money."

Both Patrick and Nix burst out laughing, and it was the most beautiful sound I'd ever heard—until suddenly, it was the most painful, as Nix's chuckles became gut wrenching sobs. I stood so fast that my chair hit the tile behind me, and was around the table in seconds, pulling my baby boy into my arms.

He'd finally gone over the edge he'd been perched on for weeks. I was just thankful that I was there when it happened.

"Nan's gone, huh?" he asked into my neck, his entire body shuddering as his fingers dug into my back through the thick robe I was wearing.

"Yeah, baby. I'm so sorry."

I heard a sniff from the table, and turned my head toward Patrick to find his elbows braced on the top with the heels of his hands digging into his eyes.

I couldn't stop the tears that rolled down my face.

"She made Patrick read Robert Burns poems to her," I told Nix softly, rubbing his back.

"Good ol' Robbie Burns, eh?" he replied in a surprisingly accurate depiction of Peg's accent.

"Yep. Still making all of us do her bidding, even at the end." I clenched my eyes tightly closed and breathed in deeply. I didn't have the luxury of letting myself lose it. I had a son to take care of.

"What happens now?" Nix asked, and it was so similar to the question that I'd heard years ago, that my eyes met Patrick's across the table as I answered.

"Nan planned her own damn funeral, so we'll do that next week sometime... and then, we'll just keep living."

"Okay," Nix said, as he leaned up to kiss my forehead. I swear I'd never get used to my child being taller than I was. "Um," he hiccupped, and pulled away. "I'm going to go shower. You okay?"

"I'm good. Go ahead and shower, but leave some hot water, would you?"

"Yup." He moved to the entry of the kitchen and then turned back to Patrick. "It was nice to meet you again, even though the reason you're here sucks."

"It was nice to see ye again, too, Phoenix."

"Sorry I stole your last name," Nix said with a crooked, watery smile.

Patrick stared at him for a minute then lifted his chin. "I'm not."

Chapter 48

Amy

"Thanks for coming," I said, looking over my shoulder at Patrick, who was glowering at the man I was speaking to.

"Of course, babe," Sam said kindly, pulling me into a hug and rubbing my back in long, sweeping motions.

The movement would have been a comfort on any other day, but with Patrick watching us, it just made my skin crawl.

"Call me tonight."

"I will."

I watched Sam walk out to his lifted pick-up truck, and sighed as he waved before pulling away. Fuck.

I'd been seeing Sam for a little over six months and things were good with us. Really good. He was handsome, smart, he knew what he was doing in bed and he treated Nix like the kid brother he'd never had—interested in what he was doing and protective, but not all up in his business like a parent. He was such a good guy. Over the past month, he'd dealt with my mood swings, breaking plans, and depression, and he'd never once faltered in his devotion.

My dating life had been pretty much non-existent the past few years. I'd dated a man for almost a year when Nix was five, but that had eventually fizzled out. I'd made him wait so long before I'd been ready to have sex with him, that when I'd eventually given in we'd realized that we weren't very compatible. He'd been a sweetheart, a man I'd met at my yoga class, and I couldn't have picked a better person for my first time after the attack... but it hadn't been good. Not in any capacity. He'd been gentle, and tender and everything I could have wanted, but he'd also had no backbone or skill. After the first time when I'd cried, and the next few times that I'd laid there in boredom, we'd both known that it wasn't going to work out.

I hadn't had sex again until Patrick had shown up a few years later, and after that, I hadn't even been open to the possibility of becoming serious with anyone else. Not until Sam.

On paper, Sam was everything I could have wanted. He was gentle, but he also knew exactly how to touch me. He didn't put up with my shit, but he didn't push, either. He was successful, driven and extremely attractive. I really liked him and I'd thought that maybe we were working toward something good.

But now, all I could see was Patrick, and I fucking hated that. I hated the pull he had on my emotions and the way he wouldn't let go.

He wouldn't let go, and I couldn't go back.

"Mum, I'm heading over to Simon's okay? His mom's leaving right now." Nix came to a stop next to me, and I leaned against his lanky frame.

He'd grown taller than me by the time he was thirteen, and now my head barely reached his shoulder. It both amazed me and drove me insane because I knew where he'd inherited that height.

"Are you sure—" my words cut off as his body grew tight against mine. I was being selfish. "Sure, baby. But you need to be home by nine, okay?"

"Mum—"

"Nine, Phoenix. No later. You've got school tomorrow and you're not staying the night over there."

"I always stayed there before—"

"Nix," I warned, and his mouth snapped shut.

"Fine," he grumbled, wrapping his arms around my shoulders. "Love you."

"Love you too, kiddo."

He ran down the steps and met Simon's mom Renee at her car, where she stood waiting for him. She raised her hand and waved back at me with a nod before climbing inside and pulling away. We had a deal, her and I. No matter where the boys were, my house or hers, we kept an eagle-eye on the two of them.

"Ye couldn't have let de kid stay wit' a friend tonight?" Patrick's voice startled me. I'd forgotten for a moment that he was there. "We've got shite to talk about, Amy. I let ye have de past couple of days, but it's time."

I shook my head and locked the front door, absently looking over the messy house. There'd been too many people inside my small home, but I'd wanted to have the reception after the funeral in my own space. I'd never felt completely comfortable at the church, and I'd wanted to get out of there as soon as I could.

"Yer makin' him a mama's boy," Patrick continued, and I felt unreasonable anger rise in my chest. I'd heard that comment before from an old boyfriend right before I'd kicked his ass out of my house.

"Simon's not Nix's friend, Patrick," I replied, walking into the kitchen for a cup of coffee. It felt like the house had dropped ten degrees without all of those bodies heating it. "He knows he's not allowed to stay the night there, he was just trying to work the sympathy card."

"Shite, de boy just lost his nan—"

"That doesn't mean that I'm going to encourage him at sixteen to go have sex!" I snapped back, turning to face him.

"What?" The look of confusion on his face was almost comical.

"Simon is Nix's boyfriend."

I watched as understanding hit him and braced myself. I was used to people saying shit—I lived in a small Texas town, for Chrissake, so it wasn't like I hadn't heard the murmurs. I was also pretty sure that Simon and Nix were together purely because it was slim pickins around here for gay teenagers.

But that didn't mean that I was prepared for any type of scorn from Patrick. It would completely sever any ties I believed were still holding us together.

"Well, shite. I wouldn't let him spend de night dere, eit'er." He growled, dropping into a chair at the table. "What's dis Simon kid like?"

I felt a small smile curve my lips as I turned back toward the counter. "He's a nice kid. Not very handsome," I looked over my shoulder with a smirk. "His ears stick out and he's fighting a losing battle with acne. But he's sweet to Nix, and that's all I can ask for."

"Little fucker better be nice to Nix," I heard him grumble as I passed him a hot mug.

"It's fine, you know? He's a good kid, and he's respectful. I can't really complain."

He was silent for a few moments and I could envision the gears grinding and the wheels turning as he processed this new information. I'd had years to process it, starting when Nix was around…eleven, I think? He'd started asking questions then, and even though it had scared me, I'd answered as calmly and reasonably as I could.

Did I care that my kid was gay? Not at all.

Did I worry about him every single second he was out of my sight? Yes, but I'd been doing that since the day he was born and I didn't see it changing—ever.

I knew that there were people out there who would hurt him just because they could. Bigots. But for now, we were tucked away here in our quiet town, and we hadn't had any problems yet. My boy was all boy, strong and masculine, and there were only a few kids larger than him in his high school. As long as he was there, I knew he was relatively safe. I didn't let myself think of when he'd leave for college. That was a whole new set of worries.

"He havin' sex wit' dat kid?" Patrick's accent was deeper, along with his tone.

"Uh, no. I don't think so," I replied, wiping off the coffee that had come out of my mouth in an arc of surprise. "He's only sixteen, Patrick."

"I was havin' sex by de time I was twelve."

"Twelve?"

"Aye."

"That's disgusting!" I looked at him in horror, but I couldn't change my expression. Ew.

"Mum worked quite a bit," he said with a chuckle, his accent once again fading.

"New subject," I ordered, my nose still scrunched up.

"Ye have de birds and de bees talk wit' him yet?"

"He's not going to be getting anyone pregnant."

"Don't be a bitch, ye know what I meant," he chastised. "He knows about condoms and whatnot?"

"Where the hell is this all coming from?"

"Because I could talk to him. Talked to some of de younger boys at de club, ye know—"

"Patrick!" I yelled, cutting off his rambling.

When his eyes met mine, they were concerned. "He can't go havin' unprotected sex, Amy. It's not safe."

"Relax, baby," I said, the endearment slipping out before I could stop it. "I've had that talk with him. More than once. He's got condoms if he needs them, but I don't think he's using them."

"Dere's AIDS and shite, Amy."

"Nix isn't going to get AIDS, Patrick. Shit."

"Or herpes."

"Could you knock it the fuck off?"

"How well do ye really know dis Simon kid?"

He was really irritating the shit out of me.

"Patrick, what the fuck is wrong with you? Simon's gay, not a serial killer!"

Patrick's chair fell over as he shot up from the table, his face a mask of angry disbelief.

"Dat boy thought I was his da," he hissed, bracing his hands on the table to lean closer. "He carries me name."

I watched him in silence as my face grew red. I knew I'd offended him, but I was fucking offended, too.

"He carries me *name*, Amy. De love of me life carried him inside her fuckin' body! It's not like he's some kid off de bloody street." He shook his head, seeming to grow angrier by the second. "I have a daughter at home and she doesn't even bring boys back to de club because dere so fuckin' terrified!" he growled, taking a step back away from the table. "Ye are out of yer bloody mind if ye believe me concern comes from anyt'in' but de worry dat someone is takin' advantage of our children."

He stomped away and out the front door before I had a chance to reply.

I felt like shit, like a complete and total asshole. I'd been so defensive for so long that I'd automatically assumed that he was being a dick, spouting off all of that STD crap. It hadn't even crossed my mind that he was being ridiculously protective. I spent so much time worrying that someone would treat Nix badly, that I hadn't even realized when someone was doing the exact opposite.

I was such a bitch.

"Patrick!" I yelled, pushing back from the table and following him outside.

I found him sitting on the front steps, smoking a cigarette.

"I'm sorry," I said, plopping down next to him. "I think I'm overly sensitive."

"No shite?"

"I'm so worried that someone is going to be an asshole— hold that thought."

I jumped up and ran upstairs to grab a small Altoids tin out of my sock drawer. When I made it back down, Patrick was watching me in amusement.

"You have a light?" I asked, setting the tin down on the wood step next to me and pulling out a small joint.

"Why, Amy Gallagher, ye rebel."

"Without a cause—I know." I shook my head as I took the lighter out of his hand and lit up, taking a small drag and coughing slightly. "It helps with my anxiety."

"Ye have a problem wit' dat? Anxiety?"

"Not really, yoga and meditation help. I haven't even gotten hives in years. You know, this is the first time in a long ass time that we've just sat shooting the shit."

"American phrases are ridiculous—and don't change de subject."

"I thought you were giving me a minute to apologize."

"Consider yerself forgiven—I've dealt wit' me own share of shite wit' Brenna."

"Really? That surprises me."

"Not so surprisin'," he commented, taking the joint from my fingers and inhaling deeply. "Her pop is part of a motorcycle club, some parents ain't too excited about dat."

"Ain't." I snorted, as he passed the joint my way again.

"Shut it."

"Sorry you've had to deal with that. We haven't had any major things happen yet—but I feel like I'm always braced for it. I just don't want him to get hurt, you know? I mean, he's big and he's going to be bigger, so I think he'll do alright physically. I just hate the thought of someone making him feel bad about something that he's got no control over."

"Ye can't shield him from everyt'in'—boy's almost grown, he can't be cowering behind his mum."

"He doesn't. If anything, he's more protective of me."

"Good. Sounds like ye raised him right."

"More like your mum did. Shit, I don't know what I would have done without her. I was so messed up for so long, I think I had a panic attack when she finally moved out."

"Ye ready to tell me what I want to know?" he asked, taking the joint from me again and finishing it off.

"Want to go inside for this?" I asked calmly, leaning back against the railing.

"Probably not. At least out here dere ain't anyt'in' to break." He shook his head at me, his eyes moving leisurely from the top of my head to the neck of my black blouse.

"It's not something I talk about—ever." I said, looking away from him. "I mean, I haven't even discussed it with Sam yet."

"Dat de jammie bastard wit' his hands all over ye today?"

"He's a good guy, Patrick."

"He know he's fuckin' a married woman?"

"Don't be a cunt, he knows that we were married."

"Cunt, huh? Yer language has gone to hell. And we're still married."

"It's a piece of fucking paper," I argued, knowing that I should be really irritated, but not really feeling it. The marijuana was doing its job.

"It was vows we spoke in front of a priest."

"A dirty priest."

"Dat doesn't matter."

"Oh, yeah?"

"We made promises," he insisted stupidly, and I had to curl my hands around each other to keep them from smacking him in the head.

"You didn't keep even one of those promises—" my words trailed off as I saw movement at the end of our long driveway, and within seconds I was on my feet and running.

"Phoenix?" I called, "Are you okay? What happened?"

He was sweaty and breathing hard, his face beet red from running in the heat, and there were dust covered tear tracks on his cheeks.

"It's nothing, Mum," he lied, passing me without meeting my eyes.

"It isn't nothing. What the hell, Nix?"

"I said it was nothing!" he turned and leaned down to yell at me, and I flinched backward.

"Mum?" he asked, his voice cracking as he tried to understand my movement.

"Don't speak to yer mum dat way," Patrick said angrily, walking toward us.

"I can handle this, Patrick," I warned, my eyes never leaving Nix's.

"Ye don't look like yer handlin' anyt'in'," he retorted.

"Why the fuck are you still here?" Nix hissed, turning to face Patrick. "Your mom no longer lives here, you need to leave."

"Phoenix Robert!" I yelled, completely caught off guard by his scathing words. Who the hell was this kid?

"Ye okay, boy?" Patrick asked quietly, watching Nix closely.

"Fuck you! I said I'm fine!"

"Ye don't look it."

"I'm fine!" Nix yelled, his hands closing into fists and his arms tightening down his sides. Tears began running down his cheeks again, and humiliation mixed with absolute grief on his face.

"Baby," I murmured, reaching out to touch his back gently through the sweaty white undershirt he was wearing. "What's going on?"

My tone, or maybe my touch, must have been the catalyst, because he began sobbing as he covered his face with his hands. He turned his body toward mine, and I took most of his weight as he wrapped himself around me.

"Mum," he moaned into my neck.

"You're okay, son," I whispered into his ear. "We'll figure whatever it is out. I promise, baby. But you've got to tell me what it is."

Patrick watched us with concerned eyes as I held Nix in my arms. He wasn't sure what to do—and I was glad for that. He may have been Peg's son, and a part of my life years ago, but he had absolutely nothing to do with Nix.

Nix was mine. Only mine.

"He broke up with me," Nix finally whispered.

On the day of his grandmother's funeral? I shook with fury, wishing that Simon was eighteen so I could go over and beat the shit out of him. What a little dick head.

"He said he wasn't really gay, that he just—" Nix began sobbing once again, and I almost didn't hear his whisper. "He said he just knew that I'd give him a blowjob."

My stomach turned at the whispered words and I saw red.

"What a prick," I said tightly, squeezing Nix tighter. "And if that kid isn't gay, then neither is Elton John."

Nix laughed once, then pulled back to meet my eyes.

"I'm so embarrassed," he said shamefully.

"You have nothing to be embarrassed about, Phoenix Gallagher. Not one thing. He's the douchebag, not you."

"But why would he say that?"

"Because people are assholes sometimes." I reached up to grab a fist full of his hair, holding it tight as I made him meet my eyes. "You're better than him. So much better. And someday you're going to meet a guy that's as handsome as you are, and he's gonna think you hung the fucking moon."

"This hurts really bad, Mumma."

"I know it does, baby. I know."

I turned him, and walked him slowly to the house as he did anything he could to keep from meeting Patrick's eyes. My kid was mortified, and I resented the fact that Patrick had witnessed something that Nix didn't want him to see.

"I think Renee is gonna call you," Nix said as we reached the front porch.

"Good, I can tell her what a little fucker her son is."

"I think she'll probably say the same thing."

I came to an abrupt stop and my gaze shot to his.

"I'm pretty sure I broke his nose… maybe his jaw, too," Nix said nervously.

I looked closely at my tall, strong son. He was so many things.

Smart and kind and handsome and funny. He had a way with people—they just seemed to gravitate toward him—and he'd never met a stranger. When he was really little he'd been kind of shy, but I sometimes wondered if it had been my nervousness rubbing off on him, because as I'd healed, he'd become more outgoing. He was the best man I knew.

"That's my boy," I said with a solid nod, reaching up to cup his cheek in my palm.

"I thought you'd be mad at me," he said in relief, his shoulders slumping as he continued to hiccup with leftover sobs.

"You never let anyone treat you like less than you are, you hear me? You stand up for yourself. Always. Now go upstairs and shower. You smell like BO and manure." I looked down to see blades of grass sticking to the bottom of his dress shoes. "Oh, gross! Take your shoes off, I'm pretty sure you stepped in some."

Nix's startled laughter made my lips curve as he slid his shoes off without untying them, then went up the stairs, taking two at a time.

"Yer a good mum," Patrick said, startling me. "Ye know just what to say to him."

"Nah, I'm just winging it most of the time."

"I wasn't sure what to—"

"I think you should probably go, Patrick," I said, setting Nix's shoes on the front porch. "I'm not sure what you're looking for, but you're not going to find it here."

"What are ye sayin'?" he asked cautiously, stepping toward me.

"I'm saying that I can't do this with you—whatever this is." I raised my hands palms up. "I have nothing to give you. Nothing. I have a son that's heartbroken, medical supplies that I have to go through and dispose of, a boyfriend who's probably wondering where the fuck I've been all week, and a yoga studio that won't run itself, even though it's been doing a pretty good imitation for the past few months."

"A boyfriend."

"Don't act like you're surprised, we just talked about this."

"I didn't realize it was serious—dat ye would choose him—"

"Are you shitting me right now?" I asked incredulously. "Choose him? Is there a choice? I swear to God, Patrick, you think you can change the past to suit your purposes."

"It has always been ye," he said, and I couldn't take one more word of his distorted reality.

"Get the fuck out of my house," I said flatly. "Thank you for coming, and for helping with everything this past week. I'm not sure how I would have done it without you. But now—now you need to leave."

He looked as if I'd just punched him, but he didn't say another word and I didn't back down as he gave me a nod. He left me there in the entryway as he strode into the kitchen for his coat, and I was still standing frozen in the same spot when he came back.

"I apologize for takin' advantage of yer hospitality—" his words were so quiet and almost embarrassed, that I had to bite the inside of my cheek to stop myself from reassuring him. "I want ye to know, no matter how much time has passed or how far away ye are, if ye ever need me, all ye have to do is call. I'll be dere in an instant. I know I've not done what I promised all dose years ago, and ye've no reason to trust me word, but ye've got it, anyway."

He leaned forward and pressed a scrap of paper into my hand as he kissed my cheek, lingering for just a moment.

"I've loved ye for as long as I can remember," he whispered before pulling away.

I didn't say anything as he strode out of the house. I couldn't.

Once again, my voice was stuck in my throat.

It was finally over. There was no longer any reason for us to cross paths again.

And I had no words left.

Nine Years Later

Portland, Oregon

Chapter 49

Amy

"Hold on a second, son," I mumbled into the phone, setting it down to pull my hair back into a massive bun at the nape of my neck.

My dreads were getting too long again, and I knew I needed to cut them—but the process involved a night in, pot, red wine, and Nix wielding a pair of yard clippers. Hands in my hair was a trigger I'd learned to live with, but over twenty years later, I still wouldn't allow a pair of scissors in my house or shop.

I was okay with that, even if it meant my hair grew too long on occasion and I had to have my son cut it when I was buzzed out of my mind.

It was funny that when I was a kid I'd so badly wanted to fit in somewhere, and as an adult I stuck out like a sore thumb. I guess that's life, though. Experiences change you, there's no way to escape it.

"Are you and Ken coming over tomorrow night for dinner?" I

asked, picking the phone back up.

"His name is Mat, Mum."

"With one T," I confirmed with a snort.

"You're such a pain in the ass sometimes."

"Ditto, kiddo."

"We'll be there as long as your house doesn't stink like incense and pot and you use one of Nan's recipes."

"What the hell is wrong with my recipes?"

"They're disgusting."

"They're works in progress," I grumbled, looking out the door to my office—that was really a utility closet I'd stuffed a desk in—to see how many we had for the 'Mommy and Me' class Kali was teaching in ten minutes.

"You're not a bloody vegetarian!"

"I could be if my son didn't insist on eating the carcasses of dead animals."

"You're nuts."

"The apple doesn't fall far from the tree." I ignored the twinge those words brought me.

"Hey, I better go. I'll call you tonight before—" I dropped the phone to my side as I caught sight of a woman walking in the door with her daughter.

She was lovely, with creamy skin and straight strawberry blonde hair, and she was wearing expensive yoga gear that only a woman with too much money and too much time would wear.

A few years ago, when Nix had gotten a job offer from a growing ski and snowboarding company in Portland, I'd packed up and followed him. There was nothing left for me in Texas by then except for the acquaintances I'd met through my old studio, so I'd sold my house and settled down in the Oregon town, even though the thought of being so close to Patrick had made me nervous. I didn't regret it, either.

I'd opened up my tiny yoga studio on the west side of Portland between an Indian restaurant and a funky thrift store, and while the space was limited, I couldn't complain about the foot traffic. We were busy from open to close, and last year I'd been able to hire Kali to teach more of the classes so I could work on the business side of the desk.

I had realized quickly that there were two types of people that came into our studio. The first type were serious, mostly crunchy people like myself that came in to do more than just stretch their muscles. They wore beards and sandals and beaded necklaces and they used the same ragged yoga mat for years.

The second type, well, they were my favorite and I also hated them a little. They were the housewives who never carried cash and bitched every time the credit card machine was down because they couldn't pay for their class without it—even though it had happened to them twice before and they should have remembered that the thing was a bit temperamental. Their hair was always styled to perfection, they wore clothing that cost more than my car, and I'd never seen one with a broken nail. I called the studio's popularity with those women *The Dharma and Greg Effect*. It was the idea that those women came in because they wanted their workout to sound sexier than it was. Their rich husbands wanted to be able to mention how their wives could put her feet behind their head, and the wives, well, they just wanted to find the hot new thing before everyone else… and what was hotter than a flexible woman?

The redheaded woman ushering her little girl into the shop was one of the Dharmas. I hadn't seen her before, but I usually worked from home on Tuesdays when I didn't have class. I wondered how long she'd been attending.

I didn't know what it was about her that made me look twice, but I knew it was *something*. I completely forgot the phone in my hand as I watched her set her stuff down. When she suddenly tilted her head and smiled, it was like being punched in the chest.

It couldn't be. I didn't even know if she lived in Portland, or even if she was in Oregon anymore. There was no way she'd walked into my shop.

I watched her for a while longer as Kali started the class, and the more I saw, the more my heart raced. The mannerisms. The head tilt. The way her hair curled into tiny little ringlets at her neck as she began to sweat.

I stumbled back inside my office and closed the door quietly, finally realizing that my phone was still clutched in my hand.

"Nix?"

"Mum? What the hell was that?"

"I'll call you back." I hung up the phone and sat heavily in my chair, reaching for the member files in the drawer next to my desk.

I checked for Gallagher first and there was nothing, but I wouldn't let myself relax. She was what, twenty-five now? Just a few months older than Nix, and plenty old enough to be married. I rubbed my hands over my face and took a deep breath before pulling out every single file for members who had last names that started with A.

I went through the files letter by letter and it took me hours.

And then there she was.

Brenna and Beatrix Richards.

Twenty-five years old, according to her driver's license.

I stared at it a lot longer than I should have.

Classes were over for the day and the studio was quiet as I stared at the little black and white photo our copy machine had printed out. She was a little blurry, and without the red hair I wouldn't have been able to pick her out of a lineup. There was nothing about her in that little grainy photo that would have made me look twice, but I had a hard time looking away.

She was the single most influential person in my life, her mere presence on the earth the catalyst of every single thing that had happened to me in the last twenty-five years.

Yet when I stared at her photo, I couldn't see anything but a beautiful mix of Moira and Patrick.

I dropped the sheet of paper on my desk and sobbed into my hands.

***

I wasn't proud of myself, really I wasn't. And I knew that I was acting like a lunatic.

But that didn't stop me from being in the office the next Tuesday morning when Mommy and Me classes started up. She was there again, with her dark haired little girl, smiling and quiet as the rest of the moms talked over each other.

I followed her that day.

And the next week.

And the week after that.

She always took her daughter to a coffee shop down the block for hot chocolate when they finished class. They'd stay for thirty minutes, while the girl drank her hot chocolate and Brenna drank an unsweetened iced tea. Then they'd walk to the lot on the other side of my studio to pick up their car.

The routine never changed. Not for two whole months.

I knew, because like the incredibly stupid woman I was—I watched them.

Then one day, Brenna brought a laptop to the coffee shop.

I sat behind her, facing the little girl I'd come to know as Trix, and tried to see what she was doing over her shoulder. It didn't take me long to recognize the website she was on, and I watched avidly as she posted her expensive car for far less than it was worth.

"I need to go potty," Trix said politely, her voice almost lost in the noise of the shop.

"Just one second, okay, baby?" Brenna answered, her fingers typing over the keyboard.

My initial thought was that her husband was going to be pissed as hell that she was selling her car for way less than she could get on a trade in… but then, it was like my sight widened. She was moving slower that day, almost stiffly, but the way she'd pulled her laptop out of its case and snapped it open had seemed a little jerky. Like she was waiting for someone to walk over and catch her. Her hair was down instead of tied back in the low ponytail she usually wore... and even Trix was quieter than usual.

A knot of dread formed in my stomach as she exited out of the website and went back in to clear her web history.

"Okay, let's go potty and then we'll head home," Brenna said shakily, putting the laptop back in its case and reaching for Trix's hand.

I watched as they walked toward the bathrooms, then grabbed my bag and left the shop. I was shaking as I pulled out my cell phone.

"Hey, Mum, what's up?"

"Nix, do you know anything about Patrick's daughter?" I asked, cringing as I crossed the street to where I was parked.

"Not much, no. Trick said she married some guy with shit-tons of money and moved up here a few years ago. Why?"

"I—" I couldn't exactly tell him that I'd been stalking the girl for months. "I think she may come into the studio sometimes." Yeah, like every single week like clockwork.

"Whoa. Small world."

"Yeah, no kidding."

"Wait, have you met her before? How did you even notice?"

I climbed into my car and locked the doors, suddenly feeling uncomfortable in my own skin.

"I knew her parents, remember? She looks like them."

"Damn, you've got the memory of an elephant."

"It's a curse."

"Well, I think I'll probably talk to Trick this week sometime—you want me to mention it?"

"No!" I gulped, shaking my head in annoyance. "Don't say anything. I don't know why you even talk to him."

"You know why," he reminded me, making me want to slam my head repeatedly into the driver's door window. "He kept in touch, even when I was a dick to him. I'm not his kid, but he came to every graduation I've ever had. I know you guys had a falling out, or whatever the fuck that was—but he's the only father figure I ever had."

"I was your father figure," I replied stubbornly.

"And you were fantastic. But in case you haven't noticed, you don't have a dick."

"Phoenix Robert Gallagher, watch your mouth."

"Look, all I'm saying—"

"Oh, you're trying to make a point? I thought you were just trying to annoy me," I said, pulling out of the parking lot and turning toward my apartment.

"All I'm saying is the guy isn't all bad. And he still asks how you're doing after ten years—"

"Nine."

"Whatever. Nine years. But still—you're the only one that seems to have an issue here, and I get it. I do. But at some point, you either need to cover up that anchor and get a divorce or forgive the guy for whatever he did."

I clenched my teeth in anger at his skewed view of the situation, but I didn't argue. I couldn't. Because for twenty-five years, I'd never said a word about the way he'd been conceived. He had no idea about the things I'd gone through, or the part Patrick had played in my agony, and if it was up to me, he'd never find out.

"You're right," I said through my teeth.

"I am?"

"Yeah. I need to cover this tattoo."

"Mum, that's not what I was—"

"I'm almost home, so I'll call you later…or in a few days. I'll talk to you soon."

"Are you angry?"

"Not at all, son. I'm just home, and I need to carry some groceries up to the apartment," I lied.

"Okay, then. I guess I'll talk to you later." I rolled my eyes.

"Love you, too. Bye, kiddo."

I hung up and sat in my car, my conversation with Nix forgotten as I remembered Brenna's stiff movements and the weird post she'd put on Craigslist.

I knew I shouldn't get involved, but as I sat there in the quiet, I realized what exactly had caught my eye when I'd seen Brenna for the first time.

She watched the world with the same haunted look that I'd had for most of my life.

That night on a whim, I posted my old, beaten-up Corolla on the same website and for the same price that Brenna had posted her car hours before.

Chapter 50

Patrick

I knocked on the door in an unconscious rhythm before pulling my hand back and stuffing it into the pocket of my jacket.

I wasn't wearing my cut. Portland wasn't our territory and I wasn't on club business, but I felt odd without it. The leather was so worn by that point that it molded to my chest perfectly, and I'd had it retooled more times than I could count as shit had frayed and ripped. Not wearing it reminded me of the feeling I'd get when I forgot my wallet at home.

"Nix you said seven—"

Amy froze with the door halfway open, and for a second I thought she was going to slam it in my face.

"What are you doing here?" she asked nervously, running her hand over her head even though there were no stray hairs to settle.

"It was ye, wasn't it?" I asked, my heart in my throat. God, she was so beautiful and it had been so fucking long since I'd seen her. I wanted to reach out and run my hand down her bare arm just so I could feel her soft skin under my fingertips again.

"I don't know what you're talking about—"

"I don't know how ye did it—" I had to stop to clear my throat. "I don't know how ye knew dat she'd need dat car."

"Who, Patrick? I'm sorry, I don't know—"

"Me sweet Brenna," I looked down at the floor and pulled my hand out of my pocket, so my fingers had room to fidget. "He would have killed her. He almost did."

"Fuck," she whispered, bracing her hand against the door.

"I know it was ye."

"I don't—"

"T'ank ye."

"What?"

"I don't care how ye knew. I don't care what ye did. *T'ank ye*."

"Is she alright?" she finally asked, dropping the pretense.

"He beat de shite out of her," I choked, raising my hand to my face to try and turn the sob into a cough. "She's in de hospital now, but she'll be alright. And she doesn't ever have to worry about him again."

She searched my face thoughtfully, then nodded. "He's visiting the good priest?"

I snorted, and shook my head at her choice of words. "Aye, dey've had similar experiences, yeah? Perhaps dey could compare notes."

"Good," she replied, her jaw firming.

I had no idea how she'd ended up meeting Brenna outside that grocery store in Stayton. It was too odd to be a coincidence, but I had no idea how she'd pulled it off. The fact was—she had—and she'd given my baby the tool she needed to get away from the sorry bastard she'd married. I would never understand why she'd done it, and I'd never be able to repay her.

She'd stepped in when she didn't have to and saved my child.

"Of course, de priest's brudder may be dere, too," I said softly after a moment, watching her closely. "Dough his experiences would make dem t'ankful for dere own."

Her lower lip trembled as tears filled her eyes and her fingertips went white where they gripped the door. My stomach clenched at her expression and I wondered for a second if I'd done the wrong thing.

I'd respected her wishes all those years ago, but that hadn't meant that I'd forgotten. It only meant that I hadn't contacted her when I'd made sure the men she feared no longer walked the earth. She'd wanted me to leave her alone, and I had. After I'd made sure that the monsters who'd hurt her had paid.

"He had a rough time of it then?" she asked through her teeth, her nostrils flaring as she took in a deep breath.

"His mot'er would not have known him," I answered honestly.

A sob came out of her mouth, but I kept my distance. Years ago, I would have taken her into my arms and comforted her, but there was a wide gap between us now that I didn't know how to breach. All I knew with certainty was that she did not want me to touch her.

"Thank you, Patrick," she said, her voice hoarse. I nodded, opening my mouth to speak, but nothing came out.

"Trick? What the hell are you doing here?" Nix called out, walking up the open stairs to Amy's apartment.

"Just stopped by to have a word wit' yer mum," I answered, stepping away from Amy's door. "Ye look good, boyo."

"Thanks, man." He leaned in to give me a hug, and I gripped him hard, thumping his back twice as I let go.

I hadn't seen the boy in far too long, though I was sure Amy would have disagreed. From the emotionless look on her face, I knew she hated that we'd kept in contact at all. I wondered if she knew that we spoke on the phone every couple of weeks, or that he always brought his bike down to Eugene for fixing up.

I hadn't set out to keep in contact with Nix. In fact, I hadn't thought of him at all in the first few weeks after I'd left. I'd been too busy taking care of first Kevin—in a warehouse outside of Dallas—and then Malcolm, in the back room of Casey Dillon's pub.

Sometimes, late at night, I thought about the night I'd caught up with Malcolm, wishing I could do it all over again. He'd been easy to get a hold of, drunk off his fat arse in a pub not far from his mum's. I'd had to wait until he'd sobered up to start in because I hadn't wanted him to miss any of it or neglect to realize the reason for my visit. By the time the alcohol had mostly left his system, he was tied to a chair with a rag in his mouth, bleeding to death from the rough castration I'd performed.

It had been too quick, and I'd left feeling unsatisfied and uncomfortable in my own skin, as if I'd missed something. The feeling had plagued me for years.

It hadn't been until after I'd arrived back in Eugene, weary and ready to be home for a while with Brenna, that I'd gotten a phone call at the shop. Phoenix had been pissed—going on and on about how I'd done something to his mother—how she'd been acting strange since I'd left, and had broken up with her boyfriend. I didn't say much during that first call, I'd just let him take out his anger and his confusion on me over the telephone lines until he'd finally come to a ragged stop.

He'd called again a few weeks later, his anger still present.

Then again a few weeks after that, his anger mostly gone.

It went on like that for months, until one day when he called the shop, there wasn't one heated word. Instead, he'd told me about school, and the dirt bike his mum had helped him buy. After that, he called regularly, just to visit, and I never gave any indication that his calls weren't welcome. At first he'd been my only connection to Amy, but it hadn't taken long before I was anxious for his calls just to know that he was doing alright. I'd begun to care for him when we'd met again in Texas, but as the calls continued, I grew to love him with a ferocity that I hadn't understood was possible for a child that didn't belong to me.

I knew even then that the lad had a long road ahead of him—especially in that tiny Texas town where being different wasn't so popular. I'd breathed a sigh of relief when he and Amy had moved to Portland—a city that got off on sticking out in a crowd.

"Are you coming in for dinner? Mum's making—"

My heart thumped hard and began to race.

"Patrick can't stay," Amy announced firmly with a small shake of her head.

"Yer mum's right, I was just on my way t'rough," I told him, respecting her choice, but hating that I couldn't speak up. I'd never understood how my da could walk away from us without even arguing until that moment, when I knew that I'd let her push me away again without a protest.

I wasn't about to cause a rift between her and Nix because I had the overwhelming urge to push her inside the apartment and tell her I wasn't going anywhere.

"Through Portland?"

"Right."

"Hey, how's Brenna doing?" he asked, looking between his mum and I as if he knew a secret. I almost laughed at his attempt to make Amy uncomfortable. He had no idea that I'd figured it out.

"She's healin'," I said with a small smile. "And she's havin' another babe."

"Congratulations!" Nix swung one of his long arms out and slapped my shoulder, and I couldn't help but be proud of the self-assured man he'd become.

He was a good lad, there was no doubt about that.

I heard a small noise, and my head whipped toward Amy. I wasn't even sure it had come from her until I saw the frown on her face.

"She's pregnant?" she asked sympathetically.

"Aye," I answered, confused for a moment. "She and Dragon—a lad from de club—are havin' anot'er."

"Wait, what?"

"They have me oldest granddaughter, and now another on de way."

"Okay," she said hesitantly, her face still confused.

"It's a long ass story, Mum," Nix said, taking off his coat as he moved inside.

"Well, it was nice to see you again Patrick," Amy declared abruptly, as if she was afraid I'd follow Nix into the house. "Thanks for stopping by."

"I'll call you later this week," Nix yelled as Amy began closing the door. "My bike is rattling and I can't figure out where the fuck it's coming from."

"Talk to ye soon, boyo," I called back. Then I met Amy's guarded eyes and gave her a small nod before I forced myself to walk away.

I'd been anxious to see her, and thankful that I'd been given a reason to do so ... but as I left her apartment complex that evening, I wondered if it would have been better if I'd not seen her at all. The pain I'd felt in my chest the last time she'd ordered me from her house came back with startling intensity as I climbed on my bike.

Christ, when would I stop having such a visceral reaction to the woman? I had any pussy I wanted at the club, my vice-president patch and big cock enough of an aphrodisiac for any of the whores—but twenty minutes in the company of one woman and I wanted to either fuck only her forever or be celibate for the rest of my bloody life.

When I looked at her, I didn't see the forty-year-old woman with laugh lines bracketing her eyes and mouth. I saw her at eighteen, smooth skinned and adoring as she'd looked at me from inside my sheets.

I missed the smell of her, the taste of her, the feel of her, and the ache for her didn't fade no matter how long we'd spent apart.

I deliberately blanked my mind as I started up my bike and pulled out of the small parking lot. There was no use trying to figure out why she affected me so strongly; it just was, and I didn't believe that would ever change.

I belonged to her no matter how much she hated me.

***

"Hey, Pop!" Brenna called out across the noisy room, making my head snap up in surprise. "Did I leave Leo's blanket in your room earlier?"

I shook my head, not even bothering to try and yell over the music and laughter that surrounded me. I was tired, so goddamn tired.

I'd been living in the clubhouse for a fuck of a long time, and the constant buzz of people in and out was finally getting old. Christ, maybe it was just me that was getting old. I'd sold my house back when Brenna had gotten married because I'd hated going home to the quiet, but lately I'd been missing that silence.

It was as if the younger lads saw me as some sort of den mother, and more often than not, they'd been coming to me with bullshite problems that I had no interest in solving. I didn't care who was fucking who, or which little prick had forgotten to pick up the kegs from behind the bar. I just didn't give a shit.

It had been over two years since the last time I'd seen Amy, and I think the visit had fucked me up more than I'd realized at the time. Before I'd stopped by her apartment that day, I'd let myself believe in the back of my mind that she'd come back to me at some point. That in some alternate reality, she'd been waiting for me to make the first move—and as long as I hadn't seen her, I'd been able to perpetuate that lie in my head.

I could no longer do so.

I'd seen Phoenix eight or nine times in the past two years, and I'd not seen Amy even once.

"It was in Slider's room," Brenna mumbled into my ear before climbing over the back of the couch I was sitting on. "Whatcha doin', Pop?"

"Havin' a beer and watchin' Casper act like a woman," I answered, pointing the neck of my bottle toward where the kid was smiling goofily at his girl.

"Be nice, they're cute."

"Don't know about cute—good thing he worships the ground she walks on, though."

"No shit—Slider would kill him."

"Slowly," I agreed.

"Everyone's settling down lately and having babies," she said tiredly, resting her head on my shoulder. "You ever wish you had more kids after me?"

"Yer ma couldn't have any more after ye," I reminded her.

"That's not what I asked."

I was quiet for a moment, thinking back to the day I'd asked Amy to marry me. "Aye, I thought about more children. At one point, I thought I'd have a houseful."

"You're still young, you know. You have time."

"Yer delusional," I said through a laugh. "That time is long gone."

"At least an old lady then."

"Not sure that'll happen either, lass." I wrapped my arm around her and kissed the side of her head. "Don't ye worry about yer old da. I've got everythin' I need right here."

"Of course you do, I'm awesome. God, I'm tired," she moaned, relaxing even farther into my chest.

"Where are the babies?"

"Vera stayed at the house with them so Dragon and I could have some adult time, but shit, he's over there playing pool with the boys and all I want to do is take a nap." Her voice was muffled against my cut, and a memory hit me of her drooling all over the thing when she was cutting teeth.

"Close yer eyes, lass. I'll wake ye up if anythin' excitin' happens."

"I knew you were my favorite."

"I better be."

She fell asleep within minutes, and Dragon caught my eye from across the room, tilting his head to the side in question. I shook my head, letting him know she was fine where she was and leaned back into the couch. It had been a long time since my girl had fallen asleep curled up against me—I was going to savor it a little longer.

I must have fallen asleep at some point, because I woke up to my phone vibrating against my chest. Brenna had scooted down in her sleep and her curly red head was resting on my thigh, one hand tucked under her face and the other clutching Leo's blanket like she was afraid she'd lose it again. My baby girl was a mum. Sometimes it was hard to believe it.

I pulled my phone from the pocket of my shirt and answered it quickly before the ringer started blaring.

"Yeah?"

There was silence on the end of the line, and I tensed as I waited.

"Patrick?"

"Amy?"

"Phoenix," she gasped as if she was trying to catch her breath, and I immediately tucked the phone into the space between my neck and my shoulder so I could use both hands to slide Brenna's head onto the couch. "They think someone beat him, Patrick. Someone hurt him bad."

"Where are ye?" I barked, knowing that I should temper my voice, but unable to do it with the panic coursing through my veins.

"We're at Emmanuel in Portland. They called me when they brought him in but—" she sniffled again. "They haven't let me see him and no one is telling me anything."

"Ye alone?"

"Ken's here. Shit. Mat. Mat's here."

Ken?

"Nix's Mat?"

"Yeah."

"Can ye give him de phone?"

There was a shuffling noise for a couple of seconds, and while I waited I walked toward the boys standing around the pool table. As they noticed me, I motioned with my head and they all nodded, moving off to talk to their women.

"Trick?"

"Hey, Mat. What's goin' on, man?"

"I don't know," the poor kid said quietly.

"Ye haven't heard anythin'?"

"I've got a friend, she works in the ER and she was supposed to text me, but she hasn't."

"Maybe she hasn't got a chance yet. Gotta give them time to see what's what. Everything's probably fine—just gotta be patient, boyo. I need you to stay with Amy, okay? I'm on my way, but I won't be there for hours yet—you stay with her even if you hear from your friend."

"I will. I will. Do you want me to call you if we hear anything? God, Trick, I don't understand why it's taking so long." He sniffed hard at the other end of the line, and my stomach clenched.

Amy's tears I understood, that was her baby boy. But if Mat was upset enough to cry, I knew that things were not good.

"Yeah, mate. Call if you hear anythin'. I'll be on the bike, so leave a message and I'll check back in a bit."

"Okay."

"Stay with Amy."

"I will. Patrick?"

"Yeah, kid?"

"I was supposed to go with him," he whispered. "We had plans but I wanted to stay home because work's been so crazy. I didn't—fuck—I should have been with him."

I stopped next to my bike and felt my stomach roll. A small part of me wanted to yell. I wanted to tell him that, yes, he should have fucking been there. As a parent, I wanted to blame the little fucker for not having Nix's back.

But I would never say such a thing aloud. Because I knew with absolute certainty that whatever happened was not his fault... and the guilt was going to poison him from the inside out without a single word from me.

"Could have happened even if ye were there, Mat," I said instead. "Could be ye in there with him, yeah? I'll call ye soon."

I hung up the phone, and had to brace myself on my bike for a moment.

That's where Slider, Dragon, Grease and Casper found me a few minutes later.

"I need you boys with me," I said, grabbing my helmet.

"What's goin' on, Poet?" Slider asked.

"Amy just called. Said Nix got jumped."

"Motherfucker. He alright?"

"Not sure—Amy's worried outta her mind and they're not tellin' her shite."

"They in Portland?"

"Emmanuel."

"You need me there?"

"No, brother. Not sure how well that would go over and I don't want to add to her worry."

"Yeah, I get it." Slider ran his hand over his short goatee. "You'll let me know when you hear somethin'?"

My life from before rarely mixed with the one in Eugene. I'd never wanted Brenna to question where she'd come from or the love I'd felt for her mother—especially after we'd lost her—but the boys at the club knew Nix. Slider had taken an interest in the boy from the very beginning, when he'd first come for a visit during his freshman year in college, probably because he was Amy's. I knew the man would be worried as hell until I got to Portland and found out what the fuck was going on.

"I'll keep ye posted," I agreed, then turned to the lads. "Ye boys up for a ride to Portland?"

"Yup."

"I'm down."

"They know who did it?" Grease asked, crossing his arms across his chest.

"Not yet, but I sure as fuck will," I said roughly.

We left immediately, and even riding well over the speed limit, it still took us hours before we were pulling into the emergency parking lot at the hospital. I hadn't heard one word from Amy or Mat, and by the time we'd stowed our colors and walked in the sliding glass doors, I was strung tight as a bow.

"I'm lookin' for Phoenix Gallagher," I told the receptionist, making Dragon's eyes snap to me in surprise.

"I'm sorry sir, we can't give out information—"

"I'm his da," I interrupted, slapping my driver's license on the countertop. "Where's me son?"

"It looks like he's in surgery. Let me make you guys some nametags so you can get there without a problem."

We were on the move again and riding the elevator to the surgery floor in minutes, but it felt like the woman had taken as long as she possibly could to write two words on a sticker with a fucking marker.

"Lucy, you got some 'splainin' to do," Dragon mumbled behind me.

"Shut it, Ricky," I snapped back, the lights of the hospital giving me a headache after riding in the dark for so long. Where was my boy? Fuck, I was losing it.

I saw Amy the minute the elevator doors opened, and my first instinct was to go straight to her and pull her against me, but I held myself back. Instead, I walked slowly toward where she and Mat were sitting quietly, not saying a word until she looked up and caught sight of me.

"They took him into surgery," she said, standing up to meet us. "His spleen was ruptured, so they had to take care of that first." Her hands came up to cover her mouth and I moved without thought.

I pulled her tight against me and dropped my face to her shoulder, the lump in my throat threatening to choke me. She felt so small there, like she was shrinking into herself, and I tortured myself with the thought that she'd been where Nix was, but with no hospital and no support past my mum and Doc. It made me want to go back and slice Malcolm to pieces all over again.

"He'll be alright," I assured her, rubbing her back gently. "Best trauma hospital in de state—dey know what dey're doin.' "

"His face, Patrick." She sobbed, "It was so swollen."

"Boy was too pretty to begin wit', yeah? It'll give his mug some character."

"I can't believe this is happening," she whispered, pulling away from me. "Thank you for coming."

"Wouldn't be anywhere else."

I glanced up to find the lads standing around uncomfortably, and Dragon watching the interaction closely with absolutely no expression.

"Boys," I said, lightly grasping Amy's arm to turn her toward them. "Dis is Amy, Phoenix's mum. Amy, dis is Casper, Dragon and Grease."

"Nice names," she commented with a snort, making me grin.

"Call me Asa, ma'am." Grease said, reaching out to grasp her hand.

"Cody," Casper followed.

"Dragon."

"Gonna stick with Dragon, huh?" Amy asked as she grasped his hand.

"Only name I answer to," he replied with a twitch of his lips.

"You guys know my son?" she asked, stepping back to my side.

She didn't touch me, but my breath still sped up at her movement. If she knew what she'd done, she'd immediately step away again, and I wanted her there next to me. The fact that she'd instinctively moved to my side after staying as far away as she could for so long was... she may as well have kissed me.

"Yeah," Grease answered her, "Known Nix for years."

"He never said anything about a gorgeous mother, though," Casper chimed in with a crooked smile.

"Watch it," I warned, making the boys laugh.

"You can call me gorgeous all damn day," Amy argued, before glancing over her shoulder. "You guys met Mat yet?"

We walked toward the man hunched over in his chair, and I couldn't help but feel incredibly sorry for him. His eyes were bloodshot, his clothes were wrinkled as hell, and the mop of blonde hair on his head was literally standing on end.

"Hey, Mat," I said, reaching out to shake his hand. "Good to see ye."

"Hey, Trick."

"The boyfriend?" Grease mouthed to Dragon.

My boys were standing silently, their chests puffed out like a bunch of roosters and theirs arms crossed over their chests.

Jesus Christ.

"Where were you?" Grease said quietly, and I honestly thought Mat was going to shit himself right there in the middle of the hospital waiting room.

"Enough, Grease—"

"I was home asleep," Mat replied, his eyes filling with tears. "I was just tired—I just didn't want to go out and watch football at a fucking bar. I wanted to sit on my motherfucking couch and watch the game in my goddamn underwear."

His words got stronger as he got angrier, and it was a relief when the broken man stood up and started pacing. The lads all watched closely as Mat ran his hand over his hair—showing us exactly how it had gotten so messy—and one by one, their bodies relaxed. Casper was new—and younger—but Grease and Dragon had been protective of Nix since the first time he'd shown up at the garage on a rusted old Honda. The fact that Nix had never brought Mat by the garage made them suspicious.

"Are you the family of Phoenix Gallagher?"

I spun around to catch sight of a man in light blue scrubs walking toward us.

"I'm his mother," Amy stated, taking a couple steps forward.

"Hello. I'm Dr. Albright. We've just finished with Phoenix, and the surgery went beautifully—"

I didn't hear the rest of the words as my legs began to tingle, and I wondered for a moment if I was going to hit the floor in a heap from the relief that made me dizzy.

"Steady, brother," Dragon mumbled, gripping my shoulder until I caught my balance again.

By that time, the doctor was already walking back through the double doors he'd come out of and I'd missed almost everything he'd said.

"Thank God," Amy murmured, a wide smile on her face. "Thank

God. Thank God." The last word was a sob, and she dropped her face into her hands, covering her entire face beneath her fingers.

My legs were instantly steady and in working order.

"Shhh," I soothed, stepping forward to pull her against my chest as she moaned into her hands. "Come on now, love, ye've gotta calm a bit or ye'll make yerself sick."

Her fingers dug into my chest as she gripped my t-shirt, but she couldn't seem to stop the sobs that wracked her body.

"Did dey say when we could see him?" I asked Casper, who was standing the closest to us.

"He's in recovery now—an hour or so and they'll let one or two people back."

"Only an hour, sweetheart," I murmured into Amy's hair as her sobs calmed to hiccupping breaths. "Ye want some coffee, or a soda maybe?"

She shook her head but didn't raise it as she continued clutching my shirt tightly, almost like she was afraid I was going to let her go. Christ, hadn't she figured it out yet? I'd continue to hold her as long as she'd allow it.

***

Two hours passed before they allowed us back to see Nix. He'd had some sort of reaction to the anesthesia and they'd wanted to keep a close eye on things for a while longer than they'd told us in the beginning.

They'd only allow two people in the room at a time, and I'd clenched my jaw as Mat and Amy stood up to follow the nurse back, but within a few steps Amy had paused and rested her hand on Mat's arm.

"I think it should be me and Patrick at first, okay, Mat?" She said it kindly, but it really wasn't a question.

"Oh, sure," he replied, glancing back to where I was getting to my feet. "I'll just wait for one of you to come out."

I took his place as we followed the dark haired nurse, and I glanced over at Amy's face as we walked, curious about where her head was at. It didn't take long before she started to speak.

"You're his dad," she said, focusing her eyes straight ahead. "I mean, as close as he's ever had to one. You should be one of the first ones in there."

I nodded, but I couldn't answer her because, for the first time since I'd gotten her phone call, I felt tears burn at the backs of my eyes. His da. To say I was honored would have been a massive understatement.

Chapter 51

Amy

Every fear I'd had over the course of Nix's life had coalesced into that single moment when I met his eyes after surgery.

He was groggy and his face was still really swollen. During the few hours we'd been apart, his skin had begun to bruise in shades varying from raspberry to almost black, and they'd set the broken bone in his wrist while he was out of it.

But none of those things were as bad as the look in his eyes. It was pure fear and confusion—like he couldn't even understand what had happened.

"Mum," he mumbled through swollen lips.

"Hey, baby," I replied gently, walking forward until I was standing next to the edge of his bed. "I'd kiss ya, but I'm afraid I'd hurt those Angelina Jolie lips you've got goin' on."

"Ma mouth tathteth like ath," he said, his words so garbled I had a hard time understanding him. "An ma tongue hurth like a motha."

"Ye probably bit de hell out of it," Patrick spoke up, finally coming into the room.

"Twick!" Nix said in surprise, one side of his mouth pulling up a little before falling again. His eyes darkened in embarrassment as they jerked back and forth between us, and I saw him swallow painfully. "You doin' hea?"

"Had to come see me boy," Patrick replied softly, stopping on the other side of Nix's bed. "Ye look like shite."

"Ya should thee the otha guy," Nix joked with no change in expression.

"Only one?"

I bit the inside of my cheek as we waited for his answer. I knew. I *knew* that there was no way one guy did this much damage to my boy. My son was big, and he was incredibly strong, and after years of visiting Patrick at the club, I knew he could take care of himself. So the fact that he was in the hospital just out of surgery because he'd been beaten so badly? There had to have been more than one person involved.

"Fow o five, I thin," Nix answered, dropping his head gingerly back onto the pillows. My stomach clenched in horror. He hadn't stood a chance.

"Ye recognize any of dem?"

"Theen couple of vem awoun. At the bah prett offen." Nix's eyes closed, and two tears rolled down the sides of his face as his nostrils flared.

"Alright, son," Patrick said gently, "Alright."

He reached out to brush Nix's wild hair gently off his forehead, and my throat felt so thick it was hard for me to breathe.

"Lads are here wit' me, we'll take care of dis—" Patrick promised.

"Don let em back heah," Nix said quietly, defeat in every line of his body.

"Nix—" I began, but Patrick cut me off.

"Look at me," he ordered quietly, leaning down into Nix's face.

My son's eyes opened, and the shame there nearly brought me to my knees.

"Ye—" Patrick stopped and cleared his throat, sniffing once before speaking again. "Ye get a few of yer own in?"

Nix nodded slightly, his eyes watering.

"Dat's me boy," Patrick said vehemently. "Ye have not one t'ing to be ashamed about, ye understand me?" His head lowered even farther until Nix had no option of looking away. "Dere is no shame in bein' outnumbered."

"Ith becauthe I'm gay," Nix whispered as if that was important, tears rolling down his cheeks. "Ca me a faggot."

Patrick reared back as if he'd been hit, and the fury on his face was overwhelming.

"Ye did not come from me body," Patrick said fiercely, staring into Nix's overflowing eyes and cupping his face so gently their skin was barely touching. "But ye are me son. And ye are exactly as God made ye. Dere is not one t'ing wrong wit' ye, Phoenix Robert Gallagher, and I'll kill any man who says ot'erwise."

Nix chest lurched as he tried to hold back a sob, and I laid my hand over my eyes to hide my despair.

I remember being afraid of every sharp corner and uneven step when Nix was a baby. I'd seen danger everywhere, and I'd been riddled with anxiety any time he'd attempt to sit up or crawl or walk. There were so many things he could hurt himself on.

As he grew older, the focus changed. It was slow, but eventually I got more comfortable with his physical safety and I'd worried more about his emotional safety. There's nothing quite like dropping your kindergartener off on the first day and forcing yourself to walk away from them. Was he scared? Was he crying? What if the other kids were mean? Did I put the right t-shirt on him or was that cartoon considered uncool? It didn't stop; if anything, that feeling of fear grew as he got older.

I couldn't protect him any more, not physically or emotionally, and now he'd been unbelievably hurt. That realization was like someone cutting out my heart.

"Mum, don' cry," Nix said, grabbing my loose shirt in his fingers. "I'm gon be fine."

"I'm so sorry this happened to you," I replied, pulling a few tissues from his nightstand to wipe my face. "Christ, Nix."

"Ith Mat here?" he asked, his eyes moving between Patrick and me.

"Yeah, he's here. He's probably pissed because I made him wait so Patrick could come back."

"He'll get ovah it." He waved his hand a little in a 'brush it off' gesture that reminded me of Peg. "I'm tiad, can you thend him back before ah path out?"

"Sure, son." I leaned forward to kiss him, but I couldn't find a single place on his face that wasn't battered.

"Lipth," he muttered, pursing his lips.

I gave him a quick peck, then leaned back. "It's like three in the morning, so I'm going to get a hotel unless you want me to stay?"

"Nah."

"That's what I figured. I'll be back after I get a couple hours of sleep, okay?"

"Love ooh, Mumma."

"I love you too, baby."

I left the room before I started crying again. He didn't need me losing my shit while he laid there in pain, unable to do anything about it. He was so protective of me, probably because it had just been me and him against the world for most of his life —so I knew that he was lying in there worried about me, even though he had to be in excruciating amounts of pain.

Patrick didn't follow me straight out, but by the time I'd reached the double doors to the waiting room, he'd caught up to me.

"Mat, yer up," he called out as we reached the group of men standing in the corridor. "Ye stayin' here de rest of de night?"

"Yeah, I'll be in his room if they don't kick me out."

"Okay, let me or his mum know if ye've gotta leave, yeah?"

"Sure." Mat didn't wait another second before he was striding quickly down the hallway and out of our sight.

"He say anything?" Grease asked, the veins in his neck becoming more pronounced as I watched. The guy was built like a brick shithouse.

"Got a description on two of 'em," Patrick answered, his jaw tightly clenched. "Said he's seen 'em around de pub he goes to. Saturday night, should be easy to find 'em. Nix got one of 'em good in de face, bet dey all have fucked up knuckles."

"Cops been in yet?" Dragon asked, and I got a good look at him now that I was a bit calmer.

That's when I realized who he was—Brenna's man. That's why I'd remembered his name. Dang, their daughter was the spitting image of him.

"Haven't been in yet—don't matter though—Nix don't remember what happened."

I looked at him sharply, and he shook his head once.

"Amy and I are gonna get a hotel, ye boys should do de same."

"Need to talk, brother," Dragon said ominously. Damn, if these boys weren't young enough to be my sons, they'd be scary as hell.

"It'll wait," Patrick dismissed him with a glare. "I'll call ye lads in a few hours."

His hand rested at the small of my back as he ushered me to the elevator, and I didn't resist. I just didn't have it in me.

Once I knew that Phoenix would be okay, my body had started to ache with exhaustion, and my head was pounding from all the tears I'd shed. Now that the nightmares that had plagued me since Nix was a child had been realized, I didn't know what to do with myself.

I was so angry, so unbelievably angry. I wanted to find those men and claw their eyes out. I wanted to parade them through the streets, yelling out their crime for everyone to hear. I wanted them to hurt for their cowardice.

I wanted them to feel the same shame that Nix was feeling for not being able to protect himself.

Those motherfuckers.

"Ye know a hotel around here?" Patrick asked as we stepped

outside the front doors.

"Yeah." My voice was hollow and I could feel the numbness sinking in.

"Hey," he called, getting my attention. "I'll grab me bike and follow ye dere. Where ye parked?"

***

He was being a bit presumptuous twenty minutes later when he rented only one room, but I didn't say a word. I knew it was a bad idea—Patrick and I in one place with a bed involved was always a bad idea—but I didn't like the idea of being alone, either.

He was the only support system I had, as pathetic as that sounded. I'd never been good at making friends, and most of the people I came into contact with on a daily basis were acquaintances at best. Making connections had never been something I'd learned to do, and after I'd been attacked all those years before, I'd lost the will to even try. I liked my own company. I didn't need anyone else.

I suppose, though, that wasn't altogether true. Because at one point, I'd needed two people more than I'd ever thought possible. One of them was leading me down a corridor at that very moment, looking for our hotel room.

"Only brought one change of clothes in my saddle bags, but if ye want the t-shirt I got, it's yers," he mumbled, pushing open the door to the room.

"I'm good in this," I told him, walking ahead of him and straight into the bathroom.

I needed to wash my face and I'd had to pee for what felt like hours. I stayed in there longer than I needed to, but eventually, I pulled off my shoes and socks and walked back into the bedroom, carrying them in my arms.

Patrick was doing something on his phone when I came out, but looked up when I sat on the edge of the bed, still holding the shoes.

"Ot'er side, love," he said, making me look up in surprise.

"Huh?"

"I sleep by de door."

I nodded absently and stood back up, remembering the first night he'd rolled over to face the door instead of sleeping wrapped around me. I told myself that I didn't care how he slept anymore, but a small part of me twinged at the thought that he still did that.

He came toward me as I sat back down, and my eyes burned as I looked up to meet his. God, they hurt. I was so fucking worn out.

"Better lie down before ye fall down," he said quietly, reaching behind me to pull the blankets down the bed. "Climb in."

He took my shoes and socks out of my hand and unwrapped my purse from over my shoulder as soon as I laid down, then pulled the blankets back up to my chin, tucking them around my sides.

"Sorry," he mumbled, taking a step back. "Forgot where I was for a moment."

I closed my eyes and passed out as I felt him lie down on the other side of the bed. Knowing he was there meant that I slept deeper than I had in the many years he'd been gone.

I instinctively knew that nothing could hurt me when Patrick was there.

It was when he left that bad things happened.

***

We spent the next day at the hospital, becoming familiar with Nix's room and the cafeteria. There was something I loved about the food there. It reminded me of school lunches when I was a kid—grilled cheese sandwiches and hamburgers that tasted satisfyingly like rubber. The coffee sucked, though, and by that evening, I was dragging ass again. I was too old to function on four hours of sleep.

"Gonna head out for a bit," Patrick told Nix, watching him closely. "Boys wanna see ye before we go."

I wasn't sure what passed between them in that look, but minutes later, Grease, Dragon and Casper were filing into the room, their large bodies crowding it a little too much for me to be comfortable.

"Jesus, Nix, they got you good," Casper said in surprise.

Nix flinched, but nodded silently.

"Hell, that's nothin'. Shoulda seen Dragon when Poet got through with him," Grease chimed in, leaning forward to shake Nix's uncasted hand. "Good to see you, man."

"Yeah, you too." The swelling in Nix's mouth had gone down a bit, his words more clear than they'd been the night before.

"I was pissin' blood for weeks," Dragon grumbled, nodding at Nix. "Have fun with that."

I watched my son's body go from completely rigid to relaxed within moments, and I could have kissed those three boys.

"Stop fuckin' complainin', ye wean." Patrick grumbled.

"I only understood about fifty-four percent of what you just said," Casper commented to Patrick in bewilderment. "Did anyone understand that shit?"

Nix started to laugh and then winced. "His accent always gets thick like that when he's around my mum. Never fails."

"Yeah, but do you have any clue what he's sayin'—"

"Met your man last night," Grease interrupted Casper and I braced myself. I'd seen the way they'd been staring at Mat. "I can see the draw—dude's almost as pretty as a chick."

Nix laughed then groaned, but the smile stayed on his face. "Mum calls him Ken."

"Yeah, he does kinda look like one of the Barbies Trix has lyin' around," Dragon commented, making all the men laugh.

"I'm mostly jealous that he's prettier than me," I joked, winking at Nix.

"Not possible," Patrick argued with a small smile. "Ye good here?"

"Yeah, we'll be fine. Mat should be back in a while with Nix's stuff."

"We'll see ye soon, yeah?" Patrick said, turning to Nix and kissing him on the forehead.

Dragon and Casper's mouths dropped open in surprise, but Grease just smirked.

"Let's go, boys," Patrick called as he walked away without waiting for them to follow.

"You didn't say your mom was hot," Casper complained to Nix as they reached the doorway, which had Grease shoving him into the wall so hard I knew he'd have bruises.

"Keep pushin' and Poet's gonna have your balls," I heard him mumble.

Nix and I were quiet for a few minutes, and the lack of noise was kind of nice. We hadn't had much time to just *be* over the past almost twenty-four hours, and it was comforting to be in the same room with my boy and not have to fill the silence with chatter.

We understood each other better than anyone else, and I wasn't sure if that was normal, considering my son would be thirty soon… but I didn't really care, either. For so long, we'd only had each other. We were a family of two, and luckily for me, I didn't seem to annoy him too badly. I knew that he had his own life outside of me—Mat was a big part of that—and he knew that I needed space. We worked in a way that only two people who knew each other inside and out could. My kid was a genuinely cool guy and even though he was grown, I still loved hanging out with him.

"I'm sorry, Mum," he said after a while.

"For what?" I pulled the scarf I was knitting out of my purse and tried to get my hands situated on the needles. It didn't matter how many years had passed since Peg had taught me to knit, I still couldn't do anything more intricate than a long piece of fabric.

"For all this."

"Don't be an idiot."

"I'm not. I know this sucks for you. You hate hospitals."

"Everyone hates hospitals."

"You hate them more than most people."

"That can't really be determined, can it? I mean, who are these 'most' people. How many is a 'most'? I mean, some people only go to hospitals when babies are born, so they don't really count—"

"Christ on a cracker, Mum! Could you shut up?"

"If I have to."

"You have to."

"Fine."

We were silent again while I stewed, but I knew at any moment he would once again bring it up. He'd never been able to stay quiet unless it was on his own terms. We could eat an entire dinner with no words spoken, but if he wanted to say something and I asked him to be quiet? He could *not* hold that shit in.

"I'm just sorry I scared you, and that you've had to be here with me all day."

I continued to knit quietly.

"You can talk."

"Oh, can I?"

"Stop being an ass."

"First, let's get one thing straight," I said, dropping my knitting to my lap and turning to face him. "You can't control what other people do, therefore you couldn't control whether or not you'd be in the hospital at this particular juncture."

"You've been reading again. I can tell by the words you're using."

"Second," I raised my voice above his, "I would rather be with you—even in this smelly ass hospital—than anywhere else on earth."

"Fair enough."

"I'm always fair… and right."

"I'm going to sleep, okay?"

"Having your buds come to visit tired you out, huh?"

"They're cool, right?" he asked, closing his eyes. I felt bad for him, because I knew he'd never be comfortable on his back. My kid was a stomach sleeper, always had been.

"Yeah, and good looking."

"Shut up."

"Did you see Casper's eyes? Good Lord."

"Mum."

"And Dragon, with that long hair? Jesus. I think I need to read a historical romance novel soon... I know who the mighty brave will be."

"I'm going to vomit."

"Don't even get me started on Grease."

"I've been trying to stop you for five minutes."

"Muscles," I sang.

"You're insane."

"Love you."

"Love you, too... most of the time."

I smiled to myself as I picked up my knitting again, listening to my son breathe. The noise on the monitors was extra, the heart monitor more of a nuisance than anything, but when I heard him breathing just a few feet away, it made me feel like all was right in the world again.

"His eyes *are* incredible," he murmured sleepily before nodding off.

***

Patrick and the boys never made it back to the hospital that night. I finally left Nix's room at almost midnight and drove straight to the hotel room that Patrick had booked for another night. I'd grabbed some clothes from my apartment during the day while Nix had been resting, and I was so glad I had. Even though I'd planned to sleep in my own bed that night, I couldn't make myself go that far from the hospital.

Nix was going to be fine. I knew that intellectually. However, emotionally I was still scared out of my mind. I'd almost lost him. If someone hadn't seen him lying in that parking lot, he could have bled to death.

I had to try and balance my need to be up his ass all the time and the need to get some actual sleep in a bed.

The hotel seemed like a solid middle ground until I walked into the room as Patrick was walking out of the bathroom, wearing nothing but a towel slung around his waist.

"You're back," I announced stupidly, letting the door swing shut behind me.

"Didn't take long, yeah? How's Nix?"

"He's good. Mat was staying with him again tonight, so I was going to try and catch some sleep. I'm pretty sure he's getting sick of me by now, anyway."

"I doubt dat," he said, shaking his head as he stepped into a pair of boxer briefs and pulled them up under his towel.

"How—" I cleared my throat as he pulled the towel away, trying to get a hold of myself. "Mums seem to annoy grown sons regularly. There are about a thousand sitcoms based on that very premise."

"Not yer son," he argued, drying his beard and hair with the towel. "Yer son t'inks yer de shite."

"That's because I am."

"Ye just made me point."

"You wear boxer briefs now? When did that happen?" What the fuck was I saying? I didn't care about his underwear. I didn't care about it at all.

"What?" he asked in confusion.

"Forget I said that."

"Ye like me underwear?"

"No, you look like you're trying too hard."

"Because I'm wearin' boxer briefs?" He was looking at me like I'd lost my mind, and I was pretty sure I had.

"You're too old for boxer briefs."

"Yer too old for dose fuckin' booty shorts I know ye have under dat skirt, cause I saw de outline of dem at de hospital earlier."

"Did you just say *booty shorts*?"

"Ye'd call dem somet'in' different?"

"Um, underwear that comes in a pack of ten. That's what I'd call them."

"Don't care where dey came from, I'd still like to see yer arse cheeks hangin' out de bottom of 'em."

I opened my mouth, then closed it again. I had no idea what to say to that. We were venturing into dead man's land, and I'd fucking led us there.

"Ye plannin' on standin' next to de door all night?"

"What?" I looked around me, then shook my head. "Uh, no."

I'd carried my bag with me from my car, and I dropped it near the dresser so I could rummage through it for some pajamas. I wasn't going to wake up again with my freaking skirt hiked up to my waist and lines from the chest band of my bra permanently imbedded in my skin.

Without another word, I scooped up my things and stepped into the bathroom, closing the door firmly behind me. I needed a shower—a cold one—and a couple of minutes to get myself together.

"Ye couldn't have grabbed an old t-shirt or somet'in'?" Patrick grumbled as I stepped out of the steamy bathroom a half hour later.

"I'm wearing shorts underneath, ya dirty old man."

"I can be much dirtier, love," he said hoarsely, sitting up from the bed. "Just say de word."

I'd dated a few men in the last couple of years, nice guys, but not one of them had caused such a primitive reaction in my body. It was as if the closer he got to me as he crossed the room, the more my body heated and softened. My fight or flight response never kicked in, and I blame the stress I was under for the way I immediately began to justify my need to run my palms over all of the smooth skin that was just feet away from me.

Maybe if he'd gotten dressed in a nice pair of pajamas instead of prowling around the room in nothing but those boxer briefs...

"I've never wanted anyt'in' as much as I want ye," he said reverently, reaching out to run his finger over the strap of my nightgown laying against my shoulder.

"Word," I choked out. I only said it once, but in my head it was ringing out over and over again.

"Yeah?" His hand slid up to cup the side of my throat and I shuddered.

"Yeah," I confirmed.

His other hand came up until they were both on my neck, tilting my head back as he stepped into me. The first kiss was tentative, our lips barely brushing, but when my hands lifted to rest on his chest, all bets were off.

His mouth pressed against mine as he groaned, and I immediately opened up, letting his tongue slide between my lips. Kissing had always been flawless with us, a choreographed dance that had us tilting our heads just so for maximum impact, and even after years apart and different lovers between us, that hadn't seemed to change.

Chapter 52

Patrick

My hands were shaking so badly and I couldn't seem to stop them.

I had her. She was right there in my arms and she wasn't pulling away. *She wasn't pulling away.*

It was a fucking miracle.

This wasn't a desire to comfort me like it had been the last time. Dear God, it had been twenty years since she'd had her hands on me that way. How could so much time pass by in the blink of an eye? It was both incredible and incredibly humbling that the minute we touched, all the years seemed to disappear.

"On de bed," I ordered, running my hands down the front of her body until my fingers were gripping her hips. I wanted to spin her around and slap her ass to get her moving so I could watch it as she climbed onto the bed, but I didn't dare let go of her. I was terrified that if our connection broke for even a moment, she'd realize that she didn't really want me.

"You're bossy," she said, stepping backward.

"I've always been bossy."

"You never needed a bed before. Too old to nail me against the wall?"

She was baiting me, pushing to get what she wanted, and my cock was so hard from her tone that it was about to rip through my briefs.

"We're gonna be at it a while, yeah?" I replied, drawing a deep breath in through my nose to calm my breathing. "I want ye spread out and comfortable."

I dropped my hand to her thigh as she reached the bed, and listened to her breathing speed up as I pushed the nightgown to her waist.

Shorts my arse. They were underwear, and just as I'd imagined, they only covered half of her cheeks.

"Dis comes off," I rasped, gripping her nightgown and pulling it over her head.

I stopped then. Everything stopped—my hands, my breathing, my heart.

She was everything I'd missed for years, and more than anything I could have imagined.

Her chest was heaving, and her breasts swayed, the hard nipples pointed toward my chest like little beacons. They weren't as perky as when we were young, but they were heavy and thick and I couldn't help the sound I made as I stared. I drew my gaze downward, over her oddly shaped bellybutton that I knew came from when she'd carried Nix, and the small white lines that zigzagged their way from the top of her underwear to halfway up her stomach.

I wanted to cry in that moment. Why hadn't I paid attention all those years ago? Why hadn't I taken the time to really see the body she was showing me and realized then, before it was too late, that I wanted to see that skin stretched tightly over our child? I hadn't catalogued her changes then; I'd been too anxious to get as close to her as I could.

Perhaps if I had been less selfish, I'd have found a way to make her love me again.

"You're staring," she whispered, running her hands down my belly.

"I'm in awe."

"It's just a body."

"It's *yer* body."

"It's getting impatient," she said slyly, running her nails up my chest and pinching one of my nipples between her fingers.

It was like a jolt straight to my balls, and I felt my cock twitch as I shuddered.

I grabbed her hand in mine, pulling it up to my head, and leaned down to pull one of her tight nipples into my mouth, drawing a moan from us both. Her fingers curled into my hair the way I'd known they would and I pushed her back gently until she was falling onto the bed. When she got there, my lips popped off her nipple and her hands fell down beside her head, raising her breasts slightly on her chest. Fuck me. Her laid out before me was every dream, every fantasy and every sight I'd believed I'd never see again.

I flipped her over.

I couldn't stop myself.

I had to see those fucking booty shorts.

Her back arched, tilting her round ass toward me. I stared for a moment, running my hand down her bare back, stopping just short of the waistband of those beautiful, beautiful underwear. When her hips began to sway the tiniest bit from side to side in an unconscious movement, staring was no longer enough.

I grabbed my cock and squeezed it hard as I leaned down and bit the meaty part of her ass just below where it was covered by fabric. The overwhelming urge to bite harder flashed through me, but instead, I sucked hard.

"Shit!" She gasped beneath me, and her back arched more than I would have imagined was possible. "Again."

I moved to the other side and bit down again, growling as she pressed back against my mouth. Christ.

I wrapped my hand around the back of her thigh and pressed her leg onto the bed, opening her up to me. The center of her panties were dark with arousal, and my mouth watered as I ran my nose down the back of her thigh. As I made my way back up, she was trembling, and I swear to Christ she screeched as I bit into the skin where her ass met her thigh.

My hand moved quickly, tugging her panties to the side and feeling no resistance as I pushed two fingers inside her. She was shaved bare, hot and soaking wet, and her muscles clamped down so tightly I had a hard time pulling my fingers back in order to thrust again. I turned my hand, instinctively moving the tips of my fingers to the spot I knew would have her crying my name. Even after all those years, I still knew exactly how deeply I needed to press my fingers inside Amy before curling them back.

"Patrick," she groaned, her hips rolling against my face and hand. As her breathing grew shallow and her body began to shudder, I wondered what the fuck I was doing.

I pulled my hand away, making her yell out in protest, then ripped her underwear down her legs, leaving them at her knees as I pulled apart her ass cheeks and pressed my mouth against her wet cunt.

Yes.

Fuck.

Yes.

I was starving.

I let her juices cover my face, knowing that no matter how much I washed up in the morning, I'd be smelling her for days. Lovely.

"Your beard," she gasped, pulling one leg from her underwear so she could spread her legs farther. "Holy hell."

I tilted my head a little and let the hair below my lip scratch gently along her clit. That was all it took to push her over the edge, silent and shuddering helplessly against the bed.

I stood as soon as her body relaxed into the comforter and pushed my boxers down my legs as I stared at her pink, swollen pussy lips peeking out at me between her thighs. I needed in there.

I stepped up and gripped her hips, my fingers digging into the sharp bones as I pulled her body high enough to meet mine.

"Patrick, no!" she said urgently, and my stomach rolled as I immediately let go of her and took a step back.

She was going to push me away. She was going to turn and tell me to get lost while I stood there with my cock in my hands. I opened my mouth, but nothing came out as I felt my chest flush and the red begin creeping up my neck.

It wasn't an ego thing. She could turn me down a hundred times and I'd not be angry. That was her right, and it was one that I respected. It also wasn't about the fact that my cock was so hard it was beginning to hurt. I could take care of it in the shower—it wasn't my first choice, but it would at least provide relief.

No, it was the idea that she was so very close to me and I couldn't make love to her that had my stomach churning and my face flushing. I wanted to be as close to her as I could. I wanted to wrap myself around her, and breathe her in and come inside her.

I was ashamed and completely devastated that she'd stopped me.

"Patrick!" she called, jolting me out of my head. "Are you going to just stand there?"

"What?" I shook my head, my heart racing.

"Condom?"

"Ye want me to wear a condom?"

"I can still get pregnant, but I'm too old for more kids, and you've had your dick in too many places to name," she said reasonably, and I broke out in a cold sweat of relief making me shudder.

"In me wallet," I told her dumbly, the fear of being pushed away making me a bit shaky.

"It's not doing any good in there," she teased as she rolled completely to her back. "Are you okay?"

"Aye," I mumbled, grabbing my wallet off the nightstand and pulling a row of three condoms out.

"You're sure of yourself," she said in amusement as I dropped them on the bed.

"Dere's a good chance I'll rip de first one in me haste wit' de way me hands are shakin'," I replied honestly, my voice quiet. "De second one we'll use."

"You're shaking?" she asked, her face growing soft as she grabbed one of my hands to study it.

"I have never been more afraid or excited in me life."

"Afraid?"

"Dat ye'll realize I'm not what ye want."

"Excited?"

"Like a thousand Christmases rolled into one moment."

"Do you want me to take care of the condom?"

"Dat would probably be best."

"Lay down," she ordered, letting go of my hand to pick up the condoms.

I lay down on the bed next to her, my feet still planted on the floor, and watched her rip the condom open carefully. The second she touched me, my body jolted.

The sensitivity was almost painful as she wrapped her hand around the shaft and pulled up slowly, making my hips rise off the bed. Then she leaned down and took me in her mouth while I watched in awe.

"I'll not last long, ye do dat," I said ruefully, gripping her jaw gently to pull her away. I both hated and loved how close to the edge I was, wishing I could watch her lips around me, but knowing that if she didn't stop, we'd be finished.

She rolled the condom down my length in one smooth move, and I helped her seat it at the base, making sure that it was situated where it needed to be.

It was the first time we'd ever used one, and I wondered briefly if it would make everything different.

Then she was there, kneeling above me while those long ropes of hair brushed the tips of her breasts and she pressed my cock inside her.

I yelled out as she dropped down, and used my legs to press into her deeper. I'd been insane to think that anything would change the way it felt to be inside her. I still felt the same rush of emotion, the same overwhelming urge to get as far inside her as I possibly could.

Nothing compared to the way I felt when I was inside her. Nothing.

I held on to her hips as she rolled them above me, but soon I was pulling my hands away so I could lean up and brace myself on my elbows. Her breasts were swaying with each movement and my mouth watered at the sight.

"Lean forward," I ordered, glancing up into her heavy lidded eyes. "I want yer nipples."

She shuddered, then rested her hands on my shoulders, bringing her breasts to my face.

Her cunt clenched as I pulled first one and then the other nipple between my lips, biting them gently and sucking them up against the roof of my mouth. She didn't wear perfume or scented lotion, and the only thing I could taste was her. The salt of her skin and the sweet of her skin were the most potent aphrodisiacs I'd ever encountered. I wanted to inhale her.

She finally leaned back and I watched one of her hands reach down to where our bodies connected, rubbing at the bundle of nerves there. Her lips were stretched around me, glistening with moisture, and I had a hard time moving my eyes away from the sight.

When her movements began to grow jerky, I glanced up at her face, and what I saw there made my entire body grow cold.

She'd hit her release and she was pulsing around me, but her head was lifted toward the ceiling and tears were running silently down her cheeks.

I was frozen for a moment, not sure what was happening, but as she shuddered one last time, one of my hands thrust out and grabbed her hip, stopping her movements.

Her head jerked down in surprise.

"What are you doing?" she asked, moving against my grip.

"Yer cryin'."

"It's okay." She rolled her hips against me, and my stomach

knotted.

"Why?"

"It was a really good orgasm," she said, trying to play it off.

I met her eyes silently as she tried to move, but with every thrust and roll, I grew softer, until I lifted her off me before the condom could come off.

"What the fuck?" she asked in confusion, looking down between us.

I shook my head as I ripped the condom off, not sure what to say. I couldn't...

I just couldn't. I knew by the expression on her face that she was hurt, but I didn't know what to say to make it better.

I would not fuck her while she cried. Ever. I didn't care what type of tears they were, the sight of them erased all arousal from my body.

"Patrick?"

I walked away, tossing the condom in the bin and wetting a towel from the bathroom before going back to where she sat silently on the bed. She shuddered as I ran the wet towel over her body, starting with her neck and ending between her thighs.

"What just happened?" she asked quietly, wrapping her arms around her chest.

"I love ye—"

"Patrick, don't," she warned.

I ignored her. "I love ye. More den meself. More den anyt'in'." I closed my mouth and tried to get my accent under control. I'd spent almost thirty years in the US, but I still found myself reverting back to the old pronunciations when I was fighting my emotions. "I've always loved ye." I continued, "I'm not sure what happened dere or why ye were cryin'. But I will not ever touch ye when ye don't want to be touched."

"I told you—"

"Ye lied."

She lifted her chin, but didn't say another word as I pulled the bedding down for her to climb in. I laid down beside her on my back and breathed a small sigh of relief when her body gravitated toward mine.

I didn't know what else to say. Every sentence that came out of my mouth seemed inadequate, and I didn't want to make the situation worse while I tried to process it.

Had I missed something—some small movement or facial expression that would have told me that she wasn't enjoying herself? As always, I had no idea whether I was coming or going, her complexities leaving me completely baffled.

When she'd arrived at the hotel earlier, I'd been surprised, but really fucking glad she was there. After the night I'd had searching the pub where Nix was attacked, we'd finally found the boys who'd done it.

They hadn't even been trying to hide, but it hadn't taken long for them to realize their mistake.

By the time we'd handled that situation I was exhausted, but the adrenaline coursing through my veins hadn't allowed me to relax.

I felt her breathing deepen and I pulled her a little closer to me before turning to my side and wrapping her arm around my waist. I needed to try and sleep so I could stop by to see Nix early the next morning. He deserved to know what had happened.

I thought about every single movement and sound that had come from Amy while I was inside her her, and by the time I fell asleep, I still couldn't pinpoint the moment that I should have known she no longer wanted me to touch her.

***

When I woke the next morning, I knew instinctually that she'd gone before I'd even opened my eyes.

My back was cool where she'd slept, and as I looked toward the dresser, I noticed that her bag wasn't resting where she'd dropped it.

Her room key was on the bedside table.

Son of a bitch.

I was up and out of bed in seconds, and it only took minutes before I was leaving the hotel for the hospital. If I knew Amy, she was already visiting Nix, and I was hoping I could pin her down there. I needed to talk to both of them, and neither discussion could wait.

"Hey, Trick," Nix said as I walked into the room. He was alone for the first time in three days, and my stomach dropped in foreboding.

"Nix, how ye feelin'?"

"A little better today. Face still hurts, stomach still hurts."

"Take a while for that shite to fade, I'm sure." My eyes darted around the room.

"She's not here," he said flatly.

"What?"

"Mum's not here. She said she had some things to do this morning," he said skeptically.

"You think that's not the case?"

"Considering she showed up here at six-thirty in the morning and left by seven, I'm going to take a shot in the dark here and assume you and her had a falling out…again?"

"I don't know why—"

"Don't bullshit me, man," he said with a small shake of his head. "I know the signs and so do you. Why do you keep doing this?"

I sat down heavily in the chair next to his bad and glanced down at my hands. I'd had my anchor touched up a few times over the years to keep it vivid, and I'd noticed the night before how faded Amy's had become.

It was a good representation of our relationship. I was holding fast, and she was fading away.

"I love her," I told him simply.

"You may love her." He moved his mouth around a bit as if he was looking for the right words to say. "I get it, man. I do. But every time you play your hand, she's a mess afterwards. For months. It never works the way you want it to, and it never gets any easier—for you or for her. So why can't you just let it go?"

I ran my hand down my beard, scratching my jaw as I tried to explain to Nix something he would never understand until he'd met the love of his life.

"I'm incomplete wit'out her—" I stopped, shaking my head. "As long as I live, I'll never give up. I can't."

"I think you have to," Nix said softly.

"It will never happen."

We passed a little time quiet with our own thoughts before I remembered why I'd wanted to see him in the first place. When I showed him the photos on my phone before deleting them, he'd grew silent, but it only took a minute before he spoke.

"You didn't kill them, did you?" he asked, handing my phone back.

"Ye asked me not to, so I didn't."

"Thank you."

"Not sure it's something ye should be thankful for."

"No—thank you for taking care of it. Thank you for having my back."

"As long as I breathe, I'll stand behind ye," I answered with a nod. "Except of course, right now, as I've got a long ride back to Eugene today. Boys said as soon as yer healed up, ye should come down and meet the kids."

"I'll see what I can do," he said with a smile.

"Ye do that." I leaned forward and kissed his forehead. "Love ye, boyo. Keep me updated on things around here."

"I will."

When I walked away from him, my gut clenched in anxiety. I hated leaving when he was still so injured, but I knew with absolute certainty that as soon as I was gone, Amy would feel comfortable at his side again. She was avoiding me, clearly, and she needed to be there more than I did.

So once again, I was pushed away.

And I left like a dog with its tail between its legs, because I'd never force her to do something she didn't want—even if that meant I had to stay away.

I called and texted her even as I braced myself for another long separation, but to my surprise, it was only a couple months before I saw her again.

It was the night that changed everything for us…the night she answered questions I hadn't known to ask, and ruined me completely.

Chapter 53

Brenna

Dragon's hand engulfed mine as he pulled me inside the clubhouse. We finally had another night without the kids, and after dinner and a movie we'd decided to stop by for a couple of drinks. Drinking at home wasn't nearly as much fun as drinking at the club, and I knew he was planning on getting me hammered by the look in his eye.

Drunk sex with my man. I couldn't wait.

"Hey darlin'," Vera said stiltedly as I leaned in to give her a kiss. "What are you two doin' here?"

"Rose and Cam offered to take the kids for the night, and you know I couldn't pass that up," I replied jokingly, leaning over to hug Slider as Dragon headed toward the bar. "Whose Prius is that outside?"

I couldn't imagine any of the members allowing their old lady to get a freaking hybrid. It stuck out like a sore, white thumb in a sea of black and chrome bikes.

She began to reply when her eyes suddenly looked over my shoulder and widened and her mouth snapped shut.

I turned my head to see what she was looking at, and caught sight of a woman with long, grey dreadlocks practically running through the doorway from the back hallway.

"I know her," I said slowly, trying to remember where I'd seen the woman before. As soon as the words left my mouth, my pop came out behind her, catching her by the arm. "What the hell?"

I began to move forward when a strong hand clamped down on my arm and I turned to see Slider holding me in place.

"Wha—"

"It's not your business. You want to stay, you'll be silent," he said emphatically, never looking away from the scene Pop was making.

"What's going on?" I asked in confusion.

"Something that shoulda happened thirty years ago."

"She's going to break him," Vera whispered, raising her hand to her mouth.

"He broke her years ago, guess it's about time for her to return the favor," Slider murmured back ominously.

Their words were beginning to scare me, and the expression on Dragon's face as he made his way back to my side multiplied my fear.

"I need to go over—"

"You'll stay right where ya are," Slider interrupted. "Or I'll have your man drag ya outta here."

"He wouldn't—"

"He doesn't, I will," Slider promised, meeting my eyes for only a moment before looking back toward Pop.

"You probably shouldn't be here for this," Dragon murmured into my ear, making me glance at him in surprise. He knew what was going on?

How the hell would he know when I didn't? And why the fuck was the woman who sold me my old Corolla standing in the club yelling at my pop?

Amy

"**H**ow could ye do such a t'ing?" Patrick yelled at me, lifting my hand up so I had no choice other than to look at it and drawing every eye in the room.

"It was time. Now let go of my arm." I tried to keep my voice level, but I was fighting a losing battle with my temper.

I'd gone to the club for two reasons, to thank him for what he'd done for my son and hand him the divorce papers I'd had sitting in my purse for a week. I knew the two reasons seemed odd, like I was thanking him by trying to divorce him—but in my head, it had made perfect sense.

I was making a clean break. Finally.

I'd covered my anchor two days before, crying the entire time, and the moment I'd eventually crawled out of my bed, I'd known it was time to finish it all.

I couldn't do it anymore, not to either of us. Staying married and wearing his mark had given him hope for too long, and it was selfish of me to let that continue. My inability to let go was dragging us both under, it had only taken me thirty years to realize it.

"I love ye!" he hissed. "I'll not divorce ye."

"I don't need your agreement."

"De fuck ye don't!"

"I'm leaving, Patrick. Let go of my arm."

His hold didn't hurt, not in any way, but I couldn't make myself pull out of his grip. If I did it—if I made that physical break—I knew it would seem as if I was running away again. He had to let me go on his own, or he'd eventually follow.

"Why are ye doin' dis? I've loved ye for most of me life! I've never stopped lovin' ye, and I know ye haven't, eit'er!"

His words were ripping me up, tearing my insides to pieces and setting them on fire inside my chest. It was painful, but the longer he held me, the angrier I got.

Why couldn't he see it? Why had he been so blind for so long?

I loved him! Of course I fucking loved him! But it didn't matter how many times I told myself I'd forgiven Patrick, I couldn't shake the resentment I felt toward him and it hadn't dissipated as years went by; if anything, it had only grown stronger.

"You want to know why?" I asked viciously, my voice rising. "Really, Patrick?"

I caught movement out of the corner of my eye, and the old, familiar face almost brought me to my knees.

"You don't want to do this here," Doc said gently with a shake of his head. "Not here, girl."

I looked at him, the way age had made his upper back curve a bit and his body narrow with loss of muscle, but as I met his eyes, I was transported back to Ireland and the worst night of my life.

The words poured out of me then.

"I woke up tied to a chair," I began, moving my head back toward Patrick in time to see his face pale. "It was one of those kitchen chairs with the arm rests. Wood. The backrest wasn't real tall, it stopped at the base of my neck."

I watched Patrick swallow hard, but he didn't interrupt me as the crowd around us grew completely silent.

"I had a belt in my mouth that was tightened around the back of my head. He said it was so I didn't bite my tongue."

I glanced to the side, and saw Vera watching me in horror, but I couldn't stop. I was purging, the words coming out of me in waves.

"I didn't know who he was—I'd never seen him before. But as soon as I was awake, he took the belt out of my mouth and explained why I was there. He just wanted to know where his fiancé was. And I remember thinking, 'Thank God, that's all he wants. I'll help him find her.'"

"Amy," Patrick whispered.

"You wanted to know, right? That's what all that yelling was about."

"I didn't—"

"The first time I didn't give him the answer he wanted, he pulled my head back over the edge of the chair. I thought he was going to slit my throat, but instead he cut all of my hair off. All of it. There were times that I could feel the metal against my scalp, that was how short he'd made it. I cried as he cut it, and he scolded me for it, but I didn't realize... I didn't realize what would come next, or I would have saved my tears."

"After that, he went for my hands. He started with my pointer finger," I said clearly, lifting my hand and wiggling the crooked digit as Patrick began to shake. "He smashed it with a ball peen hammer when I still wouldn't tell him where Moira was."

I heard someone cry out from Vera's side of the room, and Patrick reached out to brace himself against the bar, but I didn't pause.

"The middle was next, and by that time I'd already pissed myself, but I barely noticed over the pain. What's a little mess when it felt like he was ripping my fingers off one by one?"

Patrick's hand fell off my arm and limply to his side as he began to sway.

"I couldn't tell him where she was, because I didn't *know* where she was." I laughed darkly. "The two smallest fingers hurt the worst, probably because he didn't have much room to work, so he broke the knuckles."

Patrick flinched with every word I spoke.

"Please, me love—" he whispered achingly.

"Thankfully, by the time he'd reached my thumb, he asked the *right* question. It was the difference between *where is she* and *where did he take her*. I knew where you were headed, so I finally had an answer. Thank God, I finally had an answer."

"I beg ye, stop," he pleaded raggedly.

"He wasn't happy at my answer," I whispered back, leaning forward at the waist. "Perhaps it hadn't been what he wanted to hear."

"Mot'er of God." I watched his lips form the words, but he made no sound.

"So while I was out of it with pain, he stripped me from the waist down, then he *cleaned* me," I shuddered in revulsion at the memory, my voice beginning to grow hoarse. "And he raped me on his mother's couch."

"You left me in Ireland to take care of a woman you barely knew, and because of that, he tortured me and raped me until I lost consciousness." I clenched my jaw against the emotion burning in my chest. "You promised me you'd never leave me again. You promised that I'd never have to be afraid. *You promised that you'd never love anyone else.*"

I watched Patrick's face go from pale to an alarming shade of gray, but I didn't stop.

I *still* didn't stop.

"Do you remember the day you found out I was pregnant? When you spit in my face and said I was filthy?" I growled at him, tears finally falling freely down my cheeks. "I didn't say anything back, because I couldn't disagree with you. I felt filthy. The kind of filth that you scrub and scrub, but it never comes off."

"No—" Patrick whispered painfully, his voice barely audible.

"You accused me of paying you back for fucking another woman, and I began to laugh, do you remember?" I waited until his eyes squeezed shut with the memory, then hissed through my teeth, "It was *hilarious,* Patrick. Because I hadn't paid you back for sleeping with her. *He did.*"

Patrick's eyes shot open as his legs went out from under him, and he landed on his knees with a loud thump, his entire body curling forward.

"Mum?" I heard over my shoulder, and I felt my entire body pull inward in fear. "Mum?"

I turned to see Nix walking toward me slowly, devastation clear on his face.

"You never told me," he accused, meeting my eyes. "And, you."

He pointed toward Patrick, more angry than I'd ever seen him. "Get up."

As soon as Patrick was on his feet, Nix's fist hit him so hard in the side of the face that he went down again.

"Phoenix, what the hell are you doing?" I cried, "Stop it!"

Patrick climbed to his feet again, only to be punched a second time, splitting his lip so badly that blood poured down his face. He didn't retaliate or try to defend himself in any way. He just stood there, silent, as my kindhearted son continued to hit him over and over again.

Sometimes Patrick was knocked to the ground, but every single time he did, he stood back up again.

No one was stopping them, and the only sound that could be heard in the cavernous room was the disgusting sound of flesh connecting brutally with flesh.

Until, finally, blessedly, Patrick didn't get up off his knees.

"I trusted you," Nix spit out finally, holding his hand over the surgery scar on his belly. "I fucking wanted her with you, and I couldn't understand why she kept you at a distance. I continued to talk to you even though I knew it bothered her... I thought she was being unreasonable!"

"Stop, son," I said, stepping forward to rest my hand on his arm.

He shrugged me off, breaking my heart, and I turned my gaze to Patrick.

I'd never seen him look so defeated.

"I know I failed ye," he said, his nostrils flaring as he tried not to cry. "Me sins are great, and I'll burn for dem. But if ye never believe anyt'in' else, know dat I loved ye more den anyt'in'. Ye were me sanctuary. Me solace in a world gone mad. I'd endure a thousand deat's to go back and ensure ye did not feel one moment of pain."

I was too busy staring into his shattered eyes to notice the movement before it was too late. By the time I realized what was happening, he'd already handed a large blade handle first to Nix.

"I'll not stop ye," he whispered brokenly to Nix, while I watched in horror. "From ear to ear, son. It's easier den ye'd t'ink."

Nix took the blade from Patrick's hand as men rushed toward us, but before I could blink or the men could reach us, his arm was moving.

***

"Did you know he wouldn't do it?" I said quietly, standing in Patrick's room with my arms crossed over my chest.

"I prayed he would."

"He was out of control—I've never seen my son that way before. Why would you do that?"

"Takin' de easy way out, I suppose," Patrick answered as he finally met my eyes. "De guilt is worse den dyin'."

The moment Patrick's blade had stuck in the wall behind the bar with a thud, men had converged on where we were standing. Grease had led Nix away while I stood frozen, watching as Slider slid his shoulder underneath Patrick's arm and pulled him to his feet. I wasn't sure why I let Doc gently lead me into Patrick's room, but my feet instinctively carried me toward the shell of the man I loved without protest.

"I've not been de best man," he whispered, his accent, as usual, so much more pronounced in his grief. "I've done t'ings dat I'll burn for, killed men for no reason udder den to follow de task I'd been given, but nuttin' in me life has felt as wrong as leavin' ye in Ireland. I knew it before I went, and I was too young and too stupid to follow me instinct to stay wit' ye."

"You couldn't have known—"

"It doesn't matter," he whispered brokenly. "I told ye I'd protect ye and I didn't. I'm so sorry, me love. So sorry."

"I didn't understand how you could have left me," I whispered back, tears beginning to fall down my face. "I was so devastated."

The sound that came out of his throat then was the most painful wail I'd ever heard. It didn't last long, only a second, but the sound seemed to echo in the room.

"It was me fault, all of it," Patrick choked, sliding onto his knees on the floor. "And den I—and den I blamed ye. God forgive me, I blamed ye."

I watched him as he tried to hold back his sobs, lost in my own misery, until I heard voices outside the door.

"You're not going in there," Slider said.

"That's my mum." Oh, shit. Nix was out there. I turned my head toward the door.

"And she's with her man, it's none of your concern."

"He's not her man. He's just some prick that left her to be brutalized and then continued to torture her with it for thirty fuckin' years. She came here to serve him divorce papers, for fuck's sake."

"She could have mailed those fuckin' papers," Slider retorted, his tone indicating he was losing patience. "Boy, you don't want to try me. I'll fuckin' lay ya out before ya know what's happenin'."

"Ye better go wit' yer boy," Patrick said quietly, his voice ragged.

I turned back to face him, and I was drawn into the eyes I'd loved for most of my life. I was certain in that moment that he was prepared to do exactly what I'd asked of him. He was letting me go.

"I don't know how."

"To do what, me love?" he asked gently.

"I don't know how to not love you."

"Lovin' me doesn't mean ye forgive me, and I don't deserve yer forgiveness."

I lowered myself to the floor until we were facing each other, and drew in a shuddering breath. "I know that it wasn't your fault, but God, Patrick, you weren't blameless, either. But all these years, I knew what happened and you didn't. You got to move blissfully along with your life, making a family with Moira and raising your daughter... and I was just stuck. I resented you so much for that, for leaving me and spending your life with the woman who was the reason I was ruined."

"Yer not ruined," he replied gently but firmly, lifting his fingers to my cheek. "Ye were *never* ruined. Yer de strongest woman I've ever met. Kind and funny and so gorgeous dat sometimes it hurts to look at ye. Ye were never ruined, me love, just cracked open for a bit. Took a while for ye to piece it back toget'er, but ye did it."

He swallowed hard, running his fingers down my jaw. "Ye'll never know how sorry I am dat I wasn't dere to help ye find all of dose pieces ye lost."

"I don't think I can leave you." I murmured quietly.

"I don't deserve for ye to stay."

"What about what I deserve?"

"Ye deserve everyt'in'. Ye deserve everyt'in' I promised ye and didn't give ye."

"Give it to me now." I whispered, chewing on the inside of my cheek.

"Yer de best part of me. Ye know dat?" His eyes searched my face. "Yer de best part, and dat means ye'd be gettin' de worst parts if ye stayed wit' me."

"Would you ever leave me again?"

"Me love," he said tenderly, "I can't even imagine ever lettin' ye out of me sight again. But I'll do it, I'll sign de papers, if dat's what ye want."

"I've missed you so much—" my words cut off with a painful sob.

"And I've ached for ye. I've never stopped, wife. Not for one moment."

I lurched forward, and he caught me.

He caught me.

"Shhh, don't cry sweetheart," he murmured into my ear, his own voice full of tears. "I've got ye. I know I'm late, me love, but I'm here now."

Chapter 54

Patrick

I sat with Amy on the old cement floor, refusing to move a muscle even as my back began to ache and my feet fell asleep.

I didn't understand why she was still there, why she'd curled against me and cried into my chest.

I was the reason for everything terrible in her life. Every hurt she'd endured and silent pain she'd felt fell on *my* shoulders. I didn't know if I could bear the weight of that.

I wasn't sure how I was going to live with myself, knowing what I'd done and what I hadn't.

She continued to hiccup as her tears finally came to an end, but I was afraid to say a word. I'd once told her that I wasn't a writer because I lacked the talent to string a sentence together with any sort of eloquence. That fact was still true as I sat silently with the love of my life in my arms, praying that she wouldn't leave me, but unable to beg her to stay.

"Do you ever wonder how our lives would have turned out?" she asked timidly.

"Every single day of me life."

"I don't know if I would change it," she whispered.

"I love our children," I replied, kissing the top of her head. "But if I could go back, I'd never leave ye in Ireland."

"Then I wouldn't have Phoenix—"

"Ye don't know dat, me love." I argued, pulling her tighter against my body. "He may have still existed... just a bit smaller and wit' red hair."

"I'm afraid, Patrick," she confessed.

"Of what?"

"That you'll leave again. That my son hates me. That your daughter is going to hate me. That we'll never figure this out."

"Dat's a lot of fears."

"That's the condensed version," she said tiredly with a shrug of her shoulders.

"Let's lay some of dose to rest, eh?"

"Your accent fades in and out."

"What?" The change of subject startled me.

"When you're upset it gets thicker, and then it sort of fades away as you calm down."

"Aye. I've tried to master it for years. Sometimes I can keep a handle on it, but it's actually harder to keep Mum's accent out of me voice on a daily basis."

"Why would you try to get rid of it?"

"Seemed like a good idea when I got here, and now it's a tell, yeah? Not good to show emotion when ye do what I do."

"What exactly do you do?"

"Now? Mostly I keep an eye on de boys, make sure everyt'in's runnin' smooth. Used to do it all, and none of it ye want to hear about."

"Malcolm called you something—The Butcher? Something like that."

My stomach clenched at the bastard's name, but I tried not to show any reaction, and made absolutely sure that my accent didn't slip. She needed to feel comfortable talking about it if that was what she needed, without fear of me losing my shit. "It's not somet'in' I'm proud of."

"You killed people."

"Aye. Only men."

"Bad men?"

"Some of dem."

"Good men?"

"Yes."

"Do you wish you could take it back?"

"I try not to t'ink on it."

She nodded in understanding, then grew quiet again.

"I'm not going to leave ye. Not ever," I said after a few moments.

"You promise?"

"I'll not promise, dat word has little meanin' between us now." I leaned back and tilted her face up so I could meet her eyes. "Know dat I'll never live a day wit'out lovin' ye. De day I leave ye is de day dey put me in de ground."

"What if I go first?"

"I'll follow ye."

"Do you think after everything we could actually make this work?"

"Yes."

"Why are you so sure?"

"Because I won't give up. No matter how angry ye get when old hurts pop up, or how long it takes until ye trust me again, I'll be right here, lovin' ye."

Her eyes and her nose were red and swollen, testaments to the fact that she'd spent the last few hours upset, but she smiled tremulously.

"I can't believe I said all that in front of your friends," she said, shaking her head. "They must think I'm a lunatic."

"Dey don't t'ink anyt'in' of de sort," I argued in disbelief. "Dey t'ink ye lived through somet'in' horrible—ye'll find dat many of dem have dere own stories to tell. No shame in dat."

We heard someone come to the door then, and Slider's muffled voice telling them to move the fuck away.

Instinct had me moving Amy off me as the door opened, and we were both on our feet before I saw who it was.

"Pop?" I should have fuckin' known it would be Brenna. I couldn't imagine anyone else completely ignoring Slider.

I heard my president yelling as he came down the hall, and Brenna jumped before scooting inside the door.

"I went to the john for two fuckin' minutes," Slider said in apology as he stopped at the open doorway.

My mouth twitched and I turned in irritation to my daughter. "What do ye need, Brenna?"

I wanted to be alone with my wife, and I was a mix of frustration and worry as I watched my daughter fidget. I know she'd heard it all, and I wanted to explain, but not then. Not when Amy was silent behind me and I could feel her nervousness as if it were my own.

"Is it true? What she said—is it true?"

"Out, Brenna," Slider growled, taking a step forward.

"She's fine, Charlie," Amy argued, stepping to the side so she could meet Brenna's eyes.

"Were you telling the truth?" Brenna asked, her voice breaking.

I was so bloody torn. My little girl looked as if she was about to cry, but Amy's hand was shaking against my back where she'd clutched my t-shirt in her fist.

"What're ya doin', baby?" Dragon asked as he pushed past Slider.

Jesus Christ, the entire fuckin' club would be in my room soon.

"I just—" tears filled Brenna's eyes and I was suddenly grateful that Dragon showed up, because he immediately pulled her into his side and I didn't have to step away from Amy.

"You ready to go, Mum?" Nix called, making Slider throw his hands in the air and walk away.

I didn't blame him. I wished I had locked the fucking door.

"I—" Amy looked between Phoenix and I, and I knew the instant she stopped being afraid of disappointing the boy in front of her and became his mum again.

"Sit down, Phoenix," she said firmly, making his jaw drop. "We're going to need more chairs—" she glanced around the room, "—and scotch. I need a scotch."

"I'll take care of it," Dragon offered, lifting Brenna's face to kiss her on the lips before striding out the door.

I fucking hated when he did that, but I kept my mouth shut. I didn't think I'd ever be comfortable with his hands on her, but I'd realized over the last couple of years that he worshipped Brenna. I couldn't really ask for more than that.

We watched each other silently until Dragon returned with two chairs, Grease right behind him carrying the Scotch and four glasses.

"Lock de door on yer way out," I ordered as Grease left the room.

"We know you have questions," Amy said, sitting gingerly on the bed. "And I understand, I do. But to understand it all, we have to start at the beginning."

She looked at me with solemn eyes, and once again I saw the girl I'd married all those years ago.

The loveliest woman I'd ever seen.

***

Amy and I spoke for hours while the children watched and listened.

She spoke about how it was for her growing up with parents that didn't care and described the day she'd met my mum, a story I'd never heard before.

I spoke about Ireland, growing up with my da gone, and studying at University.

We both spoke about the night we met and the few months before we were married.

I explained how I'd gotten pulled into fighting for a cause I wasn't sure I believed in.

We described our wedding... and our marriage—about how young and full of dreams we'd been.

Amy described the morning my da died...I couldn't speak past the lump in my throat.

We went over everything that had happened, both from my point of view and hers... and as we discussed the years apart, I think we both learned about things we hadn't known or understood before.

By the time we were finished, the bottle of scotch was gone and I was fucking exhausted.

"I thought—" Brenna looked down at her thighs, resting on top of Dragon's lap. "I guess I never knew that my mom—"

"Don't go dere," I warned gently, leaning forward from my perch on the edge of the bed. "I loved yer mum. I did. She gave me ye, and she was a good woman. A great one. But she knew I was married—dere were never any secrets between us."

"She knew you were in love with someone else?" she asked dubiously, her hackles rising.

"Lass, ye were eight when she passed," I replied tiredly, trying to find the words to put her at ease. "Yer memories of us are dose of a child. Aye, she knew, and she accepted it."

"How could she just accept it?"

"She wasn't in love wit' me, eit'er," I answered, raising my hands palms up.

Brenna went silent then, and I turned my eyes to Nix. He was sitting close to the door with his arms crossed over his chest. His knuckles were raw and torn, and for the first time since I'd entered my room, I wondered what my face must look like.

"Do you have any questions, Phoenix?" Amy asked calmly. It seemed the farther into the story we'd gone, the more her natural self-assuredness came forward. It was such an innate part of her. I hated that it had been beaten back over and over again, and I hated even more that I'd been too blind to realize it. The backbone in that woman was amazing, staying strong and straight even as she crumbled.

"I'm the product of rape," he replied quietly. "I'm not sure what I'm supposed to say to that."

"Don't you ever say that again," she replied harshly, making him look up in surprise. "You *saved* me, Phoenix Robert Gallagher. If you hadn't come along, I would have been dead."

My stomach tightened to the point of pain at her words, the memory of her haunted eyes and shaved head like a knife piercing my gut.

"I don't understand how you can even look at me," he mumbled, wiping his hand down his face.

Amy stood then, her shoulders straight and jaw tight.

"When I look at you," she said softly, walking forward to cup Nix's face in her palms, "I see my salvation. I see the boy who looked at me like *I* was the miracle. I see the reason I was able to go on living and the sole purpose of my life. You, my son, are not a product of anything but God's mercy on a broken girl who needed something to hold on to."

He sobbed then, just once, and I looked away to give him a small bit of privacy. It was not my place to intrude on them, and as I looked toward Brenna, I saw her crying quietly into Dragon's neck. He was rubbing her back soothingly, but his jaw was clenched as he stared at the wall.

Amy and Nix whispered for a few minutes longer before he stood up and took her in his arms. He held her gently, and for the first time I got a glimpse into the way he treated her when it was just the two of them. I knew that a lot of that came from Amy and the way she'd raised him—but it had a lot to do with the man Nix was, too, down to the core of him. He genuinely cared for his mother, not only loved her but *liked* her, and he was willing to stand up for her no matter the consequences. Christ, he'd beaten the hell out of the vice-president of the Aces Motorcycle Club inside the fucking clubhouse.

"I'll be back tomorrow," he said, as he let go of his mum. He turned to me then, and looked closely at my face in satisfaction. "I'm not sorry I hit you, you deserved it."

"I did," I replied with a nod, standing up.

"I don't understand all this." He waved his arm around the room. "But I'm willing to keep my mouth shut. She loves you. Still. After everything. And I know you love her, I've known it since I was sixteen."

I opened my mouth to speak, but he shook his head. "We'll talk tomorrow. I need—I just need to get out of here for a while."

"Ye okay to drive?" I asked before I could stop myself. Shit, he didn't want me worrying about him, and I was on very thin ice as it was.

His mouth twitched in an almost smile and nodded before walking out of the room.

"We're going to head out, too," Dragon said, pushing Brenna to her feet. I was glad to see she'd gotten the tears under control because I was barely hanging onto my own as it was.

"I'm so sorry for everything you've been through," Brenna said kindly to Amy, taking a step forward. "And I want you to know that I remember what you did for me."

Amy nodded, swallowing harshly.

"You didn't have to do that, but you did. You helped me escape." Brenna shook her head. "You'll never know how much that means to me. I don't know if I would have done the same."

"You would have," Amy replied with conviction. "If the man you loved had a child, you'd do anything to protect her."

"But I was the reason—"

"You weren't the reason for anything, sweetheart," Amy interrupted. "I won't lie and say that I didn't resent you at first—I did. But I got over it pretty fucking quick, because blaming a person for being born is asinine. That's like blaming the sun for shining during a hangover."

Brenna chuffed out a surprised laugh. "Thank you."

"You're welcome."

Brenna moved to me, and I couldn't believe the feeling of relief I felt as I held her in my arms. I'd pushed it down, refusing to give it voice, but I'd been terrified that once she'd known everything, she'd hate me. I was not the hero she'd believed me to be as a child—I was a man, and not a good one.

"I'm so sorry for everything you went through," she said again, this time into my ear.

"No, I—"

"You may not have lived through it, but I know that you're going to deal with a lot of guilt... probably for the rest of your life. If something happened to Dragon, I don't know how I'd deal." Her arms tightened around my waist. "I love you, Pop, and I'm sorry that you had to live for thirty years without the woman you love. The thought of being without Dragon guts me, I can't even imagine what that must have been like."

"I love ye, too, lass," I whispered past the lump forming in my throat.

I'd felt the urge to cry more times in the past six hours than I had in twenty years.

I understood that everyone made choices that they later regretted, some large and some small. It was human to get it wrong, to not see the larger picture until it was too late. But I didn't know how to reconcile that with the decisions I'd made.

"I'm not sleeping in those sheets," Amy told me quietly after everyone was gone. "They smell like some teeny-bopper store at the mall."

My shoulders slumped as I remembered the scene she'd walked into when she first got there. Christ, I couldn't get anything right.

"I didn't fuck her," I replied, making Amy flinch.

"It is what it is, right?" she sighed, looking around the room. "But if it happens—"

"Of course it won't—"

"I'll leave you, Patrick." She said solemnly. "I can't take any more. I can't."

I stepped forward and jerked the sheets and blankets off the bed, rolling them into a ball and tossing them in the hallway. I'd make a prospect wash them in the morning… or burn them.

"I don't want anyone but ye," I told her, pulling two of the quilts Mum had made me out of a chest against the wall and laying them flat on the bed. I paused, suddenly ashamed that I didn't have somewhere nicer for her to sleep. "Honest to God, Amy? I don't see anyone but ye."

She nodded and slipped her skirt down her hips, making my breath catch in my throat. Her legs were long and strong, and she was wearing the same little shorts that she'd had on the last time I'd seen her.

"I'm sorry I don't have somewhere better for ye to sleep," I murmured, clenching my jaw as she climbed in between the quilts. "I'll find a place—"

"This is fine, baby," she replied, relaxing into the bed.

Baby.

My chest grew so tight as she watched me that I couldn't breathe. She was in my bed. I didn't deserve for her to even glance in my direction on the street, and there she was, in my bed.

"Go clean up, Patrick," she said gently as I stood there staring. "You've got blood all over you."

"Aye," I mumbled, my gaze searching the room blankly.

"Bathroom," she reminded me. "Next time, I'll help you… this time you can do it on your own."

I stumbled into the bathroom, and finally gave into the nausea that refused to calm. I'd been swallowing repeatedly for what felt like hours, able to control my body by refusing to acknowledge the churning in my gut. I could no longer do so.

I heaved and heaved until nothing was left, and then I heaved some more, tears rolling down my cheeks.

I'd been so confident when I'd left Ireland, so unbelievably arrogant in my assumption that my sins wouldn't catch up to us. I'd assumed that we'd be safe, never imagining that in the few days between our departures, Amy would be the one paying for my mistakes… I hated myself for that.

The details of Amy's attack and the memory of Malcolm's large frame in comparison to her small one made me livid, and before I was even done vomiting, I was tearing apart the room.

My fist went through the mirror and shattered the shower door.

I kicked through the flimsy cupboard doors between the sink.

I ripped the seat off the toilet and threw it through the small window.

"Poet!" Slider yelled through the door, breaking me out of my haze. "You stupid son of a bitch, you're already busted all to hell. You're gonna die of a heart attack if you don't calm your shit, ya old fuck!"

My chest was heaving as I threw open the door, and Slider's eyes widened as he got a good look at the destruction I'd caused. "Needed to remodel, anyway," he said calmly, reaching out to grab my arm and lead me toward his room. "You can use our shower. Vera's out cold, she won't even notice ya."

"I don't know what to do," I confessed, looking at the ground as we reached the door to their room.

"Ya get a handle on your shit, and ya take care of your woman, ya stupid mick," he replied sternly. "This ain't about you. This is about Amy. So you make sure she's got what she needs. The rest will sort itself out."

"How do I know what she needs, man? I fucked up so badly, I t'ink—"

"Stop thinkin', you're actin' like an asshole." He shook his head and leaned against the wall. "Ya remember when Farrah's ma came and took her away from us?"

"Dat's not—"

"It sure as shit is not the fuckin' same, you're right about that." He scratched his jaw and looked away from me. "My woman went through a different type of pain, but pain all the same. Poppin' pills and drinkin' until I'd find her passed out in the hallway… like she'd just hit her limit and hit the floor. Lockin' herself in her room until I had to break the door down with a fuckin' axe so she didn't overdose in there alone. Fuck, I didn't know what to do. I finally realized, though, they don't need ya to do anything, man."

"I hadn't known," I mumbled, shaking my head. "Moira never said shite about Malcolm, not one fuckin' word. All dese years and I hadn't known dat he'd done dat to Amy because of me. He fuckin' tortured her, Charlie."

"Let's get one thing straight, brother," Slider said, pushing off the wall to stand in front of me. "Malcolm was a sick fuck. That's not on you. You were the catalyst, and I know that eats ya up—and I understand it, I really do. But ya did what ya thought best at the time, and ya can't go back and change it. It's what ya do now that matters, understand?"

"Yeah," I answered with a nod, not agreeing with anything, but too tired to argue.

"Now, brother, you need a fuckin' shower and to get back in with your woman." He slapped me on the back and I grimaced as it jostled my ribs. "Eyes off the bed, Vera's naked."

I followed him into his bathroom and hopped in the shower, washing the blood out of my beard and hair. Thank God I had a high tolerance for pain or there was a good chance the last few hours would have gone very differently. It was a wonder that I was still awake and functioning.

I had a small wound on the back of my head where I must have hit a table, my lips were swollen, there was a small cut on my cheek and one on the bridge of my nose, and I knew for certain that one of my ribs was bruised, if not broken.

Phoenix had kicked my arse.

Good boy.

After I finished, I walked quietly back out of their room without seeing Vera's or Slider's bare asses, not that I hadn't seen them both before on different occasions over the years. Living in such close quarters with people, especially drunk people, meant that you walked in pretty regularly on things you'd rather not see.

When I finally reached the door to my room, I saw that Amy had scooted toward the wall, leaving me space on the outside of the bed. At least, I thought that's what she had done. She was asleep, and the tension lines around her mouth and eyes had finally softened.

I wanted to pick her up and hold her to me, reminding myself that she was there with me, that she was safe, but I didn't.

I knew how exhausted she was, and if she was able to sleep, I wouldn't interfere. She'd relived the worst and best parts of her life all in a couple of hours. She deserved the relief.

I pulled on a pair of sweatpants I hadn't worn in fifteen years, and sat down on the floor with my back against the side of the bed. There was no way I'd be able to sleep that night.

Instead, my mind drifted over thirty years of memories. It hadn't been all bad, not at all, but I couldn't see how good memories could ever overshadow the bad ones.

I tipped my head back against the bed and stared blankly at the ceiling.

Chapter 55

Amy

I woke up disoriented but warm, and was surprised to see nothing but Patrick's head resting beside me on the bed.

The past twenty-four hours had tested me in ways I didn't understand. I'd watched as I destroyed Patrick with the same poison that had been pulsing through me for years, I'd had to tell my son the truth of his birth—something I'd planned to take to the grave—and then I'd watched as Patrick had told our children his part in all of the horrible things that had happened so long ago, knowing that they could hate him for it, but still not willing to make any excuses.

It felt as if things had come full circle as we'd sat in the room with both of our children the night before—like that's where we were always meant to end up.

I wanted that to be our future with a fervency that I felt in my bones and a calm sense of acceptance. I was finally in the exact place I was supposed to be.

I relaxed back into the pillow and reached out to run my fingers over his soft hair. It was so long now, and he hadn't brushed it back into a ponytail before he'd fallen asleep, so it was pooled around his head on the quilt.

"Hey, sweetheart," he said quietly, keeping his head where I could reach it.

"Why are you on the floor?" I asked, equally as quiet.

It was early, the sun barely shining through the sheet covering his window, and the rest of the club was still sleeping, making the morning silent around us.

"Couldn't sleep, didn't know if ye wanted me in dere wit' ye."

"I did."

His head nodded slightly. "Couldn't lay beside ye last night. Too many demons to take into bed wit' ye."

"You'll have to get over that," I reprimanded, scratching my nails over his scalp gently. "I won't be sleeping alone again."

His body turned then, and I got a good look at his face. He'd never before looked old to me, but he did in that moment. His eyes were bloodshot, and his cheeks and lips were still swollen, hidden partially by a wild beard that he must have been scrubbing at for most of the night. I noticed for the first time that the patch of hair just below his bottom lip had turned blonde, almost white, and it was a glaring reminder of just how much time we'd missed.

"Yer sure?" he asked, searching my eyes. "De last time we… Amy, ye cried, me love."

"I was overwhelmed and exhausted, Patrick, I promise it wasn't anything more than that. I've lived too long without you already," I answered, grabbing his hand to pull him into bed with me. "I don't want to go another day."

"T'ank God," he said raggedly, pulling me against him and pressing his face into my throat.

"I'm sorry I covered my anchor," I said after a few moments of silence. "It was the hardest thing I've ever done. I cried the entire time."

"Did ye see what he covered it wit'?" he asked, his voice full of suppressed amusement.

"Not until he was done," I confessed sheepishly, "I didn't really care what he did as long as he covered it."

"Yer tattoo man had a sense of humor."

"Why?" I asked, lifting my hand up so I could look at the raw tattoo. I'd barely glanced at it once it was done, choosing instead to cover it with the ointment without looking.

"He covered it wit' a Claddagh ring, me love," he answered with a snort. "May as well have kept de anchor."

"Motherfucker."

"Only ye would cover up a tattoo of love wit' anot'er of de same," he said with a smile, leaning up until our faces were level.

"I can't believe he did that. What a dick!"

"Are ye really angry about it?" he asked in surprise.

"No, not really." My face heated in a blush at the way he was looking at me.

Like I was the best thing he'd ever seen.

"I don't want to be apart from ye, not even for a moment," he said seriously. "If ye feel de same, we need to make plans—"

"I'll move here," I said instantly, making his head jerk back in surprise.

"What?"

"Nix is the only thing I have in Portland, and he comes here already to visit you. He can do the same for me."

"But yer shop."

"I'll sell it. Shit, Patrick, people do yoga everywhere, not just Portland."

"Are ye sure?"

"I don't want to be apart from you, not even for a moment." I echoed his words.

"I love ye more den ye can possibly imagine," he whispered, dropping his forehead to mine with a shuddering breath.

"Kiss me, husband," I whispered back, smiling against his lips as he groaned.

Epilogue

Amy

Two months later

"**Y**er arse is going to kill me," Patrick groaned, squeezing my ass in his palms as he slid into me from behind. "Grab a hold of de headboard."

I moaned as I reached up and grabbed the headboard of the heavy oak bed we'd picked up the day before.

Patrick had bought a house less than a week after I'd agreed to move to Eugene and had started working on making it a home as I'd packed up my old apartment and sold my yoga business to Kali. We took our time, spending our nights between both places, until the day before, when I'd finally handed over my keys to both the shop and my apartment.

We hadn't spent even one night apart, and I had no regrets.

"Getting tired, old man?" I asked breathlessly as Patrick's body bent and his hand hit the headboard above mine.

"I'll never be too tired to fuck ye," he gasped, grabbing a hold of my hair to turn my face gently toward his. His hips thrust hard, and my back arched even further.

"Beautiful," he murmured against my lips before letting go and sliding his hand down my torso. "Goin' to be more beautiful in just a moment…"

His fingers found my clitoris gently, barely rubbing against the nerves that were so past the point of sensitive that it was almost painful. After a few thrusts, though, they fired back to life, and I was rolling my hips against his hand, almost unseating him with the movement.

It didn't take long before my body stiffened, then shuddered as I came around him wetly.

"Lovely," he whispered in my ear, running his hand back up my body until his first two fingers met my lips. "Suck."

He growled as I took the fingers into my mouth, and his hips began to jerk as he followed me over the edge.

We collapsed onto the bed in a sweaty heap, and I couldn't keep the smile off of my face. Even after all those years, we still had it.

"I may not be too old to fuck ye, but yer gonna have to do all the work from now on," he gasped and started laughing.

"Good luck with that," I retorted, smacking his chest with the back of my hand before dragging myself out of the bed.

"Where are ye going?"

"I need to clean up and get ready. Everyone's going to be here in two hours." I walked into the bathroom connected to our bedroom and caught sight of myself in the mirror.

"Nix still planning on driving down?" he called cautiously.

My heart clenched at his tone, and I took a deep breath against my irritation over my son. Even months later, Nix was still having a hard time with all that he'd learned. He visited me, and tried to act like everything was okay, but it wasn't. He'd broken up with Mat for some ridiculous reason, he was working out so much that he looked like he was going to split every shirt he wore, and he still had a hard time being in the same room as Patrick.

It killed me to see the way Patrick's eyes lit up at the sight of my son, then slowly dimmed the longer they were together.

I had to have faith it would get better. I had to.

"He said he'll be here," I confirmed, looking at myself in the mirror.

My dreadlocks had grown out and needed to be tightened, but the longer I looked at them, the less I wanted to go to the trouble. Patrick's hands were always in my hair, and he didn't seem to mind the fact that he couldn't run his fingers through it, but all of a sudden *I* minded.

"What are ye doin' so quiet in here?" my husband asked, stepping in behind me.

"Did you know that Leo put one of these," I grabbed a lock and flicked it, "into his mouth the other day and I didn't even realize it until it was soaking wet?"

"Dat boy puts fuckin' everyt'in' in his mouth," he replied with a chuckle, wrapping his arms around my waist

"I want to cut them off," I announced meeting his eyes in the mirror.

"What?"

"Do you have clippers?"

"What?"

"Patrick, pay attention!" He was looking at me like I had two heads.

"Aye, I have clippers—not dat I've ever used dem."

"We'll have to cut them first," I said quietly, chewing the inside of my cheek.

"I've got some brand new yard clippers for dose roses out front," he informed me quietly. He knew about my aversion to scissors and had thrown out every pair he owned.

"Get them."

I sat on the toilet while he got everything ready, trying to calm my nerves. It was just hair. It was just hair and I'd begun to hate how heavy it was. I wanted it gone. I did.

"Are ye sure?" Patrick asked as he set the electric beard trimmers and the yard clippers on the counter.

"Yeah, I'm sure," I answered more confidently than I felt. "Can you do it?"

"I don't know dat—"

"Please, Patrick."

He nodded, his jaw clenched, as he leaned down to kiss me.

"I'll just cut dem first, alright?" he asked nervously, 'Den we'll use the trimmers after."

His nervousness had the opposite effect on me, calming my own nerves. "Do it," I ordered.

I sat up straight as he clipped the dreadlocks, never brushing my head with the clippers. The fact that he was so very careful to not bring back any memories soothed me even more as he moved over my head.

"All done, do ye want to take a look before I—"

"No," I interrupted, clasping my hands tightly on my lap. "No, just do it."

He leaned down and tipped my chin up with his fingers, kissing me with an intensity that had my heart racing in my chest. "Almost done, my love," he murmured into my mouth.

The beard trimmers made a buzzing noise as he turned them on, and I closed my eyes tightly as I felt the first drag catch on the short knot of hair. After that, the noise became almost soothing, and my body relaxed before he'd finished.

"All done," Patrick told me hoarsely, clearing his throat.

I glanced up to see tears in his eyes, but I didn't mention them. He was trying very hard to act unaffected, and if I said anything about it, I knew I'd make it worse.

I stood from the toilet and stepped in front of the mirror. The sight that met my eyes made a sob bubble out of my throat.

I remembered this.

"I'm sorry," Patrick said quietly.

"I asked you to," I replied, reaching up to feel the short stubble that covered my head. "I should have waited until after the barbeque… everyone is going to stare."

The trimmers started up again, and I turned in surprise as he ran them up his jaw, wincing as they caught in the long hair, but not stopping until he'd run it into the long hair above his temple.

"What the fuck?" I asked, my jaw hanging.

"Ye'll have to do mine now, won't ye?" he replied with a small grin.

"You're insane."

"Where ye go, I go," he replied seriously.

***

"Holy shit, Pop! What the hell did you do to your hair?" Brenna yelled as she ushered her family into the house.

"Nan, too!" Trix screamed. "I wanna cut *my* hair!"

"Not gonna happen," Dragon said gruffly as he passed by Brenna to give me a hug. "Lookin' good," he murmured into my ear before letting go.

"Whoa, you both did it," Brenna said, looking back and forth between us.

"Small mishap wit' de trimmers," Patrick said with a smirk, his innuendo making Brenna pretend to gag.

"Nan, I wanna go in the pool," Trix said, wrapping her arm around my leg. "Can we go in the pool?"

"Let's eat first kiddo, alright?"

Her whole body slumped until my leg was holding her weight and I couldn't help the laugh that escaped me.

"Nan, huh?" I asked Brenna as she leaned in to hug me.

"Hope that's okay."

"It's perfect."

"Don't worry, everyone, the party has arrived!" Farrah called out as more people entered the house. Her face showed surprise as she got a good look at me, then she tilted her head. "Dig the hair."

"Thanks."

"Holy fuck, Poet!" she gasped as she did a double take.

"Sorry, we're still working on appropriate words," Casper grumbled, covering Farrah's mouth with his hand. "Little ears, Ladybug. Cam! Get your sister, man, she's trying to eat that plant!"

"I got her," Callie called, picking up Cecilia with her free arm, the other holding a tiny baby in a light green blanket.

"All the food is outside," I called over the noise of kids and adults talking over each other as if they hadn't seen each other in years instead of hours.

They moved like a wave toward the back of the house, except for one person that I'd come to know pretty well in the past couple of months.

"Thanks for coming, Rose," I said with a smile as she reached me, holding a bowl of some type of salad in her hands. "You didn't have to bring anything."

"Be rude to eat your food and not contribute," she said with a grin before her face grew serious again. "You look beautiful."

"Thanks," I replied, self-consciously running my hand over my hair.

"It's not the hair," she said, reaching out to grasp my hand and squeeze it. "It's the face."

She moved past me with a smile, and I turned back toward the front door that my son had just passed through.

"Hey, kiddo," I called, walking toward him.

"Hey, Mum. Place looks good," he said with a smile, leaning down to hug me. "Brought you something."

He handed me a wrapped gift, and I looked at him in surprise. "You didn't have to bring me anything."

"I think you'll like it," he replied with a smile. "Hey, Trick, nice to see you."

I watched them reach forward and shake hands, and felt an overwhelming sense of relief at Nix's open expression. It wasn't the same as it was before, but they'd get there eventually.

"Well?" Nix asked, turning back to me. "Open it."

I ripped open the wrapping, then fumbled, almost dropping the frame as I realized what it held.

"I think that's the only one," Nix explained. "I found it in Nan's things about a year after she passed, and I put it aside. You know, just in case you found it and—"

"Ye did good, boyo," Patrick said softly, reaching out to hug Nix tightly. "Real good."

I stared down at the photo of me and Patrick on our wedding day, and couldn't stop the tears that hit my eyes.

We were so young then.

Happy.

"Thank you, son," I said, finally looking away from the picture. "This is awesome."

"You're welcome," he replied with a wide smile, obviously proud of himself. "Grease outside? I wanted to see if he'd check out my bike while I was here."

"Yeah, he's out back. Are you staying the night?"

"Probably at Grease and Callie's."

"Oh, okay."

With another smile, he left us, and I walked to the window facing the back yard to watch him say hello to everyone. He was so comfortable in the group, like he'd known them his entire life.

"Good photo," Patrick murmured, coming up behind me and wrapping his arms around my waist.

"Great photo," I agreed.

"Shall we go get some food?"

"No, let's just stay here for a second, okay, baby?"

"Alright, my love."

We stood there and watched our family for a while longer, talking and laughing and teasing each other. The kids ran around like maniacs, screeching, and Rose sat off to the side, a small smile on her face.

Without thought, he'd given me exactly what he'd promised.

Four boys.
A little house with a garden.
Everything I'd ever wanted.

Printed in Great Britain
by Amazon